PR

The Betrothal

"Once again Arnette Lamb treats us to a delightful romp. She creates a strong-willed heroine who will win your admiration and a drop-dead gorgeous hero who will steal your heart. Live the adventure!"

—Susan Wiggs, author of
The Lily and the Leopard

"I HAD NOTHING TO DO WITH THIS

ridiculous betrothal . . . My father has hooked you well," Marjorie said, a trace of sadness in her voice. "How embarrassing for you."

Embarrassing for him? Why should she pity him when he'd done his damnedest to humiliate her in front of the Crown Prince of England?

"Oh, enough of this senseless banter." She tossed her head.

"Excellent." At last she would get to the business at hand. "We must settle the arrangements."

"Perhaps," Marjorie said with unconcealed distaste, "when I know you better."

"Rest assured," he took great joy in declaring, "that night will come very soon."

"You'll have none of me."

Blake stared at the delectable fullness of her lips. "I'll have every blessed succulent morsel of you."

Praise for
ARNETTE LAMB'S
HIGHLAND ROGUE

"Arnette Lamb's delighful tale wraps itself around you, holds on, and never lets go. *HIGHLAND ROGUE* is laced with spicy dialogue, sizzling sexual tension and often hilarious, but always heartwarming escapades. . . . A book not to be missed!"

—*Romantic Times*

"*HIGHLAND ROGUE* is a warmhearted, poignant, humorous and sexy story. . . . Arnette Lamb is a unique new writer who should not be missed."

—*Affaire de Coeur*

More Praise for
HIGHLAND ROGUE

"... An undercurrent of humor ... runs through this spirited love story that makes for very enjoyable and entertaining reading."

—*Rendezvous*

"... A REAL WINNER. Arnette Lamb knows how to tell a tale. ..."

—Joan Neubauer

"Arnette Lamb proves once again that what she writes are keepers of quality."

—Ann Wassall, *Ann's World*

Look for Arnette Lamb's
HIGHLAND ROGUE
Available from Pocket Books

Books by Arnette Lamb

Highland Rogue
The Betrothal
Border Lord
Border Bride
Chieftain
Maiden of Inverness
A Holiday of Love
Betrayed
Beguiled

Published by POCKET BOOKS

The BETROTHAL

Arnette Lamb

POCKET BOOKS

New York   London   Toronto   Sydney   Tokyo   Singapore

An *Original* Publication of POCKET BOOKS

POCKET BOOKS, a division of Simon & Schuster Inc.
1230 Avenue of the Americas, New York, NY 10020

Copyright © 1992 by Arnette Lamb

ISBN: 0-671-73002-9

First Pocket Books printing June 1992

10 9 8 7 6 5 4

POCKET and colophon are registered trademarks of Simon & Schuster Inc.

Cover art by Lena Levy

Printed in the U.S.A.

IN MEMORY OF
MARCELLA LAMB

And to . . .

Sandra, Sandra, and Sandra
Barb, Susan, and Joyce
Pat and Pat
Heather, Carla, and Trisha
Virginia, Vayla, and Marilyn
Candy, Andi, and Alice
Cynthia, Kathe, and Kathyrn
Caroline, Carol, and Jane
And to Janoce   . ,

Thank you for helping me say good-bye to Mom.

Acknowledgments

My special thanks to Regency writers Phylis Warady and Karla Hocker for trusting me with research books and for letting me pick their brains. Thanks to Carole Stephenson for lending me her Bath memorabilia. And as always, to the critique group to die for: Barbara Dawson Smith, Susan Wiggs, and Joyce Bell.

The Betrothal

CHAPTER 1

> *By general consent determined that Gentlemen*
> *crowding before the Ladies at the Ball, show ill*
> *manners.*

> —Beau Nash, *Rules of Bath*

February 1739
Bath, England

SOMETHING WICKED WAS AFOOT.

Struggling for composure, Lady Marjoric Entwhistle feigned an interest in the conversation between Frederick, the prince of Wales, and Beau Nash, the king of Bath. But her senses strayed from her companions and fixed on the unpleasantly familiar Welshman working his way across the crowded Pump Room.

Oh, sweet Jesus, was Papa up to his schemes again?

"Are you ill, my dear?" asked Beau.

His drooping jowls creased. Concern laced his words. The expression seemed out of place, for Beau Nash was a man suited to gaiety.

"Of course not," she lied, and her gaze slid to the doors. Had her father come at last?

"That looks like Magrath," said Beau, squinting into the crowd.

"Magrath?" asked the prince, his small head bobbing on his skinny neck, wig powder clouding around him. "I say, the chap's a bit late. Who is he?"

Through a haze of uneasy anticipation Marjorie said, "Milo Magrath is my father's herald."

"Was he invited?"

Assuming his role of local monarch, Beau Nash drew himself up. "Hardly, sir." He tugged at the sleeves of his lavishly embroidered coat. "Magrath's never invited to Bath. Always brings bad news."

"We'll have no ill tidings tonight," declared the prince. "I command it." He nodded regally and drew murmurs of assent.

Marjorie chewed her lip. Even the interdict of the heir to the throne of England could not forestall her father's schemes. She gripped the crystal goblet until the hard edges of the cut glass bruised her palm. The familiar bubbling of the fountain echoed off the stone walls. The herald seemed to be traveling in circles around a sea of panniered skirts and padded shoulders. In his wake the noble occupants of the room grew quiet.

His cheeks chapped raw by the wind, his chest heaving from exertion, Magrath stopped a few feet from her. With a grand flourish he doffed his feathered cap and bowed to Prince Frederick. "Your Royal Highness."

"No ill news on the celebration of our royal birthday, Magrath," he replied. "We've forbidden it."

Startled, Magrath jerked his head toward Marjorie. She noticed a faint blue tinge about his mouth and concluded that only the most pressing wickedness could have brought him across the Channel in the dead of winter.

He made a lesser obeisance to Beau Nash. "With your permission."

Beau grumbled, "If you must."

Milo knelt at her feet, a beribboned parchment in

his chilblained hand. "Lady Marjorie," he said, his teeth rattling with cold. "I bring you warm and sincere greetings from your sire, who most humbly prays for your continued good health and fair fortune."

Her heart slammed against her ribs. All his vile missions had begun with false felicitations. If her suspicions proved true, the present tiding would end with shattering humiliation. But what if Magrath was here for innocent reasons? What if her father was merely announcing his imminent arrival in England?

In the midst of the worst winter even Beau Nash could remember? No. Her comfort-loving father wouldn't bestir himself to cross the Channel in this weather.

Magrath rose. His apologetic smile portended disaster. Marjorie longed to fling the goblet against the wall and storm from the assembly. But she was a veteran of humiliation. No matter what scheme her father had cooked up, she would not sacrifice her pride or her livelihood for his misguided sense of fatherly duty.

The herald turned to the prince. "With your permission, sir, I would read an announcement from Lady Marjorie's father."

Eager for a snippet of gossip, the crowd pressed closer.

"Your Grace," she began, striving to keep her voice even, "I dare not trouble you with trivialities from an expatriate who hasn't set foot in England in twenty years."

She prayed he would agree. To her dismay, he waved a royal hand and said, "I'm in an indulgent mood. But be quick about it. Whatever your name is."

Magrath cleared his throat and unfurled the parchment. "Hear ye, hear ye"—he darted a worried glance at the door. Whom was he expecting?—"citizens and visitors of His Royal Majesty's divine province of

Bath. I, Sir George Entwhistle, sire of Lady Marjorie Elizabeth Entwhistle, do herewith proudly announce her immediate and irrevocable betrothal to his lordship, Commodore Lord Blake Chesterfield, most honorable marquess of Holcombe and rightful heir to His Grace, the duke of Enderley."

The chalybeate water she'd drunk just moments before turned to bile in Marjorie's stomach. Her father had staged this scenario for maximum effect. He'd backed her into a corner and blocked her escape.

Unable to drag her eyes from the door, she stiffened her spine and kept her expression bland. Blake Chesterfield! Sweet Saint Mary. The man was a master at avoiding the marriage trap. What had happened?

The crowd came to attention. Fans rattled open. Monocles and opera glasses framed curious eyes.

"It's about time he brought the chit to heel," crowed Dame Surleigh, her towering wig infested with paste fruit and faux birds, her words thick with too much brandy.

"Quite right, Dame Surleigh. Too bold by half, she is," said the widow Fontaine. A heart-shaped vanity patch dangled from her puffy cheek. "Our postmistress got herself quite a letter today."

Embarrassment chipped at Marjorie's dignity. How could you, Papa? the child in her cried. How could you do this to me again?

"Bravo, Lady Marjorie!" the prince said exuberantly. "This is jolly news indeed." A shower of wig pomatum drifted to the shoulders of his cut-velvet coat. "Your father's outdone himself. He's snared you a Chesterfield, he has." Addressing the assembly, he added, "Been at the side of the king of England since the Battle of Hastings, the Chesterfields have."

As if sensing her despair, Beau Nash moved closer. Unlike the prince, Beau could read her moods. He tilted his head back and smiled encouragingly. "I can't agree with his methods, but he's landed you the wealthiest and most sought-after bachelor in England."

Rebellion surged through her. "I will not accept his suit."

The Prince Regent's eyebrows touched his wig. Blinking, he said, "In the name of Saint George, why would you turn down Enderley's heir, Lady Marjorie?"

Dame Surleigh eased closer, anticipation glittering in her bleary eyes.

Let the gossip fly, decided Marjorie. She had survived it before. She would not demur now. "I've no wish to marry."

The prince gaped. "Never?"

Feminine whispers floated on the now-oppressive air. Marjorie drew in a labored breath; her ivory stays bit painfully into her breastbone. How could she explain to the Prince of Wales that she hoped to marry one day, but not at her father's command? "I have responsibilities, Sire."

"Responsibilities a man should shoulder," sneered Dame Surleigh. "The London mail's always late, and soggy as spoonbread."

Anger ripped through Marjorie. "You don't seem to mind so long as those wretched tabloids find their way to your door."

The older woman's mouth fell open. "Wretched?" she squealed. "I should have expected as much from you. You haven't changed in the least. You're still a—"

"None of that!" commanded Beau. "We've heard enough from you tonight."

Frigid air blasted into the room. Printed broadsides fluttered against the stone walls. Bewigged and powdered heads turned toward the doors. Like the slashing of a rapier, a collective gasp sliced through the room.

"By Rotterdam," the prince exclaimed, "'tis Chesterfield himself."

"So it is," said Beau, nervously fishing his spectacles from a pocket of his brocaded coat. "At least he's tall. Not that that counts a pennyweight, of course." He glanced up at her over his spectacles. Softly he added, "Unless you will favor him—"

"No." The word jumped from her lips. Seeing the curious stares, she knew she'd spoken too quickly. "We'll see," she amended.

"I met him in London once," crowed the widow Fontaine, plying her China fan. "A masterpiece of English breeding and continental style he is."

"Give me that betrothal." Beau snatched the document from a bewildered Milo Magrath and scanned the words. He smiled and winked at Marjorie. "It requires your signature."

Somewhat relieved, Marjorie clutched the bowl watch dangling from the fob at her waist. The tiny vibrations of the timepiece tickled her damp palm. The ominous whirl of spurs and the hollow tapping of boots sounded on the Bathstone flags. Slowly the crowd began to part. In tune with the ticks of the watch, the footsteps came closer.

The coward in Marjorie told her to ignore the approaching man, but strength, increased by a determination to rule her own life, tamped down the spiritless impulse. She had no reason to be afraid; her father could not force her to marry. He'd tried before. And failed.

She squared her shoulders and turned to meet her adversary head on. A shiver of foreboding prickled the hair on her neck. Like her, the man marching across the room stood head and shoulders above the throng.

Blake Chesterfield.

Glossy black hair, fashionably clubbed at his nape, bore the imprint of a recently removed hat. A black mustache confirmed his rakehell reputation. The aristocratic planes of his high-bridged nose and the stark lines of his slashing cheekbones were devilishly enhanced by forest-green eyes alight with purpose. That noble chin, typical of seven hundred years of English-born Chesterfields, displayed the same cleft as that of his famous ancestor who had fought alongside William the Conqueror.

Thigh-high jack boots bore a coating of lime dust. Like a second skin, chamois knee pants hugged his lean hips and muscular flanks. He shed his cloak to reveal a stark white shirt with billowing sleeves. An open waistcoat of forest-green satin, embroidered with the chevrons of Chesterfield, hugged his broad torso. On powerful legs, more befitting a horseman than a naval officer, he strode across the Pump Room.

Toward Marjorie.

He might be the scion of one of England's oldest families, and the amorous object of women from Boston to Barcelona, but to Marjorie this Blake Chesterfield was merely the newest trump card in Papa's humiliating game of matchmaking. Why, then, did she feel intimidated?

As he approached she searched his handsome face for some sign of his mood, for some hint as to the personality of the man who was not only heir to a dukedom, but the most decorated sailor in the king's navy. Her answer came when his gaze locked with hers. Malice, blatant and venomous, glimmered in his eyes.

A cold wave of fear trickled down her spine. In his

obsession to choose her a husband her father had anted up a peer of the realm. A very angry peer of the realm. The stakes were high this time. High indeed.

Compassion assaulted her, for this Chesterfield had not come to Bath of his own free will. What had he done to fall into her cunning father's trap?

Compassion fled; every man had a weakness. At the first opportunity she'd let this "masterpiece" know that his mission was doomed. Stepping to Beau's side, she confidently prepared to assume her role as honorary hostess for the evening.

Beau Nash nodded regally. "Good evening, Lord Blake. Welcome to Bath."

"Yes, yes, Chesterfield. Always room for a defender of the realm," the prince said. Grinning and wagging a finger, he added, "Although you'll have to dispense with those boots, or Nash'll sentence you to the stocks. Our king of Bath is persnickety about his dress code, he is."

In a bold move Lord Blake stepped to Marjorie's side. The rowels on his spurs ceased to spin.

"Thank you, Your Grace, for the warning. I shan't be long." His rich baritone voice stirred the hair at her temple. Why did he have to stand so blessedly close? "Pardon my ill manners, Mr. Nash, but I confess to being anxious to meet my betrothed."

She felt trapped and realized this handsome scoundrel intended to put her at maximum disadvantage. Instinctively she leaned away from him.

A cold hand touched her bare shoulder. "Good evening, Lady Marjorie."

Though she knew him only by reputation, she had not expected him to be so brazen. His long fingers, resting casually on her shoulder, felt relaxed, but his thumb pressed insistently into her back. She would gladly give up the Bristol package route to know what he truly thought.

Turning slightly, she put on her most dazzling smile and found herself nose to nose with the most handsome man in England. The determination in his eyes said he wasn't moved by her in the least. She chastised herself for not expecting that reaction. Blake Chesterfield didn't want her; he wanted to finagle himself out of an imbroglio her father had staged.

Deciding to match his polite performance, she said, "Will you share a glass of champagne, Lord Blake? Although belatedly, we're celebrating the birthday of His Highness, the Prince of Wales."

"I'd have . . ." He stopped. His fierce expression changed to one of repressed merriment. No wonder women flocked to him like children to Bartholomew Fair. His gaze dropped to her breasts. "Aye, Lady Marjorie, a drink from your hand would be delightful, or a sip from your dainty slipper would be divine. And I'd have you explain how George Entwhistle managed to sire a creature as lovely as yourself."

"That's Chesterfield for you," laughed the prince. "A cavalier of the first order."

Marjorie blushed to her waist. She hadn't counted on flattery from Blake Chesterfield. Other men had gone to despicable lengths to win her hand; their praise had fallen on deaf ears. Why, then, did this man's compliment ignite blushes?

He chuckled and reached for her hand. A disquieting shiver crept down her back.

"I'll take that flute of wine now, Lady Marjorie." He lowered his voice. "And later, I'd like a quiet place to talk to you."

She owed him that at least. "Very well, Lord Blake."

Beau Nash put away his spectacles and held out the proclamation. "Would you care to read this?"

In profile, Lord Blake called to mind a dozen coins minted in honor of his forebears. He emanated nobility, yet the hand holding Marjorie's grew tense.

"That's not necessary, for I was instrumental in its creation."

"I'd like to see it," said Marjorie. Now he'd be forced to release her hand. To her dismay, his fingers tightened around hers. She grasped the parchment in her free hand.

"So you've been wife hunting at last," said the prince. "You've picked a fine one in Lady Marjorie. She's related to us, you know—by her grandmother's second marriage, of course."

Blake's vivid green eyes made a slow and meticulous inspection of Marjorie, but beneath his regal countenance he looked surprised, she was certain.

Coolly he said, "How delightful."

"I say, Blake," said the prince, "how fares that coachman of yours? My offer to him is still open—and he can even wear those ghastly hats."

"Peddicord fares quite well," he murmured. "And I'm flattered by your interest. But the Chesterfields won't part with him."

How typical, thought Marjorie. The noble and spoiled Chesterfield thought of his servants as possessions. If he thought to own her, he'd be sorely disappointed.

Tobias Ponds stepped forward. A scoundrel, he was, from the strands of his golden wig to the diamond-encrusted buckles on his shoes. He stood to gain considerably if Marjorie married, for he wanted her job.

"If I may, Your Grace," he said, "let me remind you that George Entwhistle is not Lady Marjorie's guardian. He has not the wherewithal to pledge her troth."

"A formality. Chesterfields have a way 'round rules, Mister . . ."

Tobias bowed from the waist. "Ponds, Sire. Tobias Ponds at your service."

What trick was this? Ponds acting her champion?

Preposterous. But she might as well take advantage of it. "Mr. Ponds has the right of it." She turned to Chesterfield and sank into a deep curtsy. "Still, it's pleasant to meet you, my lord."

He did not release her hand but pulled her up again. "When my illustrious forebear wooed and won Alexis Stewart the bards said no Chesterfield hence would bring a more beautiful woman into the bower of our family." Deviltry smoldered in his eyes. He turned her hand over. "'Twould seem"—he boldly kissed her palm—"the songsters didn't realize a treasure like you would come along."

Feminine sighs spread like a blanket of calm over the room. Marjorie's hand itched unbearably. She wondered if Blake Chesterfield was hard of hearing.

"I say, Lord Blake," Beau sputtered in outrage, "we'll have no wanton seduction in the Pump Room."

Turning a bland, handsome stare on the king of Bath, Chesterfield said, "By the way, George Entwhistle sends you his regards."

Marjorie's heart sank to her knees. Had Beau played a part in this wicked farce?

Spots of color flashed on Beau's face. "He can keep his regards."

"How can Entwhistle make her marry?" Tobias squealed, staring at Blake Chesterfield as if he were dim-witted.

Sparing Tobias a disdainful glance, Chesterfield called for more champagne. When glasses were refilled he released her hand and raised his goblet high. Locking his gaze with Marjorie's, he said, "I should like to propose a toast."

Resentment flooded her, for she knew she would be the object of his insincere salute.

He smiled, looking inordinately pleased. "A toast, ladies and gentlemen of Bath, to—"

"To the Prince of Wales!" she broke in.

Someone shouted, "Long live the prince!" A chorus of cheers rang through the crowd.

Relief surged through her until Lord Blake touched his glass to hers. "You're either very clever," he murmured, "or very reckless."

"She was a reckless youth," sneered Dame Surleigh.

"Silence your tongue, madam," commanded Beau.

Marjorie's confidence swelled. "I am merely anxious to end this farce, Lord Blake."

"Hum." With a dry look of disbelief he stared at her. "I assume, then, that you wish to be alone with me. Very well." Turning to the prince, he clicked his heels and said, "Sire, with your permission, I should like to see my fiancée home."

Through gritted teeth she hissed, "Your assumption is preposterous. I wish nothing of the sort."

"Of course, of course, Blake." The prince fumbled with the latch on his snuffbox. "Nash'll be closing at eleven sharp anyway. Another of his rules, you know." He slapped Beau on the back. Champagne splattered Beau's cravat. "I say, ol' Beau, be a sport and send them off in your chariot. 'Tis blessedly cold out tonight."

Beau's long face pulled into a troubled frown. He glanced from Lord Blake to Marjorie. She expected treachery from her father, but the idea that Beau Nash, her friend and her champion, would betray her devastated Marjorie.

"I can't refuse the prince," Beau said, his eyes gleaming with regret.

Marjorie touched his hand. "I understand."

"Send along our best wishes to the dowager duchess of Loxburg," the prince said. "We wanted so to see Rowena this evening."

"I'll do that straightaway, Sire," Marjorie said. "My grandmother doesn't get out much these days. Your concern always does wonders for her health."

After bowing to the prince, Blake Chesterfield guided Marjorie through the well-dressed and curious crowd. That loose-tongued Mrs. Fieldmouth studied them through her lorgnette. Lady Cuperton-Mills took notes on a linen napkin. By tomorrow the baths, the coffeehouses, and the jelly shops would be humming with gossip. The devil take tomorrow and the gossips as well!

Given time to think, she would devise a plan of her own. With skillful maneuvering she would soon tear the betrothal contract to shreds and joyfully bid Blake Chesterfield bon voyage.

Feeling benevolent, she smiled graciously as he draped her cloak about her shoulders. "You've forgotten your cloak," she said.

Her fake sweetness needled Blake. "I'll manage," he replied, the heat of anger warming him to his toes. With a hand firmly on her waist he ushered her out the door.

A bitter, howling wind greeted them, but Blake didn't care; he welcomed the bite of the cold. The stately woman at his side seemed unaware of his volatile mood. She was George Entwhistle's get all right. Beneath that generous bosom lurked a heart as cold and clever as her father's. She could pretend innocence and play the defiant daughter until the wind ceased to blow, but nothing would change the outcome. They would be married. Blake would sacrifice his bachelorhood. Marriage was a small price to pay to avoid a humiliation that would rip his life apart.

Now that he'd met the postmistress of Bath, the rest of his mission would be as easy as riding the Gulf Stream on a summer day.

Yet sitting across from him in the close confines of the carriage, with the amber glow of the lantern illuminating her flushed face, Marjorie Entwhistle didn't seem formidable or corrupt. He had been told of her stubborn pride; her own father had warned that she would be irascible. A ploy, Blake thought, a cruel game between sire and daughter.

But why, by Saint Elmo, had George neglected to mention her beauty or her intelligence? Behind her enchanting blue eyes worked a quick mind he intended to probe without mercy. Beneath those frothy silks lay a body he intended to enjoy. The fashionable powdered wig had been styled to enhance her features rather than detract from the country-fresh beauty of her skin. Done up in sweeping waves, the white wig accentuated the alluring arch of her auburn brows and the slight upturn of her thickly lashed eyes. He liked the mystery of wigs, enjoyed the game of guessing the true color of a woman's hair. But with her the exercise was unnecessary.

Marjorie Entwhistle's hair was red; he'd stake his royal commission on that. But to what degree? Would her hair be a deep honey-gold like that of Adelle, his former mistress? Or would it match the fiery red of Caroline, his current paramour? If that was the case, he hoped Marjorie's disposition matched her hair, for he anticipated a heated nose-to-nose confrontation with George Entwhistle's wily daughter.

At the thought of his enemy Blake felt a renewed surge of anger and loathing. His fists knotted, and he shifted in the velvet seat. His knees brushed hers. They were both too long-limbed for Beau's carriage.

Her head snapped around. "Pardon me," she murmured, rearranging the heavy brocade of her skirts, her eyes avoiding his.

She seemed embarrassed. Or had he imagined her discomfort? Bloody barnacles, he swore to himself, why the devil should he give a bosun's whistle about her mood? She was an integral part of this marriage trap, and since he had no way out, he would make the best of the situation. In payment for her scheme he'd get an heir on her, situate her at one of his country estates, and return to sea. He didn't have to like her, though.

Feeling mildly content, he cleared his throat. "Have you questions, Lady Marjorie, before we discuss the wedding date? You will, of course, immediately pen your resignation to the Postal Surveyor."

She leveled him a look so bland he thought she hadn't heard. At length she said, "'Twould seem that you and my father have come to an agreement without a thought to my feelings. Yours is not an original ploy, but I must admit to being curious. How, I wonder, did such a pact come about?"

He had no intention of admitting the answer to that.

"I assume you've been in France, and that is where you fell prey to my father."

She had a bloody wicked tongue. In a tone reserved for green seamen he said, "You've played a skillful hand up until now. Don't spoil it or insult my intelligence by being obtuse."

To his great surprise, she laughed. No missish giggler, the woman before him seemed honestly amused. "You've given yourself away, Lord Blake. I knew you would."

He grew still. Where had he gone wrong? What had he said to give himself away?

"Why else, save coercion by my father, would you wish to wed a woman you find both insulting and obtuse?"

Blake relaxed. She was speaking in generalities. Reminding himself to choose his words more carefully, he said, "An anxious groom can forgive his bride many things."

She looked him square in the eyes. "I had nothing to do with this ridiculous betrothal."

Her candor impressed him. "You expect that to make a difference?" he said.

"I'd hoped it would, for you can't force me."

"Yes I can."

"He's hooked you well," she said, a trace of sadness in her voice. "How embarrassing for you."

Embarrassing for him? Christ in heaven! Why should she pity him when he'd done his damnedest to humiliate her in front of the crown prince of England?

"Oh, enough of this senseless banter." She tossed her head.

"Excellent." At last she would get to the business at hand. "We must settle the arrangements."

"Perhaps," she said with unconcealed distaste, "when I know you better."

"Rest assured," he took great joy in declaring, "that night will come very soon."

"You'll have none of me."

He stared at the delectable fullness of her lips. "I'll have every blessed succulent morsel of you."

Defiance flashed in her eyes, and with a much-needed boost to his pride he decided her hair must be very red indeed.

Leaning back in the seat, he listened to the whir of carriage wheels and the howl of the wind. Bath might be renowned as the pleasure garden of the civilized, but the notorious city held no allure for him. He preferred a deck beneath his feet, the wind at his back. The woman sitting primly across from him deserved no better than the lusty needs of a sailor too long at sea. He'd see she got a full ration of his rampant ardor.

"You had a pleasant voyage?"

The sound of her voice brought him up short. Polite conversation was the last thing he expected or wanted. He said, "As pleasant as the Channel can be in winter."

"Then perhaps," she said, her chin tilting regally, "you should have waited till spring."

"Oh, but your father would have no procrastination."

Her lower lip drooped, lending a vulnerable quality to her face. "Are we to expect him, then?" she asked in a small voice.

Against his will Blake found himself softening to her. The chit wanted her papa. They deserved each other. "He didn't say precisely."

She nodded and swallowed visibly. "I didn't expect he would. Has he convinced you to resign your commission, Lord Blake?"

Had he detected a sheen of tears in her eyes? "I do not plan to resign."

"Good," she said on a sigh. "Neither do I."

Doubt crept into Blake's mind. If outward appearances could be credited, Marjorie Entwhistle was innocent in this scheme. Even so, it made no difference. "But it is inevitable, you know."

As if she hadn't caught his meaning, she asked, "Is your ship still in England?"

"Aye. We docked in Bristol."

"We?"

Her coy questions blotted out the sympathy he had felt a moment before. "Milo Magrath and my servant are with me."

"My father hasn't changed his methods or his messenger. Have you found lodgings in Bath?"

Blake shrugged. "I suppose I'll stay with the duke of Cleveland. I assumed Magrath would stay with you."

With an indignant glare she said, "Not for all the stone in Bath quarry."

"Surely your father made arrangements for his—"

"Lackey," she spat, straightening her back. "You have been grossly misinformed." That vulnerability

17

shone through again. "I haven't seen my father in fourteen years."

Blake didn't know whether to challenge her or sympathize with her. For a reason he did not dare ponder, he chose the latter. "You would have been a child of—"

"Ten." Her dainty nostrils flared. "I'm not ashamed of my age. I am, however, disgusted by the scoundrel who sired me and the loathsome pawns he sends to Bath."

Blake cursed himself for feeling pity for her. "Calling me names will not alter your future."

"Forgive me. You obviously think you have no choice."

"Neither," he took great relish in saying, "do you."

"Lord Blake," she began hesitantly, her slender fingers absently toying with the braided frog of her ermine-lined cloak, "while finances are normally beyond the . . . ah . . . *prospective* bride's control, and oftentimes, naturally, outside a woman's realm of understanding, such is not the case with me."

Amused by her prissy dissertation and intrigued as to the point she was attempting to make, he cocked an eyebrow and said, "You're wealthy?"

"Not fabulously so." Leaning forward in the seat, she continued, "I'm certain you think you are doing the proper thing, and your motives are without doubt as noble as your line, and I wouldn't presume to cast aspersions on your character or your intentions, but . . . " She stopped, her rich blue eyes searching his, probably looking for a weakness she could exploit. Pray God she didn't discover it, he thought.

"But—" he prompted.

She pursed her lips. "But I'm certain if we try, we can reach a mutually agreeable . . . ah . . . retreat from my father's wishes."

"And why would you knowingly go against his . . . wishes?"

Only his mother had scrutinized him so closely. And like the duchess of Enderley, Marjorie Entwhistle possessed neither warmth nor generosity. Fury blossomed anew. As he had so often since George Entwhistle became aware of his dark secret, Blake felt like a hunter's quarry trapped in the deadly jaws of his own inability.

She turned her face away. "I want to choose my own husband."

"Then you'll choose me."

She turned back to him. Again he was disconcerted by her direct gaze. "Considering your social position and our audience back there, I hoped to spare your feelings. Cease bullying me, Lord Blake. As I told the Prince of Wales, I've no wish to marry at this time."

He'd do a hell of a lot more than bully her once she was his. "Oh, but I certainly will marry you. As a matter of fact, I'll do anything to get you into the marriage bed."

She gasped. "That's impossible."

Did she belong to another man? The notion did dangerous things to his disposition. Accustomed to a life of overindulgent and eager women, he recoiled at the prospect of marrying an unchaste bride, but he had no choice. "I suppose you needn't be a virgin."

"You wretched snake! I"—she touched a tapered finger to her breast—"I, who stand to lose as much as you in marriage, have gone far beyond the bounds of patience to save your exalted Chesterfield pride. But I see now that you're no better than my father."

A redhead indeed. His blood grew hot at the thought. He studied her neck, her mouth, looking for the brand left by her lover. Her cheeks flushed in response. "That may be true," he began, enjoying her temper. "I will, however, insist that you abandon your current liaison."

"You unmitigated boor."

Her anger salved his ragged pride. "I seem to have progressed from a pawn to a boor in a matter of moments. Predispose yourself, Postmistress," he said through clenched teeth. "You will become the marchioness of this unmitigated boor."

"Never." She turned away and stared out the window.

"Never?" He pondered, as if it were an important military decision. "No, I think perhaps a month away. A very telling month—if you catch my meaning."

Her gaze slid back to his. "I should slap you."

"I wouldn't," he murmured slowly, "recommend it."

"And what would you recommend?" she challenged, her lips tilted up in a sweet smile. "That I ruin my life because my father caught you in bed with another man's wife?"

Blake grew stock still and prayed she wasn't working up to the thing he dreaded most.

"Ah, I can see by your indignant reaction that your crime is not one of the heart." Her winglike brows drew together. "Have you mismanaged your duty and placed England at the mercy of France? Or have you gambled away your family's wealth?"

Realization thrummed through Blake. She didn't know the awful truth about him. "What difference does it make? Money is not what I came for. I came for you."

The carriage jerked, then halted. The proclamation rolled off the seat. Stunned and relieved, he did not move.

She snatched up the document. The carriage door opened, and the footman put down a box for her to step on. In a swirl of ermine and dignity she glided from the carriage.

Blake followed and fell into step beside her. For the second time since meeting her he considered her unusual height. And for the first time the observation pleased him. Without the wig and the stacked heels her nose would touch his chin, and her breasts would fit nicely against his chest. Her high, slender waist would put her hips—

He banished the thought; his plans did not allow for lust. In a matter of weeks he would marry her; in a matter of months he would get her with child. Once she bore him an heir he'd leave her to her own devices.

She stopped at the door and faced him.

"Whatever you've done, whatever you think you can do, Blake Chesterfield, know this." She slapped the parchment against his chest. "It will take more than fancy-worded declarations and the whim of my father to force my hand in marriage."

Startled by both her dignity and her strength of will, Blake closed his hand over hers. "I'll have you to wife, Marjorie."

"No, you won't. I'm sorry you've wasted a trip to Bath, for under different circumstances we might have become friends. Please release my hand."

He relaxed his grip. "We'll be more than friends."

"No, we won't." She opened the door and stepped inside. Over her shoulder she said, "You cannot force me. My father cannot make me wed. He's tried before."

Behind Blake the team of grays snorted. The wheels of Nash's fine conveyance crunched on the gravel drive. Uneasiness stole his breath. "Before?"

Her blue eyes softened. "You're not the first, Lord Blake. My father has sent other men to Bath to marry me. Many times."

The frosty wind whistled through the columns that adorned the front of the mansion. Had she faced those men in front of an audience? Had this lovely creature been humiliated often by her father?

She must have sensed his pitying thoughts. Her lush lips tightened, her slender hand gripped the wooden door.

"How many times has he betrothed you?"

She leveled a look at him even his haughty mother would have envied, but beneath her regal bearing he glimpsed a vulnerable young woman.

"Six times." Her voice wavered, but her posture didn't.

Respect surged through him.

"Don't look so smug, Lord Blake."

"Why not, Lady Marjorie?" Blake smiled. "Seven is my lucky number."

CHAPTER 2

By general consent, it is determined that all
Repeaters of Lies and Scandal shall be shunned
by all Company.

—Beau Nash, *Rules of Bath*

TIRED FROM A SLEEPLESS NIGHT AND DISGUSTED WITH
Blake Chesterfield's high-handed presumption, Marjorie paused outside the door to her grandmother's
apartments. How dare he expect her to fall into his
arms like some ambitious commoner eager for a noble
husband? The answer was obvious. He dared because
of her father.

She grasped the door handle. Again she hesitated.

A cock crowed in the stableyard. In the still-dark-
ened street a sedanchairman called out, "Have a care
and pay the fare." Like a hand extended in friendship,
the familiar sounds reached out to her. Desperate,
Marjorie grabbed hold.

She would allow Lord Blake to escort her to Wiltshire's and a few parties. His pride would be salved.
She would show him the futility of his cause. He
would leave Bath. Life would go on.

She opened the door and walked inside. Love and security washed over her.

A wall of pillows at her back, a sleepy-eyed terrier at her feet, Rowena, the dowager duchess of Loxburg, reclined amid an array of maps and books. Draped over her shoulder, a rope of hair, once the shade of an autumn fire, now glistened with strands of silver. In spite of a leg crippled by a fall from an ill-tempered hunter, she faced each day with the courage of a gladiator.

Her heart bursting with affection, Marjorie longed to share the fresh hurt of her father's latest betrayal, but a disquieting voice in her mind told her to take her time.

The maid Lizzie knelt in front of the hearth.

"Haven't you got that fire going yet, Lizzie?" asked Grandmama.

The maid stood. An embarrassed flush stained her freckled cheeks. "Sorry, mum. The kindling's as slow as the Claver's bootboy, but it's going now."

Marjorie smiled at the maid, who was known as the biggest gossip in Bath's servant class. "Thank you, Lizzie. That will be all."

The girl bobbed a curtsy and left the room.

Slowly Marjorie approached the bed. "The light's too dim. You should have another lamp."

Without looking up Grandmama flicked an agile wrist and tossed aside the map. It snapped back into a roll just as it hit the floor. "And another five minutes of peace and quiet without the voice of youth harping in my ears." Although stern, the voice held no rancor.

Rowena snapped her fingers. Jewels twinkled in the lamplight. The terrier bounded off the bed and retrieved the map.

Marjorie chuckled. "I'll harp as I please."

Rowena's clear blue eyes glittered with confidence. "Five pounds says harping avails you naught."

Stifling a sigh of exasperation, Marjorie said, "Agreed. Now you only owe me four thousand, nine hundred and ninety-five pounds."

Rowena stiffened. "The London post is late?"

Marjorie didn't try to hide her concern. "Yes. I suppose the wretched weather's to blame. But still, you lost the wager and five thousand pounds."

Rowena cleared a spot on the bed and held out her arms. "Of course it's the weather. It's too cold for the highwaymen to venture out of their dens. Tug probably stopped for the night in Hounslow Heath. He'll arrive today."

As she had every morning for the last ten years, Marjorie moved into Rowena's comforting embrace. The familiar smell of roses drifted to her nose. "You slept well?"

"As well as a dowager duchess with a clear conscience and an empty coffer. And you?"

Fighting back a pang of guilt, Marjorie said, "Splendid."

"Tell me how the party went."

Marjorie absently stroked the terrier. She longed to blurt out the painful truth, yet the words wouldn't come. "'Twas grand, as always, but the weather and . . . ah . . . other things prevented our trek out to Queen's Square to formally dedicate the obelisk to the prince."

"Other things? What did Frederick do? Was he angry?"

Pledging to choose her words more carefully, Marjorie said, "The prince didn't do anything, really, and he didn't mind not seeing the monument."

"Of course he didn't. Frederick's had a dozen of those fancy markers dedicated to him. He'll fawn over it before he departs, you can be sure of that, and he'll probably present Beau with another of those gaudy snuffboxes." She wrinkled her nose. "Nasty habit."

"You tell him so often enough. Perhaps he'll listen to you one day and give up snorting tobacco dust."

"Men don't listen to women, child. Now tell me who was there last night. Did Dame Surleigh behave herself?"

"For the most part. Until she emptied her brandy flask and accused Beau of being a whoremonger."

Rowena's mouth dropped open. "She didn't. What did Beau say?"

"He defended himself, diplomatically, of course." Marjorie smiled, remembering the incident, which had been the last enjoyable moment of the evening. "He said a man who has one whore is no more a whoremonger than a man who has one cheese is a cheesemonger."

Rich laughter filled the room. "Clever devil," Grandmama scolded. "Our Beau can bandy words with the best of them. Jump up. I'll sit at the vanity. You can plait my hair while you tell me the rest."

With an efficiency of movement, honed and perfected since her accident five years before, Rowena slung her good leg over the side of the bed. Marjorie reached for the crippled limb but was stalled by a slap on her wrist. "Take back that coddling hand," came the sharp reprimand. "I can manage myself, thank you."

Tenderness welled inside Marjorie, yet she knew better than to argue.

Grasping a cane in each hand, Rowena slowly got to her feet and rose to a height that almost matched Marjorie's. The older woman steadied herself, then began the slow and painful walk across the room. Once seated, she handed Marjorie a brush. "No fancy coiffure today. I'm eager for the baths."

"I think you'll change your mind once we're there." The instant the words were out Marjorie regretted them, for the talk of the town was certain to be about her and Blake Chesterfield.

"You're hiding something. What is it?"

Marjorie concentrated on the strokes of the brush. "Papa's up to his tricks again."

"What's he done now?" Rowena scoffed. "Threatened war on Bath if you don't scurry off to Calais and marry his latest choice of husband?"

Marjorie reached for a bunch of green ribbons, the color a vivid reminder of Blake Chesterfield's eyes. Discomfited by the image, she cast it away. "Don't wear these today."

"What, child, has your father done?"

Marjorie set down the brush and began separating the hair into sections. "He's betrothed me again."

"That scoundrel," spat Rowena. "You'd think he would've learned his lesson by now. I swear on your grandfather's grave I'll—"

"Be still," said Marjorie, speaking to both her heart and her grandmother.

"If your father were as adept at picking husbands as he is at cheating at Hazard, you'd've been wed at sixteen, as I was." She twisted on the stool until their eyes met. "You'll not have some simpleminded Colonial or penniless minor lord stupid and desperate enough to fall prey to your father. Who is the fellow?"

Although Grandmama would never intentionally hurt Marjorie, she felt insulted by Rowena's implication that only a desperate man would marry her. She knew she must make light of the situation. "I shan't tell you. You must guess."

Rowena's eyes glowed like those of a child anticipating a jelly tart. "And the prize?"

Marjorie applauded herself. "The prize is ten thousand pounds."

Rowena paused. Tallying her losses, thought Marjorie.

"Agreed. Is he a Colonial?"

"No."

"English, then. But mind you, that doesn't qualify as a guess."

"Very well, but the count begins now."

"How many guesses am I allowed?"

Marjorie estimated the odds. "Considering your excellent memory . . . and that lucky streak the Irish would envy . . . I'd say . . . three."

Wagging a finger, Rowena said, "Cruel girl. It pays to know things. A woman gets nowhere sewing altar cloths and birthing a babe every year."

"No worry of that in Hartsung Square," Marjorie murmured.

"Don't be missish. You should appreciate my interest in your future."

"Oh, I do. So long as it doesn't cost me any money. I might need every shilling to buy him off, as I did the others."

Rowena strummed her fingers on the marble surface of the vanity. "Does he come from a titled family?"

"Yes, he does. And you forfeit one guess."

"Above the rank of earl? And I'm just gathering information. Not guessing."

"Yes," Marjorie said, and she immediately cursed her wayward tongue.

"Oh ho!" Genuine interest sparkled in Rowena's eyes. She picked up the brush. "Is he here in Bath? And mind you, general tidbits don't count as guesses."

"Yes. He arrived yesterday . . . on the heels of Milo Magrath."

"How *un*fortunate for our Merlyn, and how embarrassing for our mystery groom. Is he handsome?"

Handsome seemed a paltry word to describe the

dark good looks and regal bearing of Blake Chesterfield. Had he been as embarrassed as she?

"I see." Rowena tapped her palm with the ornate silver brush. "That's something in his favor. Very well. Has he ever been wed?"

"The answer to that will cost you guess number three."

"Then I withdraw it. Is there a dukedom in his future?"

"Is that guess number three?"

"I shouldn't waste one of my chances on the impossible." She held up the hand mirror and with a tastidiously manicured finger examined her complexion. "George has as much chance of landing you a duke as Beau has of halting passage of the Gambling Act. And guessing the identity of your latest intended requires greater odds still. You, Marjorie Entwhistle, ask a great deal of an old woman."

It was Marjorie's turn to laugh. Rowena would never walk again unassisted, but she could stare down a prince of the realm as easily as a scullery maid. "Don't try to wheedle his name out of me, Grandmama. I know all of your tricks."

The look she shot Marjorie said she would let the remark pass. "Let's see." She put down the mirror. "I count eleven dukes with eligible sons."

"And I count two guesses gone."

"You've no respect for the infirm. Or the elderly."

"You're neither."

With a steady hand Rowena chose a flagon of perfume and set it down with relish. "Richmond's heir is a possibility." She picked up another bottle and stood it by the other. "Oxford's son is unattached." She grasped an exquisite bottle of ruby-red crystal. "Chesterfield would never force that spoiled rascal of his, but still the lad's unwed."

Marjorie went stock still; Grandmama, engrossed in her game, didn't seem to notice.

"Radcliffe's out of mourning." A jasper flagon joined the others.

The count went on until she'd lined up eleven bottles in a row and placed the most eligible men in England at her fingertips. How fitting and unique, Marjorie thought, to have a grandmother who could reduce such exalted men to a row of expensive perfumery.

Marjorie felt the power of Rowena's sly gaze. Rather than submit, she rummaged through a sandalwood box in search of hairpins.

"One of these, I assume," Rowena said as if she were merely choosing a cane.

"And one more guess," Marjorie said around a mouthful of wooden pins. "Don't fidget."

"I never fidget. You were staring at the jasper bottle—I'm certain of that. Look at me, child."

Marjorie pushed the last pin into place, then studied the effect in the mirror. "And give you the advantage?" She shook her head and adjusted the braid. "I think not."

"But your father doesn't know Radcliffe." She sounded baffled. "How did he manage a noble catch?"

Marjorie avoided Rowena's gaze. "I couldn't say. Unless, of course, that's your third guess."

As if she were a god selecting the fate of mere mortals, Rowena eliminated several bottles. "Young Atherton's still in short pants. Watson-Sykes is betrothed to . . ." Deep in concentration, she picked up a rose-quartz bottle and touched it to her lips. "A Bolingbroke, I seem to recall." Satisfied, she placed it with the other discards. She went on until five remained; among them, the ruby flagon towered grandly over the other four.

"I think I'll save my last guess until after we return

from the bath." She waited until Marjorie's eyes met hers. "The Cross Bath."

"That's unfair." All the anxiety, enhanced by a sleepless night, returned. But something new hammered at Marjorie: the feeling of being no more important than perfume bottles. "You like the Queen's Bath. We always go there. Every gossip in the city will be in Cross Bath."

"So?"

"You'll have the advantage."

Rowena reached for the ivory-topped canes. "It's the dead of winter, child. Only the infirm and the stalwart will take to the waters today. Are you feeling infirm or stalwart?"

Embarrassment twisted inside Marjorie. "I'm feeling fine. But I won't go to Cross Bath this morning, Grandmama. You know how they love to gossip about you and me. Our robes won't be wet before some loose-tongued dowager blurts out his name."

Rowena drilled Marjorie with a cold stare. "How many people know?"

"Enough, when one of them is Dame Surleigh."

Rowena grimaced. "That old harridan." She pinched her cheeks, then glanced in the mirror. "It pays to know what other people think. Not, of course, that their opinions should dictate your life."

Her head crowned by braids, her rose silk dressing gown shimmering in the pink light of dawn, Rowena looked more like a young girl than a dowager duchess. "And you will learn a lesson about how to deal with men."

Suddenly, standing up for herself meant more to Marjorie than placating the proud woman before her. "I'm saying it now, Grandmama," she stated flatly. "I will not go to Cross Bath."

"A welcome surprise," Rowena declared as she got to her feet. "'Twould seem you're learning to use the wits I gave you. Fetch our bathing robes. The Queen's Bath it is."

Cloaked in the traditional tentlike robe and chip hat of white canvas, Marjorie made her way down the steep, narrow stairs leading to Queen's Bath. Over the hissing of the chalybeate springs she heard the murmur of female voices. But the noxious odor reminiscent of rotting eggs threatened to embarrass her less than the gossip going on below.

She shivered, swallowed back the bile rising in her throat, and passed through the portal.

Dense, smelly fog rose from the bath and disappeared into the winter sky. Shadowy shapes moved in the water and lined the walls above. She grasped the damp metal rail and stepped into the bath. Blessedly warm water covered her ankles, then her knees. As she sank deeper she gleefully realized no one could see her face!

There is a God, she thought, and he's decided to favor me today.

"Put me down, you ham-fisted goosebrain," came Rowena's booming voice.

All sound save the sibilant and ancient spring ceased. Marjorie wanted to dive under the water and slither out of the bath.

"Marjorie!"

Please be quiet, she silently begged, and she regretted having been so secretive about last night's events in the Pump Room. Resigned to the degradation ahead, she turned and went to Rowena.

"I'm here, Grandmama."

A hand grasped her arm. "I'm blind as that old beggar in Lilliput Alley, child."

Marjorie wrapped a supporting arm around her grandmother. "Shall we go home, then?"

"Oh, no," Rowena said gaily. Leaning close, she lowered her voice. "And play the coward? Never. You made light of this betrothal, didn't you?"

Immediately guilty, Marjorie said, "Yes."

"I concede the wager. I won't have your future and your pride reduced to the matter of a few thousand pounds. Who is he?"

Something splashed in the water nearby. Like a frigate emerging from the fog, Dame Surleigh sailed toward them. The chip hat and voluminous robe dwarfed her painted face.

Oh, drat, thought Marjorie. She was sure the old harridan would be at Cross Bath.

"Ah, there you are, ladies," said the dame.

Rowena stiffened. "You forget your manners, Dame Surleigh."

Her eyes grew round and her mouth popped open. A mixture of chalky face powder and rouge had turned to pink paste and streamed down her sagging cheeks. "Of course, Your Grace," she murmured coldly. "How could I have been so careless?"

"A simple task for you, I'm sure."

Her face taut, Dame Surleigh turned to Marjorie. "I'm to give you a message from your betrothed. He awaits you in the King's Bath."

"He can await the Second Coming—"

"Please, Grandmama," Marjorie interrupted, unaccustomed to such rudeness.

Rowena snapped her mouth shut, but her fingernails dug into the thick canvas of Marjorie's robe.

"Thank you, Dame Surleigh," said Marjorie. "It was kind of you to relay the message."

The woman tipped her chin in the air and smiled. The concoction on her face settled into a crease at the corner of her mouth. "Certainly, Lady Marjorie." She glared at Rowena. "Now that I've discharged my duty,

I shall return to my friends. Good day." Rigid with indignation, she sank to the gunwales in tepid water and faded into the fog.

Knowing her courage would fail if she hesitated, Marjorie extricated herself from Rowena's grasp. "Excuse me, Grandmama. I shan't be long."

"You're going alone? You can't."

Rowena seemed to have lost interest in learning the name of the man on the other side of the wall. "I can, Grandmama, and I will."

Through the foggy sea of curious faces Marjorie made her way around the wall to the King's Bath. Once there, she heard the trill of feminine laughter harmonize with the deep rumble of male voices. Considerably hotter than the Queen's Bath, the water here sapped her energy. The parson sleeves of her robe billowed out; the heavy fabric weighed her down. What began as a determined march slowed to a cowardly crawl.

The elite visitors of Bath nodded to her as she passed. How like them, she thought, to forgo the congeniality of Cross Bath today for the promise of greater entertainment here.

Exchanging pleasantries and ignoring the snide remarks, she dodged the armada of floating Japan bowls that contained nosegays and sweet comfits for the female bathers.

She heard his voice long before his image came into view.

". . . Pitt the younger has the right of it. I say damn the French and their undeclared war on our trade with Spain."

Using the sound as a beacon, she trudged along until a small hand on her arm halted her progress.

"It ain't fair nor proper, the way they're acting. And them peers of the bloody realm."

The sympathetic voice belonged to Mrs. Juliana Papjoy, mistress of the king of Bath.

Surprised by the intervention of such a formidable figure in the city of Bath, Marjorie relaxed. "Thank you."

Black elfin locks peeked from beneath the chip hat and framed Juliana's birdlike jet eyes and pointed chin. "You deserve better than being bullied by a passel of witless boors."

Marjorie understood why Beau Nash had chosen this good-hearted woman. "They won't bully me." She prayed it was true.

"Not if I have anything to say about it." Those black eyes seemed to glow. "Shall we?" She held out her arm. "They're holding court over there—near the statue of King Bladud. I confess the need to speak to Mr. Nash."

Unable to resist the offer of friendship, Marjorie glided into step beside her.

As they passed, the murmur of voices quieted, reminding Marjorie of the ambience in the Pump Room as Blake Chesterfield had stormed into the room and her life. The fog thinned. She spied him lounging against the octagonal tower in the center of the bath. He dwarfed Beau Nash, who was deep in conversation with the redoubtable duchess of Marlborough.

Arms spread wide, his hands loosely hooked into the rings that hung from the tower, Blake Chesterfield seemed totally at ease. Disdaining a hat, his thick black hair fell in careless waves across his high forehead. The extreme temperature of the waters brought a flush of red to his swarthy skin. The open collar of the bathing jacket revealed a mat of dark hair on his chest and a golden compass on a thick gold chain.

"He's a prize, Lady Marjorie," Juliana said, her

voice laced with awe. "No wonder the women flock to him like sharpers to the gaming tables."

He spied her then, and Marjorie's heart clamored in her chest. His emerald eyes focused on her hat. He frowned, pushed away from the tower, and glided toward her.

The duchess lost interest in her conversation with Beau Nash. She pushed back her chip hat to reveal a diamond tiara and fixed her appreciative gaze on Blake Chesterfield. Beau turned and looked, not at Marjorie, but at his mistress.

All contriteness, Beau reached for her. "Juliana."

She knocked his arm away. "Juliana, is it?" she sneered. "I'm surprised you remember my name."

He moved closer, an odd look of pain deepening the creases of his jowls. "My dear, I must talk to you."

"Oh, you must, must you?" Her voice rose. "Well, I have no intention of speaking to a man who compares me to a cheese!" She spun around and almost lost her balance. "I'd rather live out my life in the hollow of a tree."

"Juliana!" His voice echoed off the stone walls.

Juliana faltered, but to her credit, she did not stop.

Uncomfortable, Marjorie glanced at Blake Chesterfield. His regal countenance now was like that of a precocious young man who'd learned a secret. Then suddenly his expression grew serious, and Marjorie realized he was not looking at her but at something behind her. She turned. And spied Grandmama.

"Chesterfield," Rowena spat, as if his family name were a curse. "So you're the one."

Never had Marjorie seen such an expression of loathing and something else on Grandmama's face. She turned back to Lord Blake, who continued to stare at Rowena.

"'Twould seem so, ma'am."

A strange look passed between them, and for an instant they resembled enemies ready to do battle. Marjorie had the oddest feeling of being left out, of being exploited, and yet she knew the strife between them centered around her. Uncomfortable for the second time in as many moments, she stepped back. Lord Blake stared at her. She felt compelled to stay where she was. Even when his gaze softened and, in open admiration, roamed her face and shoulders, she couldn't shake the feeling of being used.

Rowena's hand touched her arm. "Leave him to me, child. You're no match for him."

The words pounded into Marjorie. Despite the steamy haze that hung over the bath, she felt everyone scrutinizing her, awaiting her reply.

"The duchess will be in her glory again," someone whispered from behind Marjorie. "Poor Lady Marjorie."

"Aye, Her Grace does love to best her son-in-law," someone else replied.

Marjorie's patience snapped. They could wait till kingdom come. Her private life was not some sordid tale to be told in installments for their benefit. Neither would she allow Grandmama to interfere. But the King's Bath was not the place to discuss private matters.

The clean lines and elegant simplicity of the Palladian mansion seemed a world removed from the ancient mounded fortress of Chesterwood. For seven hundred years his ancestral home had stood sentinel against invasion from hostile nations, but this modern palace stood as a monument of grace and progress. Hartsung Square didn't need towers or battlements. It had the duchess of Loxburg.

Blake knew all about overbearing duchesses. He'd

been birthed by the queen of the lot. Rowena was a rank amateur in a sport dominated by the duchess of Enderley. Marjorie Entwhistle was barely a novice.

Compassion touched his heart. Yesterday, in the aftermath of Rowena's tirade, Marjorie had glided from the King's Bath, her dignity intact but her emotions a shambles. He knew the feeling well. And he knew the way to help her. But should he bother?

He turned and searched the street for Milo Magrath, who'd insisted on accompanying Blake. He didn't see the herald, but he did notice several people walking to the back of the mansion, letters and packages in hand. The drive was worn smooth by constant traffic. Curious, he rounded the corner and stopped in his tracks.

His eye was drawn to an aging stable. One door flapped open. A goose flew out, followed by a carrot-haired lad wearing green and gold livery. The bird squawked and darted for the safety of the mansion.

Shaking his head, Blake continued to survey the yard and the back of the building. The front of the mansion was well cared for, but the rest of the building was woefully neglected. Shutters hung askew on rusty hinges.

A post horn hung above the side door to the mansion. The pedestrians he'd seen were not passers-by. They were patrons. He had thought Marjorie's position an honorary one. Did she truly work for a living?

As his curiosity about the postmistress of Bath intensified, Blake retraced his steps.

Dark, billowy clouds heavy with sleet hung in the sky. The wind whistled through the cobblestone street as if clearing a path for the weather to come. Blake faced the mansion again.

Marjorie hadn't played a part in this wicked betrothal.

He turned up his collar and shut out the wind.

She hadn't lied, either.

He shouldn't concern himself with her feelings. But he did. And as sure as the bottom would fall out of the clouds overhead, he knew he'd help her. He'd learned early in life to deal with humiliation.

Shrugging, he rapped on the door with the brass knocker.

Before he could count the Corinthian columns gracing the curved front of the structure, one of the double doors swung open. Instead of a dour-faced butler there was a youthful, dark-haired man wearing mended livery and possessing an oddly familiar face. In one hand he held a lady's muff and cape.

"Who is it, Merlyn?" said Lady Marjorie. She stood behind the butler, her pretty head down, her graceful hands involved in removing her gloves. She wasn't wearing a wig or a chip hat.

Blake stood dumbstruck at the color and style of her hair: golden blond, wrapped in a braided coronet as thick as a mooring cable. Blond. How could he have thought her hair red?

"Sir?" The butler raised his brows.

Blake dry-docked his military mien and dragged his civilian voice from the archives. Slapping on a dandy of a smile, he said, "Lord Blake, the marquess of Holcombe, to see Lady Marjorie."

Her head shot up. Frayed feelings and trampled pride glittered in her jewel-toned eyes. He knew she wanted to slam the door in his face. With a jerk she whisked off the gloves and cloaked her emotions. "Show his lordship in, Merlyn."

Blake stepped inside. The butler closed the door and turned to Blake. "Welcome to Hartsung Square, my lord," he said as if reciting a poem. "Your coat, please."

Where had Blake seen that face before?

The door knocker rapped again. Mumbling an apology, the butler opened the door. Milo Magrath started to step inside. There was that face.

The butler gasped and dropped the armload of clothes. "You!"

Milo's expression grew as frosty as the wind outside. "Hello, brother dear. I came to collect the ten pounds you owe me."

Recovering quickly, Merlyn placed a well-groomed hand on Milo's chest and pushed him back. "The servants' entrance is 'round back. Even a lickspit like you should know that."

Milo regained his footing. Just as he opened his mouth to reply, Merlyn slammed the door in his face.

"You'll pay for that, you pompous ass," came the muffled retort.

Pivoting, his expression one of serene satisfaction, Merlyn wiped his hands and scooped up the garments. "There's a fire in the Hamburg room, my lady. Will you have brandy?"

The exquisite bow of her lips twitched. "Thank you, yes. I'll serve it myself, Merlyn."

"I'll take my leave." He stomped off down a long corridor, his back as straight as a newly set mast. Candle flames in the wall sconces barely flickered in his wake.

"Merlyn," she called after him. "Please let me know the moment the London post arrives."

The butler didn't break stride. "In a trice, my lady."

"Those two are quite a pair." The breathless quality of her voice complemented her dazzling smile. She tossed her head back and laughed, giving Blake a glimpse of an extremely candid and very welcome facet of her nature. She had a sense of humor. Perhaps they would manage after all.

The tension that had begun the evening before last

when he entered the Pump Room vanished like fog in the morning sun. Who would have thought, he mused, that an unlikely pair of Welsh brothers could have defused a volatile situation? "Are they always so hostile to each other?"

"Excuse me." She chuckled, holding her gloves to her face. "You looked so shocked when Milo walked in. I thought you knew about them." She laughed again, her bare shoulders shaking, the exposed curves of her breasts quivering deliciously.

"No. Your father didn't—I wasn't told." Still confused, yet utterly delighted, he found himself laughing, too. Relaxed for the first time since meeting Marjorie's father, Blake held out his hand.

Marjorie Entwhistle, postmistress of the most lucrative district in England and heir to the man who owned Blake's soul, put her hand in his. "A truce?" she queried softly.

Warmth spread through him—warmth and a spark of hope. "Aye. A truce."

"Good." She squeezed his hand. "The brothers Magrath possess enough enmity for the entire British Isles. Our troubles pale in comparison."

"Perhaps," he murmured, his senses fixed on the tilt of her chin, the curve of her neck, and his sudden preference for the fragrance of lavender. "Are they twins?"

"Yes. According to Merlyn, Milo is one 'grunt' older. Merlyn refuses to speak to Milo. If you'll follow me . . ."

She led him through a wainscoted corridor, the upper walls lined with beveled mirrors. Prisms of light from the crystal chandelier multiplied a thousand times, and in every direction he viewed a different image of the tall woman at his side. Her glorious hair wasn't simply blond, but a dozen delicate shades from corn silk to honey. She wore a well-tailored yet simple dress of lavender blue velvet. The color did wonderful things for her eyes. Her natural beauty did enjoyable things to Blake. We make a handsome couple, he thought, comparing her fair beauty to his dark form.

Couple. The ghastly reason behind this betrothal flashed in his mind.

"You promised," she chided in a melodic tone.

He caught their reflection. His wary scowl contrasted vividly with her unabashed confidence. "Promised what?"

"Promised we'd find a way," she whispered, "a mutually agreeable and graceful way out of this predicament. Now smile, and we'll put our heads together and come up with a plan."

Lusty images rose to mind, pictures that had nothing to do with the joining of minds.

"Lord Blake!"

His collar tight, his mouth dry, he cleared his throat. "Your father never told me you were so observant."

"My father doesn't even know me."

They exited the mirrored hallway and entered what he supposed was the Hamburg room. "I don't understand," he said.

"George Entwhistle never had any interest in being a father. But never mind him." She released Blake's hand and moved to a massive mahogany breakfront. "Warm yourself by the fire, if you like."

What he'd like and what she offered were different matters altogether, he thought. Even though he needed the warmth of the fire like he needed another title, Blake crossed to the mantel. He'd pursue the topic of George Entwhistle later. Behind him he heard the rustle of petticoats and the tinkle of crystal, but his gaze fastened on the painting above the hearth.

Neptune be damned! That was Marjorie in the

middle of the bizarre canvas. How many more surprises would he encounter?

In his whimsical and heartwarming fashion Hogarth had captured the postmistress of Bath in her element. Surrounded by a dozen young men clad in the traditional yellow and green livery of the postal service, Marjorie reigned as the epitome of womanly patience tossed into a scene gone wild with comical chaos. Amid a smoky plethora of winged letters sailing overhead and legged parcels scrambling underfoot—each just out of reach of a determined boy—stood Marjorie, her skin the delicate hue of ivory, her hair the shades of the noonday sun.

Spellbound, Blake took in detail after surprising detail. The background featured a wall of cubbyholes containing letters with mouselike ears, bovine snouts, and donkey tails. He chuckled out loud.

"Do you like it?"

She stood beside him, a glass in each slender hand, a pleased flush on her cheeks.

He smiled, whether in response to her or to the painting he couldn't say. "I like it very much indeed." He took the drink she offered, then touched his glass to hers. "To the postmistress of Bath."

"Thank you." She sipped the brandy; her gaze wandered to the painting. "It's enormously clever the way Hogarth fashioned Beau in the picture. He hates it, by the way." She lowered her voice and, in a tone reminiscent of Nash, declared, "Says it diminishes his position."

Blake scanned the portrait again. "This is my first visit, and I'd never met Nash before. Little gossip reaches the warship I call home. You'll have to explain about his position."

"There." She indicated a likeness of a bewigged Nash holding an unfurled parchment of exaggerated length featuring tiny squiggly lines. "'Tis a parody of the list of his *Rules of Bath."* Demurely she added, "He *does* have many rules of proper conduct—too many for that small scroll."

Did she always recover so quickly? Blake wondered. "Do you abide by them all?" He hoped she didn't abide by anyone's rules except Blake Chesterfield's.

"To the letter. The postmistress must be above reproach."

"Hum." He extended a hand to touch her cheek. She stepped back. "Above reproach and out of reach?" he asked.

She sighed, put the glass on the mantel, and clasped her hands in the folds of her skirt. "If you'll tell me why my father is blackmailing you," she said, as serious as a captain facing mutiny, "I'm sure we can outsmart him." She stared straight at him, yet her eyes were full of hurt. "I've done so before."

Blake went cold inside. God, she was direct, and clever, too. But she was doomed to failure, for George Entwhistle held all the cards. "This time it's impossible," he said mildly as his heart raced. "We have a contract. We'll be married. Resign yourself to being my wife."

She seemed not to hear. "I couldn't bring myself to embarrass you in front of all those people in the Pump Room. The truth of the matter is, he can't make me marry. Not you. Not anyone."

"He seems to think he can." Oh, and he could, Blake was certain of that.

She picked up the glass and drank again. An apologetic expression on her face, she said, "Ah, but he is not my guardian. He forfeited that right years ago."

Shock and confusion battled for position within Blake. "But he's your father." And he's my master.

"That matters not."

"Then who," Blake began, returning her kindness

44

with patience, "is your guardian?" He would bargain with Davy Jones himself for the hand of this woman.

"The king is—until I'm thirty-five or wed." Grinning, she added, "Or dead."

"The king of England?"

"Of course."

Like a ray of sunlight on the edge of a deadly nor'easter, relief surged through Blake. "Splendid. We've no cause for worry on that account. The first of April seems a nice day for a wedding."

Slowly, succinctly, she said, "Don't be foolish. The king will not even receive my father, let alone sign a document at his request."

"Oh, but he will at mine, and we mustn't tarry on this, for I do so wish to marry you."

She slapped her palm on the mantel. Sparks of anger glittered in her eyes. "That's preposterous. You don't care a brass penny for me. My life and future lie in Bath. Yours lie . . . elsewhere. Besides, I would make the worst of marchionesses."

"That will change when we are wed . . . and you will make a splendid marchioness."

"You don't seem to be listening." She took a step toward him. The fabric of her skirt brushed his knees. "The king will never gainsay me in this."

"No?" Blake said blithely, fighting the urge to uncoil her braid and bury his hands in her mane of golden hair. "Under normal circumstances I would agree, but such is not the case."

She laughed. The sound reminded him of a waterfall. "You may be the son of a duke, but who and what are you to the king of England?"

Victory, sublime and long overdue, pervaded Blake. "His godson, marchioness. His favorite godson."

Her face grew as white as a gull's throat. Like a coachman gathering in a wayward team she fought for control of herself. She won. Admirably so, Blake thought. She let out a soft sigh. Just as she opened her mouth to speak the butler stepped into the room.

"Your pardon, my lady. The London post has arrived."

The calmly spoken words belied the anxiety in Merlyn's eyes. And his coat was splattered with blood.

CHAPTER 3

FEAR HELD MARJORIE IMMOBILE. SHE WATCHED IN HORROR
as Merlyn peeled off the bloody gloves. Drawing in a
shaky breath, she said, "Is it Tug, then?"

Merlyn grimaced. "Yes, my lady," he answered
through clenched teeth. "I've sent for Dr. Oliver."

The empty glass slipped from her hand and rolled
across the rug. She rushed toward the door. "If you
will excuse me, Lord Blake, I must go."

He stopped her with a hand on her arm. "You're
white as sailcloth. Who is this Tug, and what's the
matter?"

His demanding tone set fire to her temper. She had
no intention of explaining while Tug was hurt.

"Marjorie? What's happened?"

She owed no explanation to this blue blood, no
matter whose godson he was. Besides, he'd probably
use it against her. He didn't care about her problems

with the post. He didn't care about poor Tug Simpson.

She jerked free of his grasp. "Nothing to bother yourself with, Lord Blake." She made a slander of the address. "I must hurry."

His green eyes narrowed. He opened his mouth, but she didn't dally to hear his retort. By the time she reached the door Merlyn had disappeared down the hall to the east wing.

She picked up her skirts and ran. Grisly possibilities flashed like nightmares in her mind. Tug battered by highwaymen. Tug flung from a horse. Tug bleeding and hurt.

Dread settled like a stone in her stomach, and tears blurred her vision. At the base of the stairs leading up to the dormitory she reached blindly for the newel post.

A hand grasped her elbow and propelled her up the stairs. "You'll break that pretty neck if you don't slow down."

Blake Chesterfield!

"What the devil are you still doing here?" she rasped.

"Continuing our conversation, Postmistress."

Fury erupted in her. "I haven't the time to exchange pleasantries with you." And obviously she couldn't hide the disaster. She shot him her most withering stare. But the blighter wasn't looking at her. She whirled around.

Lining the upper railing, their young faces registering shock, worry, and anger, stood the postboys of Bath. Some had just returned from morning deliveries and still wore their green and gold uniforms. Others had donned work clothes for the multitude of chores the post demanded.

An agonized groan rumbled through the grim silence. *Tug!*

"Come along," said Lord Blake. Ushering Marjorie ahead, he started up the stairs. "Make way, lads. Where is he?"

A wide-eyed boy pointed. They rushed through the door and between the rows of unmade bunks. A broken kite dangled from a bedpost. The room smelled of boot polish and smoldering coal fire. The groans grew louder. Marjorie bit her lip. Dear Tug. At six he'd been a battered and hungry child. At fourteen he was becoming a responsible and confident man. There'd been accidents before; postboys were always at the mercy of the elements and man. Tug had had an armed guard; the London-to-Bath run demanded a trained mercenary. What, then, had gone wrong?

Ignoring Blake, she trudged ahead, picking a path through a forest of shoes and books and posthorns. Tug didn't sleep huddled in a corner anymore. His bed occupied a place of importance in the room. As leader, he slept on the only featherbed.

When she saw him she cried out, "Tug!"

"Bloody barnacles!" came the curse from beside her. "Stand aside, lads."

Wick Turner, Albert Honeycombe, and a dozen others shuffled away from the bed, bewilderment clouding their eyes. Merlyn, bearing a similar expression, hovered nearby. Knees wobbling, Marjorie grasped the soft mattress and dropped to the floor.

Tug turned toward her. Winter sunshine cast a soft light on his battered face. One eye was swollen shut. A sliver of brown showed through the other. He smiled but winced as fresh blood oozed from a cut on his puffy lips.

Her heart leapt into her throat. "Oh, Tug."

Merlyn came to life. His hand shot out. Using a soft cloth, he dabbed at the wound.

"I'm aright, Merlyn," he squeaked.

Blood, dirt, and dried grass matted Tug's fair hair,

and a lump the size of a goose egg bulged from his temple. He tried to lever himself up. "Your hands!" Marjorie exclaimed. Whether their blue was from cold or bruise, she couldn't decide.

Gingerly she began to roll up his sleeve. Tug flinched. "Your skin feels cold as ice," she said. "Wick, build up that fire."

"I'll be aright," Tug mumbled again.

"I know you will," she said, feeling his pain and sensing his embarrassment. "I've sent for the doctor. He'll be along straightaway to fix you up. I'll make sure you get shepherd's pie for dinner. It's your favorite."

A shadow loomed over her. "Who did this to you?" Blake's voice boomed through the quiet dormitory.

That slitted brown gaze swung to Blake. "Who're you?"

Praying he'd lie convincingly, Marjorie said, "Just answer him, Tug."

"A posting nag," he said, squinting to focus on Blake. "I fell off the beast."

"And I suppose a fairy dropped an acorn and gave you that goose egg."

Wick and the others again closed their protective circle around their leader.

Marjorie held her breath. Her critics kept a keen eye open for any weakness in her management of the post. An instance such as this would be blown out of proportion. They'd say she wasn't fit. They'd say she was too young. They'd say she'd made a muck out of a man's job. Tobias Ponds would yammer for her resignation.

As if reading her thoughts, Tug whispered, "'Twas the nag they gave me in Reading, my lady. She fair balked like a jennet when I headed her onto the heath."

"If you could lie as well as you bleed," accused

Blake, "you'd be dancing a jig, not wasting abed with a broken face."

"That's enough." Marjorie turned to him and was surprised at the worry on his handsome features. His distinctive mustache accentuated the grim set of his mouth. She wished he'd go away. "Thank you for your concern, but we'll manage."

Taking his cue from her, Wick stepped forward. He puffed out his chest and said, "Lookit here, Mister—"

"No," said Lord Blake. "You look."

Wick took a step back but didn't alter his belligerent stance.

"This man needs brandy, and a river of it from the looks of him." Lord Blake drew himself up and clasped his hands behind his back. "Scuttle yourself downstairs and fetch it."

Wick's eyes bulged, and his mouth fell open. Rage mottled his youthful face. "I don't take orders from you," he spat. "And I ain't got a key to the spirits cabinet."

"Merlyn," Marjorie broke in. "Give Wick the key."

The butler did as he was told. Angry grumbles turned to whispers of surprise.

Lord Blake turned in a slow circle, scrutinizing every face. "You'd rather stand about and watch him suffer? What kind of men are you?"

Chins jutted out, hands balled into fists, and in that instant Marjorie understood why Blake Chesterfield had achieved command of the Atlantic fleet. He towered over Wick. "Will you still loll about when the doctor cuts off his hands?"

Wick looked as if he'd swallowed a buzzing wasp. "No, sir," he stammered, his glance darting to the others. "I won't let no one take Tug's hands."

Blake's countenance screamed authority. "How, lad, will you prevent such a thing?"

"Please," said Marjorie, her patience dwindling. "I

appreciate your concern, but we'll make do until the doctor arrives."

"Marjorie," he began in a reasonable tone. "The lad's hands are frostbitten. Most likely his feet, too. He needs warm, damp cloths—now." His voice dropped. "You're on the verge of tears. The lads don't know what to do. Merlyn'll swoon if Tug bleeds again."

She gnawed on her bottom lip. Every instinct told her he was right, but she hated yielding her authority to her father's pawn. She glanced at the butler. His pallor had developed a greenish tint. "Go wait for the doctor, Merlyn."

Blake's stern countenance softened to entreating charm. "Marjorie?"

"I'm not leaving here."

"No one asked you to." Blake turned to Tug. "Who's second-in-command here?"

Tug ran his tongue over his lips. He glanced at Marjorie, then rasped, "Honeycombe."

Blake's brows shot up. "Honeycombe?"

"'Tis the fellow's name," Tug declared.

Blake scanned the expectant faces. "Honeycombe," he barked. "Front and center."

Albert cleared his throat and stepped forward. A lanky, good-natured lad, he never grumbled, even when the other boys teased him about his carrot-colored hair. "It's me, sir. I'm Albert Honeycombe."

Blake looked him up and down. "Very well, Mr. Honeycombe." Blake draped an arm over the boy's shoulder and led him toward the door. "We'll need brandy, towels, and boiled water. You're to . . ."

As Blake gave careful instructions Marjorie turned her attention to Tug. "Hang on." She smoothed out his blanket. "This will earn you a pound's worth of lemon taffy."

"That spark looks familiar. Who is he?"

"I'll tell you later," she said. "It's a long story."

A trace of the familiar, plucky Tug shone through the damage. "He don't seem like a regular spark. He ain't fawning about and romancing you."

Marjorie smiled. "He's not exactly . . . a spark. More like an explosion."

Tug rolled a knowing glance at Blake, who had moved out of earshot. "Don't take a Mr. Goldsmith to reason that out, my lady. He's a blooded spark, I'll wager."

Despite the serious situation, Marjorie chuckled. Quietly she said, "That he is. Now. What happened to Horace Newton? He was supposed to ride guard for you."

His swollen lips curled into a sneer. "A serving wench at the Swan with Two Necks offered him a tumble . . . uh . . ."

Bemused affection thrummed through her. "I understand. You could have waited for him."

"I waited for him, I did. For two wretched days."

She couldn't fault his judgment. Garbed in the distinctive uniform, a postboy was easy prey for the rowdies in London. Tug couldn't have paraded in Lad Lane looking for another guard to accompany him home to Bath. "Who attacked you?"

"'Twas Claude Drummond who snatched the post. Every last letter. He caught me at the twenty-two milestone out of Marlbor—" He stiffened and looked beyond her. Raising his voice, he went on, "But it doesn't hurt much, my lady, truly it doesn't."

Blake Chesterfield loomed behind her. "Here, Tug," he said, holding a brimming tumbler of brandy to the boy's lips. "Drink hearty, now. Marjorie, hold up his head."

She slid her hand around his neck. He felt fragile. Tears stung her eyes.

Grinning crookedly, he said, "I always favor a spot

of the good stuff, I do." He gulped down the liquor as if it were water.

His unflagging humor broke her heart.

"So it would seem," mumbled Blake.

Tug looked guiltily at Marjorie. "Not that I'm given to drink, of course."

Her spirits lifted. "Of course you're not given to drink."

"But I'll not be coddled."

"Coddled?" Blake shook his head. "You'll be bawling like a teething babe when the frost begins to thaw from your hands."

"Huh!"

But an hour later Marjorie saw Blake's prophecy come true. Hot compresses covered the boy's hands. Tears poured forth. So did the brandy. Tug alternately groaned and whispered, cursed and cried. When the doctor couldn't come, Blake stayed beside Tug, giving encouragement and asking questions. The lad babbled like Dame Surleigh's pet parrot.

When at last Tug slept Blake escorted Marjorie back to the Hamburg room. He paced the floor, his mind obviously on other things. At length he spoke. "I'm taking Honeycombe and six others. We're going after Claude Drummond."

Marjorie sprang from the chair. "You'll do nothing of the sort. The sheriff of Wells will deal with Drummond."

"And when I return," he said calmly, "you'll go with me to Wiltshire's." A smile twinkled in his eyes. "I've a hankering to see how well you dance."

"I couldn't possibly. I have to tend Tug."

"Merlyn can watch the lad."

"The Bristol mail will arrive by then."

"Let the boys handle it."

"I'll need to tell Grandmama. She's waiting for me

now. I'm certain of it." That wasn't completely the truth. What Marjorie had to say to Rowena had nothing to do with Tug's misfortune.

Blake folded his arms over his chest, sighed, and shot her a level gaze. "Six hours to Marlborough, Postmistress. Toss in an hour or two to find this Drummond's lair, six to get back . . . that should give you ample time to make your explanations to Rowena."

Irritation welled inside her. But how could she refuse him? He had helped Tug today and had taken control of the others. He had offered to find Drummond and retrieve the stolen post. She hadn't a better plan. "I hate being indebted," she blurted.

"Ah." He smiled and lifted her chin. "Then perhaps," he whispered close to her lips, "you'll enjoy being courted."

A log popped on the hearth. She opened her mouth to protest. Blake drew her against his chest and kissed her. She shivered and stiffened with outrage. He relaxed, and his warm, soft mouth coaxed her to join in the lover's play.

Maybe one kiss was a small price to pay for all he'd done. Besides, his roguish mustache felt too delicious to resist exploring. And he was Blake Chesterfield, after all. Any woman would want to kiss him.

Logically resigned, she balanced on her toes, grasped his broad shoulders, and allowed him his kiss. With a groan deep in his throat he acknowledged her participation. Her body went liquid at the soothing sound. His mustache began to tickle her, and just when she thought she could bear it no more his lips soothed away the itch.

His kiss didn't mash her lips or smother her as other men's had. He smelled and tasted of brandy, and her head began to swim, as if she'd drunk a pint of the drink. The strong and gentle hands that had tended poor Tug now roamed her pliant back and held her steady. His supple lips moved to her ear. He whispered, "I won't have time to sup before I leave you, Postmistress. But if you could slip your tongue into my mouth, the taste of you will sustain me."

His lusty words both embarrassed and excited her. She should push him away and order him to leave. But she was hungry herself, now that he mentioned it, and his lips tasted so divine.

His hands slid from her back to her waist, and his fingers splayed beneath her breasts. Dots of light flashed behind her closed eyes. She breathed deeply and smelled the delightful aroma of his lemony soap. He didn't smell like other men, and he didn't act like them, either.

She couldn't think sensibly, not with her breasts tingling and his lips trailing kisses over her neck. Her forehead dropped to his shoulder. Her eyes drifted open. She shivered and drew in a shaky breath. Sweet Saint George. No wonder her breasts felt strange; he was caressing them!

"Lovely," he murmured.

His head started down. Blessed virgin! He was going to kiss her there!

"Oh, no, you don't." She gave him a mighty shove.

Taken by surprise, he toppled to the floor, his legs sprawled, his eyes wide. He blew out a breath, shook his head, and said, "If you dance as well as you kiss, Postmistress, we're in for a merry time."

He was making fun of her. The spark. "'Twas a kiss of gratitude, nothing more."

He grinned and combed a hand through his already tousled hair. "In that case, I'll bring you Claude Drummond done up in ribbon bows and tinsel."

"Get up and behave yourself."

He frowned. "Don't get prissy on me again."

"I am not prissy. I'm appalled. Don't you ever kiss me again."

"Why not? I enjoyed loving you with my mouth."

"Love? Ha! You were lusting after me. You wouldn't know love if it knocked you down in the lane."

He toyed with the corner of his mustache, and his eyes shone with mischief. "Like you just did?"

She had enjoyed his kiss, but he'd never know it.

"You enjoyed kissing me. Admit it, and I'll take off anything you like."

Indignation barreled through her. Steadying her voice, she said, "I thought you were going to Marlborough."

He slapped his thigh and got to his feet. "Very well, fair Postmistress. I'm off to slay your dragon."

She fretted with the lace on her bodice. "Yes, well . . . thank you very much. You're very kind to offer, and I do hope you'll have a care with your person. I wouldn't want the post blamed for injuring a peer." She was yammering like a ninny! And he was grinning like a loon.

He tipped his head to the side. A lock of curly hair, black as pitch and shining like silver, fell across his forehead. "Worried about me, are you?"

Oh, why didn't he just go? Much more of his seductive innuendo and she'd melt into a puddle at his feet. "Of course I'm worried." She glanced at the fireplace. "I would worry about my grandmother's terrier going out in this weather, and after a ruffian like Drummond."

"Hum. Very encouraging." His lips pecked her cheek. "Polish your dancing shoes, Postmistress, I'll be back."

During his absence her opinion of him swayed like the pendulum on the lantern clock. He was a fine actor performing in her father's play. He was a smooth-tongued rascal trying to seduce her down the aisle.

Back and forth her opinion vacillated. He was a womanizer. He was a gentleman. He'd gone after the menace who'd stolen the post. He was a rogue. He'd threatened to compromise her. Her father owned him. What horrible act had he committed? How badly had he blackened his family name?

She didn't truly care about reputations. When she found the man she wanted to marry, his past would be his own business. As would hers. She had no intention of marrying Blake Chesterfield. The point was moot.

She wanted a proper husband with a kind nature. She thought of a dark-haired scoundrel with a tickly mustache. She needed a settled, quiet fellow. She thought of reckless, domineering Blake Chesterfield. He was the wrong man for her. He was another of her father's pawns.

But she was curious. What ugly secret had Papa discovered about Blake?

Hours later, when she sat at Tug's bedside, she still wondered. If Blake found Claude Drummond and recovered the stolen London post, she'd be grateful. An evening of dancing at Wiltshire's was a small price to pay. No more kisses, though.

With the matter settled and Blake Chesterfield relegated to the status of harmless cavalier and transient acquaintance, Marjorie made her way to Grandmama's rooms. Each time she pictured that wretched scene in the King's Bath her temper flared. How could Grandmama have been so thoughtless? Her cruel set-down still rang in Marjorie's ears. What could she have done to deserve such treatment from the grandmother she cherished?

The dowager duchess of Loxburg sat at her Queen Anne desk, a pile of opened letters before her, the terrier at her feet. Dressed in a tea gown of royal blue, coiffed in a powdered wig styled to perfection, she looked every inch a duchess. Though she seldom went calling, she dressed every morning as if she were meeting the king.

"Hello, my dear." She waved Marjorie into the room. "I was just about to find you. I feel wretched. Sit." With the ivory top of a cane she tapped the velvet cushion of a nearby chair.

Summoning a cool demeanor, Marjorie said, "Thank you, no. I didn't come to visit."

As if she hadn't heard, Grandmama said, "The duchess of Marlborough is leaving Bath tomorrow." She folded a sheet of parchment, applied the seal bearing the egrets of Loxburg. "Have Tug take this to her."

Marjorie's good intentions fled. Grandmama knew perfectly well what had befallen Tug; thanks to Lizzie, gossip in the mansion traveled as fast as the waters in the King's Bath. Bewildered, Marjorie asked, "Why are you being so insensitive? It isn't like you."

Rowena shook the ducal seal. "You should have come to me for help with Drummond instead of going to Blake Chesterfield. Time was you relied on me."

Grandmama had got her feelings hurt, but that didn't excuse her rudeness. "Yes, I did rely on you," Marjorie said calmly. "When I was a child."

"Oh, pardon me for forgetting that you've outgrown the need of an old woman's help. What use is a cripple?"

Marjorie sighed. "I'm sorry. I do need you. But why did you act so abominably in the bath?"

The egrets of Loxburg hit the desk with a thud. "Whatever are you talking about?"

"You embarrassed me in front of everyone I know." The words she'd rehearsed came pouring out. "I'm old enough to be a spinster. I can certainly deal with Chesterfield, just as I dealt with his predecessors."

"Of course you can." Her expression softened. "And I'm just a nosy old woman who loves you more than Beau loves a run of winning hands." Her eyes filled with tears.

Guilt swarmed Marjorie's defenses. Confused, she rose and walked to the dresser. The ruby flagon was gone. Her search for it ended at the hearth, where shards of red glass winked in the firelight. She knelt and picked up the pieces. "Why do you hate him so?"

Grandmama sniffled into a lace handkerchief. "He's your father's pawn, don't you forget."

"The others were, too."

"How dare he be so bold? Those tales of him carousing with loose women and sporting with the youngbloods must be true. And who does he think he is, comparing you to that notorious Scotswoman his grandfather kept? Alexis Stewart." She shivered. "Disgusting."

Marjorie felt a stab of compassion for Blake Chesterfield. She knew firsthand the cruelty of gossips. Even if he had committed an indiscretion, it shouldn't be everyone's business. "Surely you know he's not here of his own free will."

"He should have used his resources. His father could buy and sell a hundred George Entwhistles. I wonder what he has on the boy." She sighed. The terrier sprang onto her lap. Absently she stroked his ears. "Lord Blake must be a prideful sort. It will earn that boy naught, though. He doesn't stand a chance with you. I'll—you'll deal with him, of course."

Boy? An insulting word for such a formidable man. Offended anew, Marjorie didn't care if her words were bitter. "You're treating me like a child."

"I know more about men and their lustful ways than you." She tapped the cushion beside her again. "You're too busy with the post, what with that thieving Claude Drummond on the loose again. You ought to have sent the sheriff of Wells after him."

That bit of information surprised Marjorie. "How did you know about Drummond?"

Grandmama's hands fluttered about the dog's head. "I know what goes on in this house."

Realization dawned. "Then Lizzie also told you Blake has gone after Drummond."

Grandmama raised a dignified graying brow. "Blake, is it? How cozy. Dame Surleigh said you weren't good enough for him."

Not good enough. The heartless words hurt. "I thought you never bothered with Dame Surleigh," Marjorie managed lightly. "Blake offered his service, and I accepted."

"He'll be offering his personal services soon, and if you don't watch out, young lady, you'll find yourself too enchanted to refuse. That's the way rakes are. I thought you'd learned your lesson with the other suitors." At her angry tone, the dog jumped down and settled at her feet.

Was Blake bribing her? Marjorie laughed to herself. He most certainly was. But goodness, he possessed the charm to carry it off. She still pictured him sprawled on the floor and grinning like a boy caught with his hand in the jam jar.

"You like him."

Not a question, an accusation. "He's entertaining."

Grandmama snorted. "I know all about entertaining men. Your grandfather, God rest his lecherous soul, was forever trying to dip his hand into my bodice. The more crowded the room, the quicker his hands."

Marjorie blushed at the accuracy of Rowena's insight. To hide her feelings she ducked and patted the terrier's head. When she'd composed herself she faced Rowena again. "Don't fret, Grandmama. I'm merely having fun with Blake Chesterfield. As soon as he tells me why Father is blackmailing him I'll send his lordship packing and the betrothal back with Milo."

A beringed hand closed over Marjorie's. The gesture brought to mind a thousand fond memories. The day Marjorie received her first postal commission in her own name. The afternoon she'd been presented to the king. That miserable night years ago when she'd disgraced herself in the gaming room at Wiltshire's.

"Just mind you don't fall into George's trap. I care too much for you, child, to watch him continue to humiliate you." She raised her eyes to the stuccoed ceiling. "Lord knows when he'll realize you're perfectly capable of choosing your own husband."

"Don't worry. I'll be careful of Blake."

"I'm certain you will. And we've more important things to be about." She picked up the envelope. "Will you send this to Her Grace before she leaves?"

Feeling oddly unsatisfied, Marjorie said, "Certainly. But it will cost you fourpence."

"'Tis robbery," Grandmama scoffed. "Fourpence would send it to London." She reached into an embroidered pouch. "I'll give you tuppence."

Marjorie shrugged, took the pennies, and had the letter delivered.

At day's end she lay awake wondering what had gone wrong. She'd confronted Grandmama, fully prepared to learn the reasons behind that humiliating scene in the bath. She'd expected Grandmama to explain them and apologize. But Rowena hadn't done either. Somehow Marjorie had ended up feeling defensive and comforting Grandmama.

Confused and unable to sleep, Marjorie dressed and spent the rest of the night sorting the mail, tidying the posting room, and wondering how Blake Chesterfield was faring. By the time he arrived the following afternoon she had worked herself into a bundle of anxious nerves and wondered if he'd killed Drummond or vice versa.

Her worried frown was for him, Blake was certain of it. He'd ridden into the stable yard and entered the mansion through the sorting room. Marjorie was unaware of his presence, and he took the opportunity to study her.

Dressed in a modest gown of yellow silk, she sat in a leather armchair, a ledger on her lap, a lead pencil in her hand. Rays of the setting sun filtered through the fan-shaped windows of the Hamburg room and bathed her in a rosy glow. How, he wondered, could this intelligent woman have sprung from the loins of George Entwhistle? The wastrel didn't deserve the credit for siring so lovely a woman. She had her father's quick temper and derisive tongue, but the similarity ended there.

After riding six hours through a snowstorm he intended to get a personal and satisfying thanks from the postmistress of Bath.

Touching a finger to the bloody cut on his cheek, he asked, "How's our patient?"

She gasped. The ledger snapped shut and fell to the floor. Jumping to her feet, she said, "Tug's better, but what happened to you?" She took a step toward him. Sweet concern furrowed her brow.

He should feel guilty for deceiving her, he thought, but her sympathy felt too good. He couldn't pass up the opportunity. "That Drummond packs a wicked right."

"Oh. You should have ducked."

"I wasn't quick enough."

"You delivered him to Mr. Nash, I suppose."

Less than twenty-four hours before she'd melted in Blake's arms. What the hell had happened? Drum mond might as well have blown a hole the size of a sixty-pounder in Blake for all she cared. "No, I let him go."

The graceful column of her neck stiffened. "You what? I sent you there to—"

"Excuse me. We retrieved most of the mail." He pulled out a crumpled letter with a broken seal bearing the egrets of Loxburg. "I scared Drummond properly."

Marjorie stared at the envelope, which bore no address.

"Henceforth," Blake declared, anxious to regain her attention, "Drummond'll be plying his trade on the Great North Road instead of Hounslow Heath."

She wadded the letter and threw it into the fireplace. "Oh. I suppose that's something."

The circle she made of her lips was enough to make a monk rethink his decision.

"Then you approve?"

"Yes. 'Twas best you did that."

Patience, Blake told himself. You made her feel desire, and now she's embarrassed. Go slowly, and she'll jump into your arms like a tamed ship's cat. "Uh, yes. 'Twas Tug's idea—under the influence of brandy and thawing frostbite. He said Ponds would use the incident with Claude Drummond against you."

She smiled fondly. "He knows what he's about. Ponds will do anything to discredit me. He wants my job and loves stirring up trouble."

Blake wondered why the thought of trouble with the post made her so uncomfortable. Matrimony to Blake Chesterfield stared her in the face. "It won't come to that, Postmistress, and even if it does, I'll protect you."

She glanced nervously at her hands. The soft light

turned her hair to a crown of gold. The ship's cat came to mind again. Suddenly he was glad her hair wasn't red.

She looked up. Her gaze roamed his face. "You should have that cut attended to."

That she hadn't offered to minister to him herself spoke volumes about her feelings. If that meddling Rowena had had a hand in freezing Marjorie's heart, he'd exile the old witch to the Colonies. That is, once he'd managed to get Marjorie's signature on the betrothal and Marjorie herself into his bed. And not necessarily in that order.

"'Tis only a nick," he said, hoping she would argue.

She peeked at him from under fanlike lashes. "Doesn't it hurt?"

He shrugged, enjoying her advance and retreat. "Not as much as Everson's stitchery will."

"Everson?"

If she didn't pick up those dainty feet and make a move toward him, he thought, he'd compromise her here and now. "My valet. He stitches skin as if it were canvas."

"Oh. You'll have a scar then."

Not bloody likely. "Yes, and a bad one, I'm sure."

"I could summon the doctor again."

Even if he had to stand here bandying words all night, she'd sew him up herself.

"Perhaps I could put a small stitch or two there." Her turquoise eyes still avoided his. "Then you wouldn't bear Drummond's mark or Everson's."

He tried to remember if he'd ever romanced a shy woman. Or a woman with brains. Common sense told him to make her forget that kiss. Manly urges demanded he give her lesson number two. But other thoughts intruded. He'd expected to lust after Marjorie Entwhistle. Her beauty and sensuality appealed to his base needs. But he hadn't anticipated the thrill of holding her close, or the pleasure of getting to know her.

"Since you offer, I would rather bear your mark." He nearly choked on the humble words.

"Oh, very well."

She dashed to the door and called to a maid. Blake gave himself high marks for strategy. He was still applauding his clever tactics when she returned with a sewing box.

"Sit here, under the light." She indicated a chair near a candelabrum.

"We could do it standing up." The image of that love play set his loins afire.

A rosy flush blossomed in her cheeks. "I'm not quite tall enough." Her eyes grew wide, and the bow of her lips turned up in a smile. "I never thought I'd say that to anyone."

You're perfect for me, he said silently. He tucked away the romantic thought to ponder later. If he didn't keep a sharp wit about him now, Marjorie Entwhistle would dash away again.

Settling himself comfortably in the wing-back chair, he said, "Say what you will, Postmistress, as long as you don't stitch me up with pink thread."

She laughed and rummaged through the box. "How about green to match your eyes?" She held up a length of thread. The color reminded him of the forest along the James River.

Struggling for lightness, he said, "Would green comply with Mr. Nash's dress code?"

"Rest assured that if it doesn't, all of Bath will know it."

"How?"

"He'll slap up posters all over town."

"Imagine that," Blake said, "one man bringing about another of Nash's rules."

"One woman did."

"Were you that woman?"

Her mouth snapped shut like a clam, but he suspected the answer. "Tell me what you did."

She spent an eternity threading the needle. When she turned to him again she was all the postmistress of Bath and none of the shy cat. "It was a long time ago, and not a pleasant tale or one I'll repeat to a visitor in my life."

"I'm no visitor, Marjorie."

Her slender fingers touched his cheek. "Be still or we'll be here all night." Her eyes locked with his. "This will hurt."

He sat still as a stone while she plied her needle, but his mind whirled like a water eddy. Her nearness did delicious things to his senses and kept his mind off the pain she dealt him. Her neck smelled of lavender and her breath of sweet mint. She didn't paint her face, as was the fashion, but simply dusted her cheeks with a fine, light powder, beneath which peeked a freckle here and there. He longed to draw a finger down the elegant slope of her nose and trace the gentle sweep of her lips. The pink tip of her tongue darted out as she tied off the first stitch. Oh, what he could do with that tongue.

She blinked in confusion. "You're enjoying this?"

If he set her straight on that, she'd run like the wind. Coughing away the lump in his throat, he managed, "I'm thinking how lucky I am that it's you rather than Everson wielding that needle."

"Oh."

She sounded disappointed, and little furrows appeared on her brow. Bloody barnacles! The cat had come out of hiding. And he intended to dole out the cream. "You're doing splendidly," he said.

Her lips bowed up again. "How would you know? I could be sewing your ear to your cheek."

He laughed.

"Be still!" Her eyes flashed with mirth. "Don't move again or I'll botch this, and you'll look like a patched-up cloak."

His gaze fell on her breasts. "The navy wouldn't care."

She took a deep breath. "The navy's lucky to have you. I imagine you're a fine officer. You must be eager to get back to your command."

He was more eager to get her into the marriage bed. "Not especially."

"You were splendid with the boys. Thank you again."

His pride-swelled chest strained against his buttons. Shafts of desire rocketed to his loins. Discreetly, he folded his hands in his lap. "You needn't thank me. We're going dancing, remember?"

She reached for the scissors and, with an air of finality, snipped off the thread. "I'll meet you at Wiltshire's, but you mustn't try to kiss me again. You're a visitor in my life, remember?"

Belay that. He intended to kiss her from head to toe and suckle the sweet spots in between.

"I wouldn't think of it, Postmistress."

CHAPTER 4

*Snobbery based on birth has no place in the
civilized and commodious town of Bath.*

—Beau Nash, *Rules of Bath*

"LORD BLAKE PASSED ME HIS PISTOL AND BADE ME SHOOT
off Drummond's balls should the lubber move so
much as a finger."

Whoops of boyish laughter erupted from the posting room.

"Quiverin' in his jackboots Drummond was," Albert Honeycomb boasted. "And whimperin' like a gin
sot on Sunday morn."

Unnoticed, Marjorie paused in the doorway to
listen.

Squatting on the sorting table, Albert gave a de-
tailed and obviously embellished version of the cap-
ture of the postal brigand. A score of younger boys
gathered close, their faces all rapt attention. Albert
made a fist and, grunting loudly, jabbed the air with a
fierce uppercut. "Knocked him near to 'ell from
whence he came, we did."

Marjorie cleared her throat and stepped into the room.

"Cor!" Albert sprang to the floor. His audience turned and gawked at her.

Albert ducked his head sheepishly. The stacks of letters and magazines on the workbench and the empty slots in the sorting cabinet told her he'd spent the afternoon reliving his adventure rather than bagging the mail.

She sent him a commanding stare. "Albert, the mail *is* going to Bristol at daybreak, is it not?"

"Aye, milady. Sure as the king's another George." Hastily he grabbed a bundle of magazines. "Let's be about it then, lads."

Like geese fleeing a fox they scattered to their appointed stations. Letters flew from nimble fingers.

Cumber Stokes, the youngest at nine years old, took a step toward her, a stack of letters in his hand. "My lady. Look at you, all tricked out in black and pearls."

She beamed at him. The black evening gown and matching high-heel slippers had been a gift from Grandmama. Marjorie had never worn them. The shoes added two inches to her already formidable height. Tonight, though, she didn't have to worry about towering over her dance partner. Blake Chesterfield was the tallest man she'd ever gone dancing with.

Cumber shook his head. "You're grander than a fairy queen."

"And you're quite the gracious young flatterer, Mr. Stokes."

The bells of the abbey church rang out. The boys stopped and counted each peal out loud. At twenty-four Albert said, "The duke of Richmond has arrived. Lizzie said so."

The ringing of the bells to announce the arrival of titled guests was another of Beau's customs. But tonight Marjorie couldn't worry about ceremony.

"Cumber," she said, "have you counted the bye letters?"

Enormous hazel eyes stared at the clusters of pearls on her velvet petticoat. "Eek, no, my lady." He jumped back. "Bless me, I've just pulled 'em out of the local sack. I won't send 'em on to London again by mistake, I promise."

"What have you been doing?"

He pointed to the other boys. "Albert was telling us about how he caught Claude Drummond and run the blighter off the heath. He couldn't let ol' Drummond get away with robbing the mail and takin' money out of the hands of poor folks."

Gratitude and annoyance sat like a stone in her stomach. She would dismiss Lord Blake, just as she had his predecessors. But she couldn't do it right away, not when he'd gone to such trouble to help her. He was too important to shun.

She began pulling off her gloves. Without Tug's supervision they'd be here for hours. She couldn't enlist Merlyn; he was attending Grandmama and the parson, who'd come to dinner. "The mail should have been bagged by now, gentlemen." Resigned, she put away her gloves and reticule.

"We can manage, my lady," Albert pleaded. "You're going to Wiltshire's." He glanced at the clock. "'Tis ten minutes of six. You'll be late."

"A lady is always late, Albert. The mail, however, is not."

His thick brows drew to a point in the center of his forehead. "Lord Blake said you'd be dancing with him. Is it true?"

The notion did funny things to her insides. Resolutely she stilled the fluttering. Why should she be anxious? He'd promised not to kiss her again. In return, she'd make certain he left Bath with his great Chesterfield pride intact. "Perhaps I will."

Hands on his hips, Albert said, "I'll wager he can set the ladies' fans a-clickin'. He was tellin' me as how he almost fought a duel over a lady in the Colonies at harvest time. A shipbuilder's daughter set her sights on him, and her other suitor objected."

Under her breath Marjorie murmured, "Then I'm sure she needed spectacles."

She walked to the table, picked up a stack of mail, and turned to the sorting cabinet. Official documents on heavy parchment with fancy seals shared a cubbyhole with private letters on perfumed stationery with spidery writing. *Gentlemen's Quarterly* joined the *Cole Street Journal* and the *Racing Calendar*. The sound of paper sliding against wood and coins rattling in envelopes filled the room.

So much work, she thought, for so little compensation. Then she spied the boys, dedicated to their tasks. These young men would have a chance in life—so long as she was postmistress of Bath. Thinking of the dangerous ramifications of the robbery, she said, "Gentlemen."

"Look sharp," declared Albert, his chest puffed out.

They stood at attention, their trusting faces turned her way. "We must keep the robbery a secret. Should Tobias Ponds or anyone learn of Tug's misfortune—"

"None of us'll be talking, my lady," said Albert. "Any mate who spouts a word'll answer to me. Got that, lads?"

Eyes wide, they nodded.

From the corner of her eye Marjorie spied Albert glancing again at the clock. Guilt drew down the corners of his youthful mouth.

"Lord Blake said you were a great help with Claude Drummond," she said.

He grinned crookedly. "We gave that rotter Drummond a taste of the king's justice, we did."

This phrase, too, reeked of Lord Blake. Hero worship wouldn't do at all. These boys must see that Lord Blake was simply a man. She didn't want a house full of long faces once he was gone. "I understand Mr. Drummond packs a wicked right."

Albert shrugged. "Drummond never laid a hand on the commodore."

The commodore. If she didn't do something, these impressionable boys would soon be singing ballads about her misled suitor. "He did so, and Lord Blake has stitches in his cheek to prove it."

"You mean that nick on his face?" Albert squeaked.

"Yes. The product of Drummond's wicked right, I believe."

"Cor! He's having you on, my lady." He slapped a copy of *Gentlemen's Quarterly* on the table. "That Drummond never had a chance to fight back. The commodore slipped on the ice outside, he did, and smashed himself on the bootscraper."

Marjorie's hand stilled. "What?"

Over his shoulder Albert said, "Ain't it so, Cumber?"

Cumber paused, his pudgy fingers tangled in a ball of twine. "Albert said it straight, my lady. Saw it with me own eyes, I did."

Wicked right, indeed. That cunning devil. To think that she'd fretted over his being injured in her defense. He'd duped her into feeling sorry for him, then he'd tricked her into feeling gratitude. How could she have been so gullible?

Once fooled, always warned. Perhaps she didn't even owe him his pride.

"The commodore lied?" Albert looked like a hungry child peering into the window of a jelly shop.

She couldn't disillusion him. "No, the commodore didn't lie. He was, as you say, having me on."

He hitched up his breeches. "That's aright, then," he said, copying Tug's favorite expression.

She wouldn't go to Wiltshire's. She didn't have to deal fairly with a liar. That decided, she resumed her task.

But as the evening waned her anger grew. She wanted to sling the magazines across the room and rip the racing forms to shreds. Baffled by her strong reaction, she tried to temper her anger. Destroying love letters and mercantile catalogs wasn't the solution. Still, she flicked the letters into the slots with more force than necessary and tied the bundles so tight the string creased the letters.

She pictured Blake Chesterfield strutting about the crowded ballroom and praising himself for making a fool of her. He expected her to fall into his arms and dance the night away. She glanced at the clock. It was half past seven. Her anger cooled. She would teach Lord Blake Chesterfield a lesson. What better place than Wiltshire's Ballroom on Friday night? And who better for an accomplice than the king of Bath?

She went to the desk and penned a note. Folding it, she called for Cumber. "I want you to take this note to Mr. Nash. Put it in his hand yourself."

She paused before the wall of potted palms that separated the foyer from the ballroom. Strains of a minuet floated above the well-bred murmurs and trilling laughter. Familiar sounds. Festive sounds. The sounds of Bath at play.

Secure in her own element, Marjorie strolled into the throng. She didn't have to look for Blake Chesterfield. She knew where he was. Let him find her—when and if he got the chance.

Dame Surleigh nodded formally. "Congratulations, Lady Marjorie. Lord Blake informs us that we'll be invited to a wedding feast soon." She looked behind Marjorie. "Her Grace didn't accompany you? How disappointing. Isn't that so, Georgina?" Puckering her mouth, she turned to her companion, Lady Sheridan of Wells.

Rather than tip her head back so her eyes would meet Marjorie's, Lady Sheridan directed her response to Marjorie's bosom. "My felicitations."

Anger began a slow burn in Marjorie. How dare that verbose cockscomb? Speaking to the peacock perched on Lady Sheridan's wig, Marjorie said, "Don't believe a word of it. He's a renowned prankster. You told me that Blake Chesterfield swore he was to wed Marianne Bolingbroke last year, didn't you?"

Lady Sheridan looked up then, impotent hope in her eyes. "I had heard rumors of a wedding."

"Of course you did," Marjorie replied. The woman told so many falsehoods, she wouldn't remember one more. "And you were kind enough to pass the information along. Now, if you'll excuse me."

She nodded and walked away. Only in Bath did nobility mix so freely with common folk. By dictate of Beau Nash, merchants mingled with minor lords, peers shared tables with printers. Class barriers were breached, weapons banished. Pleasure and manners were the order of the day, every day.

She spied the king of Bath holding forth near the dance floor. Decked out in white brocade and a rolled wig that fell almost to his lapels, he looked every inch a monarch. Leisurely she started toward him.

Like sparkling raindrops, candlelight from the crystal chandeliers illuminated the elegantly appointed crowd. Stark white walls served as a fitting backdrop for the prancing dancers garbed in every hue of an artist's palette.

A deep blue uniform caught her eye. Amid an ocean

of jewel-encrusted silks, frothy laces, and quilted velvets, the coat trimmed with golden epaulets and dangling braids made a picture of masculine dignity. Blake wore no wig, but had clubbed his thick black hair with a simple tie at the nape of his neck.

As he led the countess of Beauly through the steps of the minuet Marjorie stared at his broad back and admired his graceful moves. His left hand rested at his waist, and with his right he drew the elderly woman close, then turned in a half circle. An assortment of ribbons, badges, and medals decorated the front of his uniform. Four stitches of white silk thread adorned his cheek.

Scoundrel. Lying, conniving knave.

"A striking couple, wouldn't you say?"

Marjorie smiled at Beau and took the cup of punch he offered. "Oh, the uniform is striking, but the man leaves something to be desired," she lied.

Beau rolled his eyes. "I was speaking of Mrs. Papjoy and Squire Morton."

Amused at his comic expression, Marjorie said, "Juliana and anyone make a striking couple. I haven't seen her wear those sapphires before. Has she forgiven you, then?"

Unabashed affection glowing in his eyes, he stared at his mistress. "Bold as brass she is. Sent me a pair of goats with a parchment proclaiming me the Lord High Goatmonger of Bath."

"What did you do?"

He chuckled. "I donated the beasts to the royal menagerie, and then I came to my senses. 'Twas either the bauble or a season of cold shoulders. She's a proud woman."

Envy settled inside Marjorie. Once she had dreamed of giving her heart to a man who would love her, cherish and respect her. He'd laugh at her jests, buy her gifts for no reason at all, except that he loved her. Thanks to her father, that dream had become a nightmare. "You're well suited, Beau, and both very clever."

He rested folded hands on his portly midsection. Surveying his kingdom, he said, "You're the clever one. I received your note, and as you can see, I've instituted your plan."

"I just hope it works." She touched the embroidered sleeve of his formal coat. Since the day she had arrived in Bath ten years before, Beau Nash had been a constant in her life. "He has so much pride."

"And you don't? He lacks something or has committed a grave error, else your father wouldn't have caught him." Beau paused to nod to the duke of Cleveland, who was guiding Lady Sheridan onto the dance floor. "He's been prating about marrying you."

Familiar weariness engulfed Marjorie. "I know."

"What could your father have on Chesterfield's heir?" whispered Beau, awe and confusion in his voice. "'Tis baffling."

"What indeed," she murmured as she watched Lord Blake bow deeply over his partner's hand. How had one so revered, so well fixed in England's nobility fallen beneath her father's yoke? She searched his broad form, his regal features for a speck of weakness. She found naught but a scandalously handsome blackguard.

The music stopped. He tucked the countess's arm in his and escorted her from the dance floor. Craning her neck, she spoke to him. He laughed, setting the gold braid on his shoulders to jiggling. Leaning close, he whispered a reply. The older woman shot him a look of disbelief; then she drew her fan to her lips to hide a chuckle.

Beside Marjorie, Beau stiffened and huffed his

disapproval. "The martinet," he spat. "If he oozes any more of that Chesterfield charm, he'll have the women swooning where they stand."

"Agreed." Marjorie scanned the room. "Lady Sheridan's batting her eyelashes so hard and fast that patch on her cheek is flapping. Cleveland thinks she's flirting with him."

"Lord Blake told everyone you'll be married at month's end."

Marjorie almost dropped her reticule. "How dare that blabbering jackanapes make such a commitment!" Now he'd definitely forfeit his pride. "By month's end he'll be wallowing—" She stopped at the sight of Dame Surleigh an arm's length away, her beady eyes in a squint, her ear turned rudely to their conversation. Worse, Tobias Ponds stood beside her.

Wearing a scissor-cut coat of dark brown velvet, he looked more like a carefree nobleman than a shiftless cheat who'd stoop to treachery to become the postmaster of Bath.

Beau looked up at Marjorie, then followed the line of her vision. He spied the dame and her companion. "No eavesdropping here," he commanded. "'Tis the pastime of jades and Peeping Toms."

Dame Surleigh's eyes bulged. "Well, I never." Chin in the air, she turned away. The unsmiling Tobias didn't move.

Behind his hand Beau whispered, "Don't fret, Marjorie dear. You won't be dancing down any aisle with Lord Blake. You won't be dancing with him here, either. Unless you've changed your mind since sending me that note."

A few hours earlier she'd wanted to dance with Blake Chesterfield. She'd even worn her fanciest dress. Throughout the day her thoughts had strayed to him. He was a traveled man, and he had a sense of humor. She'd envisioned them becoming temporary friends.

"Marjorie?"

How silly of her. "No. I haven't changed my mind."

"That's just as well," said Beau. "In the new order of things, four more countesses await him."

Revenge tasted sweeter than the punch to Marjorie. Her plan to teach Lord Blake a lesson was succeeding. "How many baronesses?"

A smile of pure confidence wreathed Beau's face. "Five."

"I do so love your propensity for rules."

"You, my dear, created this new one. I only enforced it. And when the country dances begin I'll take him to the gaming room. Tobacco and carousing have a way of relaxing a man." Dropping his chin, he said solemnly, "I'd like to see what this Chesterfield is about."

"He's desperate."

He didn't seem desperate, though, moments later when he handed the countess into Beau's care. Clicking his heels together, he bowed from the waist and said, "A pleasure, madam."

She flushed, and her keen gray eyes met Marjorie's. "Lord Blake was just telling me the good news. So uncontrived he is. Why, he even told me how he received that ghastly cut."

From his spot behind Beau Tobias Ponds glared at Marjorie and said, "Do enlighten us, Lord Blake, about your injury."

Oh, God. Tobias had found out about the robbery. But how? From whom? No, she decided, he couldn't know. He was too much of a braggart to play coy. If he knew that the post had been robbed, he'd spread the tale like the plague. He was merely hoping to see her embarrassed.

Addressing the group, she said, "Oh, don't believe a word Lord Blake says. He's as full of tales as a fisherman's dory."

Blake crossed his arms and shifted his weight to one booted foot. Smiling congenially, he surveyed every face in the small circle. Except Marjorie's. Beyond her, glasses clinked and laughter erupted, but in this tiny group expectant silence reigned.

Why was Lord Blake ignoring her? He should be like the others her father had sent. He should play the suitor and grumble good-naturedly about not being able to dance with her. Suddenly uneasy, she awaited his tale of derring-do.

He chuckled and touched his stitched cheek. "Very well. I know when I'm caught dead to rights. Let me say first that I've been at sea too long. I'm still clumsy on land."

"You wouldn't guess it from the way you were dancing," Marjorie snapped, hating herself for making such a prissy remark.

"Imagine," trilled the countess, waving her fan, "he collided with a bootscraper and had the honesty to admit it. Most men would make up an unlikely tale of heroism."

The guilt Marjorie had felt earlier returned in full force. He hadn't revealed the postal robbery. He also seemed resigned to the social order of the dance. Still, that didn't make up for the lie he'd told her.

"Lady Marjorie stitched him up. Didn't you?" added the countess.

A run of notes from a flute signaled the next dance. A tight-lipped Beau mumbled, "Excuse me," and he wandered into the throng.

"I'm surprised, Lady Marjorie," said Tobias. "I didn't realize you practiced the womanly art of stitchery."

Now the center of attention, Marjorie knew she

must reply. She gazed at Blake. He didn't look her way. What was wrong with him? And what was so bloody interesting about the countess's wig that he continued to stare at it rather than at Marjorie?

Growing uneasier by the moment, she said, "'Twas my boot scraper he fell upon. The least I could do was tend the wound. Isn't that so, Lord Blake?"

Staring straight ahead, he smiled. "A perfect account of the tryst, my dear—considering we're in mixed company."

The women tittered like girls. Marjorie fumed.

Beau returned, a matriarch of the neighboring gentry at his side.

Without a glance or a motion toward Marjorie Lord Blake came to attention. "Ah, Nash," he said, as regally as a king on parade, "I see you've brought me another victim. How do you do, madam?"

Beau yanked at his waistcoat. "May I present Lady Markham, countess of Wells?"

Despite her age, which rumor estimated at seventy, the matriarch dropped into a graceful curtsy. "My lord." Rising, she said, "The devil with Mister Nash's new protocol. I'm delighted to make your acquaintance, Lord Blake, but I'm absolutely certain you'd rather dance with Lady Marjorie than with an old woman."

The clock of time seemed to stop, and he turned his head so slowly toward Marjorie that she had an endless moment to anticipate his expression. He's handsome indeed, she thought, awaiting the instant their gazes would meet. Expecting a winsome smile, she was unprepared for the cold glitter in his green eyes.

Her flagging spirits soared, for the scoundrel was as angry as she. Hallelujah! She tipped her head to the side and smiled innocently.

He didn't move so much as a spiky eyelash. "That's

very kind of you, Lady Markham, but my betrothed has her entire life to dance with me. Don't you, darling?"

"Oh," Marjorie said primly, "I have my life ahead of me all right. Go ahead, Lady Markham. He'll be leaving us soon."

His wrathful countenance hit her like a blow. The intimate address was a scam. Good, sweet Lord, he was angry. She'd played his game and outfoxed him. He didn't like it.

He leaned close. His breath tickled her ear. His mustache raked her cheek. "I'll be leaving true enough, and I'll take you with me."

She couldn't stop a blush from creeping up her cheeks. "Let us hope your brains match your boldness, my lord."

Pulling away, he gave her a saucy wink.

Lady Markham smiled knowingly. Tobias frowned in confusion. Dame Surleigh sighed. With sinking dread Marjorie realized they thought Lord Blake played a game of seduction rather than a contest of wills.

Jowls quivering, Beau blustered, "Stop this knavery, Lord Blake. Kissing and other forms of affection are strictly forbidden. You shan't dance with her either."

"You stop, Mister Nash," complained Lady Markham. "This new rule is senseless. We are bored silly by it. And it hardly applies here, since Lady Marjorie and Lord Blake are betrothed. They should dance."

Marjorie almost groaned. She'd be hard put to gracefully escape this marriage trap if it became a foregone conclusion. "Please don't cause a stir, Lady Markham," Marjorie said. "Lord Blake is accustomed to dancing with many women."

Lord Blake grasped the countess's hand. "Don't chide Nash too much, Lady Markham, for I'm fast learning that without his discipline Bath would descend into a den of iniquity. Please, do me the honor."

As if nothing were amiss he strolled with his partner to the dance floor and took the foremost spot in the set.

"Your cup is almost empty, Marjorie." Beau held out his arm. "Come, let me escort you to the punch bowl."

Exhausted, Marjorie allowed him to lead her away. As they wended through the throng of familiar faces she nodded, doll-like, and uttered meaningless phrases on the proposed Gambling Act, the departure of the Prince of Wales, the repaving of the road to London. She ignored the comments about her marriage to Blake Chesterfield. All the while her mind ran the gamut of reasons for his ire. Let him get as angry as he pleased. She had a life in Bath, and if the mighty Lord Blake thought to strip her of it, then he was in for a long bout of annoyance.

Feeling suddenly better, she sipped the mock ratafia.

"I believe," said Beau, "that I'll have them play an extra minuet or two." He shuffled off to the musicians' gallery.

Staring at the almond-rich drink, Marjorie vowed to ignore her perplexing suitor. But the moment her mind strayed from the pledge, her attention turned to the dance floor. Smiling as if he hadn't a care in the world, and moving with the grace of a cavalier, he executed the steps of the minuet to perfection. Sea legs indeed. He seemed to absorb attention, to thrive on it. Had she underestimated him? Oh, yes, she admitted, dreadfully so.

A flash of orange satin caught her eye. Looking left, she spied Edward Luffingham bearing down on her. A tailor by trade, a nitpicking grouch by nature, he was the second-to-last man she wanted to talk to. Topping off the garish suit, he wore his hair bunched like turnips beneath a dusted Falbala periwig.

"Lady Marjorie," he blustered, "I must speak to you about the mail."

Although she knew he meant to cause trouble, she clung to the safe topic of her work. "How may I help you?"

Drawing himself up, he said, "That snip of a postboy hasn't been by to fetch my letters."

She put down the cup. "That young boy is Cumberland Stokes, and he hasn't been by because you refused to pay him the postage on your letters going to London."

"It's to be paid on the other end." Chuckling, he added, "Unless you've taken it upon yourself to change the law."

Poor Cumber often bore the wrath of this grousing ne'er-do-well. She ached to call him a selfish bully, but name-calling wasn't the answer. The ever-ardent gossips of Bath would spread the rumor that she couldn't manage her job. Even now her conversation with Luffingham was drawing a crowd. Lady Sheridan and Dame Surleigh sidled closer. The sight of Juliana Papjoy edging up gave Marjorie courage.

"You know very well that I haven't changed the law, or bent it." Dropping her voice, she continued, "Your letters have been refused by your solicitor in London. Master Stokes apprised you of that when he returned the last batch to you. At considerable expense to me, I might add."

His eyes bulged. The ridiculous wig slipped back over his forehead, exposing a shock of carrot-hued hair that clashed miserably with his coat. "I gave him fourpence apiece for my letters when he fetched them. You look for my coin in that boy's pockets. You'll find it there."

Protectiveness rose in Marjorie. "That's a serious

accusation, Mr. Luffingham. Cumber Stokes is no thief."

"Well, I'm saying he is. Had he begged a few coins, like his mother was wont to do, I'd've given him a penny, generous soul that I am."

Generous? she thought. This penny-pinching louse made a practice of scratching out addresses and using the envelopes twice. But no matter his methods, she would not lose her temper. Quietly she said, "This is neither the time nor the place for a business discussion, Mr. Luffingham. I shall look into the story and call on you tomorrow."

Suddenly cognizant of the bystanders, he said, "Yes, well, until tomorrow, then." Righting his wig, he walked away.

Tobias Ponds stepped into her line of vision. "When I'm postmaster I'll put that Stokes back in Lilliput Alley with the other beggars and thieves."

The crass statement sapped her patience. She'd had enough boldness from thoughtless, arrogant men. "You'll be postmaster when the baths run dry."

He sneered and clutched the wide lapels of his coat. A familiar diamond ring glittered on his little finger. "I don't have to bandy words with you."

"True," she snapped. "You always lose."

"I'll overbid you."

"You could never offer as much as I can for the commission, but you're welcome to try."

Juliana Papjoy moved between them. "Do go away, Tobias, or I'll tell Mister Nash you've been crowding before the ladies."

He whirled and stomped away, the tails of his suit coat flapping

Juliana slid her arm through Marjorie's. "That one has the gall of a sedanchairman."

Marjorie sighed and glanced down at her companion. "And you have a lovely necklace."

Smiling proudly, she said, "It's new."

Marjorie thought about the jewels she'd once owned. She didn't lament, though. Losing her mother's gems had taught her a valuable lesson about men and herself. "Let's retire to the ladies' sitting room, and you can tell me how you managed to parlay a pair of goats into a string of sapphires."

Juliana sighed coyly. "Of course. But you must tell me all about Lord Blake. I think he's a lambkin—a gorgeous lambkin."

Blake felt as if his face would crack if he had to smile at one more simpering chit or fluttery matron. Damn that bold Marjorie Entwhistle and her supercilious champion. No wonder she'd been so eager to accept his invitation tonight. She'd known all along that he couldn't dance with her. Damn Nash and his ridiculous social order. Damn Marjorie for not warning him.

Damn me for underestimating her, he thought.

Never again, he swore. He knew the way to put her in her place. Try and best him, would she? Oh, yes, his little postmistress was in for a shock. And Beau Nash needed to be taught a lesson.

An hour later, as he held another winning hand of cards, Blake savored his revenge. That Ponds fellow and the tailor Luffingham had dropped over four hundred pounds apiece. With the king of Bath as his partner Blake couldn't lose. Ponds and Luffingham were pigeons ripe for the plucking.

Feeling inordinately pleased, Blake clamped his teeth down on the square end of a cheroot and stared at his winnings, which he estimated at almost one thousand pounds.

Ponds leaned back in his chair. "I say, Lord Blake. Since you and our postmistress have set the date, I'd be happy to print the announcements. I print all of the timetables for Marjorie. Luffingham and Nash can vouch for the quality of my work."

Nash, the consummate gambler, kept his attention focused on the cards. "Let's not be hasty, Tobias. *This* betrothal is a serious and private matter."

The printer drew back as if struck.

The tailor blinked and drew his hungry gaze from Blake's stack of markers. "I thought this betrothal a jest—same as the others." Baldly he added, "You ain't truly shackling yourself to that woman?"

"Be silent!" said Nash.

Blake said, "There are different kinds of shackling, you know."

Eyeing Blake, the tailor said, "She's got the tongue and ways of a viper. Ponds can vouch for that."

"Chesterfields have a way of taming women," Blake murmured, wondering what had caused the enmity between Ponds and Marjorie. Surely not the post, not if Marjorie patronized Ponds's business.

Luffingham rested his elbow on the table and leaned toward Blake. "Plucks up thieves and beggars from Lilliput Alley—like that Cumber boy—then dresses them in fine livery and sends 'em amongst honest folks. That's what she does."

Nash slammed his cards facedown on the felt. His cool facade vanished. "Luffingham!" he roared. "How dare you? You've no grounds to criticize Lady Marjorie. She's an angel of mercy."

Ponds watched the interchange and smiled as if pleased. Why? What had Marjorie said? That the printer wanted her job.

The ruddy-faced tailor licked his lips. "Maybe I spoke out of turn, but I'll tell you this." He shook his hand, foolishly exposing his cards. Blake knew what to lead next. "She oughtn't to take on a man's job. When Ponds here is postmaster we'll see an improvement in the comings and goings of the mail."

Curiosity forced Blake to say, "What happened between you and Lady Marjorie, and what's this about a thief?"

Beau said, "I'm certain 'tis a misunderstanding, and quite obviously a business matter between Lady Marjorie and Luffingham."

Marjorie a woman of business. The notion still seemed odd to Blake. But then, his life had taken an odd turn, hadn't it?

Emboldened, the tailor said, "'Tis that Cumber Stokes, that's who. Blood tells, I always say. He's no better'n the thievin' slut that birthed him."

Cumber a thief? No. When Blake had lost his footing and cut his cheek the good-natured lad had almost cried. The boy wasn't devious enough to steal.

"Have you spoken with Lady Marjorie about the boy?" Blake asked.

"Briefly," said the tailor. "She's to report to me tomorrow morning."

Blake intended to be there. "I'm certain she will, then."

"I'm certain that'll put an end to it," said Nash, his face devoid of expression. "'Tis your lead, Tobias."

Ponds shrugged and wrongly led a ten of clubs.

Luffingham, who'd been holding his two remaining cards as if they were a talisman to ward off goblins, smiled and mopped sweat from his brow. He played the jack.

"Hooray!" yelled Nash, playing the eight. "Let's see that king, partner."

Sweet satisfaction thrummed through Blake. "If you insist, partner." In one smooth motion he lay down the king, swept the trick aside, and played his remaining card, the queen and last of trumps.

A porter passed, ringing a bell and signaling the final dance.

Blake put out his smoke and pushed his winnings toward Nash.

"What's this, Chesterfield?" asked Nash, eyeing the markers.

Feeling delightfully wicked, Blake said, "I'd like you to commission Luffingham here to provide new cloaks —warm wool ones—for all the postboys. Give the rest to your favorite charity."

Nash's mouth dropped open. The tailor, seeing he could recoup some of his coin, blew out his breath. Ponds pinched his bottom lip, his eyes staring at nothing. He seemed the crafty sort to Blake. "Ponds," he said, "you needn't scheme to discredit Marjorie. She'll be resigning her post soon."

The printer glared at Blake. "My quarrel with Marjorie is my affair."

"Any conniving from you, Ponds," warned Beau, "and I'll make it my affair."

The bell sounded again. Blake rose and excused himself. As he strolled into the main room he looked for Marjorie. She walked arm in arm with an older man who looked familiar to Blake. She'd probably spent the last two hours dancing with any man who asked her.

Seething, Blake intercepted them on the dance floor. "Hello, Marjorie . . . darling."

She gasped, causing her breasts to swell provocatively over the bodice of her dress.

Her partner didn't seem to notice. "I'm Marshal Wade, at your service, my lord."

Blake knew of the famous road builder-cum-parliamentarian, and he hoped the man wasn't as set on protecting Marjorie as Nash. Smiling cordially, Blake grasped Marjorie's hand. "If you don't mind . . ."

Wade nodded in understanding. "Of course you'll want to dance with your fiancée."

She tried to pull her hand away. Blake held her fast. "I dislike French words," he said cordially to Wade. "I prefer good English terms." He faced the fuming postmistress but addressed the throng. "Let us simply say that Marjorie is . . . mine."

Movement around them ceased. A fire like Saint Elmo's glowed in her blue eyes, and her fingernails gouged his callused palm. He'd trade his medals of valor to hear her thoughts right now. Pride momentarily salved, he lifted his eyebrows and waited for her to speak.

Pretty red lips parted. At the base of her exquisitely long neck her pulse pounded like a tiny drum. In a parody of his own expression her brows arched. "'Tis poetic! The last dance of the evening is to be our last dance forever—contrary to what you've told these poor people."

A pregnant pause ensued.

Chuckling at her clever reply, Blake waited as the dancers lined up on either side of them. The musicians struck up a reel. When their turn came Blake recovered from the shock and led her to the middle of the floor. "I'll have you for more than a dance, Marjorie," he threatened.

"Your bark is worse than your bite." She laughed gaily and, without missing a step, skipped backwards to her spot in the reel.

He wanted to throttle her. But at the prospect of putting his hands around her graceful neck his mind turned to lustier pleasures. He'd like to peel off that black and white concoction and see if her waist was as small as it looked, her breasts as lush as they appeared. He watched her skip to the center of the dance floor and twirl arm in arm with another partner. Oh, yes, he thought, I'll enjoy getting heirs on this long-legged beauty.

When his turn came Blake met her in the center of

the dance floor, grasped her waist, and swung her around.

"You're gawking at me," she said, flitting away before he could reply.

By the time the reel concluded and Blake escorted her to the cloakroom his anger had cooled. Other parts of him, however, burned like a flame.

"Beau will see me home," she said, and she gave Blake her back.

He spun her around. "He'll see you in hell first. I'm taking you home."

"Now is as good a time as any," she spat. "I've a few things to say to you."

CHAPTER 5

Gentlemen of Breeding shall not force their attentions on the Ladies of Bath.

—Beau Nash, *Rules of Bath*

A TORRENT OF ANGRY WORDS PERCHED ON MARJORIE'S tongue. She held them back. When she singed the blackguard's ears she'd do so without an audience.

Collecting herself, she pulled her cloak snug around her and marched out the ballroom door. A line of street lamps shone like bright square moons against the dark blue sky. Following their familiar path, she headed for Hartsung Square. The cool night air bathed her flushed face and tugged at the curls of her stylish coiffure.

She didn't care that she was unraveling in front of him.

The clickety-click of her high-heel shoes on the smooth stone street set up a harmony with the solid crunching of Lord Blake's boots. Sedanchairmen raced past, their empty conveyances bobbing recklessly as they hurried to pluck a fare from the crowd pouring out of Wiltshire's.

One of the men halted and set down the poles,

then motioned for one of his cronies to stop. "Smoothest ride in Bath, my lord," he called out to Blake. "We'll take you, and my friends'll take Lady Marjorie."

Blake pitched the man a coin. "No, thanks, mate, my fiancée and I are taking a more secluded route."

He grasped Marjorie's arm and guided her across the street.

"I don't want you to call me your fiancée."

"That's unfortunate," he ground out.

"Where are you taking me?" she demanded, trying to yank her arm from his.

"To task."

She tried to pull away again, but his hand gripped hers like a manacle. "Let go of me, you conceited, thoughtless beast."

"I? Thoughtless? But I've a whole host of thoughts regarding you."

"I don't wish to hear them."

"I suggest," he said smoothly, "that you begin by explaining to this conceited, thoughtless beast why you were two hours late."

Looking for eavesdroppers, she glanced over her shoulder. The others still stood in front of Wiltshire's, a block away. "You can suggest until your fancy medals tarnish for all I care."

He walked faster. Marjorie easily kept pace with him. "You were late on purpose," he accused.

Staring at their elongated shadows, she applauded herself for choosing the shoes; she stood as tall as he. "Perhaps I was. And since you seem determined to break my arm if I don't salve your precious pride, I'll tell you why I was late."

She stopped and faced him. Light from the street lamp formed a halo around him. What a silly notion, she thought, for if Blake Chesterfield were an angel, posting nags could fly.

"I'm waiting."

Furious, she said, "I had to bag the Bristol mail. That's why I was late."

He pulled her close, his mouth a white slash beneath his jet-black mustache. "Sorting the mail is Albert's job. You'll have to invent a better excuse than that."

Hold your temper, she told herself. She couldn't. "You're just a privileged nobleman. You've never worked a day in your life."

"How would you know?"

"I'm gifted with the sight."

He looked her up and down. Smiling lecherously, he said, "You certainly are, and I await the 'sight' of you in our marriage bed."

She threw up her hands. "Why do I argue with you?"

Shaking his head, he said, "'Tis a wonderment to me, Postmistress. You haven't answered."

Maybe he would go away if she did. "Bagging the mail is Albert's responsibility—until Tug's back on his feet. Albert, however, spent the afternoon recounting his adventure with you instead of doing his job."

"You could have sent word to me."

"I considered it. Until I found out you lied about that cut on your face. You were never in any danger with Drummond."

He started walking again, tugging her along. "Would you have stitched me up? Would you have laughed with me? Would you have agreed to go to Wiltshire's had you known the truth?"

Unprepared for honesty from so despicable a man, she said, "Of course I would have ministered to you, especially after what you said about Everson stitching you up. I took pity on you. Foolish me."

His hand relaxed, but not enough to allow her to escape. "But your pity felt so good. Especially when you kissed me."

That he would discuss their past intimacies appalled Marjorie. "If you insist on seeing me home, you're going the wrong way. Turn left. Then right at Horrid Tom's. And no more talk of kissing."

As they rounded the corner he said, "Did you instigate Nash's social order tonight?"

The icy wind whistled around them. Marjorie tucked her chin beneath the collar of her cloak. "The rules are posted all over town. You should have stopped to read them."

"He changed the rules tonight. Why?" His voice dripped scorn.

"Why not? You ignored me until the last dance. Then you embarrassed me to my toes."

"I was angry."

"Do tell."

"I still am. And you still didn't answer my question."

"Then we have something in common. And I don't intend to answer."

"We could have more in common."

So, thought Marjorie, persistence was Lord Blake's strong suit. Fine, because frankness was hers. "What did you expect to gain by telling everyone in Bath we were betrothed?"

"We are betrothed," he said smoothly. "And I don't think I have to tell what I'll gain. You're not that naïve."

"You scoundrel!"

"Perhaps. But I'm your scoundrel."

"If you speak so frankly when you're upset, I shudder to think what you say to your lights o' love."

"You could find out, you know."

"I've found out all I need to know about you, and I don't like it."

"You're getting prissy, Marjorie."

She was also walking so fast that her feet hurt. She slowed. "Go to the devil."

"Look." He sighed and loosened the collar of his uniform. "I'm sorry."

His apology sounded forced. She said, "And you'll be that way for the rest of your pampered life."

"Pampered?" he choked out. "Ha. You've never been on a warship, or you wouldn't say such a thing. I awake at dawn in an opulent stateroom, which is the size of a broom closet. If I'm lucky, I don't bash my head on the ceiling beam. My cabin boy, an admirable fellow dragged from the bowels of a Spanish galleon, dresses me in my fine uniform, which is unfortunately as damp as a used Bath robe. I eat a mouthwatering breakfast of flat beer and vintage ship's biscuit. Sometimes, just for a treat, there's a worm in it. Then I stroll above decks." His voice dropped. "Where the scenery is predictable and the companionship less than enchanting."

She wasn't about to feel sorry for him. She was still too angry. "Well, you certainly took your fill of enchanting company tonight."

"Jealous?"

She shot him a look reserved for postal bandits.

"I guess that would be too much to hope for. Listen, Marjorie. I went there to be with you. I hoped we could get to know each other better."

"That would have been a good idea—before announcing our betrothal. I have no intention of marrying you. I had hoped to allow you your pride, but you've botched that yourself."

"Are you finished?"

"With you? Yes."

"I'm not finished with you," he said ominously.

"I see. And that's why you stayed in the gaming room for hours."

"Nash rooked me into playing whist. That was probably your idea, too." Shrugging, he added, "At least we won."

"Nash always wins. He's a professional gambler, but that hardly excuses your behavior."

"I think it does, considering we nicked Ponds and your friend Luffingham out of almost one thousand pounds."

Her stomach grew queasy at the thought of Ponds. "They are not my friends, and I care nothing about money won at gaming. It's a vile, destructive pastime."

"How would you know?"

The old shame flickered to life. She could tell him a tale that would make him cringe in disgust. "Believe me, I know."

"I gave my share of the winnings to charity. An admirable trait in your husband, no?"

"You can give it to the Pope for all I care. I will not marry you."

"Why not? You don't even know me. I could be the man of your dreams."

"You could be the goblin in my nightmares, too."

Hartsung Square came into view. Security and confidence flowed through her. Perched atop a rise and dwarfing the other residences, the mansion looked like a queen surrounded by her subjects. The columned facade fashioned of Bathstone glowed like rich ivory in the moonlight.

"Mark my words, Marjorie, once you're in my bed you won't be troubled by goblins."

"Are you deaf? I will not marry a man I loathe. I won't marry a liar, either."

"You're getting prissy on me again," he said with too much familiarity. "Besides, no one marries for love. It's simply not done in the best circles."

"Circles make me dizzy. And I shall marry for love!"

He laughed, low and seductive. "Then I'd best be about making you fall in love with me, hadn't I?"

Marjorie stopped, the echo of his promise ringing in her ears, the romantic voice in her heart crying out for love. Light shone through the windows of the Hamburg room. "Pistols and petticoats!" Dismissing his empty words, she changed directions.

"Hum. Two of my favorite things," he mused. Seeing that she'd walked away, he said, "What's wrong? Where are you going?"

"Grandmama's still awake. I don't want her to see us together, so I'm going 'round to the back door. You can go back to sea."

His deep laughter rang out. "Not without you, darling."

"Good night, Lord Blake!" She marched to the side yard and the public entrance of the post office. He followed.

A brass post horn gleamed beneath a pair of globe lamps. She heard voices inside.

Frustrated, and eager for a few moments alone, she crossed the shadowed yard to the stables. Blake dogged her footsteps like a seasoned lecher. Mud seeped into her shoes, but she didn't care.

"I'm not leaving you outside."

She drew back the bolt, yanked open the door, and stepped inside. "There. You've seen me inside. Now go away."

"Marjorie," he growled.

In the darkness horses whinnied and stamped. "Oh, very well," she said. "But if you insist on making a

nuisance of yourself, at least be useful. Light the lamp.
It's there by the door to the tack room."

Behind her and to the left she heard him bark his
shin on a mounting box and swear. A bucket rattled
noisily. He cursed again. A moment later flint struck
steel. Light filled the room. The horses poked their
heads out of the stalls, their ears pricked. A still-
dripping cloak hung on a peg outside the first stall.

The London post had arrived. No wonder lights
were on in the posting room. Grandmama was sorting
the mail when she should be abed. The boys were hard
at work. Marjorie would have to help them.

Suddenly weary, she went to the first stall and
leaned against it. Out of habit she mentally listed
tomorrow's tasks. Rise before the sun. See Wick
Turner and the Bristol mail cart on its way. Remember his lunch. Eat breakfast with Grandmama. Skip
the bath. Take Cumber to confront the wretched
tailor. Sit with Tug. Give geography lessons to the
boys. In the afternoon, make the round of titled guests
and residents. Collect their letters and packages. Tally
the fees.

"Is something wrong?" Blake asked.

She laughed without humor and shook her head.
The horse nuzzled her neck. She stroked its nose.
"Everything. Nothing. Will you please leave?"

He scooped up a handful of oats and walked toward
the horse. Against her will she found herself admiring
Blake Chesterfield, his handsome form—long, lean
legs, trim waist, broad shoulders, a thickly muscled
neck, and a face more recognizable to any Englishman
than the newly come Hanoverian king's.

Standing beside her, he offered the oats to the horse.
"Tell me what's bothering you."

She tried to summon her former anger but couldn't
"I want you to leave Bath."

A rakish smile lit up his face. "I will, as soon as you marry me and conceive me a son. Step aside."

Irritated at his persistence, she moved back. He opened the door of the stall, walked inside, and removed his coat. Speaking softly to the brown horse, he picked up a handful of straw and began dragging it over the animal's damp coat. "You should take better care of your horses."

"That is not my horse. It belongs to an innkeeper in Chippingham."

"He's your responsibility when he's in your stable. You should also demand better mounts."

"And you should listen to me. This is not your business."

"Anything that concerns my betrothed is my business."

"I refuse to be your betrothed. I won't be used as a pawn between you and my father."

He propped his elbow on the horse's withers and laid his head against his palm. Seemingly unperturbed, he said, "Would it make any difference if his honor rested in the balance?"

A lifetime of paternal neglect flashed before her. From the day she could pen the alphabet she'd written to Papa, first asking and later begging him to visit her at the convent. Each year on her birthday a letter containing a little money arrived. But the note was written by a clerk, and she had nowhere to spend the money. Choking back the remembered sorrow, she said, "My father has no honor. He's given me nothing."

He spread his arms wide. "He gave you me."

"I don't want you."

"You do. You just don't know it yet."

"You're daft."

He stiffened and kicked the stall. The horse side-stepped. "Easy, old mate. What if I told you that he'd forfeit his castle and his vineyards to me if you refuse to marry me?"

For years she had prayed for such circumstances, anything to have her father remember that she existed. But after all the betrothals she felt used. "I'm not some serf's daughter to be bartered away for a patch of land."

"You would stand by and let him lose everything he holds dear?"

"I care nothing for a pile of stones and a winery in France. If he lost them to you a-betting, that's none of my affair. I'm surprised he lost, though. They say he'll cheat to win."

Solemnly he said, "Those are harsh words, Marjorie. He is your father."

Suddenly ashamed, she looked away. The nuns had told her she asked too much of her father. An obedient daughter knew her place. And oh, what a place her father had chosen for her. A tiny, dark room in a remote convent in France. Her only companions had been the aged nuns, a cantankerous goat, a few chickens, and a sorrel mare appropriately named Fire. She had given names to the trees and rocks and pretended they were her boon companions. In spring she draped them with daisy chains and thanked them for proclaiming her the queen of the May. By day's end she told them of her loneliness.

"Here," he said, holding out a handkerchief. "Dry your eyes."

She hadn't known she was crying, and as the hot tears poured down her cheeks she wondered again what awful sin an infant girl could have committed to warrant such a desolate childhood. Ironically, her greater sin had come many years later, here in Bath.

Strong arms surrounded her, and before she could

protest he pulled her against him. "Shush," he murmured against her ear. "Don't cry. Nothing's so bad as that. Talk to me. What has upset you so?"

"Nothing you'd understand. And stop being so considerate."

He stroked her hair. "All will be well, Marjorie."

He spoke the truth, and although she knew it was wrong to give in to such weakness, she couldn't help herself. He offered comfort and solace. She needed both. She might as well take them while he was here. Like most of her other suitors, he'd leave Bath soon. She'd never see him again.

His hands roamed her back. "That's a girl. Relax."

She did, and as her mind cleared her common sense returned. She pulled back. "You maneuvered me into a moment of weakness. Still, I won't marry you."

"You're repeating yourself." His lips touched her temple.

"You humiliated me tonight, with everyone looking on."

"I'm sorry. I won't ever do it again."

"True. Because you're leaving. Just tell me why my father is blackmailing you, and I'll set things right. And don't tell me that lie about forfeiting his vineyards. I don't believe you."

"You don't like me either. You probably curse me to hell every night."

The self-deprecating statement struck a chord of irony in her. Any woman would want Blake Chesterfield. Marjorie Entwhistle just couldn't have him. Not on the terms he presented.

She took a deep breath, and her nose filled with his lemony scent. "I don't curse. Ever."

"Hum." The vibrations of his deep voice rumbled in her ear. "An admirable trait, Postmistress."

Be reasonable, she told herself. You've vented your anger. You have work to do. Let him leave with his dignity. "It's not that I don't like you. I meant it when I said we might have been friends—had circumstances been different."

His lips touched her cheek, and the drag of his mustache soothed her skin. He seemed so safe now, and yet so dangerous.

"We could try," he said, his mouth very close to hers, "and make a new start. You liked it when I kissed you."

"No, I didn't."

His eyes glowed with a peculiar light, and if she hadn't known better, she might have mistaken the look for tenderness. "You did so."

"I kissed you because I was grateful for what you did. And it turns out you didn't even do as you said."

He smiled and cupped her head in his hand. "Something in your eyes tells me that wasn't the only reason."

Now that they were conversing civilly, she could speak the truth. "I was merely curious about your mustache."

"I see," he said gravely. "Did you like the feel of it against your skin?" He took the handkerchief and dabbed at her eyes. "Did it tickle you or scratch you?"

At his tender ministrations she grew warm, listless. "I don't recall thinking about it."

"Because you were only feeling grateful toward me."

"Yes. That's it exactly."

"I understand perfectly."

She couldn't tear her eyes from his, couldn't escape or deny the interest glimmering in their cool green depths. He was a selfish liar, she reminded herself. He was trying to placate her so he could seduce her.

"I was glad to help you, Marjorie."

His lips settled on hers and moved slowly, seductively, giving her time to see if she liked the feel of him. She did. His lips were warm and soft, and he tasted of sweet French brandy and exotic tobacco. Emboldened and curious, she followed his lead and moved her lips across his. He tilted his head and deepened the kiss, his tongue nudging her lips apart. The soft brushing of his mustache against her cheek set her skin to tingling. She opened her mouth to ask him to stop, but his tongue slipped inside, robbing her of words and igniting a fire that warmed her from inside out. She grew weak, and her hands clutched at him like talons, crumpling the soft silk of his shirt and straining to get closer.

His hands rubbed her back and circled her waist, holding her up, drawing her out. She labored for every breath and fought to keep her mind alert, but thoughts drifted through her head like flotsam in a raging sea of sensual pleasure.

"How do you feel?"

"Like flotsam in a . . . Oops. I feel very odd, actually," she confessed.

"Remember," he whispered, "it's only gratitude."

She whispered back, "If this is gratitude, Blake Chesterfield, the king is a Turk."

He chuckled. "You're a prize, Marjorie Entwhistle." He kissed her again, and her senses reeled. As inexperienced as she was, Marjorie recognized desire pouring through her. In not so subtle ways her body responded: Her breasts felt heavy, eager for his touch, and her secret, womanly parts craved a greater intimacy. Of their own accord her hands moved up his neck and to his hair. The ribbon tie slipped free, and her fingers threaded into the thick, wavy strands.

He growled and sent his tongue deeper into her mouth, and she welcomed him, willingly playing the student to his tutor, caressing, stroking, reveling in the passionate lesson.

Cursing softly, he tore his mouth from hers and

trailed his parted lips down her neck and lower. Then his hands were pushing aside her cloak, reaching into her bodice and scooping up her breasts, lifting them, cradling them while his fingers teased the tautened nipples. Her senses seemed centered there, and when his tongue darted out to lave the straining buds she gasped and shuddered.

In answer he breathed gently against her nipple, then drew it fully into his mouth.

Her back arched like a tightly strung bow.

"You could nurture our son here, Marjorie," he said against her breast, "or suckle a daughter as lovely as you."

Yes, her heart cried. I would love a child; I would cherish and care for a babe.

"Say yes, Marjorie."

He swung her into his arms, and her "yes" turned to a gasp of surprise. In a daze of passion she watched him fling open the stable door and heard the sound of his boots tramping across the muddy yard. Easily he carried her, and through a dreamy lethargy she drew the edges of her cloak over her naked breasts and shuddered when the soft fur touched her tender nipples. The post horn and globe lights above the door gleamed up ahead. Stars twinkled above. Wind whistled around them.

He carried her up the steps, and when he reached the landing he leaned over. "Open the door, love."

Lost in the sensual message glaring hotly in his eyes, she reached down, grasped the handle, and flung open the door.

"Bloody barnacles!"

His curse brought her to her senses. And when her eyes adjusted to the light she groaned. For there in the posting room sat Grandmama and the parson sorting the London mail.

* * *

The next day Blake still felt naked to his toes. He hadn't been so ashamed of himself since the day he'd been caught cheating on an exam at Cambridge. Weariness engulfed him. He hadn't slept, for each time he closed his eyes he pictured the ghastly scene of the night before. The dowager had been indignant, bitter to the extreme in her condemnation. The look of disgust she'd aimed at Marjorie still made his blood boil.

Oh, Marjorie. His stomach bobbed like a cork when he thought about her, about the night before. She'd felt as light and cuddly as a kitten in his arms, her eyes dreamy with yearning, her lush body ripe for the taking. He could have taken her, too, there in the sweet-smelling hay with only the horses to witness their loving. But no. He wanted her in a warm, soft bed where he could spend hours learning her secrets, telling her some of his own.

The moment they entered the posting room her desire fled. He had complied with her choked-out request and put her on her feet. In awe he'd watched as she addressed the goggle-eyed parson, then excused herself and, with the dignity of a queen, marched from the room. Her explanation about slipping on the ice and injuring her ankle was as lame as a blind navigator.

Everson cleared his throat, jolting Blake from his reminiscences.

"Perhaps, my lord, we should commission a horse-hair shirt while we're here. That should fit your mood."

The all-too-familiar and sarcastic voice made Blake smile. "Stow it, Everson."

"No matter," he replied, a thumb and forefinger gingerly turning the pages of a fashion book as if they were covered with ants. "This Luffingham chap would probably ask you to bring in your horse for a fitting."

Blake chuckled. His extremely improper valet could find humor in a ship's fire. "And you, no doubt, would lead the hapless creature through the door and into this fitting room."

"I could never be so bold."

"Liar," Blake said good-naturedly.

Everson closed the book, wiped his gloved hands, and fished an overlong sheet of paper out of his pocket. Rattling the parchment, he said, "I brought along Nash's rules. Care to hear them?"

Ruefully, Blake said, "Do I have a choice?"

"No." He held the page at arm's length. "Quoth Mister Nash, 'Gentlemen of Fashion never appear in boots before the ladies.' " Snickering, he said, "You've broken that one."

"I was in a hurry, and the Prince of Wales didn't seem to mind."

In an imitation of Nash, Everson poofed out his stomach and rested his hand there. "That was the first night. What about last night? You wore your boots again."

"Dress boots and my uniform should be exempt from his rules."

But Everson was reading on. "Ah, here's another you've violated," he said solemnly, and he wagged a finger at Blake. " 'Ladies coming to the ball should appoint a time for their footman to see them home.' You walked her home yourself. And arrived later at Cleveland's in quite a state of pique."

Remembering his raging lust and boiling anger, Blake said, " 'Twas hardly pique."

"Hard is right," snapped Everson. "You popped a button on your breeches."

"That's enough, Everson. Just repair the damned things."

"Cleveland's parlor maid offered to do it— and

other things." He smiled hugely. "I accepted, of course."

Blake murmured, "You always do accept the 'help' of comely female servants."

Turning up a palm, he said, "Who am I to deny them?"

Blake didn't reply; he was more interested in the arrival of Marjorie Entwhistle than the amorous adventures of his valet.

"Listen to this," said Everson. " 'Gentlemen of breeding shall not force their attentions on the ladies at the Ball.' I think he penned that rule with you in mind."

Blake pounded his fist on the arm of the chair. "Will you cease!"

Everson folded the paper and put it away, then began examining swatches of fabric. Ten years Blake's senior, Oscar Everson had been friend, servant, and companion for as long as Blake could remember. The fair-haired, brown-eyed Everson could stare down any butler in the realm. He could also get up a parlormaid's skirts before she could turn down the lamp.

His hawklike nose bore an interesting kink, the result of an unwilling maid wielding a brass candlestick.

"What do you think of this shade of green?" asked Everson, holding up a scrap of lime velvet.

"I'd look like a parrot."

"True." He cast it aside. "Black most adequately suits your mood. Ah, there's the bell." He took out his watch. "Perhaps your quarry has entered the trap. I still say she won't notice anything different about you."

Excitement thrummed through Blake at the prospect of seeing Marjorie again. "She'll notice. She rather likes my face."

Everson held aside the curtain that separated the

fitting room from the main part of the tailor's shop. "Good luck, my lord, and leave Luffingham to me."

Blake stood motionless, the curtain at his back, Marjorie in his sights. She wore a wool gown in a shade of red reminiscent of sumac berries. The modest panniers drew his eye to her slender waist, which was bound by a black satin bow with sashes that framed a petticoat of gray velvet. Her thick golden hair peeked from beneath a demure gray bonnet. She held a leather mailbag in one hand, Cumber Stokes's shoulder clenched in the other.

From his vantage point Blake could see the profile of her lovely face. Even though she'd dusted her complexion with powder, he didn't miss the dark circles under her eyes. She'd probably lain awake fretting all night.

Behind the counter Luffingham looked up. "Do join us, Lord Blake."

Her back grew stiff as a harpoon. "Finish your statement, Mr. Luffingham," she said.

"'Twas my fault entirely, Lady Marjorie," said the tailor, slapping the counter. "I put the postage money here, and my clerk, not knowing what it was for, inadvertently returned it to the money box. Here." Smiling falsely, he pushed several coins toward her. "You do understand, I'm sure."

She took the money and gave it to Cumber. "I understand how accidents happen, Mr. Luffingham. But you did call Cumber a thief, and in front of a number of people. I think you owe him an apology, and I expect you'll have the decency to clear his name."

Blake remembered the harsh treatment and neglect of his own childhood. Why couldn't he have had a champion like her? He couldn't turn back the clock, but he could make sure his children had a loving, protective mother.

Cumber shoved his hands into the pockets of his green and yellow uniform and waited, his chin held high, his shoulders squared. When he saw Blake his mouth dropped open. "Cor! You scraped off your mustache! Wait'll I tell the others. Oops! Sorry, my lady." He resumed his pose, but anticipation glittered in his eyes.

Over her shoulder she glanced at Blake. Her gaze fastened on his mouth.

"Looks a smooth spark now, don't he, my lady?" said Cumber.

She shrugged and turned back to the tailor. "You were saying, Mr. Luffingham . . ."

A dip in the North Sea would have been warmer than her attitude, thought Blake.

The tailor tripped over his tongue in his haste to enumerate Cumber's fine qualities. "I was most certainly mistaken about this lad. He'll look the smart one, too, in his new cloak."

She frowned. "I have no idea what you're talking about, sir. I commissioned no apparel for Cumber."

Feeling like a condemned man approaching the gallows, Blake stepped to her side. "I did, Marjorie."

When she didn't offer her hand, he took it. And found it trembling in his own. Their eyes met. He expected embarrassment; what he got was continued indifference. He made himself a promise at that moment: One day very soon this gorgeous, complex woman would look at him with love in her eyes. She'd never learn his black secret. He could hide it from her just as he'd hidden it from everyone. Except her father and Everson.

"The boys need new cloaks," Blake said, hoping she'd open her pretty mouth and talk to him. He wanted to know what had made her cry in the stables last night. He wanted to make sure she never cried again.

"Uh, yes," stammered the tailor, "Lord Blake's ordered cloaks for all the postboys, warm ones with good, strong linings and hoods. Charitable soul, he is."

"How generous," she murmured. "I'm sure your conscience feels better."

"In that case, Mr. Luffingham," announced Everson, right on cue, "I suggest that you and I select the wool." He tapped Cumber on the shoulder and said, "Come along, lad, we'll need to match the cloth to your jacket, take measurements and such from all the boys. We'll begin with you, Mr. Stokes."

Marjorie faced the valet. "Who are you?"

Bowing, he said, "Everson, my lady."

Her gaze darted to Blake. "Let go of my hand."

He waited a moment to comply, giving Everson time to discreetly lock the front door, then usher Cumber and Luffingham into the back room.

Quietly Blake said, "You didn't sleep well."

She gave him a halfhearted smile. "I did nothing well last night."

He noticed a trace of redness on her cheeks. His mustache had taken a toll on her tender skin. He patted himself on the back for shaving. "That's a matter of opinion. How are you feeling?"

She toyed with the strap on the mailbag. "Actually, I'd say I feel rather well—for a charity case, that is."

Her pride sparked tenderness inside him. "The lads need cloaks, Marjorie. Nash said you didn't complain when Ralph Allen bought those cots for the dormitory last year."

"That was different. Mr. Allen is a resident of Bath."

"Look at me." He put his hand under her chin and lifted it.

Her eyes were great pools of regret. At that moment he started to fall in love with her. As his heart swelled his confidence soared. "You're beautiful, you know, and you're mine."

Beneath his knuckles the delicate muscles in her throat contracted. "No," she said, but she didn't pull away. "What I did last night was wrong. I should never have kissed you."

That was like her, forthright and honest enough to admit her part. Pleased to his fingertips, Blake said, "I'm sorry I was rough, but I liked it when you kissed me. I've shaved, you see? I'll never scratch your face again."

Her gaze dropped to his clean-shaven lip. "No, you won't. We shouldn't kiss."

"You mean we shouldn't get caught."

"Both."

From the corner of his eye he saw passersby on the boardwalk and hoped none would seek out the tailor shop. "You wanted me last night, Marjorie. Say it, love. Tell me truthfully."

Not batting an eyelash, she said, "I did feel desire for you, about that I cannot lie. Now you tell me the truth. Why do you want me? Is my father blackmailing you, or am I truly part of a gaming debt?"

He couldn't hold her gaze. God, if she only knew. "What if I told you I wanted you for myself? That I love you?"

She blinked, then laughed. "How original. Suitors one through six said the same thing."

CHAPTER 6

A Gentleman of Quality who takes unfair
advantage of a Lady of Breeding is no better than
the creature who forages for food.

—Beau Nash, *Rules of Bath*

IN THE QUIET CONFINES OF HER UPSTAIRS OFFICE MARJORIE studied the sketch of the mail coach, a sleek, high-wheeled, four-horse vehicle designed for speed. The drawing raised in her mind a vision of fast-spinning wheels, straining horses, and the hilly landscape of Wiltshire racing past in a blur. The swift coach was hopelessly trapped on a square of foolscap.

Her fellow postmasters proclaimed her idea folly. They said a mail coach traveling between London and Bath would bog down in the mud or shatter a wheel before it reached Brentford, the first of eleven stops. Her peers were partially correct, for the road had once been too badly rutted for a quick travel. Large carriages with the fastest of mounts had required three days to reach Bath.

Marshal Wade had changed that when he paved the road. Marjorie could now afford the coach. Beau had raised the money to pave the Great Bath Road, and Marjorie had convinced General Wade to oversee the work. Soon the mail coach would leave the drawing board and fly along the road to Bath.

It would take longer to get the mail to Bath by coach than by horseback, but the safety and profit it offered would offset the delay.

Feeling proud for taking the initiative and confident that her concept would soon become a fact, Marjorie traced the elegant lines of the carriage. She pictured four passengers inside. Their fares would cover the costs of feeding and stabling the extra horses. Tug, Wick, and Albert would be trained in the art of coaching. They were bright, responsible boys. They would learn. But who would teach them?

Marjorie Entwhistle would be hailed as an innovator for her progressive move. No one would criticize her management of the post. Not even Grandmama.

Marjorie imagined the surprised look on Blake Chesterfield's face when he learned of her achievement. She shouldn't want his approval, but she did—as much as she'd wanted his kisses in the stable.

A thrilling sense of anticipation had filled her that night. It filled her again. She thought of his soft lips, of his sweet words, of his tender ministrations. The feel of his hands caressing her, supporting her when she grew helpless in his embrace. He'd nurtured her passion and readied her for his loving. He'd suckled her breasts and enticed her with the promise of children. Like a Romeo overcome with love for his Juliet, Blake had swept her into his arms and carried her across the courtyard.

And brought her face-to-face with an affronted Grandmama and the gape-mouthed parson.

The memory turned sour. Marjorie winced, thinking of how close she'd come to surrendering to him, to disgracing herself, to sacrificing her life and her plans for the future.

The blackguard. Blake Chesterfield had probably seduced more women than Charles II, only because the last Stuart king hadn't ventured to the Colonies for his conquests.

Marjorie would not become the victim of a heartless rogue with some loathsome secret who'd struck a dishonorable alliance with her father. She had almost fallen prey to Blake Chesterfield, but she would never succumb to him again.

Even in the tailor shop he had tried to work his magic. He'd seemed so sincere in his guilt over the episode in the stable, but that hadn't stopped him from renewing his quest to marry her.

Out of practicality she'd accepted his donation of the cloaks; the boys needed warm clothing. But she understood the gesture for what it was: a bribe. Credit him with originality, she thought, for none of her other suitors had tried such a clever and, yes, generous ploy. They all had admitted to loving her. She knew a hollow declaration when she heard it.

A knock sounded at the door. "Come in."

Merlyn entered wearing a pleasant smile and a white apron over his black butler's habit. In his hands he held a silver chafing dish and a blackened rag.

"I'm sorry to interrupt, my lady, but Her Grace would like to see you in the Hamburg room."

Marjorie's first impulse was to refuse. Driven by shame and the need to be alone, she had concocted the excuse of falling on the ice. Drawn by a mountain of work, she had declined to take meals with Rowena or accompany her to the baths.

Cowardice had not influenced Marjorie's refusal; a new sense of privacy had. But sooner or later she'd have to answer Rowena's questions.

Merlyn cleared his throat. "She's in quite a pleasant mood." Embarrassment pinkened his cheeks. "If you're at all interested, that is."

Marjorie smiled. Surely Merlyn knew that she'd made a spectacle of herself with Blake Chesterfield; gossip traveled like the plague in Hartsung Square. How far would the tale-telling go? Probably all the way to Westminster. "Thank you, Merlyn. Tell her I'll be there directly."

"As you wish."

He started to leave but stopped at the sound of church bells. Pivoting, he walked to the window and looked down on the street. The pealing of the bells of Bath Abbey continued. "Twenty-four times," she mused. "Who is our titled visitor, Merlyn?"

His face was pressed so close to the window that his breath fogged the glass. "I can't make out the crest on the carriage door yet. But the coachman's a sight to see. He's wearing a black hat with a roguish red plume. Must be one of those Stuart dukes."

Now Marjorie *knew.* The finest coachman in England, the Prince of Wales had said of the man who wears flamboyant hats. Had Lord Blake summoned his father to Bath?

"Ah, now I can see." Merlyn paused and turned to face her. Smiling apologetically, he said, "'Tis the coach of the Chesterfields. My brother is inside."

Marjorie sagged with relief. "'Twould seem that Lord Blake intends to stay awhile in Bath."

Merlyn nodded. "So his man Everson said."

"I'm surprised. Where did you see Everson?"

"Why, here, just a few moments ago, Lady Marjorie. He came with Lord Blake."

Jolted, Marjorie said, "Lord Blake was here? Why?"

He sniffed. "I'm sure I wouldn't know. According to Lizzie, his lordship came 'round to the postal office and asked for Master Tug."

"Did Lizzie offer details about the visit?"

"Only that 'twas a brief meeting. She said Lord Blake spoke too quietly to Master Tug. She couldn't overhear." Eagerly, he added, "But I could summon Master Tug, if you like."

So Merlyn was curious about the visit, too. As ruler over the maids and the cooks he was privy to all of the household gossip at Hartsung Square. Only the post-boys lay outside his jurisdiction. "No. Don't summon him," Marjorie said. "I'll speak with him before he leaves for London."

"As you wish, my lady. I'll be off, then." He bowed and left the room.

Marjorie rolled up the drawing and slid it into its leather tube. She looked for her new satchel, and, not finding it, she put the drawing in her old leather pouch. She tidied her desk and returned the stacks of ledgers to the bookcase. Tomorrow she would have to begin the tedious job of auditing the figures from last year's postal receipts so she could prepare her annual bid for the postal surveyor. She would win the concession again. Her critics could find another victim. Tobias Ponds be damned.

Free of worry over her rival, Marjorie made her way downstairs. But when she spied Grandmama her suspicions sharpened like thorns on a bilberry bush.

Rowena lounged on the settee, her hands steepled and her fingertips tapping nervously. She stared into the fireplace. Around her neck she wore a choker of thumb-size topazes which caught the firelight and winked like miniature suns. She'd donned a gown of golden velvet over a white satin petticoat shot through with threads of gold.

Putting on a cheerful expression, Marjorie said, "What has you so deep in thought, Grandmama?"

Rowena flung her hands apart, then patted the

space beside her. "Marjorie, darling. Come sit down. We haven't shared cocoa in a monk's age."

Expecting censure, Marjorie wanted to refuse. Grandmama didn't appear to harbor any condemning notions about Marjorie's conduct with Lord Blake. Why not?

"Sit and rest your poor injured foot."

Grandmama had believed Marjorie's tale of a slip on the ice. Marjorie remembered to limp. "I'm fine, truly. I didn't hurt myself in the least."

Rowena's lips turned up in a smile reminiscent of a patient governess. "So you said. But as a precaution I had that Honeycombe boy sand the pavement."

Mildly affronted, Marjorie said, "You asked Albert? Oh, Grandmama, he's much too busy for such a task. Cumber or any of the younger boys could have done it."

Her face settled into a pout. "I was only trying to help. And I'm too old to distinguish one boy from the other. Time was when the post needed only a handful of laborers, and grown men at that."

"Grandmama, that's—"

"I agree, my dear," she interrupted. "That's neither here nor there. Being postmistress of Bath requires hard work and dedication. The people can't understand a smidgen of that. But I certainly do. After all, I *was* postmistress myself." She fished beneath her skirt and found Marjorie's new satchel.

"Where did you get that?"

With a self-satisfied smile Rowena said, "Merlyn fetched it from your office this morning while you were still abed. If my poor old legs could climb the stairs, I'd've gotten it myself."

Instantly offended, Marjorie said, "But it's mine."

"And very serviceable, too. Look what I've done. I was so concerned about your foot that I saved you the trouble of making rounds. See?" She pulled out a stack of letters. "I hired a carriage and collected mail from the dukes of Cleveland, Kingston, and Richmond, and several others. It's all here—the correspondence from all of the dukes in Bath."

Grandmama knew that Marjorie fetched mail from anyone in the household of a duke, not just the peer himself. Puzzled, she said, "Are you being snide?"

"Me?" She slapped the letters to her breast. "What can be snide about me trying to help? What's gotten into you? I was only following *your* rules. *You're* the one who decided to fetch mail personally from titled residents—if, of course, they happen to be dukes or better and are willing to pay a premium for the service."

When Marjorie had begun the rounds Rowena had objected strongly. "The boys needed boots and books," Marjorie said defensively. "That's what I used the money for."

"Of course they did, and you're always the clever entrepreneur. You took the responsibility off my back."

"But you never bought cloaks for the postmen under you," said Marjorie.

"They had their own. You're wise not to stop at the duke of Cleveland's just now. I don't mind going there for you. How is the audit coming along?"

Marjorie had avoided the duke's residence because Blake was there. Distracted, she said, "The sums cross my eyes."

"Will we show a profit for last year?"

"Of course. I expect I collected almost ten thousand pounds."

"My, my," Rowena said breathlessly, putting the letters and pouch in Marjorie's lap. "You've done a fine job. Almost as good as I used to." Sternly she added, "And kept meticulous records, unlike your counterparts in some districts I could name. Lizzie tells me you're commissioning a mail coach for us. When will work begin?"

Marjorie decided that worry over her own vulnerability toward Blake Chesterfield had been the reason behind her doubts about Grandmama's sincerity. She was only trying to help Marjorie. Eagerly she latched on to the exciting subject of the mail coach.

Just when she finished the story Tug stepped into the room. He'd donned leather riding pants and a green and gold livery jacket. In his gloved hands he held a newly polished post horn and a patched woolen cloak. Marjorie grew depressed at the yellow bruise that rimmed one of his eyes and the thin pink line that scarred his lip. She hoped he carried no inner bruises from the incident, for Tug needed all the confidence he could get.

"Excuse me, my lady. May I have a moment with you?" From his pocket he withdrew several envelopes.

"What are those?" Marjorie asked.

"Lord Blake's letters."

"Do come in, Tug," said Rowena. "It's beastly cold out. Have a cup of cocoa."

He blinked, looking at her as if she'd spoken in Greek.

"Come now, Tug. I insist," she declared. "You're scarcely out of your sickbed."

Hesitantly he approached. "That's very kind of you, Your Grace, but I'm off to London straightaway. That's where these letters are going. But I haven't listed them in the book yet, Lady Marjorie."

Why hadn't Grandmama taken Lord Blake's letters? Had she refused them? That was odd, since she loved to know who wrote to whom. Blake had brought his letters himself. "Thank you, Tug. I'll put them in the ledger," Marjorie offered.

"I'll bundle them with the others," said Rowena.

She snatched the letters from Marjorie's lap and held out her hand to Tug. "Give them to me."

Reluctantly he obeyed.

With a seemingly casual air Rowena studied the top letter, examining the wax seal and the texture of the paper. "He has a neat hand. Very military, I'm sure." She moved the envelope to the bottom of the stack.

Appalled, Marjorie said, "Don't examine those."

She waved her hand. "It's just a letter to his mother. How nice and dutiful. Perhaps the duchess will visit Bath." She held up another. "Ah, this one's interesting. It's to his mistress, Caroline Sharp. Dame Surleigh told me about her."

A wicked pain pierced Marjorie's heart.

Glancing up, Rowena said, "You don't suppose he's sending for her? What's wrong, child? You look ill."

Ignoring the hurt, Marjorie said, "I'm fine. And you're speculating."

"Don't you care if he brings that woman here?"

"Of course not," she lied. "And you have no business reading his mail. Hand them over."

"I'm not reading them." She peeked at the other envelopes, then handed them to Marjorie. "I suspect she's a tart, if her hair's as red as they say. I'm told she's petite, though, and given to swoons. She's also never worked a day in her life— except in intimate positions. They say she keeps to herself. He's also written to the king. That doesn't bode well, my dear. According to the duke of Cleveland, Lord Blake is the king's godson. If anyone can allow your father back into England, it's George."

Marjorie glanced at the top letter. The fancy lettering seemed contradictory to the man himself. He obviously saved his best penmanship for his mistress.

"Interesting, no?" asked Rowena.

Marjorie intended to upbraid Rowena, but not in front of Tug. "Not to me."

Rising, she passed him the letters and walked him to the door. "You'll be very careful."

Looking older than his fourteen years, he said, "Aye, my lady." He lowered his voice. "Lord Blake offered me half a crown to deliver one of those letters personally."

Her heart pounded fast. "The one to Mrs. Sharp?"

He ducked his head. "Aye, that one."

"Do you want to?"

His tongue peeked out and traced the scar on his lip. "If I did earn the money, I could visit that fancy confectioner in Oxford Close."

"And buy enough lemon taffy and sweets for everyone?"

Nodding vigorously, he said, "That was what I thought to do."

"Then you have my permission. Just remember, don't let the postal clerks in London give you any heavy packages, even if they're addressed to the Bishop of Wells himself. Tell them the parcels will have to wait for the package wagon."

Squaring his shoulders, he said, "No chance of them trying to sweet-talk me, my lady. They wouldn't dare risk another tangle with you."

"Very well. Be on your way." She handed him several pennies. "And take a hot meal in Hungerford."

She watched him march away and said a silent prayer for his safety. Each time she said good-bye to him she died a little inside. She might never see him again.

"It's not polite to whisper," admonished Rowena.

Marjorie braced herself and turned around. "And it's rude to examine other people's mail. How could you gossip so, and in front of Tug? He needs a good example, not a lesson in snooping."

Rowena's eyes filled with tears. "I thought it might help to know what Lord Blake's about. Besides, I'm just an old, crippled woman with nothing to do. I love you, and I can't bear to think of you being tricked into a marriage you don't want."

Sympathy for Grandmama diluted Marjorie's resentment. Still, she had a point to make. "You must promise me you'll never pry into anyone's letters again."

"We must know what he's up to, and I couldn't take his letters since he isn't a duke yet."

"You should have taken his mail out of respect for the duke of Cleveland."

"Lord Blake won't be as easy to discourage as the others," Rowena said. "Imagine, the Chesterfield heir is here to marry you."

"I don't care if he's a crown prince."

"He might as well be."

"As I said, snooping is a breach of trust, Grandmama. I can't afford any mistakes just when I'm about to make another bid."

Rowena sniffled and dabbed at her eyes with a handkerchief. "It's also evil of your father to use you like a piece of property to be bartered at his whim. Why, you must feel dreadfully put upon. I hate that blackhearted devil."

Marjorie wasn't sure what she felt about a man who'd never been more than a name on an envelope or a signature on a betrothal. She'd escape this trap as she had the others, and as always without interference from Rowena. "Promise me you won't pry into anyone else's mail."

"I swear on the duke's grave I'll never embarrass you again, or be a burden."

"You're never a burden, Grandmama."

* * *

Later that day, feeling dreadful over Rowena's callous treatment of Lord Blake, Marjorie rapped on the door of the duke of Cleveland's residence. No matter what had brought Blake to Bath, he should be treated with the same respect as any peer of the realm.

The butler opened the door. "Good day, Lady Marjorie. Won't you come in?"

"Hello, Sanford."

He ushered her into the foyer. The smell of wood wax mingled pleasantly with that of hothouse roses. Gold fabric embossed with unicorns adorned the walls.

"I'm sorry, but His Grace just left for the country, my lady."

"Actually, I'd like to see Lord Blake."

"Oh, come with me, then. His lordship said you are always welcome."

As she followed the butler down the portrait-lined hall Marjorie couldn't stifle a twinge of guilt. Grandmama had acted abominably toward Blake by falling back on the dukes-or-better rule so she wouldn't have to take his mail. But why? She'd been anxious to read them.

Marjorie had phrased her apology. She had also thought of a proposition.

"His lordship is exercising with Everson," said the servant. "I'll announce you."

"What kind of exercise?"

"Fencing, my lady. And quite expertly—if I may say so."

Marjorie had always appreciated the sight of a finely wielded foil, but since Beau Nash had outlawed weapons, local interest in the sport had fallen off. "May I watch without you announcing me?"

"By all means."

He led her up a flight of stairs. She heard the slide of

steel against steel. He ushered her into a gallery overlooking the ballroom. In the room below tables and chairs lined one wall; fine rugs had been rolled up and pushed against the other.

Hoping the men wouldn't see her, Marjorie stood still as a statue, but her blood sang with the thrill of the contest going on below.

Lord Blake wore a gathered shirt of stark white silk, the full sleeves billowing like sails. His breeches were of black leather, and they fit so tight she had to squint to see where his boots began. Jet hair hung in disarray about his shoulders. He grunted and, with a move befitting a dancer, leapt upon a table. Everson's foil sliced through empty air.

"You were better at leapfrog," taunted a breathless Everson, his own sleeves rolled to the elbow.

Blake brought the slender foil to his nose, then flung his arm wide in an exaggerated salute. "And you were better at reading the classics."

Laughing, Everson stepped back and assumed the position. "I had no competition from you there, but swordplay is a different matter. *En garde*, you wretched knave, and I'll nick away your wavy locks until you look like an Iroquois. Then we'll see how that postmistress falls for you."

Arm pumping, Blake fended off the blows, then became the aggressor. "She'll fall, all right. I have great plans for her."

Through a clenched jaw Everson said, "She won't be as easy to get into bed as Caroline Sharp."

Blake jumped onto a chair. "Marjorie's a lady. I'll get her into a marriage bed."

Everson grunted, "You'll have to pry her away from her job first."

Blake sprang from the chair and landed as smoothly as a cat. "Boast now, fool." He rotated his wrist, drawing small circles in the air with the blade. Bearing down on his opponent, he said, "I'll snip your balls and make a eunuch of you."

"I think not." Everson took a step back.

Blake came on. "Retreating so soon, old man?"

Moving to the side, Everson drew back his foil, then lunged.

Metal rang out against metal. Marjorie held her breath even as they panted in their exertion. Curses and grunts punctuated the eerie screeching of steel. She clasped her hands. Her fingers tangled in the strap of her satchel. Heart pounding, she watched in admiration as the advantage seesawed from one man to the other.

She felt exhilarated and exhausted at once.

Twang. Twang. Twang. Relentless in his pursuit, Blake backed his opponent into a corner. Everson squatted low, dived beneath Blake's arm, and somersaulted out of reach. Blake turned. Everson sprang to his feet. He brought up his hand to strike.

Caught up in the excitement, Marjorie yelled, "Watch out!"

Blake's head shot up. His eyes found Marjorie, then shot back to his opponent.

He twisted to the right. Everson's blade swept down.

White silk parted like thin air. The length of the blade slashed his arm.

Blake winced.

In horror, Marjorie watched blood well from the cut and stream down his arm.

Everson threw down his foil. "My lord!" He rushed forward.

Blake dropped his weapon and clasped a hand over his wounded arm. Blood seeped between his fingers.

Marjorie's stomach roiled. Sure that her legs would give way, she grasped the railing for support.

"It's just a scratch, Everson. You've done worse, and I've done better." Lord Blake waved him away, his eyes never leaving Marjorie. Smiling, he said, "You're as white as a new topsail. You won't faint, will you?"

Everson glared up at her.

Words wouldn't come. Her hands curled on the wooden rail in a death grip. She managed to shake her head.

"Good," said Lord Blake. "It's a long fall." He walked toward her.

Marjorie gasped, but then anger took over. "How can you be so flippant? You're hurt."

Everson spat, "Of course he's hurt. You almost got him killed!"

"I'm so sorry. I shouldn't have distracted you. I only wanted to watch." She turned to leave.

"Wait!" yelled Blake.

Marjorie stopped. Filled with remorse, she faced him. "I'm so sorry."

He strolled across the empty ballroom, blood running down his arm and dripping onto the marble floor. "Everson, go fetch a towel," he said. "And come back tomorrow morning."

Grumbling, Everson disappeared beneath the balcony. A door opened and closed. Blake stared up at her, sweat streaming down his face. He reached up and grasped the banister. With the agility of Dame Surleigh's pet monkey he swung himself over the rail and landed beside her.

"You're mad!"

Grinning like a spoiled aristocrat, he said, "And you're beautiful. I like that dress. You should always wear red."

Angry retorts flashed in her mind, but Marjorie couldn't stop thinking about his wound. "You'll bleed to death."

His eyes widened. "And leave you to spinsterhood? Not a chance, Postmistress."

She stared at his bleeding arm. "Give me your shirt," she commanded.

"My shirt, my heart, my life. They're all yours, Marjorie." He ripped off the garment and handed it to her.

Her breath caught at the sight of his naked chest adorned with the gold compass. Curling black hair fanned out toward his shoulders and dwindled to a point before disappearing beneath his scandalously tight breeches.

"What's on your mind, Postmistress?"

She gasped at his suggestive tone. Seeking a diversion, she spied an old injury on his shoulder, the scar smooth and neatly stitched. Everson's stitchery, she guessed. "Not what you think. You lied. You said Everson stitched skin like it was canvas. He sews a perfectly lovely stitch."

"I never said he sewed a poor seam. I said it hurt like hell. Look at me."

"I'm busy." She did look at him, though. Seeing the blatant invitation in his eyes, she dropped her gaze and made a bandage of the shirt. Halfway between elbow and shoulder the cut angled over a thickly muscled arm that both her hands wouldn't span. "Hold still."

"I'd rather hold you."

She wrapped the shirt around his arm and applied gentle pressure to the wound. "I'm neither interested nor available. Besides, you'll stain my dress."

"You are interested. The look in your eyes proves it."

"Don't confuse me with your other women."

"You *are* my only woman."

She whipped her gaze to his. "Wipe that grin off your face, Lord Blake. You don't need my help or stitches. And I wasn't looking at you per se. I was looking at your cheek. I see Everson removed the stitches. He can patch you up again."

"You wouldn't be so heartless."

"You've a lot to learn about my heart, Blake Chesterfield."

An emotion she couldn't define glimmered in his eyes. "That's encouraging, for I'll enjoy every minute of it."

"You're a flatterer."

"Will *you* bandage me, Postmistress?" he quietly asked.

Knowing she shouldn't, certain she would, Marjorie said, "Yes, I will, if you'll put on a fresh shirt and do something for me."

He licked his lips. "I can do lots of things for you. Just tell me what you want, but you needn't barter for my attentions."

He wasn't the only one who could set verbal traps. "You can allow me to hire your coachman. The one the Prince of Wales praises so highly."

"What?" Confusion and the absence of his mustache brought a youthful look to his face.

"I've commissioned a mail coach, and I'd like for your man to teach Tug and the other older boys to drive a team. Saturday afternoons are convenient. 'Tis the only day they're all in Bath at the same time."

Choking with disbelief, he said, "You ask the damnedest things, Marjorie Entwhistle."

Pleasure rippled through her at the sound of her name on his lips, even if the compliment was crosswise.

"Well? Do we have an agreement?"

Smiling, he said, "All I have is yours, my coachman included."

"Thank you, but the coachman's services will suffice—and a shirt."

"You're welcome," he grumbled. "I'll join you downstairs."

Later, as she sat on a stool in the study and put a proper bandage on his arm, Marjorie congratulated herself on striking a good bargain. The coachman, Reuben Peddicord, was at her disposal, along with Blake's fine conveyance.

"Tell me about the new coach," he said, eyeing her handiwork.

She got to her feet and fetched her satchel. "I'll show you." Taking out the drawing, she handed it to him.

He studied it. "Did you draw this?"

"No. The coachmaker did."

At length he pointed to the top of the cab. "What's this?"

"A spare wheel. 'Twas my idea, and I sketched it in, but I don't draw very well."

"Very clever, and impressive."

Marjorie wanted to preen, but she had the good grace not to. "Thank you. 'Twas actually common sense. I can't afford to buy a spare wheel for every inn between here and London. I can't afford delays either."

He flattened the paper on his thigh. "Have you thought about putting the wheel between the cab and the boot, rather than on top?"

She frowned, trying to picture the design. "I don't think I understand."

"Come here." He motioned her over and patted the arm of his chair. When she didn't move he said, "On my word as a sailor, I won't bite you."

"I've never taken a sailor at his word."

His eyebrows shot up. "On my word as a gentleman, then?"

She laughed at that.

"I'm wounded."

"You certainly are." She eased down on the arm of his chair.

He gave her a warm smile, and she was shocked to see a dimple on his cheek.

"What's so funny?" he asked.

"Nothing," she said.

He touched his bare upper lip. "Do you miss my mustache?"

"Like I miss the brigands on Hounslow Heath. Show me your idea for this wheel."

He pointed to the drawing. "If the wheel is stored here, wedged upright between the carriage and the boot, it would take up less room, and it wouldn't bounce around." He sketched a wheel so perfect it looked as if it would roll off the page.

"Yes, I see." She pointed to the roof. "It also wouldn't scratch the paint. Where did you learn to draw?"

"I don't remember learning. It seems I always knew how."

"You have a great talent."

He put his hand over hers and squeezed gently. The tender, spontaneous gesture set off a heated reaction in Marjorie. She remembered the feel of his hands on her. He'd been insistent then. He seemed affectionate now, almost like a husband.

Looking up at her, he said, "We make a good team, Postmistress. Dine with me tonight."

"Thank you, no."

"The cook's prepared a rack of lamb," he wheedled as he rolled down his shirtsleeve. "There's thornback soup, and a dozen other delicacies so tasty they should be banned. Say yes, and over the ox cheek pie I'll tell you about the time Peddicord won a race and landed a viscount's daughter for his eldest son."

She should decline. She had no business dining with Blake Chesterfield. But she yearned to celebrate the coach. She'd felt jubilant all day and wanted to enjoy the feeling a little longer. "I do not eat ox cheeks."

"No problem," he said magnanimously. "Consider them scratched from the menu. There's almond custard with raspberry cream for dessert."

Her mouth watered, but not for the dessert.

"Say you'll stay."

She could share her joy with him, couldn't she? That didn't mean she was encouraging him, did it? She wasn't sure.

"Marjorie?"

"Grandmama will expect me to come home."

"She'd best get used to doing without you. We'll let her know you'll be late."

Ignoring the innuendo, Marjorie addressed the morning's offense. "I'm sorry for the way she treated you about your letters this morning. It's just that she's loyal to me."

"It was a rather awkward situation."

Mildly put, thought Marjorie. "No matter what the circumstances between you and me, she had no right to refuse to collect your letters. She knows that I even take Sanford's love letters."

"This was quite different."

Of course it was, for Lord Blake had written the love letter in question. Melancholy pulled at her good spirits, and she wondered why she should care that he'd written to his mistress. It only reinforced the fact that he was courting her because her father was blackmailing him. "Yes, well, your correspondence is your affair. I told Grandmama that. I assure you, Lord Blake, that should she make the rounds in future, she'll take your letters, too."

"No, she won't, and you won't change my mind, either."

Confused, Marjorie said, "'Either.' What do you mean?"

"Her Grace insisted I give her my letters. I refused —for obvious reasons."

"But Grandmama said—" Marjorie knew he spoke the truth. The floor seemed to cobble beneath her feet. The one person she trusted had lied. Grandmama hadn't fallen back on the dukes-or-better rule. She'd tried to get his letters. Humiliation had caused her to lie.

"I take it you heard a different version," he said quietly.

"No wonder," she said defensively. "You hurt her feelings."

He opened his mouth but stopped. A moment later he said, "We won't let Rowena's poor hurt feelings ruin our evening or interfere with our bargain, will we?"

Still wrestling with Rowena's lie, Marjorie said, "Bargain?"

"I'll lend you Reuben Peddicord. You pick up my mail, even though I'm not a duke yet. You also dine with me tonight."

"I haven't agreed to supper."

"Trouble yourself no more about your grandmother," he said expansively. "I'll send her a note."

Staring into his eyes, as green as oak leaves in the summer shade, she wondered how she'd ever be able to resist him. Vulnerability assailed her. Tersely she said, "You can't write her a note."

He started; then his eyes narrowed in unexpected fury. He studied her so closely she wondered what she'd said wrong. "Why are you angry?" she said in confusion.

He withdrew his hand and looked away, but not before Marjorie saw the fire fade from his eyes.

"I'm not angry," he said. "I'm hungry."

Puzzled by his changeable moods, she longed for the chance to uncover the man behind the myth.

Perhaps his arm hurt. She wanted to talk about it, about him and his life. She wanted to ask if he felt different without the mustache. She wanted to know why she felt drawn to him.

But in her heart she did know. She was lonely. In her role as postmistress she had achieved a goal today. She had wanted to celebrate commissioning the mail coach. Thinking she could do that with Blake Chesterfield had been a mistake.

"I just don't understand Rowena," he said quietly.

"You can't expect her to tolerate you simply because I agree to dine with you. If I agree."

"I don't expect anything of her except interference. You write the note, and I'll see that it's delivered."

He seemed enveloped in sadness. Or was he lonely like her? The possibility touched her heart. "Enough about Grandmama. I told you we could be friends. Can't you see I'm trying to do just that?"

"Then have dinner with me."

She shouldn't. She should go home and work on the audit.

"Marjorie," he said, taking her hand again. "We'll be more than friends. We'll be man and wife."

"No. I won't marry you at my father's bidding."

"Would you marry me at *my* bidding?"

"No."

"Then what about the bidding of your heart?"

"My heart is neutral." His brows rose, and she knew he would challenge her. "I know what you're going to say, Blake Chesterfield, but it won't work."

He smiled, and that rare dimple appeared. "What was I going to say?"

Marjorie ignored the fluttering in her heart. "That you'll ravish me here and now if I don't agree to marry you."

"Wrong. I was merely going to ask if you preferred a lead pencil or a quill."

Amused, she said, "A pencil. And put on your coat, too."

"Certainly, and I promise not to ravish you until after dessert."

After she'd written the note and he'd had it delivered, he escorted her into the formal dining room. The long table was an endless stretch of polished wood. A single candelabrum illuminated two place settings, one at each end. Marjorie remembered the last time she'd been in this room as a guest of the duke of Cleveland. She could almost hear Grandmama's breathless laughter as she chided all the men for having danced her to the point of exhaustion. One week later the accident had put an end to her dancing and so much more.

"What are you thinking about?" asked Lord Blake as he pulled out her chair. "You look so pensive."

"I was thinking about how much Grandmama liked to dance, and what fun she had before."

He waved Sanford away. When the butler left, Blake picked up his plate and silverware and brought it to her end of the table. He sat and poured the wine himself. "What happened to her?"

"Five years ago her hunter balked. She was thrown onto a slab of Bathstone. She broke a leg and her hip."

"She was riding near the quarry?"

"No. At Prior Park. 'Twas still under construction at the time, and Ralph Allen had hosted a picnic and hunt on the site."

"I'm sorry for her. She did, however, seem quite well this morning—hardly limping at all."

Marjorie's once-fierce anger over the accident had mellowed to regret. "The warmth of the bath helps, if she goes every day. Sometimes she limps worse than others. The winter is always bad."

"Cleveland swears she was the queen of Bath once."

Memories tumbled through Marjorie's mind. "She

was. There were plays, masquerades, and dinners at Hartsung Square that went on for hours." The images slowed and faded to dark pictures. "We laughed over nothing. We gambled and wagered on the most trivial of matters."

His brows rose in question. "You? Beau told me you never gamble."

Filled with remorse, she said, "Not anymore."

"Because of your grandmother's infirmity. Why should that change your fondness for gambling?"

He was too quick by half. Let him believe what he would, for she wasn't about to share her thoughts on the matter; they were too private, too painful. She told him a partial truth. "I haven't the money to gamble with." She lifted her glass. "What shall we toast, or whom? Perhaps my father for engineering this meeting."

In a deep, insistent voice he said, "No. That intelligent mind of yours snaps shut like a man trap at the mention of him." Smiling, he continued, "Let's toast the new mail coach." He touched his glass to hers. "And the clever woman who designed it."

A blanket of delight smothered her dark thoughts. "I only thought of it."

Over the rim of his glass he said, "Reason enough. You're not afraid of progress, are you?"

"Of course not. We'd still be living in caves if someone hadn't thought of tools and words and the like."

"Just so."

When the fish soup was served and the butler had again departed Marjorie said, "Do you miss the sea?"

Lord Blake sighed fondly, a faraway look in his eyes. "Some things I miss very much. Others I could live three lifetimes without."

She put down the spoon. "What do you miss?"

Absently he stirred his soup. "I miss the sky, so

brightly blue from horizon to horizon that it invades a man's soul with serenity. And the nights, often so clear, and the constellations so vivid you can almost reach out, snatch up the big dipper, and take a drink."

The wistful quality of his voice surprised her. "It sounds wonderful."

"It is, on many occasions."

Intrigued, she said, "What about the other occasions? What don't you miss about the sea?"

He pushed the bowl aside. "Would you really be interested?"

In repose he was gorgeous. "I once called you a pampered nobleman. Here's your chance to prove me wrong."

He looked at her with what she deemed a proprietary air. "It's not pretty," he warned.

Her independent nature rebelled. "You might discourage underlings with that commanding stare, but not me."

He laughed.

"Life isn't always pretty," she said. "Tell me what you don't like about the sea."

With his index finger he realigned the silverware beside his plate until the tines of the forks were even. "I don't miss ordering a man flogged because he fell asleep at his post and endangered the crew. I don't miss finding debris from a harmless merchantman seized and scuttled by pirates. But most of all I don't miss the sight of Englishmen herding Africans onto floating death traps and transporting them to a life of slavery in Spanish America." He traced the delicate scrollwork on a salad fork. "Poor souls."

Marjorie quaked inside at the despair he didn't conceal and at the grim picture he painted. "Stop them," she said. "You have the power over English ships."

He shook his head. "Ah, but our countrymen are

only a drop in the bucket. The Spaniards ply the trade hard, yet they run a far second to the Portuguese." Closing his eyes, he said, "May they rot in hell for their sins against the Africans."

Fired by a need to right the injustice, she grasped his arm. "You must do something. At least stop the English."

He took her hand, and she was surprised to feel dampness on his palm.

"I can't. Not from the deck of the *Reliance* or any of my fleet."

"Then from where?" she asked.

"Only Parliament can put a stop to such disregard for human dignity."

"You have a seat in the House of Lords if you choose to take it."

"Aye. But I'm not sure I could change things."

"Of course you can. Write letters and petitions."

"I'm not eloquent with the pen. And enslaving Africans is a business, Marjorie. Englishmen won't easily part with their livelihood because a wealthy nobleman says 'tis wrong."

His attitude shocked her. She pulled her hand from his. "Don't tell me that, Blake Chesterfield," she said vehemently. "Only a coward refuses to fight for what he believes in. And I don't think you're a coward."

"What am I?"

He wouldn't trick with words again. "You're a clever man who's trying to seduce me."

He gave her a sad smile and reached for his wine-glass. "Hardly. I'm losing my touch."

No, he wasn't, but she'd keep that to herself.

"What qualities are important to you, Marjorie?"

She couldn't remember anyone having asked her such a question. But the answer was easy. "Honesty. Independence. Loyalty."

Tipping his glass in a mock salute, he said, "As your

husband, I promise not to curb your independence too much."

He wouldn't trap her with his wily ways. "So I should settle for one quality out of three? What of honesty and loyalty? You can't give me those."

"Of course I can," he said.

"Then tell me the truth," she shot back. "Why is my father blackmailing you?"

With a delicate pop the stem of the wineglass broke in his hand. The footed half clattered to the table and wobbled like a crippled spinning top. "I'll tell you this honest truth, Marjorie Entwhistle. I want you, and your father be damned."

She felt as if she were both pawn and prize in a game of chess. Hurting, she said, "So now we're back to seduction, are we? I'll tell *you* the honest truth, Blake Chesterfield. You can't seduce me, for I don't intend to be alone with you."

He waved a hand about the room. "We're alone now."

"Ha. You're not desperate enough to bring ruin on us both by compromising me in Cleveland's dining room."

"I could compromise you in yours."

The resolve in his eyes frightened her, but she refused to back down. "Don't threaten me."

He leaned back in his chair, the lingering promise in his eyes belying the casual pose. " 'Twasn't a threat, but a promise."

"We'll see about that."

They managed civil conversation throughout the twelve courses, but to Marjorie's sadness, they never regained the spontaneity they'd shared earlier. He related the story of his coachman winning a wealthy noblewoman as wife for his son. She countered with a tale about Merlyn and Milo. By the time the almond custard was served, Beau Nash arrived.

Holding his white hat in his hands, the king of Bath said, "Her Grace said Lady Marjorie was dining here and asked if I would see her safely home."

Blake yawned. "Yes, it has been a rather long evening."

Feigning exhaustion to mask her disappointment, Marjorie declined dessert and left with Beau. An hour later she fell into a troubled sleep.

She awakened the next morning to find a silver serving dish on her dressing table. She lifted the dome lid and discovered a portion of almond custard with raspberry sauce.

Later in the day, when she made her rounds, she returned the clean dish to Lord Blake. "How did you get this into my room?" she demanded.

"I delivered it myself."

"No one saw you."

Grinning like a cavalier, he kissed her nose and said, "I was very careful."

"I forbid you to do it again."

He gave her a look that said he could invade and conquer France if the notion suited him.

The next morning she found a sketch, signed with the initials BAC, painstakingly drawn and framed in a chevron, the Chesterfield hallmark.

CHAPTER 7

By General Consent, Ladies who appear in
public in aprons, expect no quarter from the
advances of Gentlemen.

—Beau Nash, *Rules of Bath*

AFTER DAYS OF BLISTERING COLD, BRIGHT SUNSHINE
streamed through the fan-shaped windows of Marjorie's office. Icicles fringed the roof and drip-drip-
dripped in a slumberous rhythm so captivating she
had to force herself to look away.

Her gaze fell to her desk and the items there. In the
center lay the stack of schedules for the Royal Mail, a
different one for each posting station in her district.
To the public the timetables were useful tools; to the
brigands they were agendas for robbery.

She must deliver the originals to Tobias Ponds
today so they could be printed, then distributed
throughout her district. Her jaw clenched at the
thought of doing business with her nemesis, but
Tobias employed the finest engraver in Bath, and she
refused to accept inferior service for the sake of her
own bias.

To the right of the timetables lay Blake Chesterfield's ludicrous sketch.

In a style similar to Hogarth Blake had drawn a likeness of Marjorie languishing abed, her hair in disarray, her mouth captured in a smile of sheer bliss, and in her eyes an expression bordering on ecstasy.

Fear rumbled through her. Her hand shook, and the paper crackled, for the look was reminiscent of Juliana Papjoy gazing at Beau Nash when she thought no one was watching.

Like a weight around her heart, bitterness dragged at Marjorie. How dare he picture her in such a scandalous pose? She had hoped someday to gaze at a man with such love and passion, but he would be the devoted husband of her own choosing, not the minion of her father.

At the thought of Papa she snatched up the drawing, crumpled it, and pitched it into the rubbish bin beside her desk.

Feeling somewhat mollified, she turned her attention to the other item before her: Mrs. Caroline Sharp's reply to Lord Blake. Tug had brought the letter to Marjorie immediately upon his arrival from London.

His description of the tiny woman and her unexpected reaction to Lord Blake's message still played in Marjorie's mind. The cheeky tart! The envelope, modestly scented with lilac and addressed in a governesslike scroll, intrigued Marjorie. Oh, she'd deliver the letter, to be sure, and she had a message of her own to relay.

The door swung open. Tobias Ponds strolled into the room. Few ventured to this upstairs corner of the mansion. It was her domain, and she resented his intrusion.

"Good day, Marjorie."

She slapped her hand over the letter and raked it into a drawer. "Don't you ever knock?"

He tucked a leather portfolio under his arm and began pulling off his gloves. "You needn't hide your love letters from me, my dear," he said with a familiarity that always rankled, even after six years. "It is ironic, though, don't you think?"

He wiped his hand over the bookcase, then examined his fingers for dust.

He wore a fashionable wig, dusted gray and styled with three pigeon rolls over his ears and a neatly clubbed tail at the nape of his neck. He never painted his face as some men did; the cosmetics would be wasted, for Tobias had been blessed with flawless skin. He always dressed himself elegantly, but in conservative shades. Today he wore breeches and a well-tailored coat of dark blue velvet. Thanks to Marjorie, he had prospered in Bath.

Frowning, he helped himself to one of her pencils. "You have the manners of a sedanchairman with blistered feet."

"Such a wit, Marjorie, but then everyone says so. Why, just this morning in Cross Bath your grandmother was boasting of your cleverness and telling one and all how dreadfully busy you are. Poor dear, she had to hire a guide—a stranger, as she put it—to help her stand upright in the water."

Poor Rowena, indeed. Marjorie appreciated the sentiment behind her grandmother's helpfulness. Lately, though, Rowena's efforts always backfired. The episode over Lord Blake's letters came to mind. Once the postal concession was again secured and Lord Blake sent on his way, Marjorie promised herself she'd spend more time with Rowena. Until then Marjorie could hire a companion to accompany Grandmama to the bath. First Marjorie had to deal with her enemy "Thank you for that report, Tobias."

He made a fist and crumpled the gloves. "You're as rude as ever."

Applauding herself, she slid the new timetables toward him. "I assume this is all you came for."

"You needn't thank me for saving you a trip to my shop. I was in the neighborhood." Without waiting to be asked he seated himself on the parson's bench near the door and craned his neck to examine the wall. "You should paint and drape the windows. 'Tis ghastly puritan in here."

Even the youngest of the postboys could sit comfortably in the room without disturbing knickknacks or soiling the furniture. Besides, she couldn't afford velvet drapes with golden cords or plush sofas with mats from Doyley's. She glared at him. "This is a place of business, not a club for lolling about. The room is precisely the way I like it."

"Suit yourself, while you can."

His sarcasm annoyed her. "I'll need the schedules as soon as possible."

"You certainly have changed over the years, haven't you, Marjorie? Once the belle of the ball. Now it's business, business, business."

"Yes. I have work to do. You know the way out."

Innocently he said, "But I haven't told you why I'm here."

"If it's about how I run the post, I don't care a fig. If it's about my past, I care less."

"I expect," he said derisively, "that your marriage to Lord Blake will leave little time for posting letters and sheltering street urchins—if your spotted past doesn't make him think twice about marrying you."

Weakling, she thought. He'd never admit his part in what had happened to her years before. Maintaining a smile, she said, "I expect you should mind your own business. The timetables." She held them out to him.

He yanked up the pages and began examining each one.

Hiding her irritation, she said, "You may take those with you."

He opened his mouth to reply but stopped, his attention focused on one of the schedules. "You've incorrectly listed the time between London and Brentford. It's much too slow." He glanced at the next page and the next. "See here, you've done it wrong again at Hounslow and Colinbrook."

Marjorie smiled, for Tobias assumed the mail would still be carried on horseback. Although the coach was slower, service would be improved. She considered telling him about the new service and decided against it. "The times are correct, Tobias, but thank you for your concern. I'm making a few changes."

"Like what?" An overconfident grin revealed his chipped tooth. "Saddling tortoises instead of horses?"

Since his arrival in Bath six years ago he'd put her through hell on more than one occasion. She could forgive his past indecencies; he'd been reckless and desperate. But now he wanted her job. She'd give him no quarter there. "Just print the schedules. I must get back to work."

"But they're wrong," he blustered.

"You needn't concern yourself."

"I certainly will concern myself," he said smoothly, "when I'm postmaster."

Even if he offered a higher price than she did for the concession, the addition of the mail coach assured her success. The boys would have a home, an education, and hope for the future. She would have her livelihood and her self-respect. It had to be enough.

"I never forget that you're ambitious, Tobias. Now, if there's nothing else . . ."

With the skill of a thespian he pulled his face into a smile. "Yes, there is, as a matter of fact." From the portfolio he produced several pieces of paper. "Lord Blake commissioned these announcements. I thought you might like to have a look at them." He put them on the desk and slid them toward her. "Very thoughtful, don't you agree?"

In beautifully drawn letters was a formal announcement of her betrothal to Lord Blake Chesterfield. She bit her tongue to keep from saying something she'd regret, something Tobias could use against her. "Pity this will go to waste. Your engraver does splendid work, as always."

Preening, he said, "Lord Blake also ordered new stationery for you, Lady Marjorie Chesterfield. Has a nice ring, doesn't it?"

She looked at the paper and spied her monogram tucked beneath the hated chevron. That did it. Her temper snapped. She swept the stationery off her desk and onto the floor at Tobias's feet. "Get out! Take those and your presumptions with you."

Like a miser who'd dropped his gold he dived for the papers. Sickened, Marjorie walked to the window and stared out at the street. Behind her she heard him scrambling on the floor. In his clumsiness he knocked over the rubbish bin.

"I'll get this cleaned up in a minute." Papers rustled.

Outside in the yard Cumber carried a pail of water toward the chicken coop, one arm held out straight for balance. Would Tobias never leave?

She heard his footsteps tramping to the door. It opened.

"I'll print the timetables exactly as you wrote them," he spat. "You'll have them in a week or so."

The door slammed. When she heard his retreating footsteps Marjorie slumped onto the window seat.

She had to put a stop to this betrothal. She'd been patient and understanding. It hadn't worked. Now she'd be stubborn and assertive.

Blake paced the carpeted floor in Cleveland's library, the emptiness of the house closing in on him. After living with constant noises and volatile tempers on the *Reliant*, the false comity of the city made him restless. The longer he stayed here, the greater the risk, for eventually he'd give himself away. He cringed at the thought of the gossips learning his secret.

Bath held but one pleasure for him: Marjorie Entwhistle. The prospect of seeing her again roused his emotions and stirred his blood. Originally he'd planned to marry her, get an heir on her, then go about his business. Now he wanted to woo her, cherish her, and take her with him everywhere. When had the turnabout come? He, who'd always shied from lengthy entanglements, found himself wanting to see her every day and love her every night.

The clock struck ten. His prim and proper and oh-so-punctual postmistress had better be here soon to pick up his mail, he thought. Christ, he hadn't composed so many letters since Captain Jenkins had lost an ear and promised to start a war between England and Spain. Blake had started his own war, too, and if Marjorie didn't call on him herself, he'd step up the offensive.

Black humor engulfed him. What would she say to his latest midnight foray into her bedchamber? What would she say about the drawing? She'd be shocked to her prissy undergarments to know how close he'd come to stripping off his clothes and crawling into bed with her. Anticipation shivered within him at the thought of her long legs wrapped around his waist, her luscious body yielding, welcoming him.

Even as desire pumped through him his conscience

147

effectively stemmed the flow of lust. Forcing her was wrong. Seducing her was immoral. But Blake had to have her, and for reasons that had little to do with his own repulsive flaw or her father's selfish whim.

Of late he'd glimpsed the precocious little girl in Marjorie. Like an image floating below the surface of the ocean, a loving, passionate creature lived beneath the stern trappings of the postmistress of Bath. He intended to be the man to discover her.

In an attempt to fit himself into her life Blake had memorized the social calendar and made the acquaintance of her foes and friends alike. He even visited the baths every morning, but she no longer accompanied her grandmother.

He gritted his teeth at the thought of Rowena. That harridan made Macbeth's witches look like benevolent godmothers. The dowager duchess of Loxburg bestowed no favors on her granddaughter. Didn't Marjorie see the manipulative cruelty behind Rowena's twisted sort of love?

He thought of his own parents, too caught up in their pleasures to bother with a rambunctious boy who'd favored adventure over the classroom. A boy who'd excelled in leadership and failed miserably in self-worth. Not until he'd gone to sea had Blake been comfortable.

He envisioned his mother's expression when she opened the letter and learned of his upcoming nuptials. She'd smile, then celebrate by ordering a dozen new gowns. The only times she remembered she had a son were when he received another decoration and when his father handed him another property to manage. Other than chance meetings on his infrequent visits to London, the only regular communication he had with the duchess of Enderley was the letter she sent every year on his birthday. Hardly a greeting, though, for her message was always the same: When would he produce an heir and fulfill his obligation to the house of Chesterfield?

How, Blake wondered, could parents so desperately seek heirs, then carelessly banish them to nurseries and nannies? He'd always felt like a utensil in their lives, dusted off and polished up when needed, then packed up and shipped off when the party was over. The duke and duchess of Enderley showed more concern for their personal servants than for their only son. But Blake had become guilty of that, too, for Everson was more of a father to him than his own.

He and Marjorie were alike in that respect; neither of them had known familial love, at least not genuine affection or thoughtful nurturing. That didn't keep him from wanting both, and more. He'd be a good father. He'd cherish his children, keep them with him. He'd love them and never be shy about showing his affection.

What did Marjorie want? Three things, she'd said. He couldn't give her honesty, for she'd be repulsed by the truth about him. Independence was out of the question, for he wanted her with him every day and every night—a far cry from the estranged marriage he'd expected to share with her. But he could and would give her loyalty. He'd stand behind her until sailing ships could fly, and he'd challenge anyone who dared blacken her name. He'd love her till the end of time.

Only one small obstacle stood in his path: He had to win her first.

The door opened. Excitement shot through Blake.

Everson strolled into the room, a stack of letters in his hand, a knowing look on his face. "You look disappointed to see me. You must be expecting someone else."

Blake started pacing again. "Where is she?"

"Let me rephrase that. Disappointment is a poor

description for you," said Everson. "Actually, you look like that caged panther we saw at the May Fair last year in Boston. Had rather green eyes, the cat did. Do you perchance recall the creature?"

"Aye, and I recall a skinny lad poking a stick at the cat. He paid for his foolishness."

Pretending fright, Everson raised his hands. "Oh, no! Did the cat take off his hand? That animal had a ghastly disposition."

At the familiar banter Blake felt his tension subside. "And you have a rather macabre sense of humor. Have you seen her?"

Grinning, Everson picked up Blake's jacket. "Here, put this on. She's next door at the duke of Kingston's."

Blake turned around and slipped his arms into the sleeves. Everson smoothed the shoulders and fussed with the lapels. Any time now she'd sail through the door, her letter pouch slung over her shoulder, her chin in the air, her eyes gloriously blue and distant, her official duties shrouding the woman he longed for.

But a few moments later, when Sanford ushered her into the room, Blake realized he'd miscalculated one aspect of her: the eyes. No longer aloof, they glittered like turquoise in the sun.

"Good day, my lord," she said with less warmth than an ice storm.

"Hello, Marjorie."

Everson stepped between them. "May I take your cloak and gloves, my lady?"

"This is not a social call. However, you may."

She put the pouch in a chair. After handing over her hooded cloak and gloves, she said, "Please excuse us, Everson. I should like to speak privately with your master."

Blake's senses sharpened. What cleverness was going on behind her lovely eyes? He studied her closely.

She had fine taste in fabrics and chose styles that complemented her unusual height. Today she wore a gown of shiny, stiff cotton in a shade more rust than orange. Fashionably split at the waist, the skirt revealed a petticoat of yellow satin that matched the puffy sleeves. Without bows, festoons, or intricate embroidery, the gown accented but did not overshadow her beauty. Cut square across the neck, the bodice revealed the exquisite line of her collar bones and hinted at the luscious mounds of her breasts.

He thought a jewel would look good there, nestled between her breasts. He grew warm thinking about the shape and texture of her nipples and the feel of them in his mouth.

"Are you hungry, my lord? Shall I bring tea?"

Everson's sarcasm snatched Blake from his lusty thoughts. It also warned him of the transparency of his desire. "Yes."

"Don't bother on my account," she said with a directness that dragged like an anchor at Blake's patience. "What I have to say won't take long."

When the door closed behind Everson Blake knew the valet wouldn't return.

Marjorie reached for her mail pouch. In a graceful motion she'd probably performed a thousand times, she freed the buckle and lifted the worn leather flap.

He gazed at her hair, unpowdered and swept up in a thick golden coil that seemed too heavy for her slender neck. He noticed that she again wore no jewelry, just a ribbon, and was glad, for she needed no ornamentation. Someday, though, he'd present her with the famous rope of Chesterfield diamonds. Those gems would send her flying into his arms where conversation wouldn't.

She held out a letter. "Your mail, my lord."

The unwelcome scent of lilac drifted to his nose. Stunned, he allowed his future wife to place in his hand a letter from his former mistress. Sweet Saint Crispin, how much odder could this courtship get?

Like a green sailor caught smoking in the gunpowder hold, Blake jammed the condemning evidence into his pocket. "Thank you," he murmured.

Still holding out her hand, she smiled much too sweetly and said, "That will be fourpence, my lord."

So, she wanted to play, did she? "You are bold, Marjorie."

"So what? You are typical."

"What do you mean by that remark?"

"Never mind. Fourpence, please."

"Fourpence for what?" he asked.

"For the postage."

Feeling as dumb as a post, he retorted, "Will you take a kiss instead?"

Her smile faded, and her dainty nostrils flared. "Don't be glib. Correspondence to or from your mistress is your affair. Collecting postal fees is mine."

Shame cooled his attempt at flirting. "I'm sorry." From the desk he fetched a gold coin and placed it in her palm.

"Two guineas?" she said. "I haven't change for this."

Gently he closed her fingers around the coin. "Use the rest to pay for the mail coach." *And to forgive me for being a buffoon.* When would he learn how to deal with this woman?

She stared at the coin for a moment, then shook her head. "No, I can't take it. Send it to Mrs. Sharp. She and your son need it more than I . . . especially now that you've turned them out."

Aghast at the censorship in her voice, Blake said, "I had no idea you'd stoop to reading other people's mail. And Robert's not my son."

She drew herself up and took a step toward him. The pleasant odor of lavender obliterated every trace of lilac. "I did not read your mail, Blake Chesterfield. I never read anyone's mail but my own. Tug personally delivered your letter. He told me that Mrs. Sharp cried, then laughed, because you had dissolved the relationship. And what do you mean that boy's not your son?"

Be patient, Blake told himself. She's accustomed to protecting defenseless children. "The boy is five. I've only . . . ah . . . *known* Mrs. Sharp for a year or so. Nevertheless, I've arranged for his schooling. I'm certain that's what her letter to me is about."

Marjorie's chin dropped, and a frown marred the smooth plane of her forehead "Oh. Forgive me. I shouldn't have jumped to such a conclusion.

Since meeting Marjorie Entwhistle, Blake had been continually taken off guard by her forthright manner. He wanted to embrace her, wanted her to depend on him. He wanted to ask why she shouldered the enormous responsibility of the postal service. Wooing her with words wouldn't be easy—not if unsuitable topics such as his former mistress kept creeping into the discussion. On second thought, though, when had he had a normal discussion with Marjorie?

"You're forgiven, my dear," he said cheerfully. "Now that we've cleared that up, tell me what you've been doing since I saw you last."

She slipped the coin into her pouch. "The last time you saw me, I was sleeping."

He remembered how sweet and angelic she looked, her lips parted, the covers pulled up to her chin. "And very prettily, too."

"You're a troll."

"I am not."

"I tossed your scandalous drawing in the trash."

"In the trash?" Her words struck a blow. He hadn't drawn a line in years, and the piece was not up to his ability, but with practice his skill would return.

"Oh, I've hurt your feelings."

Now she wanted to be coy, did she? He could match her in that. "I guess that means you won't sit for me again."

She advanced on him, dignity shimmering around her like a nimbus. "I didn't sit for you in the first place. You barged into my room—"

"No, I didn't," he interjected, hoping to stall her anger. "I was very quiet."

"I'm glad breaking and entering is so humorous to you."

She looked as formidable and determined as she had in the tailor shop when she'd defended Cumber Stokes. The remembrance pleased Blake. "You're enchanting when you're angry."

She laughed, and the fire in her eyes turned to mirth. "Do you expect me to be moved by such unoriginal flattery?"

Floundering in uncharted seas, Blake realized that winning her didn't get any easier. The challenge inspired his idle brain. Humor had failed. Would a direct approach succeed? "What will it take to move you?"

She walked to the fireplace. Trailing her hand over the mantelpiece, she touched the assortment of iron soldiers, which were Cleveland's pride and joy. The dark and masculine room seemed brighter with her in it. So did Blake's life.

"If," she declared, "I wanted to be moved, 'twould not be by a man who possesses the talent of a burglar and the imagination of a swineherd." She whirled and shook her finger at him. "Take my advice, Blake Chesterfield. Confine your artistic urges to carriage wheels and bowls of fruit. And your amorous attentions to the bedchamber of someone who welcomes them."

If pride was a good fair wind, he was dead in the

water. Defensively he said, "'Twill take more than prissy insults to discourage me. Especially after you so recently fell into my arms, almost kissed my face off, and certainly encouraged the tender feelings I have for you. Had your grandmother and that bumbling pastor not been in the posting room, I would have kept right on walking up those stairs, carried you to your frilly bed, and given you a full measure of my amorous attentions."

She held her ground, and the only hint of her anger was the quick rise and fall of her breasts. "I would have come to my senses long before you ravished me."

She would have come all right—several times. "Then you admit that you were moved, that you wanted me."

A furious blush stained her cheeks. "I was . . . curious. And much too angry for my own good."

"You're angry now, too."

"I'm always angry at you."

Look out, Marjorie, he thought. You're in over your head. "Then it follows that you always want me."

She threw her hands in the air. "I don't know why I even bother to talk to you."

His body tense with the need to hold her, Blake took her into his arms. "You *bother* because you like me."

"No." She tried to pull away. "I don't like you. At least not in the way you're thinking that I like you. Oh, bother it! What I mean to say is, you're wrong in what you're thinking."

When she didn't move away he pressed his point. "What do I think?"

She stood so close he could see the feathery texture of her eyelashes. Softly she said, "You think you'll wear down my will. You think I'll yield my virginity to you. If not, I believe you'll try to take it."

His racing mind screeched to a halt. *Virginity.* Why had he assumed she wasn't a virgin? Because of that first meeting. Aside from her lush physical attributes, she was the most independent and resourceful woman in England. He'd assumed she had a paramour, and why not?

Stunned, he let the exceedingly welcome knowledge sink in. One night very soon he'd introduce this exquisitely unique and perfect woman to the joys of passion. His body responded with the subtlety of a randy goat.

"Well?" she demanded, stepping back. "Have you nothing to say? Will you try to take my virginity here?" A dare glittered in her eyes. "Now?"

He swallowed and opened his mouth to answer, but her expression stopped him. He watched with interest as her gaze fell to the placket of his breeches.

"How quintessentially predictable you are, my lord."

Her astuteness riled him. "Now, look here, Marjorie."

"I already have looked, thank you, and I'm not in the least interested in my father's latest offering."

Blake laughed to cover his discomfiture. "Trust me, darling, your father has nothing to do with my offering."

"I wouldn't trust you if the Archbishop of Canterbury vouchsafed your character."

"The king, then."

Casually she said, "You wrote to him. Why?"

"Worried?"

Confidence wreathed her. "Not in the least."

"Oh, I think you're worried." And well she should be. "I think you're frightened of me, too."

"Bah! You flatter yourself. You think I'll fall in love with you."

"Yes, I do. I'm a good catch, and you're a prize, Marjorie."

She made a fist and pounded the mantel hard

enough to topple the infantry. "I'm not a prize, Blake," she said, righting the soldiers. "I'm a pawn, just like you."

The truth of her words exhausted him. His hands fell to his sides. "It's the betrothal, isn't it?"

Her expression softened, and she seemed so vulnerable, he thought she might cry. "Yes, it's the betrothal. Why else would you want me? You can have any eligible and not-so-eligible woman in England. Probably France and Spain as well. Don't pretend. We know why you're here."

A bold idea came to mind. "Don't move. I'll be right back."

Before he could ponder the consequences he marched to his suite and returned with the document. "Here." He thrust it into her hands. "It's not worth a brass penny without your signature. Tear it up. Throw it into the fire. Hoist it on a flagpole, Marjorie. I don't care."

Injured dignity brought color to her cheeks. "I knew you didn't want to marry me." She shook the document. "Your indifference to this proves it."

She'd misunderstood. Blake's patience snapped. "Of course I want to marry you. I've made no secret of that. But when have I actually proposed to you?"

"You didn't precisely propose." As she spoke she fondled the rolled parchment in such a suggestive manner, Blake cringed. "In front of the entire town of Bath you told me we would be man and wife."

Although he knew the gesture was innocent, he couldn't help but picture her hands on him in a similar fashion.

"Do you deny what you said?" she asked.

His knees threatened to buckle, and if he didn't get that paper away from her soon, he'd be sorry. "No, I don't deny it, but how do you know that you wouldn't want to marry me? You won't even get to know me."

"Trust me. I know enough. In case you've forgotten, I've played out this scenario six times before."

"I'm different from the others."

She looked him up and down. "Oh? How are you different?"

She'd never know the answer to that. "I want you. The others weren't worthy of you. And I'm willing to prove I am." He looked pointedly at the document. "Tear it up."

Instead she hugged it to her breast. "You can't mean it. You don't know my father. He ruined four decent men and bankrupted all but one. He's ruthless when it comes to finding me a husband and getting a grandson."

Cold fear seeped into Blake's bones, but he schooled his features into a smile and lied. "I'm not afraid of your father. And I understand that you won't be forced into marriage."

"Then what's your point? How did you get forced into this?"

Would that he could tell her. He took the document from her and tossed it to the safety of Cleveland's desk. Relieved that his bluff had worked, he said, "My point is this. We don't know each other. You're an intelligent woman, and I'm a reasonably bright troll." At her smile he hurried on. "I say we have a trial courtship. See if you don't like me."

"It's not that I don't like you, Blake. I can't marry a man with a lie on his lips."

"How do I know if I can trust you with my 'lie'?"

"You don't."

"I'm willing to risk it. We'll begin by going to Simpson's Rooms on Tuesday night."

"No, I can't." She began righting the soldiers on the mantel. "I have to meet with Mr. Nash and Marshal Wade."

"Then Wiltshire's on Wednesday night."

"Sorry, you'll have to go alone. I must accompany Albert to Bristol. We won't be back until Thursday."

"Those are excuses."

"They are not. The clerk in Bristol is new. I must examine his records."

"Then Simpson's on Thursday."

Her pretty white teeth toyed with the corner of her mouth. "You've been reading the social schedule."

His bravado sagged, but he refused to give in. "Will you go with me?"

"I'll go dancing with you on Friday, but you must agree to two conditions. You must promise to cease your midnight visits. And cancel the printing order for the wedding announcements and the stationery."

Taken aback, he said, "Who told you about those?"

"Tobias was quick to bring them to my attention."

"You don't like him. Why not?"

She sighed. "It's a very old and clichéd story." She moved a tiny cannon into the vanguard she'd created. "You would find it boring."

"I'm curious. Tell me."

"No," she said sharply.

He should retreat while he was ahead. "Very well. You keep your word, Postmistress, and I'll keep mine."

She extended her hand. "We'll be friends, and someday when you do marry and return with your marchioness to Bath we'll feel comfortable. Shall we clasp hands on it?"

Her fingers slipped into his, and he immediately anticipated a more intimate embrace. She'd be his marchioness, by God. "Of course. I'll call for you the morning after your return. We'll go to Cross Bath."

"How nice. Grandmama will be pleased with our escort."

Revulsion swept over him.

"Why do you look so distressed, Blake? She doesn't bite."

That was an understatement, for Rowena of Loxburg would chew up her enemies and spit them out. He knew her kind. He also knew how to deal with her. But could he, without harm to Marjorie, make her see the truth about her grandmother?

"Blake . . . ?"

Banishing thoughts of the cruel woman, he said, "Of course she doesn't bite. Where are you going now, and how does the idea of an escort strike you?"

She shrugged. "I'm off to the coffee shops to deliver the latest editions of the *Tatler* and *Gentleman's Quarterly*. I don't need an escort."

"Ah, but you do."

"Why?"

He rubbed his naked upper lip. "According to Dame Surleigh, the coffee houses are unsuitable to the delicate constitutions of the fairer sex, and rife with weighty conversations on religion and philosophy."

Marjorie laughed. "They never even notice my presence unless the *Quarterly* is torn in transit. And I'll be in and out before the weighty conversation can drag me down."

Suddenly he felt as if he could shinny up a mast with one hand tied behind his back. "I'm going there anyway," he lied.

"Suit yourself."

He took her arm and walked her to the door. Teasingly he said, "I think I'll call on Tobias myself and ask him why you don't like him."

She clutched his lapel. Alarm sparkled in her eyes. "You mustn't."

He covered her hand with his. "Why not?"

She glanced nervously from his cravat to the smoking stand to the portraits on the wall. At length she said, "He wants my job."

Blake lay his hand on her cheek. "Look at me." When she did, he said, "What else? You're hiding something about him."

She mustered her innate dignity again, but she didn't fool him, for Blake Chesterfield knew shame when he saw it. A deep sympathy thrummed to life inside him. "Tell me."

"Six years ago my father sent Tobias here to marry me."

CHAPTER 8

*Cheaters and charlatans will forfeit thirty
guineas of their ill-gotten gains and, for the
future, visit their vices on Tunbridge Wells.*

—Beau Nash, *Rules of Bath*

STANDING NEAR THE SOLITAIRE TABLES IN WILTSHIRE'S
gaming room, a glass of Scotch whiskey in his hand,
Blake watched the noisy crowd. A pack of young
gamesters plied the dice. Their clothes were carefully
mended but had seen better days. One wore a badly
frayed wig; another sported scuffed shoes and hose
with holes at the heels. They laughed and chided each
other, but when the dice fell into friendly hands the
jests stopped. They leaned over the table, fists knotted
in concentration as if they could will a winning roll for
their comrade. A hand flew open. The dice tumbled
across the felt.

"Point!"

The swains cheered. The losers grumbled.

Blake was reminded of his own youth. At twenty
he'd had two pursuits in mind: serious gaming and
frivolous women. Even though he hadn't needed the

winnings to survive, as these fellows obviously did, he had needed a respite from **amb**itious mamas who paraded their daughters before him like yearlings on the auction block. In London's most notorious gaming rooms he'd found plenty of women eager to fill his bachelor bed, and scores of gamesters anxious to test his skill.

He'd enjoyed his youth—even the mornings when he'd awakened with a queasy stomach, a pounding head, and a shapely bedmate whose name he couldn't immediately recall. In retrospect, he wished he had followed fashion and braved the rutted road to Bath years ago, for he could have made the acquaintance of Beau Nash. With the king of Bath as his friend, Blake might already be married to Marjorie Entwhistle and free of her father's yoke.

The thought of having George Entwhistle for a father-in-law made Blake's stomach turn; the prospect of taking Marjorie to wife softened his heart.

He sipped the whiskey. The glass obscured his view. His thoughts turned inward. At one time any reminder of the betrothal garnered bitterness and feelings of being trapped. Now the prospect of marriage to Marjorie brought a sense of rightness and satisfaction to his soul.

"You look as if you're enjoying yourself, my lord," said Tobias Ponds.

Blake's first instinct was to slam his fist into Pond's too-pretty face, beat the bastard senseless, then break the hands that had touched Marjorie. But violence wouldn't change her past, and it could have an adverse effect on her future.

Blandly, Blake said, "There's entertainment aplenty here."

"Always." The printer smiled, revealing a chipped tooth. "Although I'm certain the company would be more to your liking were Marjorie not in Bristol."

What new mischief was Tobias about? "She'll be home tomorrow," Blake said.

Tobias stared into his drink. "She wasn't too happy about the announcements or the stationery. 'Tis best you canceled them."

That was an understatement. She'd been livid. Had Blake known the extent and the duration of the enmity between the postmistress and the printer, he wouldn't have given the man the commission. "You're not her favorite person, Tobias."

He laughed. "Neither is anyone who wants her job or her hand in marriage. I was her first betrothed, you know."

The offhand statement triggered Blake's ire. "I'll be her last."

"I'm sure you will. Now. Take that fellow there." Tobias pointed to the crowd at the dice table Blake had been watching earlier. "The one in the green waistcoat. Shelbourne's his name. He pranced into Bath, a confident viscount with a betrothal in his hand. Marjorie wouldn't marry him, but I happen to know that she gave him money to pay off George Entwhistle. Still, her father ruined the poor wretch."

Blake's legs felt as limber as saplings in a gale-force wind. Knowing that Entwhistle could wreak havoc was one thing; seeing the destruction was something else. Poor Shelbourne, indeed.

Blake searched for an innocuous reply—anything to foil Ponds's attempt at intimidation. Swallowing back a knot of cold fear, he said, "Is he one of the Kensington Shelbournes?"

Ponds grimaced with disappointment and grumbled, "He was the earl's son and heir, but not anymore. The family disowned him, and the crown took away his title."

Titles be damned! If Blake's dark and repulsive curse became known, the ancient and noble house of

Chesterfield would bear the shame. Such illustrious men and memorable women deserved an honorable heir to carry on their name, not a liar who would tarnish their glory. Why couldn't he have been a second son?

Ruthlessness firmed his resolve. "'Tis a pity, to be sure, about Shelbourne, but his affairs are his own. You and I have better things to discuss, Tobias—such as Marjorie. You want her job."

He shrugged and turned a palm up. "I've made no secret of my ambitions. She knows I intend to bid against her—and win."

And Blake could use the printer's zeal to his own advantage. But would he? Probably. "She'll make as fine a marchioness as she has a postmistress, don't you agree?"

Ponds looked as if he'd eaten a bowl of broken glass. "She'll ruin you. Our Marjorie has a bit of a reputation, you know."

Blake threw back his head and laughed. "Then we're well suited."

Sputtering, Ponds said, "I'm surprised your family went along with the betrothal."

"And I'm surprised," Blake snapped, "that you're privy to the preferences of the duke and duchess of Enderley. I had thought you traveled in lower circles."

A flush of embarrassment stained Ponds's cheeks. "I wasn't giving myself airs, Lord Blake. I was merely repeating something Her Grace, the dowager duchess of Loxburg, said."

So, thought Blake, Ponds still had his pride. What had been his weakness? How had he slipped Entwhistle's trap? Marjorie said her father had ruined some of the men and bankrupted others. Ponds didn't appear to fall into either category. "You shouldn't repeat women's gossip, Tobias."

"Point taken. However"—his voice dropped—"I

know the old witch better than you. And believe me, my lord, she'll spend every waking minute turning Marjorie against you."

Oh, no, she wouldn't, for Blake had a plan. He knew someone who would keep Rowena occupied and quite possibly gain her support for the betrothal. "I'll handle Rowena."

Tobias turned toward the entryway. "Mrs. Papjoy has arrived. Isn't that a becoming dress?"

Blake spied Nash's consort surveying the crowd. She wore a concoction of enough crimson taffeta to outfit the *Reliant* with a new topsail. "Just so," he said, wondering how she navigated with panniers as wide as ship's boats. "Shall we pay our respects?"

"You go ahead," said Ponds. "I'd like to dance with Wallingford's daughter. They're leaving on Saturday."

Blake faked a smile and watched Ponds stroll toward the ballroom.

Had Ponds wooed Marjorie? How far had the seduction gone? Had he kissed her? Had he touched her breasts?

Ugly, vindictive thoughts rose in Blake's mind. She belonged to him. He wanted her right here, right now, and once she stepped through the city gates he'd never let her out of his grasp again.

Knowing he'd go after her if he didn't otherwise occupy himself, Blake decided to seek out Juliana Papjoy. She had moved to the dice table and was involved in a discussion with the man named Shelbourne.

Curiosity and some perverse inner need drove Blake across the room to meet another of George Entwhistle's victims.

As he made his way through the crowd Blake stopped to exchange pleasantries with Dame Surleigh, Ralph Allen, and several other local residents. When after ten minutes he'd moved no more than twenty feet, Blake understood the reason for his slow pace: He was afraid. The closer he came to the dice table, the higher his anxiety rose, and by the time he stood next to Juliana Papjoy his stomach was churning like the sea in a hurricane.

"Good evening, Juliana," he said, unable to look Shelbourne in the eye.

Satin rustled as she turned. She smiled, and her shoulders sagged. "Oh, good evening, my lord." Her eyes darted to the dice table, then back to Blake. "How very nice it is to see you."

Bolstering his courage, Blake allowed himself a glimpse at Shelbourne. And wished he hadn't, for the young man stared back with an expression of utter hopelessness. Blake had seen similar looks on the faces of Africans who'd spent months in degradation and starvation in the hold of a Spanish slaver.

A quake of sheer terror rocked him to the roots of his soul.

Juliana gasped and said, "Oh, dear me." She had realized the irony of the situation. "This *is* awkward."

Blake swallowed and commanded himself to smile at her. "May I say you look enchanting?"

Relief smoothed out her worry lines. "Thank you."

He glanced pointedly at Shelbourne, then back at Juliana.

Hurriedly, she said, "Forgive my manners. Lord Blake, may I present Viscount"—she stopped, her eyes wide with embarrassment—"may I present Thomas Shelbourne."

Blake couldn't unclench his fist, so he didn't extend his hand. He managed a nod. "A pleasure, Shelbourne."

"Chesterfield."

The magic word. *Chesterfield.* Centuries of family

pride glowed within him. He could almost feel Edward, the Black Prince of Wales, clasping his shoulder, saying, "Stand for your own, lad."

By God, he would.

He focused on Shelbourne's unkempt hair and grease-stained clothing. He wore a brocade waistcoat that had once been a popular shade of lime. The poor fellow's soiled cravat looked as if it had been used to scrub tables.

Juliana cleared her throat. "Mr. Nash hasn't arrived, and I was wondering if I could impose upon you. . . ."

Understanding perfectly, Blake said, "Would you care to dance?"

Shelbourne turned back to the table. A ragged ribbon held back his hair.

"Oh, no," she said, with a tiny shake of her head that didn't dislodge a speck of dust from her towering and quite becoming wig. She spoke behind her fan. "You see, Lord Blake, someone at this table is cheating, and were Mr. Nash here, which I'm certain he will be soon, he would put a stop to it."

The incongruity struck an odd chord of humor in Blake. He'd just been thinking of one of his famous ancestors, and as far as missions went, ferreting out a crooked gambler in Bath seemed child's play compared to Edward's brilliance at the Battle of Crécy. But it was a purpose for Blake.

Strangely flattered, he said "'Twould be my pleasure to act in Nash's stead. Are the men using loaded dice?"

"Yes, they are," she said derisively. "I'm certain of it. The one in the ghastly wig and the one with the rundown shoes made their point five out of five times. They were bold enough to let the pot ride when that poor woman's turn came. No one else has won so much as a shilling. She's begun to wager her jewels."

The girl held the dice. When she saw him she smiled invitingly. Before her lay the pot, which consisted of about five hundred pounds in coins, a pearl earring, a ruby stickpin, and a gold snuffbox.

Blake identified the swains he'd been watching only moments ago. They stood side by side, discussing the accommodations at the White Swan Inn. They seemed unconcerned about the next roll of the dice. Why not? When their turn came again they'd be assured of success. But which man had the loaded dice?

The girl, her expression rife with desperation, tossed her remaining earbob into the pile. Just as she closed her hand to shake the dice Blake grabbed her wrist. "A moment, please," he said.

She gasped. Her fingers flexed and the dice tumbled down the front of her dress. But Blake didn't worry about those dice; the swains had the ones he wanted.

"Here, now," said the fellow wearing the rundown shoes. "You'll have to be waiting your own turn. The colleen's rolling the dice." The lilting brogue marked him an Irishman.

The others at the table looked up at Blake. Their eyes grew wide. Like puppets whose strings had been yanked, they came to attention. Chatter in the room ceased. At the surrounding tables wigged heads bobbed this way and that as everyone sought a better view.

"Stash it, O'Donnell," said the one in the frayed wig. "He ain't just a lord. He's a Chesterfield. Can't you see that?"

The Irishman stepped back and suddenly became interested in the scuff marks on his shoes.

The men were friends, just as Blake suspected. Or partners in crime. He scanned the other occupants of the table. He couldn't single out these two swains. What if they had other friends among the players?

He'd have to accuse them all.

Addressing the table, he said, "Gentlemen, please empty your pockets."

Gasps and huffs of outrage followed. Shelbourne grimaced as if he'd swallowed bilge water.

"Empty your pockets," Blake repeated. "All of you."

Shelbourne said, "Uh . . . certainly, my lord. But I prefer to do it in private."

Had Shelbourne been brought so low that he now cheated at dice? He'd already lost more than most men could earn in a lifetime; the least he deserved was the benefit of the doubt. "Very well," Blake said, "but the rest of you be about it."

Everyone except Shelbourne began turning their pockets inside out. Snuffboxes, calling cards, an assortment of timepieces, and a king of hearts hit the table. But no false dice. When a burly Scotsman fished a beribboned condom out of his coat, laughter rippled through the tense silence.

Only Shelbourne remained.

To Juliana, Blake said, "Keep everyone here until I return." Then he guided Shelbourne to the cloakroom.

His face a picture of abject misery, the younger man said, "I'm a bit down on my luck, as you probably know. I couldn't afford supper, so I filched half a chicken from the buffet. It's in my waistcoat pocket."

Shelbourne had asked for privacy to spare himself the shame of being caught with food in his pocket. Blake tried to disguise the pity he felt, for he knew what shame was like. Ruefully he thought, but for the grace of God, there goes Blake Chesterfield.

"How much did you lose?"

Shelbourne blew out his breath. "Ten pounds last night at Simpson's Rooms. Twenty-five so far tonight."

"I was told someone was playing with loaded dice. Is anyone here who played last night?"

Shelbourne's eyes popped open. "The girl. And she walked away with four hundred pounds and those earbobs. My father was right. I am a stupid fool."

Sadly Blake thought about his own father. Unlike his forebears, the current duke of Enderley seemed uninterested in leaving his mark on England. He always spoke in trivialities, unless he was railing about his duchess. Early in life Blake had sworn that when the title passed to him he'd use the power to better the lot of all Englishmen. Lately, though, his thoughts had turned to poor Africans and what he could do to help them.

Feeling merciful, he said, "If you're going to gamble, Shelbourne, you'd best learn to spot the cheats—even the appealing ones."

With a self-deprecating laugh the young man said, "Would that someone had told me that before I sat down to play cards with George Entwhistle. He took every pound I had. If Marjorie hadn't come to my rescue, I'd be wasting away in debtor's prison."

Blake winced. "I'll strike a bargain with you, Thomas Shelbourne."

Hope glittered in the man's eyes, then vanished. "But you're a Chesterfield, and I'm—I'm a nothing."

Kindly Blake said, "You're still a man."

"But why would you help me?"

"Why not? Call it mutual dislike for George Entwhistle. We could start a club."

"Don't look for me to join, unless the subscriptions are low."

"I'll give you five hundred pounds and furnish you with a letter of introduction to a shipbuilder I know in Boston. In exchange you answer truthfully any questions I ask about your betrothal to Marjorie Entwhistle."

Shelbourne's mouth fell open. "Horrid Tom said you were betrothed to her now, but I thought 'twas a rumor or a jibe at me. Did you lose to him at Hazard?"

Blake would trade his castle in Wales if it would change his debt to George Entwhistle. "No. I'm only interested in marrying his daughter."

"She's a prize, my lord."

"Will you agree to immigrate?"

Shelbourne blew out his breath, and his gaze turned inward. A moment later he smiled and squared his shoulders. "I can start a new life in the Colonies."

"Aye, you can," Blake said with confidence. "And I think you'll like the Americans. They don't stand on rank as we do."

"God bless you, my lord, for helping me, and . . . sparing my pride."

"You're welcome. Now I'd like some answers."

Five minutes later Blake returned to the gaming table where Juliana stood guard. The girl with the dice was a bold one, thought Blake, eyeing her slack mouth and false confidence.

He held out his hand and said, "Give me the dice from your bodice."

She wiggled her hips. "You can have all my playthings, m'lord. But dice ain't among 'em."

"Just the dice." She made no move to comply. Blake warned, "I'll take them from you."

"You wouldn't dare," she spat, her expression as hard as the whores in Lilliput Alley.

Blake crossed his arms. "Try me."

He counted to five. She stared him down. He plunged his hand into her cleavage. The sickly sweet odor of jasmine drifted to his nose.

"Hey, there. That's no way to treat a lady," she said, wiggling against his hand.

She drew in a breath, trapping his hand between the

globes of her breasts and the neckline of her dress. "Oh, my lord," she squealed, "that's a fine hand you got there."

His fingers waded through the moist mounds of flesh, then closed over the dice.

Noise in the room ceased. A cane thumped loudly on the marble floor. Blake looked up. The tart girl stared at the floor. He froze, for on the threshold stood Beau Nash, decked out in gold brocade. Beside him loomed the towering figure of Rowena, her eyes focused on Blake's trapped arm.

He freed himself. Hefting the dice, he knew they were weighted, the tools of a cheat.

A gloved hand touched his arm. A dark red skirt came into view. Juliana Papjoy said, "Thank you. Shall we pay our respects to the new arrivals?"

Blake almost laughed out loud. "By all means."

"But first you must collect a fine of thirty guineas."

"Why?" Blake asked.

"'Tis another of Mr. Nash's rules," she said.

Blake snatched the coins from the dice table. "Does Nash keep the money?"

She drew in a breath. Indignantly, she said, "No. It goes to his favorite charity, of course. The Mineral Water Hospital."

Most of the people had left their tables and were moving to greet Nash and Rowena. The professional gamblers swooped down on the king of Bath like gulls after a fishing boat. The citizens, intent on reaching the dowager duchess, looked like pilgrims hastening to a shrine.

Blake laughed.

"What's so funny?" asked Juliana.

He leaned to the right and said, "I was just thinking that if this room were a ship, it'd be listing dangerously to starboard."

She looked at the mass of people now gathered on

one side of the room. Laughing, she said, "How clever of you. Do you think we'll sink?"

"Only those who can't stay afloat in ceremony."

Her eyes softened. "I like you, Blake Chesterfield."

"Good. I need a friend." He squeezed her hand and guided her to a spot at the end of the crowd. A few moments later only John Wood stood between them and the duchess.

The architect bowed over Rowena's hand and said, "Your presence is a harbinger of spring, Your Grace."

She smiled, revealing teeth as white and straight as Marjorie's. A choker of baroque pearls complemented her fair skin and drew attention to her gracefully long neck. She wore Marjorie's black velvet dress and elaborately embroidered white petticoat. Marjorie had gotten her height from her mother's side of the family, for George Entwhistle was little more than average in size. Marjorie favored her grandmother in many other ways. Both were stately and elegant, with eyes the same enchanting shade of blue, and slender noses perfect enough to challenge an artist's skill. Their temperaments, however, were as different as a shark and an angelfish.

He remembered what George Entwhistle had said of Rowena. He'd called her a crafty and bitter old woman who'd lose the use of her arms before she'd let go of Marjorie. According to Shelbourne, Rowena had called George an old battered rake who would sacrifice his daughter to the same fate as her mother: death in childbirth, all for the price of an heir. All opinions considered, Blake thought George and Rowena a matched pair of self-indulgent wastrels who couldn't be bothered about the feelings of a vulnerable young woman with a heart full of love and no one worthy of it. Blake intended to fill all her needs.

He had been at a disadvantage every time he'd seen Rowena. But the second meeting swam vividly in his mind. He'd swept into the posting room, Marjorie in his arms, lust in his heart. Tonight was different, though, for without the exceedingly pleasant distraction of Marjorie he could focus his attention on Rowena.

Eager to do just that, Blake ushered Juliana into Nash's care and grasped the hand of the dowager duchess.

"Good evening, Your Grace," he said. "'Tis nice to see you out and about."

She nodded regally and sniffed. "And you, Lord Blake. I see you've partaken of the hospitality of Bath." Glancing at his hand, she added, "The smell still lingers about you. Jasmine, isn't it?"

The wicked old bag! She was trying to turn his mission of law enforcement into a tryst. He shrugged and said, "'Tis the price one must pay to uphold the rules of Bath."

"A likely story." She turned to Nash and murmured, "George Entwhistle certainly sends us the most verbose of visitors, doesn't he?"

Juliana gasped.

Beau dropped his white hat.

Blake dropped Rowena's hand. Leaning close, he said, "Have a care, Your Grace. This visitor may surprise you."

She waved her cane and said, "I doubt that."

If she thought to intimidate Blake Chesterfield, she could think again. "Perhaps you'd care to discuss it further over a glass of punch?"

Icy challenge glittered in her eyes. Eyes like Marjorie's, and yet harder, colder. "I wouldn't dream of keeping you from your dicing friends. You seemed so covetous of their company."

Juliana said, "That ugly blemish was cheating. She wouldn't yield the dice, so Lord Blake went after them."

Beau Nash leveled a gaze at Blake. "Did you get the dice?"

"Of course. Here you are." Blake handed over the fine and the dice.

"My thanks," said the king of Bath, his long face pulled into a frown. "Scurrilous riffraff," he grumbled. "They think they can come into Bath and pluck us like pigeons."

"Hardly, sir," said Blake, "so long as you're in charge."

Nash stood taller, but not, Blake sensed, out of any puffed-up notion about himself or his reputation. He was, after all, a gambler, albeit an honest one. "I think," Nash declared, "that I should survey this mob of carousers and invite the cheats to ply their trade in Tunbridge Wells."

The king of Bath held out his arm to his queen. Together they disappeared into the crowd.

"Tobias Ponds is here. He's dancing with a baron's daughter," said Rowena. "He's another of George Entwhistle's friends, you know. I thought you were going to fetch me a cup of punch, Lord Blake."

She had the oddest habit of firing off a sally, then following it by an innocuous statement. He, too, could play her game. "Ponds speaks so kindly of you, Your Grace. Did Marjorie perchance tell you that I gave her my horse for the trip to Bristol?"

Rowena's mouth turned down. "Of course she told me. She tells me everything. I tried to talk her out of harnessing the ill-behaved animal to that cart, but she would hear none of it. She hasn't handled such a spirited beast in years."

Good for Marjorie. She had stood her ground with Rowena. Pointedly he said, "Marjorie can control the beast in question."

Rowena thumped her cane. "Ah, but does the beast wish to be controlled?"

He grinned rakishly and held out his arm. "I'll gladly give her the reins."

Rowena placed her hand on his sleeve. "She won't marry you."

"Aha." He began the slow walk to the punchbowl. "Now we're getting to the heart of the matter."

"She won't sign that betrothal, even for the exalted Chesterfield heir."

The magic word again. Inspired, Blake nodded to the passing Edward Luffingham and said to Rowena, "One would think you didn't want Marjorie to enjoy the luxury and the advantages my name can afford her."

The cane quivered in her hand. "Your name won't be worth a mended sock when George Entwhistle gets through with you."

If she kept up those kinds of barbs, he'd be a damned bloody warrior by the time he was done. Using the information he'd gleaned from Shelbourne, Blake said, "What's this? You championing George? I thought you despised him."

"Of course I do. He's a scoundrel, but he was sly enough to get something on you. I wonder what it is."

Blake stiffened his knees to keep from shuffling his feet. If Rowena knew . . . He wiped away the unthinkable.

Shelbourne had been a wellspring of information. "You know what I think, Rowena? I think you enjoy playing games with George Entwhistle. What I don't think you see is the harm you're doing to Marjorie."

"You impertinent pup!" Indignation poured from her, but she pasted on a smile for the crowd. "That's the most absurd thing I've ever heard. She's a strong, fine woman. Far better than you deserve."

One hundred pairs of eyes looked on, so Blake kept his voice reasonable. "She'd have to be strong, considering the trials you and George have put her through."

Her fingers clenched on his sleeve. "Marjorie and I have survived George's games. **What** do you know about that scoundrel?"

"Call it the opinion of an objective observer."

"Call it whatever drivel you like. Marjorie will marry for love, not at her father's behest."

Blake played one of the trumps Shelbourne had given him. "As you did?"

She paled. They reached the refreshment table. A crisply turned out waiter poured the punch. Blake took the glasses from the waiter, then handed one to Rowena.

"My marriages were arranged, both of them." With aged but supple fingers she toyed with the cord of her fan. "I never even laid eyes on either husband until the wedding day."

She'd been hurt badly. What if she didn't know any better than to treat her granddaughter as she'd been treated? Fishing, he said, "You're angry about those marriages, aren't you?"

Her chin popped up. Baroque pearls shimmered in the candlelight. "I survived them, and with my help Marjorie will never be bought and sold like a heifer at market."

For the first time he speculated on the pain this proud woman had suffered at the hands of men. But did her experiences give her the right to toy with Marjorie's life? How odd that he, who'd always viewed marriage as a business arrangement, could now look upon it as an emotional union.

Even though he agreed with Rowena, he couldn't tell her so; she'd see it as a weakness to exploit. Instead he decided to fight power with power.

Rowena sipped from her glass and turned to face the crowd.

Smoothly, Blake said, "King George favors the match."

Her gaze snapped to his. "He answered your letter? I didn't see it come through the—" She stopped quicker than a frigate on a sandbar.

He couldn't resist the urge to smile. "Reading other people's letters is no better than stealing."

She pouted like an angry, spoiled child. "I'll tell Marjorie you called me a thief."

"You may also tell her I offered you the estate of your choosing. After she and I are wed."

"And I'll tell her you tried to bribe me."

"Chesterfields," he said proudly, "don't stoop to bribes."

"Unless they have a secret to hide or a rakehell reputation to uphold." She drained the cup and handed it to him. "Good night. I wouldn't think of keeping you from your pleasures."

Oh, yes, you would, he thought, watching her limp away. So warped was Rowena of Loxburg that she would even hurt the one person who loved her most.

His heart ached for the postmistress of Bath, and for the years of suffering she'd borne.

Nearby conversations faded to a distant hum. Suddenly he felt empty and alone, even in the crowd of merrymakers. He set aside Rowena's glass.

Were Marjorie not in Bristol tonight, she'd be here, probably chiding him for his black mood, certainly drawing him out of it. When, Blake wondered, had he stopped wanting her out of necessity and begun needing her for himself?

Like a loose cannonball on a pitching deck, the weighty thought rolled across his mind. Affection for Marjorie hadn't come in an explosion of passion but had crept up on him like a calm settling over the ocean. At first he'd hated her and himself and the circumstances that brought them together. Then he'd come to know her and respect the vulnerability she so closely guarded. After that he'd been so inexorably drawn to her that blackmail and dark secrets hadn't mattered. Now he desired her, he needed her. With a yearning so intense it staggered him, he loved her.

I love her.

Stunned, he sought the nearest empty chair and plopped himself down at a vacant backgammon table. Perspiration dotted his brow. He drained his drink in one gulp. Tender emotions swelled in his chest. Denial rose up to meet them.

He'd had no experience with love. Duty and devotion were his matrimonial tools. Warmth and affection were the romantic watchwords of a cavalier, not the devices of a cripple scurrying for cover beneath a marriage of necessity.

He loved Marjorie Entwhistle. Thinking the words, admitting the truth, served as treaty to his warring spirits. He loved her, and she'd be home tomorrow morning.

The next day she'd accompany him to the baths. That evening he'd make her his own.

CHAPTER 9

*Seducers of women shall refrain from spouting
their pretty words in the public rooms of Bath.*

—Beau Nash, *Rules of Bath*

THIS MORNING SHE'D GO WITH HIM TO THE BATH. THIS
evening she'd make him leave her alone.

It was the right choice. It was her only choice. Why,
then, did her heart ache?

Marjorie stepped into the tailor-made robe and
threaded her arms into the voluminous sleeves. Her
shoulders drooped, but not from the weight of the
canvas garment. Pigeons cooed and stirred from their
nests beneath the tiled roof of the mansion. Even the
weather seemed determined to mock her melancholy
mood, for the faint light of dawn seeped into a sky as
clear as a looking glass.

As she slipped the buttons into place she made
excuses for the doubts that gnawed at her resolve. She
tried to tell herself that she still pitied Blake Chesterfield. She knew better. Genuine affection for him
formed the root of her pain.

181

She hadn't expected him to take an interest in her work, let alone put himself in danger to apprehend a bandit and retrieve the stolen post. His care of Tug, his defense of Cumber smacked of true concern. Blake Chesterfield wasn't a scoundrel at heart. She knew feigned affection when she saw it. Her father had made her expert at false devotion.

Blake seemed to care for her. Why else would he take the time to accompany her on her afternoon rounds? He certainly desired her. Why else would he kiss and caress her with such abandon and speak of the children she would bear? Why else indeed? Because he had to marry her.

She could delude herself until the sun ceased to shine. Then she could stumble about in perpetual darkness, always believing he'd fallen in love with her for honest reasons, and never finding the courage to admit that he hadn't.

Regret nagged at her. But when faced with the choice of living a lie or living alone, she knew what she would do.

Resigned, she gathered her reticule and her gloves and went downstairs to wait for him with Grandmama.

Rowena stood before the fireplace, her attention focused on the painting over the mantel. Lizzie had tinted Grandmama's cheeks and lips and done up her hair in a fashionable twist. Rubies twinkled from her ears. Her bulky Bath robe hid the grate; nothing could hide her dislike for the Hogarth.

"I still think you should let me move it to my office," Marjorie said, coming to stand behind her grandmother, "since it bothers you so."

Rowena glowered at the painting. "He's a vulgar cartoonist. He should have pictured you as a respectable, intelligent woman, not a saucer-eyed paragon of innocence—even if you are rather naïve."

Marjorie cringed inside. "Oh, Grandmama. That's a wicked thing to say."

She still didn't look at Marjorie when she said, "The people of this town always say wicked things about you. They can't forget your foolish behavior, even though it was years ago. If I don't defend you, child, who will?"

Marjorie stared at Rowena's rigid back. "I'll defend myself, Grandmama. I'm an adult now. I'm not afraid of the gossips of Bath."

Rowena bowed her head and revealed great streaks of gray in her auburn hair. Sadly, she said, "But you must admit, it's been so demeaning. All these betrothals. I wonder if I'm . . . if you're up to another. What will become of us?"

Each of the betrothals had been hard on Grandmama. "I'll be the postmistress of Bath, and you'll be my favorite grandmother. Just remember, I'm not the same innocent girl Hogarth painted years ago."

Rowena rapped her cane against white marble. "I should have burned the ridiculous thing. When I think that I sold my jade necklace to commission it . . ." She sighed and shook her head. "It's disgusting."

A slap would have hurt less. Marjorie had always appreciated the satirical style of Hogarth. She stepped back. "You don't mean that."

"Not the way you interpreted it, no. I'd never hurt you." Rowena turned. Distaste curled her mouth. "You're not wearing your hair like that, are you?"

Suddenly self-conscious, Marjorie said, "What's wrong with my hair?"

"It looks like a plaited-up horse's tail. You'll get it wet, and then Lizzie'll have to spend hours drying it."

Marjorie touched the braid that started at the crown of her head, fell to her shoulder, then looped back up again. "I thought the style rather becoming. I don't intend to swim in the bath, and Lizzie never dries my hair."

Rowena shrugged. "Suit yourself. But if your erstwhile admirer doesn't get here soon, we might as well stay home. By seven o'clock people will be packed in the water like herring in a barrel of brine."

Marjorie glanced at the clock. "It's only six-thirty. We've plenty of time. And he's merely a friend."

"Bah. Women and men are never friends. You of all people should understand that. He's your father's wretched puppet. You don't think he really cares for you, do you?"

Marjorie bit her lip to steady it. "No," she murmured. "Of course I don't. You taught me better than that."

Grandmama patted her hand. "Good. Because that rogue will say and do anything to get you to marry him. If you're foolish enough to believe his compliments and promises, my dear, you'll find yourself stuck away at that estate of his in Wales, a babe in your belly and no one to care for you." She shook the cane. "I did tell you the tight purse offered me a cottage in Northumberland, didn't I? Imagine me in a crofter's hut. I'd be dead of lung fever in a year. Then you'd have no one."

Marjorie's heart seemed to wither in her chest. Hoping to rally herself, she stared at her favorite thing in the room: the Hogarth. But the expected joy didn't come. "Such a thing could never happen to you, Grandmama."

"I knew you wouldn't forsake me, darling. You're all I have, and I do try to help you." Grandmama limped forward and gave her a quick hug. "I've no intention of standing elbow-to-elbow with clucking hens like Miranda Surleigh while your 'friend' tries to seduce you." She winked and said, "She might peck out my eyes."

Marjorie forced a chuckle. "You're so tall, she'd have to stand on her guide's shoulders to reach you. And don't worry about Blake Chesterfield. I have no intention of marrying him." Saying the words should've brought relief. Instead Marjorie felt an odd sense of loss, like spotting a rainbow only to have it vanish.

Rowena glowed. "You're too clever for the likes of that rapscallion. He's shameless. Did I tell you I saw him fondling one of those London tramps? No sooner were you on the road to Bristol than he breezed into Wiltshire's gaming room and sought out the first willing woman. Why, his hand was buried to the wrist in that woman's bosom. Now smile, dear, and tell me how the bid's coming along."

Grateful for the respite from her emotional turmoil, Marjorie latched onto the safe topic. "The Bristol ledgers are tallied to the pence. The new clerk has a fascination for mathematics."

"Did we show a profit?" asked Rowena.

"Yes—especially on the package route. I may even commission a wagon. The mail cart's seen better days."

Rowena braced both hands on the cane. Leaning forward, she said, "That Honeycomb fellow's quite young. He can't be ready to drive a team."

He would be, Marjorie thought, with the help of Mr. Peddicord. But if she mentioned the coachman, the conversation might return to Blake Chesterfield. Grandmama would call him names. Marjorie would defend him. Best to let the matter rest. Besides, she might opt to use the profits from the Bristol package route to give the clerk a salary increase. "I won't worry about the wagon until summer," she hedged. "Albert will be experienced enough by then."

"Do we have enough money to pay for the London mail coach?"

"Yes. It'll be ready by the end of the month."

Rowena raised her eyebrows. "That fast?"

"'Tis the slow season for the carriage maker. He was eager for the commission."

"Let's hope he knows what he's doing." She cocked her head toward the window. "What's that sound?" She walked to the gold velvet drapes and parted them with her cane. "Ah, here's his lordship's carriage now. I must say 'tis a fine conveyance." She gasped. "Will you look at that outrageous driver? Whoever heard of a ducal carriage driven by a man dressed as a jester?"

Come Saturday, Peddicord, plumed hat and all, would be a regular visitor to Hartsung Square. Behind her she heard the front door open. In low tones Blake conversed with Merlyn. Boot heels clicked in the foyer. As Blake made his way down the mirrored hall Marjorie thought of his first trek down that corridor. She remembered seeing the reflection of his stiff carriage, his furious expression. She remembered observing that even anger couldn't mar such a handsome face.

She'd pitied him the night he arrived in Bath. Today she pitied herself.

"Smile, darling," said Rowena. "He'll expect it. Chesterfield men are accustomed to having women fawn over them."

When he stepped into the Hamburg room Marjorie didn't have to force herself to smile. Just as Grandmama said, the reaction came naturally.

He wore the traditional garments of the bath: a jacket and ankle-length trousers of white canvas. Only Blake's were tailor-made, too, for the rented robes available to visitors at the baths wouldn't be long enough for him. The pale fabric gave his complexion a swarthy look that enhanced his already overwhelming masculinity. His shoulders seemed inordinately wide, and she suspected the stiff fabric to be the cause.

Under one arm he carried a large bundle wrapped in brown paper.

Smiling, he approached and held out the package. "Hello, Marjorie. I brought you something." His green eyes scoured her face and settled on her hair. "Lovely. You look like a goddess with your hair done up that way."

Her flagging spirits soared.

Rowena's cane thumped loudly. "Harumph!"

Marjorie took the package. "What is it?"

A mischievous grin wreathed his face. "Open it and see."

Rowena cleared her throat. Blake clicked his heels together and bowed. "Good morning, Your Grace. How nice of you to join us."

"Good day to you, Lord Blake, and yes, it *is* nice of me." Her cheerful tone smacked of indulgence. "Are you buying my granddaughter's affection with gifts?"

"Grandmama!"

"That's for your granddaughter to say. Well, Marjorie. Open it."

He seemed oblivious to Rowena's disdain; his attention was focused on Marjorie. Unable to hold his expectant gaze, she looked at the package. Curiosity brought a flush to her face. She plucked the string free of its bow. The paper fell away to reveal a canvas Bath robe with full parson's sleeves that narrowed to tight-fitting cuffs. Rather than the traditional white, the garment was dyed a mouth-watering red.

"Do you like it?" he asked eagerly, standing so close she could smell the tangy fragrance of his shaving soap.

He'd complimented her dress the day she'd worn red, the day she'd watched him fencing with Everson. Warmed by the memory, Marjorie traced the fine stitchery on the collar and the front placket. Gold buttons winked back at her.

She lifted her head. Their eyes met. "Thank you. 'Tis a luscious color."

"I thought so myself." He smiled and touched her cheek. "And you're welcome."

Rowena poked her cane between them. "What've you got there?"

Marjorie turned so Rowena could see. "'Tis a Bath robe."

Rowena's nose wrinkled. "But it's red."

"Aye," said Blake. "A color perfectly suited to Marjorie. Don't you think so?"

Rowena huffed up and gripped the cane so hard her knuckles turned white. "Only a strumpet would wear red in the baths. She'll be a laughingstock."

"Come now," he said cordially, taking Marjorie's arm. "She'll stand out in a crowd of pinched-face hags. Most people paint their faces for the baths. Some wear wigs under those chip hats. The duchess of Marlborough wore her diamond tiara." Bending from the waist, he looked pointedly at Rowena's earbobs. "You're even wearing rubies yourself."

"What I wear is none of your concern. And Marjorie is a postmistress, not a duchess."

"Yes, and the finest in England, I suspect. But things change, people change," he said conversationally.

Rowena smiled confidently. "Marjorie's father never changes. He seeks out the weakest of men, then sends them here for us to deal with."

Blake stiffened, and his fingers squeezed Marjorie's arm. "He always speaks so well of you, Your Grace."

"Bah! He's a devil. He hates me."

"That's enough, Grandmama," Marjorie said.

"You needn't wear the robe today, Marjorie, or at all, for that matter. I simply thought it would please you."

"You're full of sweet words," Rowena grumbled.

His sincerity pleased Marjorie more than any gift. If

only he'd tell the truth about why he'd come to Bath. Knowing he never would, she said, "Thank you for the thought."

Rowena spat an expletive in French, then whirled so fast she almost lost her balance. Blake reached for her. Marjorie stopped him.

Rowena righted herself. With a quick jab of her arm she used the cane as a pole and snared the cord of her reticule. "I won't go if you wear that ugly thing."

Blake said, "Come now, Your Grace. One would think you didn't want Marjorie to have any fun."

"That's absurd. Marjorie always has fun. She doesn't need a red robe or a duke's son for that."

Although she'd only been awake an hour or so, Marjorie felt exhausted. "It isn't like you to be so rude, Grandmama. Perhaps you should stay here."

Tears welled in Rowena's eyes. "You know how hard I work." Her shoulders slumped. "I don't know what's gotten into me. I'm as churlish as Dame Surleigh. Must've been staying up so late and sorting the mail the other night while you were in Bristol. I do want to go to the bath. I'm dreadfully sorry, Lord Blake."

He smiled winningly. "Don't think of apologizing, Your Grace. I generally keep company with crusty seamen. Thank you for making me feel at home." He held out his free arm. "Shall we mingle with the masses?"

That evening, Blake handed Marjorie into the carriage, then climbed inside and took the opposite seat.

Peddicord still held the door. Built like a Spanish bull and blessed with the disposition of a Cotswold lamb, he had one vanity: hats. Tonight he wore a cavalier's chapeau, perched at a jaunty angle and sporting an ostentatious red plume.

He jerked off the hat. Freckles dotted his balding

pate. "Let's get you tucked in, my lady." With fingers more suited to reining in steeds than playing the lady's maid, he arranged her cloak around her ankles. Then he indicated the straps. "There's the handhold, my lady. Hang on tight if the going gets rough." Turning to Blake, he said, "You'll be blowing out the lamps if there's trouble, my lord. We don't know about the brigands on these roads, and we won't risk a fire."

Familiar with the routine, Blake nodded, "I'll douse the lamps at once, Peddicord."

"Unsuspecting folks get hurt in carriages. You won't be moving about unnecessarily?"

"Certainly not, Peddicord."

"There's two loaded pistols in the side compartment."

"Very good, Peddicord."

The stableman slapped the panel beneath Blake's seat. "Everson packed a bottle of wine and a light repast in here. Blankets and water are there, too."

"That should take care of us nicely, Peddicord."

"The moon's full, and two armed guards with torches are leading the way."

"As usual, you've thought of everything, Peddicord."

The coachman beamed at Marjorie. "No accident'll befall you in this carriage," he said. "I intend to take special care with the commodore's lady."

Marjorie smiled indulgently. "I'm told the commodore treats all his ladies very well."

"Oh, aye. Like queens. I remember that Irish heiress—"

Blake cleared his throat.

Peddicord screwed up his face as if he'd swallowed a thistle and said, "'Tis a fine night for a jaunt in the land schooner, eh, Commodore?"

"Just so, Peddicord. Take the helm."

Bobbing his head, the coachman stepped back and closed the door. "Batten it down, sir."

Blake threw the bolt. Peddicord tested it, then walked around to check the other door, which Blake bolted.

"Is he always so thorough in his duties?" asked Marjorie.

"Always. Make yourself comfortable, because he won't climb into the box until he's checked every harness and trace. If we're lucky, he'll forgo examining the horses' hooves."

"What if you're in a hurry?"

Blake shook his head. "There's no such thing with Peddicord."

"Has he always been so persnickety?" Marjorie asked.

"Yes. Since I was a child, and even before that. His father drove for my grandfather. The carriage overturned. Peddicord's father was killed."

"How dreadful. Carriages are so unsafe."

"Not," Blake said confidently, "when Peddicord's in charge."

"He's gone to a great deal of trouble for such a short journey."

Blake turned down the flame on the lamps. "Unless you have your heart set on Wiltshire's tonight," he said, "I thought we might take a drive out to Claverton-on-Avon. Lord and Lady Claver are having a party. Cleveland's attending."

"What's the occasion?" she asked, unfastening her cloak.

Blake watched her slip the garment off her shoulders, revealing a low-cut velvet gown in a shade of blue that reminded him of heaven. "I believe the tulips have flowered."

The carriage swayed. Marjorie grasped a restraining strap. Peddicord had climbed into the seat.

"I'm surprised you'd be interested in flowers," she said.

"Actually, I'm more interested in a long drive alone with you in this carriage."

A knowing smile adorned her pretty mouth. "A favorite ploy of my third and fifth suitors." She glanced pointedly at the interior of the coach. "Although their carriages weren't lined with brocade and trimmed in gold."

Blake dodged a stab of jealousy. "My motives are pure."

"I know." She tipped her head back and laughed. *"Pure* blarney."

Very soon this witty, entertaining creature would be laughing in his bed and conceiving his children. "Come now, Marjorie. Shall we take a drive in the moonlight with Peddicord as chaperon, or will you hide in the crowd at Wiltshire's?"

With a flick of her wrist she raised the window shade and peered through the glass. Her exquisite profile should grace a cameo, he thought. He'd take her to Italy someday and commission the finest craftsman to carve her image on a delicate pink shell.

"I'd love to see the tulips," she said.

Reaching behind him, Blake slid open the panel. "Cast off, Peddicord. Steer a course north by northwest."

The coachman plied the reins. As smooth as a ship in a southerly breeze, the conveyance began moving. Horses' hooves noisily clip-clopped on the stone streets.

Heated bricks below the tin floor radiated warmth through the coach. Tiny flames in the vanity lamps bathed her in golden light, bringing a glimmer to her unpowdered and upswept hair—hair that would one day soon drape his pillow.

He patted the seat beside him. "Sit here."

Her brows rose. "Why? Are you afraid I'll fall overboard?"

He chuckled, thinking the only falling she'd do was in love with him. Lust tightened his groin, but his heart beat for more than physical pleasure from Marjorie Entwhistle. "Can you swim?"

"Yes," she said meaningfully, "even in the most turbulent of waters."

"I'll remember that. Now come here, so you can point out the sights to me."

Eyeing him curiously, she brought a gloved hand to her neck and toyed with the ribbon tied there. The coffer of Chesterfield gems would change that. He thought of one stone in particular. Thanks to his ancestor, Edward the Black Prince of Wales, Blake possessed a sapphire as big as a robin's egg. He pictured the gem strung on a long chain and nestled between Marjorie's breasts.

Bathed in family pride, he said, "Well? Surely you're not afraid of me."

"Move over," she said confidently.

He could read her like the currents of the Atlantic. Blake raised up and pulled the greatcoat from beneath him. He scooted to his left and held out his hand. She grasped it and eased onto the seat. Only the modest panniers of her skirt separated them.

"Comfy?" he asked, breathing deeply of her lavender fragrance and wishing the bodice of her gown was indecently low so he could lift out her breasts and nibble them.

"Yes." She turned until her eyes met his. "Has Peddicord the patience to teach Tug and the others?"

In the lane a group of revelers bellowed a bawdy tune about Queen Elizabeth and one of Blake's ancestors. Everyone made merry in Bath except the postmistress. Blake intended to change that, too. "I'm sorry. What did you say?"

"About the coaching lessons. Don't think I'm not grateful," she said. "It's just that the boys know nothing of driving a team of horses."

Fond memories flooded Blake. As a child he'd often escaped the cold corridors of Chesterwood for the cozy family room of the Peddicord cottage.

"Why are you smiling?" she asked.

"I was thinking about Peddicord and his eight sons, all of whom are taller than he, and fine horsemen. Trust me. He has patience to spare."

"I don't trust you at all, but I'll believe you this one time."

His gaze kept straying to the elegant column of her neck and the enticing swell of her breasts. "That's a perfect place to start."

She laughed. "Your lecherous nature is showing, Blake Chesterfield." Leaning forward, she raised the other shade and looked out the window. "Tell Mister Peddicord to veer right at the next fork. It's a bit out of the way, but the road leads up into the hills and offers a beautiful view of Bath."

Blake opened the panel again. "Stay to starboard, Peddicord, and steady as she goes."

"Aye, aye, Commodore."

Blake pitched his greatcoat onto the other seat. The heavy, dark wool covered her more feminine wrap, much the same as his body would soon cover her womanly form. Anticipation kindled his desire. Her nearness added fuel to the flame.

They passed through the city gate and onto the smooth dirt road. The clippity-clop faded to muffled tramping. Blake squinted into the darkness. "Tell me what's out there, Marjorie. I can see shadows and an occasional light speeding past."

"Ha!" she said, leaning back and staring at the lamps. "We're traveling at a snail's pace. At this rate it'll be midnight before we get to Claverton-on-Avon."

He couldn't resist saying, "I wouldn't want to go too fast for you."

Her eyes twinkled with mirth. "You're too fast— even for a penniless and lonely widow."

He took her left hand and absently trailed his thumb over her ring finger. "How about a postmistress with eyes bluer than cornflowers and a mind quicker than lightning?"

Lowering her lashes, she turned away. She seemed shrouded in vulnerability. "That's not me at all, and you needn't resort to flattery. I've heard volumes of it."

The carriage rocked gently through the night. Close to her ear he said, "Even the part about your lightning-quick mind?"

She drew up her shoulder and rubbed her ear against it. "Well, no. Never that, exactly. One suitor thought to woo me by reciting Shakespeare."

Seeing her, so kittenlike, brought a softness to Blake. "A mongrel beef-witted lord, no doubt."

"He was only a rascally knave," she said, a note of sympathy in her voice. "I'm well acquainted with the type."

Six men had romanced her out of desperation. Had any taken the time to discover the sensitive and gracious woman beneath? Surely not, else they would have persisted. Had any fallen in love with her?

Suddenly possessive, he put his arm around her and pulled her close. She tried to draw away. "Don't," he said. "You're safe with me."

She gazed out the window. "Safe from what, Blake?"

Caught off guard by her directness, he decided to respond in kind. "From the thing you fear most. Being forced. You're very stubborn about that, you know."

She sighed, causing her breasts to swell gently. "I've had to be. I had no choice. Besides, if I'd fallen into the arms of the first suitor, we wouldn't be sitting here tonight."

The coach lurched, tipping them forward. Blake held her fast as the carriage started the climb into the hills. "Then we've something in common."

She turned so quickly her nose brushed his cheek. Frank disbelief shone in her eyes. "That's preposterous. You're a duke's son. What would you know about coercion?"

For the first time in his life he wanted to share his private thoughts with a woman. He wished they were embarking on a long journey to the Highlands of Scotland or to his estate in Wales, for it felt natural to sit beside her in the warm nest of the coach.

"Dodging marriage traps is a fact of life for me, too, Marjorie."

Leaning back, she studied him intently. "I hadn't thought of that." Understanding sparkled in her eyes. "Of course. You're wealthy, titled." Pursing her lips, she added, "And you *do* have the Chesterfield looks."

Pleasure thrummed through him. "Does that mean you find me pleasant to look upon?"

"For centuries women of several cultures have been looking pleasantly upon Chesterfield men."

"You didn't answer my question."

"I don't intend to encourage you. Just remember, you're very good at evading marriage."

The irony of his present situation baffled Blake. Ruefully he said, "I've had to be. Women can be ruthless."

She shot him a sidelong glance. "Most women have no choice. Most men do. You're what? Thirty-five years old? Tell me why you never married."

"I was waiting for you."

Her laughter vibrated through the carriage.

She'd never know the reason behind his lengthy

bachelorhood, for to tell her, he'd have to reveal his ugly secret. "I'm thirty-three."

"Oh." She lowered her lashes. "I'm sorry."

"Don't be. You didn't insult me. I'm wiser now. I don't get trapped as easily as I used to."

She settled herself in the curve of his arm, and he thought again of how perfectly suited they were. Now he had to convince her.

"Would you care to share some of your narrow escapes?" Demurely she added, "You know some of mine."

She'd been humiliated by Rowena and George. So had he. They'd both dodged marriage traps. Yet perhaps he'd overestimated how well she'd weathered her father's games and her grandmother's manipulations.

"What are you thinking?" she asked, all rapt attention.

When would he learn to anticipate bluntness from her? "I was thinking that my stories would probably bore you." When she lifted her brows in challenge he added, "Then again, you might find a few of them entertaining."

"Then tell me. Did any of the episodes . . . change you?"

Harnesses jingled. The carriage slowed, then made a sharp turn. Blake held her tighter. He perceived a statement in her question; her father's machinations had affected her deeply. Blake wanted to make her forget those times.

"When I was twenty-one and living at one of the family townhouses in London a countess drugged both Everson and me with laudanum. Several hours later I awakened in my bed, groggy and naked as the day I was born. The daughter of the countess lay beside me, equally naked and deeply drugged."

She slapped her hand to her mouth to hide her laughter. "What did you do?"

"I roused Everson and told him to rush downstairs and inform the countess that I was dead."

"You didn't."

"Yes. And I was a very convincing corpse."

"Oh, surely they didn't believe you."

"Yes. The countess wailed as she got her daughter dressed and Everson carried the girl to their carriage. To prevent further entrapments I gave the townhouse to a cousin and moved in with my uncle, the earl of Westchester."

She grew thoughtful. "You were forced to give up your privacy."

He should've expected the deductive statement from her; Marjorie Entwhistle spent her life assessing situations and making decisions. With Chesterwood and fourteen other estates to oversee, he needed a helpmate like Marjorie.

"Yes, I did. But a year later I went to sea, where there's never any privacy."

"But you had to go ashore sometime. Your . . . ah . . . reputation for attracting women is legend."

Feeling absurdly flattered, he said, "I'll take that as a compliment."

"I meant it to be so," she said candidly. "Women everywhere want you."

"But do you?"

"Tell me what happens when one of *them* won't take no for an answer."

Odd as it seemed to Blake, he didn't feel he was laying himself open to ridicule or a fit of jealousy from her. "Well," he began easily, "I became an expert at climbing out of windows in the middle of the night."

She jabbed him in the ribs. Blake winced. "That's how you got into my room when you left the custard and the drawing."

His side smarting, he looked out the window and said, "Isn't the quarry around here somewhere?"

"Don't change the subject. I'm not done with you."

"Nor I you," he said with quiet intensity. "Let's talk about that bed of yours. I've been curious about it. It's very long, but then you're very tall. The perfect size for me."

Her mouth fell open. "You're a rogue!"

He shrugged and stretched out his legs. "True. I'm also getting cramped in here." Looking out the window, he said, "Have we reached your scenic spot yet?"

"I should insist you take me home."

Eagerly he said, "To Chesterwood?"

She laughed, dislodging a curl from her elaborate coiffure. Pinning it back, she said, "You'd have to abduct me."

No, he wouldn't. She liked him, and tonight he'd show her just how much. "I don't abduct my friends, Marjorie. They come willingly."

"You're a trickster with words, but you can't fool me." She peered out the window. "Tell Mister Peddicord to drop anchor."

He kissed her quickly on the cheek. "And you're as clever as a certain viscountess who picked the lock on my bedroom door."

"I'd never do such a thing."

"You wouldn't have to, sweetheart." His green eyes glowed seductively. "I'd never lock you out."

As he relayed the information to the coachman Marjorie struggled to compose herself. Blake Chesterfield was impossibly charming, and with every encounter she liked him more. Oh, but his words were as smooth as lemon pudding. He seemed so sure of himself, not a man with weaknesses to hide. Or was she so smitten with him that she no longer cared why he'd come into her life?

No, she wasn't smitten. She was in love. Hopelessly,

foolishly, she'd let down her guard and welcomed him into her heart. With his caring ways and friendly conversations Blake Chesterfield had accepted her invitation. He made her laugh; he made her feel proud of her accomplishments. He made her see the good in herself. She couldn't pinpoint the exact moment she stopped seeing him as another visitor in her life and started thinking of him as the husband she would cherish. But somewhere along the way she'd put her future in his hands.

What would he do with it?

Possibilities of the worst and best kind came to mind.

The carriage rolled to a halt. Eager for a reprieve from questions she couldn't answer, Marjorie threw back the bolt on the door. Blake snatched up his greatcoat as if it were a handkerchief and laid it across his knees. Then he picked up her cloak and draped it over her shoulders.

"Are you ready to play the guide, Marjorie?"

He shouldn't wear green, she thought contrarily. He should wear drab brown. "Only if you'll play the gentleman."

He winked, drawing her attention to eyelashes so long they probably had to be groomed.

Peddicord swung open the door. His smile faded when he spied Marjorie on the seat next to Blake.

"Don't fuss, Peddicord," said Blake. "And no lectures about staying put in a moving carriage."

The coachman smacked his lips and said, "Fine night for a stroll, Commodore. Let me help you with your coat."

Blake stepped out of the carriage and stooped down so the shorter man could play valet.

Blake Chesterfield should wear rags, Marjorie determined, and forget to wash his face. He shouldn't wear fine silk shirts of blazing white and intricately tied cravats and emerald stickpins. He was elegant. He was gorgeous. He was manly. He could give her sons and daughters to fill her waning years. He would go to any length to wed her.

He held out his hand. She grasped it and felt the hard edge of his signet ring, an immense circle of gold bearing the chevrons of Chesterfield above an emerald the size of her thumb. With the proceeds from that ring she could send all of the postboys to universities or trade schools.

"Marjorie?"

She glanced up. Tender concern creased his brow. "What mean thoughts about me are racing through your brilliant mind?"

Miffed that he was so astute, she snapped, "You flatter yourself to imagine I'm thinking about you."

He leveled her a look that said he knew she'd lied. "Give me a smile," he cajoled. "Frowning women bring out my most lecherous nature."

How could she insist he leave her alone when she wanted the night to go on forever? Having no reply, she let him lift her from the carriage, all the while wondering how she'd ever manage to refuse him anything.

CHAPTER 10

Young ladies take notice of how many eyes observe them.

—Beau Nash, *Rules of Bath*

"LET ME." BLAKE BRUSHED ASIDE HER HANDS TO FASTEN her cloak.

His fingers touched her neck, and she was again surprised at the roughened texture of his skin. His were the hands of a laborer, not a nobleman.

He loomed before her, a giant shadow in his caped greatcoat, and even before her eyes adjusted to the darkness she knew he was smiling. Her senses filled with awareness of him, of the lemony soap he favored, of the warmth his body offered, of the honest pleasure her presence gave him. Honest? Impossible, for Blake Chesterfield was just another suitor intent on using her as payment for her father's blackmail.

Would she, for a few precious hours, forget why he'd come to Bath? Reasons didn't matter now, and like a weight falling from her shoulders her guard slipped away.

Behind her she heard Peddicord addressing the outriders, but she couldn't decipher his words; her attention was focused on the man before her.

He pulled up her hood and said, "I'm yours to guide, Marjorie."

Tamping back excitement, she walked around the carriage and started down the open road. Coming up beside her, he put his arm around her and draped his wrist over her shoulder. He didn't draw her close but seemed content with the companionable contact.

You might like me, Marjorie, if you'd give yourself the chance.

He'd said as much the night she dined with him at Cleveland's. Tonight, with tender gestures of affection, he seemed determined to prove it.

They were of a complementary height, she observed, studying their moon shadows—he a snippet or so taller. Their steps in harmony, they strolled toward a well-worn path.

A pleasantly cold breeze stirred the air, rustled through the barren limbs of beech and elm, and set the firs to swaying. Patches of hard-packed snow dotted the landscape, but for the most part winter lay behind them. Low on the horizon, the moon hung like a battered plate of gold in a star-strewn sky.

He tipped his head back and breathed deeply through his nose. Exhaling, he said, "I love the smell of England. Don't you?"

Vehemently she said, "Yes. Especially compared to France. It smelled . . ." She searched for a word to describe the unpleasant odor that had permeated the convent.

With his thumb and forefinger he pinched his nose. "Like a spring house when the cheese is ripe?"

Laughter bubbled up inside Marjorie. "In summer, yes. But in winter it smells like a vat of sour wool."

"With crusty things floating on the water."

Marjorie held up her hands and wiggled her fingers. "And awful steam rising from the top and burning your eyes."

"And the food." He guffawed and fell out of step, the weight of his arm coaxing Marjorie along. In the path their shadows wobbled like gin sots who'd topped off a pail. "For my fare," he declared, "I'll take a hearty bowl of ox cheek soup."

Weak with laughter, she groaned. "You can't possibly like that swill. It's French."

He stopped. "No."

Marjorie fell against him. "I say it's French."

He put his face a breath away from hers. Silvery light glistened in his dark hair and twinkled in his eyes. "Tell me it isn't so."

She felt devilishly happy. *"Oui, monsieur"*— choked laughter stopped her—"I have it on the best authority."

He grasped her shoulders. "But I hate French things!"

She was amazed that he could be so animated, so free. Hoping to inspire him further, she said, "Whatever will you do?"

"Well," he said with finality, "that's the end of it. I'll never eat ox cheeks again."

"What will you eat instead?"

An evil chuckle rumbled in his chest. "I could take a bite out of you."

"I'd taste as bitter as old rhubarb."

"I'll take my chances."

She twirled away. He raced after her, his boots crunching on dead leaves and twigs in the path. They ran the last few steps to the top of the hill. When he reached her he halted in his tracks. And sucked in a breath.

He wasn't winded, though, she realized when she turned to look at him. He was spellbound by the view, his noble profile now serene, his regal bearing gone lax.

"The valley of the Avon," he whispered reverently. "'Tis beautiful."

A white-breasted owl sailed into view, then hovered in the wind, its wings tipping slightly for balance.

"See the spires of the Abbey Church?" she asked, pointing toward the center of town.

"Yes," he said, wonderment in his voice, "and the steam rising from the Klug's Bath. And the river . . . Oh, my, it glistens like quicksilver."

"Some say the Avon is curved like two sickles laid handle against tip."

Absently he said, "I can see that."

Caught up in the excitement, she said, "The Great Bath Road to London is off to the west, but you can't see it from here."

"Yes, I took that road to fetch Drummond and the post."

She'd hardly known Blake Chesterfield then.

Craning his neck, he searched the sky. "Which way's north?"

Surprised, she said, "I thought sailors steered by the stars."

He blew out his breath and stared at his boots. All animation vanished from his face. "Too many clouds, and actually, I've never steered a ship. An underling sits at the helm of the *Reliant*."

"Where's your compass?"

"I don't always wear it," he said tersely.

She wondered at the cause of his abrupt change in mood. Perhaps he was sorry for revealing so much of himself—especially to her. But he'd said he wanted to be friends.

Shelving her disappointment, she showed him the direction. "There's Lansdown."

He followed her outstretched hand. "A century ago the Royalists fought the Parliamentarians there," he said, seemingly preoccupied. "England lost all the way 'round."

"Your ancestors participated in that battle, didn't they?" she asked.

"Yes. Five Chesterfields died."

Awed, she realized that Chesterfields had fought in every battle in English history. "Your family is as much a part of the fabric of England as this valley is of the earth," she said. "You should take a princess to wife, not a postmistress with a notorious past."

"You, notorious?" Laughter rumbled in his chest. "I don't believe you. What did you do, lose a letter meant for the king?"

Her shameful past rose up to meet her. She'd tell him, but at a price. "Tell me your secret, and I'll tell you mine."

"I withdraw the question," he said. "Let's don't talk of secrets tonight."

"No," she said, her heart brimming with hope and love. "Let's just be with each other."

The owl hooted a lonely song. The sound faded into the tune of the night wind. She searched the barren trees to find the bird, but her gaze stopped on Blake Chesterfield.

In deep concentration he studied the lay of the land, his eyes constantly returning to Lansdown. At last he pointed south. "There." His eyes sparkled with discovery. "That flat triangle of land is Little Solsbury Hill. That would put the Roman road . . . there." He pointed to the northeast.

Puzzled, yet eager for a return to the playfulness they'd shared moments before, she said, "I don't think you need a guide."

He chuckled and shook his head. A lock of sleek black hair fell across his brow. "Then let's talk about you." He bumped her shoulder with his.

"Where did you grow up?"

"In a convent near Tournai, in France."

"Was ox cheek soup on the menu?"

She laughed. "Once a week. I fasted."

He bumped her again. "Did you always want to be the postmistress?"

He did want to be friends with her, unless he wanted to learn her secrets without telling his. "No, I didn't."

"Dame Surleigh told me Rowena was postmistress here then."

Tenderness warmed Marjorie. She remembered the lonely waif she'd been, ready to trust anyone. "Yes, and she wanted me to live with her."

"Do you have other relatives?"

Only a father who cared more about a grandchild than his daughter's happiness. "No."

"You helped her with the post."

Marjorie said, "Yes. She had the most wonderful ideas, but she hadn't time to implement them all."

"Such as . . ."

"Expanding so we could better support ourselves."

"How does one expand the post?"

"One increases one's district. Now we have Wells, the Bristol package route, and very soon a London mail coach."

"Which was your idea, I'll wager."

Marjorie remembered the arguments. "Grandmama was against it, but not anymore."

"You became postmistress when she had that dreadful accident."

"Ah, no. I was already the postmistress by then."

He whipped his gaze to her. "You were only nineteen at the time of her accident. When did you become postmistress?"

"Officially when I was eighteen."

"Truly? Weren't you awfully young for such responsibility?"

Ghosts of her first year in Bath haunted her, and even if she and Blake became fast friends she'd never reveal the awful things she'd done that summer, the summer that drove her to seek her independence. Hedging, she said, "We . . . I needed the money and something worthwhile to occupy my time. You see, Grandmama has only a small pension from Loxburg, and after her accident . . ."

"I can't imagine Her Grace playing tutor to Tug and the other lads as you do."

"She didn't. When Grandmama was postmistress she hired grown men to carry the mail. But you see, the only route we had was Bath to London. I was too inexperienced to manage men. So I found Tug and the others."

His arm circled her again. She wanted to lean against him but couldn't bring herself to be so bold.

"You gave them a home and hope for the future. That's very noble."

"I'm not noble at all. As Grandmama says, I'm a clever entrepreneur."

"That sounds like an insult. You performed an act of compassion, and she makes it sound as if you acted out of greed." He squeezed her shoulder. "Did it seem so to you?"

"Originally, yes." Truth poured from her. "But I just misunderstood. Grandmama would never hurt me."

"Do you often take umbrage at what she says?"

Shame stole over her. "Only when I'm prideful and selfish."

"Oh, come now." With the flat of his hand he drew

small circles on her shoulder. "I don't believe you're either."

She'd been honest with him; he shouldn't argue. "Believe what you like."

On a half laugh he said, "I used to believe that the devil left me on the doorstep of Chesterwood."

"Why would you believe that?"

"Because my mother told me so."

"That's wicked. How could she be so cruel to you?"

He stared, not directly at her, but at the fur peeking from the lining of her hood. Quietly he said, "I suspect she was jealous because she was no longer the center of attention." He smiled crookedly and rolled his eyes. "The Chesterfield heir always causes a stir. My father, my uncles, even her family could speak of nothing else but me. So you see, sometimes even those who love us can hurt us."

He said it with such frankness, Marjorie wondered if he hadn't been speaking for her benefit.

"Enough about me," he declared. "Tell me how old you were when you took in Tug."

Her life had changed that day, for the better. "I'd just turned seventeen."

A frown gave him a stern look. "You bought the postal commission at seventeen?"

She almost laughed at such an absurdity. "Well, no. I just managed it. Grandmama was generous enough to sign that first bid for me and give me a start."

"You're all she has," he said plaintively.

Miffed at his dismal tone, she replied, "Yes, and she's all I have. Why did you threaten to send her to Northumberland?"

His mouth dropped open. "Northumberland? I never said anything about Northumberland. One of my cousins and his family lives on the estate there. I offered to buy Rowena a home anywhere in England. I thought she'd choose Tunbridge Wells."

Grandmama had lied again; Marjorie knew it. What was it about the betrothal to Blake Chesterfield that pushed Grandmama to lie and scheme? She was probably afraid of living on her own, no matter how elegant the place. The meaning behind the move was the important thing. "That's just geography. You want to get rid of Grandmama."

"I thought she'd like Tunbridge Wells. The waters are considered curative. It's closer to London, where we'll be living. Many of the people who visit Bath come to Tunbridge—Beau Nash does. Cleveland has a place there. So does the duchess of Marlborough." As if confused, he rubbed his forehead. "I just wanted her to have a home of her own."

Marjorie had no intention of addressing his assumption about living with him in London. "Grandmama has a home."

"No, sweetheart. Your father owns Hartsung Square."

"That's a lie," she said, embittered once again by her father's deceit. "Grandmama spent all of her money—sacrificed everything to buy a home for me."

He shrugged. "Perhaps I was misinformed. Speaking of your grandmother, did you hear what she said to Tobias Ponds in the Cross Bath?"

Was he changing the subject on purpose? No matter; she was weary of the strife between him and Rowena. "All of Bath heard them. She shouldn't have called him a crab."

Blake chuckled. "But he called her a sour-faced—" He stopped abruptly. "They were quoting Shakespeare, the one about the shrewish woman."

Ruefully she said, "They often do."

He snapped his fingers. "Tobias was the suitor who quoted Shakespeare to you."

"I told you that."

His eyes narrowed. With a stiffened jaw he said,

"You told me he was a suitor. You didn't mention the details of your liaisons with him."

Feeling absurdly pleased, she said, "If I didn't know you were desperate to marry me, I'd think you were jealous, Blake Chesterfield."

His hand tightened on her arm. "I'm fiercely jealous of anyone who knows you better than I."

"Then you'll be jealous of half the people in Bath."

"That will change."

"I don't know why you persist in troubling yourself. I'm not at all interesting." But she did know: He had no choice. Her father had seen to that.

"Why do you think so little of yourself, Marjorie?"

Because she'd done things in her youth that could never be undone. Grandmama had forgiven the wicked young girl, cared for her, accepted her, but Grandmama loved her as no one else ever could. Knowing he would expect an answer, she said, "I'm just an ordinary woman."

"And I'm a frigging foundling left by Lucifer."

She laughed. "You're a rogue, and a sly one, too."

"That being the case," he said, wiggling his elegant eyebrows, "let me remind you that you're beautiful." His voice dropped to a seductive whisper. "That your intelligence puts most scholars to shame. That you're generous with your time and so free with your heart that you would give a batch of orphans a chance at a better life. You're a woman to respect, Marjorie Entwhistle."

Her heart beat so wildly she thought it might fly from her breast. "I certainly am not."

"Then I'll prove it." He breathed the words into her ear. "Come here." He drew her in front of him, then opened his coat and pulled her against his chest. His body blazed like a furnace at her back, and his arms held her fast.

He laid his cool cheek next to hers and rested his

chin on her shoulder. Wrapped in a cocoon of sandal-wood-scented wool, they gazed out over Bath.

"Now," he said, "that you're all cozy, and precisely where I want you, point out the buildings where we've been, and start with Hartsung Square."

Names of familiar places and ancient landmarks became a jumble of meaningless words, for her senses were fixed on the man and the feel of his arms around her. Perception and coherent thought fled like mallards at the first touch of winter.

"I can't show you," she said through a haze of languor. "My arms are trapped."

"Hum." He kissed her neck, then edged upward to the tender spot beneath her ear. "It *is* impolite to point."

Her earlobe tingled in anticipation of his touch. Her fingers curled into fists. "But you wanted to see the sights," she said lamely.

"Forget Bath," he whispered. "I've a much more beautiful sight before me."

A moan escaped her lips, and when her knees threatened to buckle she gave him her weight. In response he slipped his hands inside her cloak and stroked her arms from wrist to shoulder, shoulder to wrist. Then he massaged her hands until the tension fled and fingers unfurled and now-damp palms lay flat against her thighs. His agile fingers trekked upward and cupped her straining breasts, gently kneading and fiercely arousing.

His chest swelled as each ragged breath was seemingly hauled, with great effort, into his lungs, and all the while his nimble fingers continued to play a magic tune. "Turn around."

Like a hopelessly lost traveler searching for a signpost on a lonely stretch of road, Marjorie heeded his words.

His hands locked behind her, pulling her with a force she couldn't fight. "Put your arms around my neck, Marjorie, and open your eyes."

When had she closed them? She'd been so caught up in sensual pleasure that she'd become blind to any visions save those in her mind. Now aware and eager to obey, she looked at him. And fought the urge to drift back into sweet oblivion, for a forest of tender emotions gleamed in his eyes.

"Tell me what you want, sweetheart."

"I want you to kiss me," she heard herself say.

"I was hoping you'd say that." His mouth settled gently on hers, his lips slightly parted, his breath as sweet as clover in the morning. It occurred to her then that he'd once worn a mustache. Intrigued, she trailed her hand across his cheek to touch the spot where their lips were joined.

Sensory excitement scurried from her fingertips to her brain until erotic fantasies shimmered like moonbeams in her mind. Blake, taking down her hair and smoothing it over a satin pillow. Blake, presenting her with a chest of jewels on their wedding night, then insisting she model them, naked, before him.

She gasped in surprise and delight. His tongue plunged into her mouth, then twirled and foraged like a hunter seeking precious prey. Lured by the promise of pleasure, she rushed headlong into his trap. Once snared, she grew bold, straining against him, testing the limits of the desire he nurtured.

Then he was dragging her hand from around his neck and drawing it back down into the heat that blazed between them. Cold fingers touched the warm velvet of his breeches. Beneath her palm, he pulsed to life, vigorously sending the one message she couldn't ignore: He needed her.

Realization spawned an ugly truth. She was weak

where men were concerned. Grandmama had helped her see the truth. Because Papa had forsaken Marjorie, she sought out other men to take his place.

"Marjorie?"

The sound of Blake's voice jolted her back to the moment.

"What's wrong?" he asked.

"Nothing." Everything, she thought.

"Stay with me," he entreated, and he began kissing her again, moving deliciously against her hand. "I need you."

Swept up by the plea in his voice, she gave him what he asked for. Eager to catch up with his passion and discover the extent of her own wild cravings, she fought against the boundaries of inexperience. Her breasts ached, and she felt too weak to stand.

He must have sensed her struggle. Yearning rumbled in his chest, and he dragged his mouth from hers. "Stop," he groaned.

Puzzled by his urgency, she opened her eyes. Strain tightened his mouth and made ropes of the tendons in his neck. "What?" she stammered.

Through his teeth he said, "Move your hand. Now."

She did, and he gasped as if in pain. She hurt, too, and realized his palms still lay flat against her breasts. Suddenly she understood the source of her distress. "Move yours. Now."

He seemed to shake himself. Then a smile spread across his face. "I don't want to."

"You're not being fair to me."

His fingers squeezed her gently, the fabric of her gown softly abrading her tautened skin. "Were we in my bed, sweetheart, I'd be more than fair to you. And if you weren't a virgin, I'd take you here, standing in the moonlight."

He was speaking of making love to her, but what

did fairness have to do with it? Feeling out of her depth, she said, "That would be impossible. We'd tumble into the valley."

"Practical women drive me wild."

"Release this practical woman."

"No. You feel wonderful." He kissed her nose. "You also don't think I can make love to you standing up, do you?"

Embarrassment bathed her in new heat. She looked away.

"My God, woman," he rasped, "you're enough to drive a sane man crazy."

"You're making fun of me."

"No, I'm not. I'm doing my best to seduce you." He blew out his breath. His hands fell from her breasts. "Let's go." He turned toward the path, pulling her along.

With her mind fixed on a man she couldn't have, and her body yearning for an intimacy she couldn't fulfill, she dared not risk facing a houseful of people. "Wait. I'd rather not go to the Clavers."

"Good." He continued walking. "I have no intention of taking you there."

"Do you promise?"

"Yes. Don't you believe me?"

"Actually, no."

Stopping, he said, "Very well. I swear on my credentials as a sailor."

He said it so cheerfully, so proudly that an awful possibility occurred to her. Had Papa forced Blake to resign his commission? He'd done worse to poor Shelbourne. "You love the sea."

He wrapped her in his arms and kissed her temple. "Yes," he said softly, seriously, "I do. I told you how I feel about the sea."

Tenderness welled inside her, and tears sprang to her eyes. What if he had to give up his brilliant career?

What would he say to his father, the duke of Enderley? She hugged him, squeezed him as hard as she could. It wasn't fair that he should have to sacrifice so much. It wasn't fair that she should love him so.

"Here now, what's this?" His cold hands framed her face. She shivered. He tipped her head back. "I've made you cry. Oh, Marjorie. I want us to be friends."

Exhaustion swept over her. She was no match for Blake Chesterfield. Why hadn't she listened? "Grandmama was right," she said, tears clogging her throat. "And you'll lose everything because of me. Don't you know that? You'll loathe me."

"Impossible, sweetheart. You didn't give me a chance to explain. I do love the sea, but I also hate it. Every sailor does. I won't miss it. Truly, I won't. Not if I have you."

Every word was a lie, said only to spare her feelings and to manipulate her into marrying him. The story wasn't new, but her old defenses didn't seem to work. She wanted to believe Blake Chesterfield loved her, if only for tonight.

He hooked his arm through hers and followed the path back to the road. When they reached the carriage he yelled, "Peddicord, haul out the sheets and set a course for home port."

Once they were seated side by side in the coach Blake pulled a blanket from the compartment under the facing seat. He extinguished the lamps, drew Marjorie close, and tucked the cover around them.

"Are you cold?" he asked.

She felt chilled to the bone, but not because of the weather. "No," she lied, laying her head on his chest. Even through the heavy coat she could hear the steady beat of his heart. Wrapped in the solid strength of his arms, she felt cherished, protected.

No other man could measure up to Blake Chesterfield. But Papa had bested him. Then how, she wondered, would she go on with her life once Blake was free of the betrothal?

Was her career enough? She wasn't sure.

"Look at me." He put his hand under her chin and lifted it.

Moonlight lent a majestic softness to his overtly handsome face. She smiled in admiration and asked, "Are you warm yet?"

He smiled, too, and murmured, "I've been aflame since the night I walked into the Pump Room, Marjorie Entwhistle." Then his lips touched hers, moving gently, testing, as if searching for the perfect fit. "Help me fuel the fire," he whispered, and he laid into the kiss.

When he drew back she said, "What I need to help you do is give my father the slip."

"Then marry me."

"No."

"Then love me."

Her eyes drifted shut, and into the darkness sparkled images of a lazy summer day. She and Blake languishing on a pallet in a flower-strewn meadow, she and Blake basking in the radiance of love. A contented sigh passed her lips, and he answered with a groan of need that shattered her serenity and kindled her desire.

Wheels whirring, harnesses jingling, hooves thudding on the earthen road, the carriage rocked gently through the hills, and inside the coach hearts pounded, hands clutched, and senses reeled until Marjorie felt herself come to life for the first time.

Whispering, "Touch me, touch me," he guided her hand inside his shirt. The tips of her fingers met the hard wall of his chest and threaded through a pelt of silky hair.

He shivered and sucked in his breath.

Knowing she might never love again, she became the aggressor, stroking him, twining her tongue with his and fanning the fires of passion. He matched her ardor and sent his hands on an achingly slow journey that began at her breasts. He detoured around the cumbersome folds of her skirts and ended his travels at the sensitive skin of her inner thighs. His chest heaving, he pulled his mouth from hers. "Slide your legs apart," he murmured urgently, "and let me touch you here."

When his questing fingers stroked her intimately she stiffened. "Blake, no!"

"Shush," he soothed. "Relax, sweetheart. Don't close me out. You want me, you know you do."

Her eyes drifted open and found his heated gaze focused intently on her mouth. He grinned, his teeth gleaming in the dark, the warmth of his smile melting her inhibitions.

"That's my girl," he hissed, and he eased a long finger inside her.

She shivered at the exquisite touch of him.

Then his mouth was on hers again, his tongue plunging between her lips in tune with the wicked rhythm of his hand. Lights winked in the darkness outside the carriage. Bells clanged in her head. He stroked deeper and faster, while his thumb found a place that instantly became the nucleus of her desire.

Her legs felt weak and useless, but her mind grew keen and alert. A great discovery awaited her, a hand's length away, a prize just out of reach, and yet—she sensed it coming closer, closer, so near she could almost glimpse its shiny edges, almost make out its shape.

A moan of frustration escaped her lips.

"You're beautiful, sweetheart." He breathed the

words into her mouth. "Think only of the pleasure. It'll come, I promise you."

She whispered back. "No. I can't. It's there, but—"

"Yes, you can." He hugged her tight, his cheek next to hers. "Concentrate, love," he said softly. "Reach out for it. The relief is waiting for you."

Rapture engulfed her, unraveling the knots of tension and drenching her in sweet, blissful comfort that brought peace to her soul and joy to her heart.

A ragged moan passed her lips, a shudder vibrated through her. The cadence of his caresses slowed, prolonging her pleasure, draining her, bringing forth a slick wetness between her legs.

Awash in a dreamy languor, Marjorie said, "Oh, Blake . . . I feel so . . . so . . ."

"Wonderful?"

It was an everyday word, and much too ordinary to describe the unique sensations coursing through her. "I feel different, as if I've somehow discovered something new about myself."

He righted her clothes and pulled her onto his lap. "Ouch!" He jumped. "These damned panniers."

"You don't like them?"

He shifted her to accommodate the dress. "Yes, but not just now. Where were we?"

"I was confessing that you helped me discover a womanly part of myself."

Staring out the window, he said, "This man wholeheartedly concurs, so don't lose that womanly thought."

The carriage stopped. Blake kissed her sweetly on the nose. "Hold on to me," he said. Clutching her to his chest, he stepped from the coach.

Light blinded her. She ducked her head into the cradle of his shoulder. Through slitted eyes and a passion-induced stupor she watched him carry her up the stairs to Cleveland's front door. It opened. Without breaking stride Blake passed a startled Sanford, then proceeded up the staircase and down a long corridor. Gilt-framed portraits sped by, the subjects a blur, much the same as the thoughts dashing through her mind.

She shook her head to clear it.

"Be still," he commanded, "or we might fall in a heap. My legs feel like jelly."

Another door opened to reveal a surprised Oscar Everson. Blake jerked his head toward the door. Still holding a clothes brush and black velvet jacket, the valet scurried from the room. The lock clicked. Blake set her on her feet, then tore off his greatcoat and jacket and pitched them onto a dressing bench.

She was alone with him. In his bedroom.

Like a rock hurled through a window, reality shattered her lassitude. Sweet Saint Mary, what was she doing?

She felt like a child who'd wandered too far into the woods and couldn't find the path home. *Think!* She looked around. She recognized nothing, but she'd never been in this room before. *Think!* She spied a table with a backgammon board. Two empty chairs. Lush crimson drapes and a matching counterpane gave evidence of Cleveland's wealth. The counterpane. The bed.

A twinge of remembered euphoria shot through her. On wobbly legs she staggered to a high-backed chair and gripped the rough fabric of the upholstery. She had to get out of here, but how could she, when her mind wouldn't function and her legs wouldn't hold her weight?

Fire irons clanged. She turned to see Blake kneeling before the fireplace, his elegant profile limned in a golden glow. With quick, jabbing motions he stoked the fire. Moments ago his hands had ignited a different kind of blaze.

Longing pulled at her anew.

Using the tool as a brace, he pushed himself to his feet and faced her. A frown scored his forehead. "You look frightened. What's wrong?" he asked, coming closer.

She stepped back. "You shouldn't have brought me here."

"No?" Although spoken in a silky whisper, the word was meant as a challenge.

"No," she said, holding her ground. "I thought you were taking me home."

He flung the fire iron. It slammed into the hearth, sending a plume of sparks up the chimney. His nostrils flaring, his heated gaze boring into hers, he said, "After your 'discovery' in the carriage I could hardly take you anywhere else. I want you in that bed, Marjorie, the soft mattress at your back, your naked belly flush with mine, your endless legs clutching my hips."

Hoping to tame his ardor with bravado, she said, "You make lying together sound so . . . coarse. I don't want that."

"You're belittling what can be a beautiful act. Admit you want me to make love to you."

She did, but a broken heart was high payment for surrender. "We were laughing and enjoying ourselves. You said you wanted us to become friends."

"The instant you cried out my name in that carriage we became more than friends."

"I did no such thing. You took advantage of the friendship I offered. You seduced me."

His jaw grew taut. Anger flashed in his eyes. "You were doing a damn fine job of seduction yourself."

Shame assailed her, but she'd learned to deal with

that villain years ago. Now she had to deal with Blake Chesterfield. "I merely kissed you," she said reasonably. "You misunderstood."

He stalked her. "You opened your legs to me. You let me give you pleasure. Tell me you don't tingle inside, Marjorie. Deny that you ache for more."

Words failed her. She swallowed and stared at the backgammon board, another old nemesis.

"Tell me you don't throb with emptiness. You want me to fill you."

"No."

Grasping her wrist, he placed her hand on his stomach. Muscles contracted, and lower, he surged with renewed vigor. "Sweetheart," he crooned, "I hurt with wanting you, and you can shake that pretty head of yours until the stars fall out of the sky, but you can't deny that you yearn for me, too. It's dragging at your belly." He touched her stomach and pushed gently.

She bit her lip to stifle a groan.

"I know, I know." He hauled her against his chest and held her there, his hands a soothing waterfall on her back, his intimate words a peacemaker to her warring thoughts.

"Give me your heart, love. I promise to cherish it always."

His mouth closed over hers, and his tongue slipped between her lips, luring her, enticing her to cast aside her inhibitions and rush headlong into the passion-induced delirium she'd experienced a few moments before.

With shaking hands he cradled her face. "Open your eyes, sweetheart."

She did. Lush green eyes smoldered with promise, and soft, sensuous lips nibbled at hers. "Say the words. They're here on your lips, Marjorie. Tell me what we both want to hear."

Powerless, she clutched him and cried, "All right! I admit it. I want you. But it's wrong."

He smiled, and his eyes glittered with happiness. "Wrong? No, love. You and I are as right as the warm waters of Bath on a winter day. Trust me. I'll make it like Christmas morning for you."

God save her wicked soul; her heart belonged to Blake Chesterfield. "Tell me what to do."

"Help me undress and I'll teach you. Here." He put her hands on his chest. "Unbutton my shirt."

Wild cravings and urgent need drove her onward. In jerky motions she removed the emerald stickpin and fancy cravat, then stripped the shirt from him. She stared in wonder at his sun-darkened skin and the furry mat of hair.

Holding out his naked arms, he said, "I'm yours to explore, Marjorie. You want to—I can see the curiosity in your eyes."

He shouldn't be able to read her so easily, she thought. But he could. She shouldn't be so weak where he was concerned. But she was.

Enchanted, she traced the contours of his broad chest, and when his muscles rippled she grew bolder, exploring a trim waist and lean hips still sheathed in soft, verdant velvet.

"Lower," he said, his voice thick with need. "Put your hands where I want you the most."

As she touched his raging heat he slapped his hand over hers, growled, and moved against her, showing her his power, letting her feel his strength.

"Enough." His hands traveled with delicious slowness, divesting her of cloak, dress, panniers, and petticoats until she stood before him clad only in chemise, stockings, and shoes.

He knelt before her, his hands sliding from her ankles to her knees and higher, clasping her thighs and teasing the sensitive places between. Tipping back his head, he said, "I've dreamed of seeing your legs. Sweet Neptune, you're magnificent."

Self-conscious, she said, "Now what?"

He grinned rakishly. "You stand here and let me look my fill. You're so slender. Legs like yours should be banned—to everyone but me."

She should have balked at such possessiveness, but she had no weapons against the allure of Blake Chesterfield. "I want to be yours," she said.

He mouthed the words, "You are."

Then he scooped her into his arms and fastened his mouth on hers in a kiss that set her heart to racing. She burned and begged him to take her there and then.

"Shush, sweetheart," he replied. "We've plenty of time."

As if he were on a Sunday jaunt in Spring Gardens, he strolled to the bed. To her further frustration, once there, he let her slide slowly down the length of him. By the time her feet touched the carpeted floor she could think of nothing save the power of the man, the feel of his naked skin next to hers, and the emptiness he'd promised to fill.

His tongue stabbed into her mouth and began a rhythm she welcomed and matched. Strong hands cupped her bottom and drew her against him; then he undulated his hips in an exotic motion that sent a shiver down her spine and brought a sheen of wetness between her legs. Sweet fantasies swamped her, and she swayed in his arms, her hands clutching at him, tracing his broad form, learning the contours of his back, the flexing muscles of his buttocks.

"Unbutton my breeches—quickly."

Boldness invaded her. If he could take his time with her, she could move at her own pace, too. "Shush, sweetheart," she said against his mouth. "We've plenty of time."

He chuckled in agony. "That's what you think, my virgin girl."

Flattered, she resumed the kiss and curled her fingertips so that her nails lightly scraped his skin, leaving a trail of goose flesh up his back, over his ribs, across the planes of his chest, and down to the placket of his breeches. With one hand she toyed with a button; with the other she toyed with him.

His chest heaved, and his belly quivered. Dragging his mouth from hers, he spread lavish kisses over her face, and then his lips closed over her ear. "I hope," he rasped, "you understand the trouble you're in."

She trembled. "Show me." Cuddling closer, she worked his buttons free.

A relieved breath gushed from him. "'Tis my pleasure."

He grasped her waist, turned, and sat on the edge of the bed. She swayed. He steadied her. Then he worked the chemise up, baring her thighs, her woman's parts, her stomach. Stopping, he kissed her there, his tongue darting into her navel, his breath cooling the dampened skin.

She clutched his shoulders and looked down, focusing on the crown of his head, the breadth of his back and the way it tapered to his waist, the way the firelight glistened in his coal-black hair. He's beautiful, she thought, and he wants me.

Pride brought tears to her eyes, and as the heated drops rolled down her cheeks Marjorie looked into her own soul and truly understood how lonely her life had been . . . until Blake Chesterfield.

She wanted to tell him, to pour out her heart to him. But then his hands moved higher, exposing her breasts, and his mouth hovered there, teasing, his hot breath tantalizing her. She could stand the anticipation no more. She leaned forward, meeting him, offering herself up to his loving, and an instant later he took her into his mouth. Her nipple caught fire, but he laved the hardened peak and suckled gently, insistently, and all of her senses sped to that one spot. Then he switched to her other breast, nurturing it in the same fashion, and honing her desire to a rapier's edge.

No longer able to stand, she bent her knees, pushed him back, and settled herself on his lap. His hips lunged upward, then rocked against her, touching hardness to emptiness.

"Now," she breathed, tipping her head to the side so their lips could meet.

An agonized groan passed his lips. "No, not like this. Not our first time."

He stripped off the chemise and lifted her, holding her in the air while he suckled leisurely at her breasts. An eternity later he laid her on the mattress. He loomed over her, his gorgeous face a picture of intense need, his hair hanging loose about his shoulders. He touched his forehead to hers. "A moment, love. Give me a moment."

Staring into his eyes, she thought of the joy he'd brought into her life, and she knew, no matter what the future held, she'd never forget Blake Chesterfield.

Instinctively her legs parted, and he settled into the nest she'd made for him. "Your moment is up, Blake. Love me now."

He closed his eyes and gritted his teeth. "Oh, God. I still have my boots on."

He sounded so frustrated, she giggled. His eyes snapped open, then narrowed. "Don't move," he warned.

Jumping from the bed, he yanked off his boots and hose and stripped the tight breeches from his hips. Below his tanned back his buttocks gleamed white. He turned and stood before her, magnificent in his nakedness, a bold warrior ready for the conquest. The clock rolled back seven hundred years, and she imagined herself a Saxon maiden gazing upon the first Chesterfield to step foot in England. The importance of it all staggered her.

His eyebrows shot up. "What weighty thought has captured your mind, Marjorie? You're not afraid of me, are you?"

She smiled in admiration. He was large, to be sure, but what did that have to do with fear? He was a man; she was a woman. God made them to fit. "Come here," she said, "and take off my garters and stockings."

"Absolutely not. They drive me wild." He eased down beside her and gathered her into his arms. Their lips met and fused in a kiss of such searching intensity that she suspected he'd tarry with her no more. The hot, hard length of him straining against her thigh gave proof of his readiness.

Then his knee slid between her legs and nudged them apart, but she needed no further inducement and opened herself willingly. He settled over her, belly to belly, just as he'd said.

"Wider, sweetheart," he whispered, "open yourself wider, and bend your knees. Let me feel those stockings against my skin."

She did, and she felt him find his place and push slowly into her. She gasped.

"Don't be afraid," he said. "It'll be . . . uncomfortable for a moment, but you're ready for me, sweetheart, and I'm . . . oh, sweet Neptune, I'm desperate to have you."

She cupped his face and, staring up into his eyes, said, "I'm desperate for you, too."

He smiled and blew out his breath. "Then lift your hips and hold on to me."

Enchanted by the promise in his eyes, she grasped

his shoulders and rose to meet him. In the next instant her bewitchment ended, replaced by a fiery stab of pain that stole her breath and curled her toes.

Through gritted teeth he said, "Stay with me, sweetheart. The pain's almost over. Just an inch or two more and—" With a quick, sure thrust he buried himself inside her.

She cried out and clawed his back and tried to push him away.

"There, there, my love," he crooned, "give it a moment. It'll be better, you'll see. You're just so small."

Her loins continued to throb with tormenting regularity, but as she thought about what he'd said her mind forgot the pain. "I'm not small. I tower over most everyone I know—except you, of course." He was a giant of a man, the same as his legendary forebears.

"You're perfect for me." His lips brushed hers, coaxing her to kiss him, to forgive him. "I told you it wouldn't last long. It's better, right?" he asked.

She didn't feel the pain now, merely a fullness and an odd disappointment. She had expected to feel more pleasure from lovemaking. "Yes, and I'd like to brush my hair."

"Now?" he squeaked, a frown creasing his brow.

Why was he surprised? "Well, what else is there to do?" She didn't know what to say.

His forehead smoothed. "You think our loving's over, don't you? Well, it's not, sweetheart. We've just begun."

As if to prove his point, he moved against her tentatively, and all the while he watched her closely, searching her expression, she knew, for any sign of discomfort.

The pain had gone. "Oh!" she gasped, suddenly tingling to life beneath him.

"I told you."

His melodious voice soothed her, but the erotic cadence of his lovemaking had quite the opposite effect. She felt deliciously wanton, eager to follow his lead.

"Better?" he asked.

"Wonderful."

Blake understood perfectly, but all the insight in the world could not forestall the demands of his body. Lust clawed at his belly, raking deep and sending arrows of pain to his loins. He'd wanted her for too long, and the weeks of expectation had taken a toll. He felt like a powder keg left perilously close to a flame, and if he didn't master his passions, he'd explode.

Where would that leave her?

She was on the verge of experiencing complete satisfaction, and he must give her that pleasure. But Lord, now that he'd breached her maidenhead and her pain had subsided, she took to lovemaking like a frigate to the ocean swells. He'd sooner face a keel-hauling than disappoint her.

She moaned and tossed her head and whispered that he hadn't lied about the pleasure.

His heart constricted with unexpected tenderness. He had intended to enjoy Marjorie Entwhistle, but he hadn't counted on cherishing her so much. Staring down at her lovely features—blue eyes mirrors of her inner joy, her mouth turned up in a glorious smile—Blake wondered if a man could die from too much happiness.

Before he could ponder the thought she stiffened and cried out. Quickly he set his lips to hers, muffling her sounds of rapture. Then he began a rhythm destined to give his own body ease and his mind fulfillment. She met his rapid thrusts, and when he asked her to lock her legs around him she complied without a second's hesitation. Lacy garters tickled his sides and brought to life a fantasy he'd often dreamed of.

Knowing his stamina was at an end, he braced himself above her and locked his gaze with hers. Then he set himself free and gave his seed to the only woman he'd ever loved.

Exhaustion swept over him, and he collapsed like an old sail in a hurricane. "Am I crushing you?" he asked between gulps of air.

She hummed a negative answer and slid her fingers through his hair. He trembled beneath her touch.

"Did you feel the same way as I did?" she asked, a note of shyness in her voice.

He rolled to his back, bringing her with him. Feeling playful, he said, "I don't know. I felt gloriously strong and hopelessly weak at the same time. How did it feel for you?"

In deep concentration she stared at the canopy. "At first I hated lovemaking, but after a moment or two I liked it very much."

Love swelled within him until he couldn't hold back the words. He took her hand, cleared his throat, and said, "Marjorie, I—"

A knock sounded at the door. "Lord Blake!" Beau Nash's voice blasted into the room. "Open this door at once!"

CHAPTER 11

All squabbling over women and pride are private concerns.

—Beau Nash, *Rules of Bath*

MARJORIE FROZE AT THE SOUND OF BEAU'S VOICE. WHAT was the king of Bath doing here?

Shame engulfed her and abraded her naked skin like a coarse blanket. "Dear God," she cried. "He mustn't find me here."

"Why not?" Blake leaned over her, his powerful arms supporting his weight. Perspiration glistened on his brow. Determination shone in his eyes. "You've nothing to be ashamed of. You've given yourself to the man who will become your husband. I'll deal with Beau Nash."

Her heart beat like a drum. The warm euphoria she'd felt faded to cold reality. For years she'd deftly avoided being compromised. She knew the rules. She knew the risks. She'd gambled and lost again, but this time the stakes were her heart and her soul.

231

"Lady Marjorie!" Beau bellowed. "Are you in there?"

"Go away, Nash," Blake yelled back. "She doesn't need your help."

"I don't believe you."

Looking for an escape route, her gaze frantically swept the room. The fire had dwindled to smoldering coals and provided scant illumination. The rest of the room lay in shadows, except for the eerie bar of light that seeped under the door. Beau stood in the hallway.

She had to get out of here. "Let me up."

"Sweetheart," Blake said, his face close to hers. "Your place is here with me. You're mine now."

"Yours? I wanted a man who would cherish me for myself. What I have is a desperate scoundrel who spouted love words and performed courtier's tricks to force me into marriage." Witless fool that she was, she'd fallen for his every ploy.

"I know you, Marjorie Entwhistle," he said seductively, smoothing her hair over the pillow. "Tell your heart not to listen to your mind. Listen to me instead."

"I might as well listen to my father." Blake had compromised her, but that didn't mean she had to marry him—or have her folly thrown in her face. She'd survived disaster before. She'd do so again. "I'm not yours, and I have no intention of listening to you. Get off me."

"Be reasonable, darling. You were a moment ago. What's done is done."

"Reasonable?" Beyond rational thought or normal action, she threaded her fingers in his chest hair and made fists of her hands. When he winced she said, "The only man I've ever trusted in my life is standing outside that door. Since the day I came to Bath Beau has been like a father to me. Even when I didn't deserve his respect, he gave it. I'm ashamed he had to find me here, but I cannot, will not, further disappoint him." She flattened her palms and pushed.

Blake spat a vulgar expletive and flung himself from the bed. Magnificently naked, he stomped into an adjoining room.

"Beau," she called out, "please wait for me downstairs. I'll join you in a moment."

"Are you hurt?" he asked, his voice shaking with rage.

Hurt? She was ruined, betrayed by her own weakness for a smooth-talking rogue. "No," she lied. "I'm perfectly fine. Please don't worry."

"You're certain? I'll break down this door . . ."

"That won't be necessary."

"I'll be in the parlor, then." The sound of his footsteps faded.

On the edge of her vision she saw movement. Wearing a dark green dressing robe and an expression that bordered on fury, Blake stood in the doorway. "You're not going anywhere tonight, Marjorie."

His imperialistic tone set her in motion. "You don't own me, Blake Chesterfield." Wincing from the soreness between her legs, she eased from the bed. Blood stained her inner thighs. Her pride rallied at the visible proof of her stupidity. She still had her dignity. A graceful exit seemed her only salvation.

Clothing littered the carpeted floor. With shaking hands she donned her chemise and petticoats and picked up her dress. In his haste to remove the garment Blake had ripped off most of the hooks and bent the rest. Dizzy with despair, she stepped into the now-wrinkled dress and fumbled with the fastenings. The back gaped, but her cloak would hide the damage.

Blake walked toward her. "Let me help."

She held up her hand. "Don't touch me."

He sighed but came on. "Isn't it a little late to push me away, Marjorie?"

Shoring up her courage, she said, "Coming here with you was a mistake, but what happened changes nothing."

"Mistake?" he hissed, all bruised male pride and Chesterfield confidence. "You didn't think loving me was such a mistake half an hour ago. Why have you changed your mind?"

"Because Beau caught me here with you. I shouldn't have surrendered to you. 'Twas wrong."

"'Love me now, Blake,'" he said in imitation of her, "'come here and take off my stockings, Blake.'"

She confronted his mockery with fury. "Go to the devil, Blake Chesterfield."

"'I'm desperate to have you, Blake.'" He grasped her wrists and held them. "You got what you asked for, Postmistress."

Blind fury enveloped her. She tried to jerk free. "Let go of me."

"So you can slap me?" He chuckled without humor. "I'm afraid not."

She kicked him in the shin.

He grunted. Releasing her, he clasped his injured leg.

Satisfaction flowed through Marjorie. "You seduced me, Blake Chesterfield, and I may have been witless enough to fall into your arms—"

"My *bed,*" he growled, hopping on one foot. "You fell into my *bed.* You loved every blessed minute of it. There's your proof." He pointed. "Your virgin blood stains my sheets."

She saw a vivid image of Blake suckling her breasts, of Blake urging her to spread herself wide so he could give her all of his love. Her skin tingled at the memory of his powerful body easing into hers, belly to belly.

Blake Chesterfield had introduced her to a sensual freedom as consuming and destructive as the desire to gamble. She'd wandered into temptation, and if she didn't get out of this room quickly, she'd be on her back again.

He caressed her shoulders. "We were both too eager, sweetheart. I tried to go slowly, but I'd waited so very long to love you."

She jerked away and yanked on her cloak. "You thoughtless, despicable rake. You probably say such drivel to all your women."

He limped toward her. "Marjorie," he cajoled, "be reasonable. This isn't going to end with one night."

Her weary heart pined to believe his tenderness, but her mind screamed that warmth was another of his tricks. "Don't try to charm me with more of your lies, Blake Chesterfield."

He smiled sadly and held out his arms. "You're overwrought, Marjorie. Come here. Let me comfort you."

The lure of his embrace beckoned, but she couldn't trust him with her heart. She danced perilously close to spinsterhood in her determination to marry a man she loved. She wouldn't give in now, not for a man who'd march her into marriage for all the wrong reasons.

"Don't try to beguile me. It won't work anymore."

His arms fell to his sides. "I've spoken nothing but the truth to you."

It was her turn to mimic him. "'You're beautiful, Marjorie. Your intelligence puts most scholars to shame.'"

"You *are* beautiful," he said, as if it were an absolute. "And too stubborn for your own good—or ours."

Afraid to turn her back on him, she eased blindly toward the door. "There is no 'ours.'"

He smiled roguishly and reached for his breeches. "The door's locked, sweetheart."

"I am not your sweetheart."

"Yes, you are. You love me."

He could have been summoning his pipe, he said it so lightly.

"That's another original piece of fiction."

"'Tis not. You know how you feel."

Obviously the esteemed Blake Chesterfield thought all women loved him. He'd underestimated Marjorie Entwhistle. "Yes. I loathe you."

He drew in a deep breath, then exhaled. "That's unfortunate, because you're going to marry your loathsome lover."

"Will you never understand? I don't have to marry you."

"No?" he queried smoothly. "What if you're carrying the next Chesterfield heir?"

Her hand flew to her stomach. "Of course I'm not." The confident gleam in his eye forced her to say, "You're merely trying to frighten me."

"Does the thought of having a babe of your own to cherish frighten you? I thought you wanted children."

In one reckless evening she might have frittered away her girlish dreams of a devoted husband and precious children. Perhaps she didn't deserve such happiness. Past diplomacy, she said, "I do want children, but their father must be a loving and honest man."

He stared at his bare toes. "You think I'm neither."

Never had the truth hurt so much. Oh, why couldn't he have been the prince of her dreams instead of the knave of her nightmares? "You know the answer to that."

"I can give you everything you want."

Regret for all of the things that could never be clogged her throat. "You can't give me the truth about why my father sent you here."

He looked up. And revealed a disturbing vulnerability. "No, Marjorie. I'm sorry to the bottom of my disgusting heart, but that's the one thing I can't give you."

Hitting her would have been more merciful than the pain his admission dealt. "I can help you, Blake."

"The same as you helped Shelbourne?"

"No. Shelbourne lost at cards. He had no secret."

"The only way you can help me is to marry me."

"That's not true. My father blackmailed Tobias and another suitor. I helped them trick Father into handing over the evidence. Please, Blake. Confide in me."

"I am not," he ground out, "like Tobias Ponds or the others."

Exhausted, dejected, Marjorie whispered, "Then unlock the door and let me go."

He recoiled. "I can't let you go, surely you know that."

She searched the room. "Is there another way out?"

He smiled crookedly. "Metaphorically speaking . . . yes. You can marry me."

"Save your metaphors and your proposals for a woman who appreciates them."

His brows rose, lending an endearingly handsome aspect to his face. "You're certain you're ready to walk out that door?"

Did he think she'd relent? If so, the mighty Blake Chesterfield was about to be disappointed. Still, she was wary of him. Perhaps he had one more trick to play. "I am absolutely ready to walk out that door and out of your life."

"No second thoughts? No unfinished business?"

Patience, she told herself. You're probably the first woman who ever walked away from him. And she'd bet the new mail coach that he'd try to maneuver her into a verbal trap or seduce her again. An ache throbbed in her belly when she thought of his lovemaking and the pleasure he'd given her. "We've quite finished any business we had in this room."

"You're prepared to walk out that door and never look back, never think of what you left behind here?"

She'd look back all right. With soul-wrenching dread she knew she'd relive this evening for the rest of her life. Her only hope was that someday soon the heartbreak would go away.

Holding out her hand, she said, "Give me the key, Blake. Beau is waiting, and I want him to take me home."

"I shouldn't do this." He raked his hand through his hair and schooled his features into what seemed a parody of sorrow. "I'll regret it. I know I will."

Marjorie wasn't fooled. Blake Chesterfield was desperate. "The key."

He walked to a desk and fished in a drawer; then he retraced his steps and unlocked the door. When she pulled it open he blocked her path. "I'll bring Peddicord and the coach in the morning. Have Tug and the others prepared."

He seemed capable of carrying on as if nothing had happened. Nobility, she thought, have strange ways. But by tomorrow morning she'd get control of herself and her emotions, too. The postboys would have their training tomorrow. She had learned her lesson tonight.

"Unless you've changed your mind about unfinished business . . ."

"Nothing has changed," she said, unable to look at him. "The boys will be ready and waiting in the stable yard at ten o'clock."

He stepped out of the doorway.

Clutching her cloak, she walked into the hall.

"Marjorie . . ."

She turned. "Yes?"

His eyes twinkled with mirth. "You've forgotten your shoes."

* * *

Bryan, the Irish footman, handed Marjorie into Beau's carriage. The last time she'd ridden in the opulent conveyance Blake Chesterfield had sat across from her and sworn he'd have her to wife. On the night of his arrival in Bath she'd been confident that she could elude him. She'd even offered to help him escape her father's trap. In return, he'd trapped her.

Beau climbed into the carriage and sat facing her. Cursing, he slammed his white beaver hat onto the seat. The tiny flames in the lanterns flickered.

Her heart constricted. "Beau, I'm so ashamed." Tears clogged her throat and blurred her vision. "You must be disappointed in me."

He leaned forward and took her hands. His merry blue eyes glowed with affection. "Now, now, Marjorie, dear. I'll hear none of that. No man's ever been prouder of his own flesh and blood than I am of you. You know very well that I'd trade all my luck at cards for the privilege of boasting that I'd sired you myself."

"Oh, Beau." Her voice broke. "I don't deserve your loyalty."

"Bother it." His thumbs pressed into her palms. "You said as much when you were sixteen, remember?"

The black days of her youth hung like shadows in her mind. She'd been drowning in a sea of overindulgence until Beau had rescued her. But the crimes of her youth paled in comparison to her folly with Blake Chesterfield.

"We settled the matter of what you deserve and what you don't, didn't we, Marjorie?"

An ember of her old courage glowed to life. "Yes, but I get so angry when I think of the trouble I always cause."

"'Tis not you, but your father who causes trouble."

"You have other responsibilities."

"Oh, I certainly do," he said facetiously. "Such as

239

Dame Surleigh and her pet monkey. Did you know that the creature got loose in Sally Lunn's bakery? 'Twas a ghastly mess, I'll tell you—cakes and tarts flying everywhere. I didn't assume the responsibilities here in Bath to settle monkey business."

The absurdity of the story made her smile. "I take it you handled the dilemma with your usual flair for diplomacy."

"Just barely, and don't you fret. We'll remedy your problem with Lord Blake."

Dear, dear, optimistic Beau. "You don't understand. He didn't force me."

"No. He seduced you," he said, his face as dark as a thundercloud. "I knew of his reputation, Marjorie. Hell, the meanest cabbage farmer knows about Blake Chesterfield's penchant for beautiful women. I should have protected you."

A compliment from the king couldn't have flattered her more. "It wasn't your fault."

"Were I twenty years younger, I'd call out the martinet," Beau swore. "A slash across his noble cheek would teach him not to toy with the ladies of Bath."

She thought of Blake's skill with a foil. Even in his youth Beau Nash wouldn't have stood a chance. Still, the sentiment soothed her raw spirit. "I knew what I was doing. The blame is mine."

Eyeing her closely, Beau said, "How do you feel?"

Hollow. Insignificant. "I'm weary."

"Do you love him, Marjorie?"

Half an hour ago she would have shouted yes, signed the betrothal, and followed Blake Chesterfield to the end of the world. Now she knew the difference between love and lust. "Same as half the women in England, I was captivated by the idea of being courted by Blake Chesterfield. But love him?" She stared at her hands. "No," she lied.

Beau gave her hands a final squeeze, then relaxed in his own seat. Thoughtfully he said, "How would you like to take a dip in the Cross Bath?"

"Now?"

"Yes, now. Juliana swears the waters there of an evening are God's curative to a woman's soul. We'll have the place to ourselves. You can relax before you see your grandmother."

The prospect of facing Rowena drained what little strength Marjorie had left. "But the bath is closed."

The king of Bath said, "Nothing in this well-watered town is closed to me."

"But my robe is at home."

"Not to worry. There's a closet full of robes for the tourists. You can wear one of those."

Peace and quiet and a pool of hot water sounded wonderful. "Yes, let's go to Cross Bath."

Beau gave instructions to his driver, who snapped the whip. As one, the team of six grays pulled the carriage through the streets of Bath. Street lamps raced by like yellow comets. She breathed a sigh of relief at the empty streets. The hollow clip-clop of iron hooves on stone rang in her ears.

"Thank you, Beau, for fetching me. But how did you know?" She couldn't put her sin into words.

He gazed out the window. "Bryan, my footman, has an affection for Kingston's parlormaid. He was standing on Kingston's doorstep when you arrived."

She braced herself against the jostling of the carriage and the battering of her pride. How must she have looked, dreamy-eyed and as limp as a spineless fool in Blake's arms? She shivered, thinking of how easily she'd fallen into his bed. Yet even when faced with the consequences of her indiscretion she relived the intense pleasure he'd given her. Lust, she thought, is a fitting memento of Blake Chesterfield, but a poor souvenir of a broken heart.

Afraid to ask, yet driven to know, she said, "Did anyone else see us?"

"No. What with the Clavers's tulip bash and the ball at Wiltshire's, everyone of consequence was occupied. Besides, even if the tale got out, no one would believe it. They'll remember the rumors about you and Tobias in that inn."

"But Tobias tried to force himself on me."

"An unfortunate occasion," he said. "Still, it'll serve a purpose tonight if need be."

"Thank God for small favors," she said.

The carriage rolled to a stop. The Irishman opened the door and pulled down the step. Marjorie climbed out and walked to the arched doorway. The familiar odor of the chalybeate springs didn't seem so noxious tonight.

"Go on ahead, Marjorie," said Beau, then he spoke quietly to Bryan.

She walked through the arched doorway and into a torchlit hallway. Echoes of dripping water and the slip-slap of her shoes filled the narrow corridor. Stone faces of ancient gods adorned the walls: The fair Luna smiled down in welcome; the fierce image of Gorgon appeared to roar in the wavering light.

Thousand of city madams and honorable knights, country squires and celebrated beauties had passed this way, but not in the dark of night. Only an elite group were privy to such luxury.

Tradition embraced Marjorie, and by the time she entered the ladies' dressing room she'd begun to feel whole again. Two stone benches, an empty brazier, and a dress rack comprised the furnishings in the cozy room.

She was greeted by a smiling and vaguely familiar servant who held a bucket and brush.

"Hello, Lady Marjorie." The woman bobbed a

curtsy. "Come for a late dip with Mr. Nash, have you?"

"Do I know you?"

With a clang the woman set down the cleaning tools and wiped her hands on her apron. "I'm called Peg, my lady. I'm Cumberland Stokes's aunt."

"Of course, Peg. Cumber's told me about you. How do you do?"

She smiled, puffing out apple cheeks. "Gettin' on famous as gentry in our own way. I got eight children —all of 'em healthier'n goats in high grass, they are. We ain't got cause to complain."

"I'm glad to hear that."

Stepping forward, she said, "I'll take your cloak."

Marjorie unfastened the garment and handed it over. Peg walked around her and gasped. "Now look what you've done to yer fine dress, my lady. Nothing untoward, I hope."

Marjorie's heart leapt into her throat. "No. I . . . I caught it on the hand of one of the statues."

"Happens all the time. But don't fret. I'll take a needle and thread to it, and by the time you've had your soak the dress'll be good as new. I sew days at the mantua maker in Pierrepont Street."

Breathing a sigh of relief, Marjorie said, "Thank you, Peg."

"Don't be thankin' me. You've a heart o' gold, my lady. Everyone says so. 'Tis grateful I am to you for takin' in Cumber when his mom passed. I had no room for the lad."

So many of the boys had no kin at all; in that respect Cumber was lucky. "He's a fine young man, Peg."

Peg squared her shoulders. "Ain't none prouder of Cumber than me. I heard that you stood up for him with that rickety-legged tailor."

Marjorie coughed to cover a laugh at the apt

description of Luffingham. "He had no right to call Cumber a thief."

"I said the same thing to my Thomas, I did. And you bide by what Peg's a-sayin', my lady. You feel the need for a soak of an evenin', you come to Cross Bath any night 'twixt ten and midnight. Peg'll see you ain't disturbed."

"Thank you, Peg."

"My pleasure." She cradled Marjorie's cloak as if it were a cuddly baby. "You wait here, and I'll fetch you a bathin' robe. It'll be too short, but there's none but Mr. Nash to see. Everyone knows he's like a father to you."

A few moments later, the heavy robe falling at her calves, Marjorie entered Cross Bath. Torches illuminated the rectangular room, and the low ceiling offered an intimacy unavailable in the open air of the King's and Queen's baths. A minimum of steam rose from water, cooler than that of its royal counterparts. The hollow-eyed bronze head of Minerva stood sentinel over the pool, and from the shadowed alcoves peeked statues of Aesculapius, the Roman god of healing, and his parents, Apollo and Coronis.

Marjorie grasped the handhold and stepped into the heavenly warm water. The minor soreness and stiffness of her muscles began to ease. The ache in her heart remained.

Submerged to his shoulders, Beau lounged on the other side of the pool. Sans wig and elaborate clothing, the king of Bath seemed an ordinary man. Marjorie knew better.

She waded toward him. "Thank you for bringing me here."

His eyes were wells of fun. "It'll be our secret, same as anything else that occurred tonight."

"What about Cleveland's servants?"

Beau laughed. "Sanford's devoted to you."

"But the others."

He shrugged. "If rumor leaks out, I'll blanket the town with broadsides proclaiming your innocence."

Feeling lucky and revived, Marjorie floated to the edge of the pool and took a spot next to her friend.

At length Beau said, "I have to go to London tomorrow."

"Will you be away long?"

"Long enough to halt passage of the Gambling Act, I hope."

Of late she'd been so involved with the enchanting Blake Chesterfield, Marjorie had forgotten about Beau's trouble. She vowed to put Blake out of her mind and resume her ordered life.

"Parliament's called for a vote?" she asked.

"Yes," he hissed. "A passel of straitlaced haystackers and country squires who have nothing better to do than foist their bumpkin morals on the whole of England. Gamesters will take their purses to France."

"Surely the conservatives will be voted down."

"Who knows? I'll do what I can. But if the act does pass, Bath is in for the same sorry times Cromwell dealt us."

Marjorie shuddered at the thought of how dreadful life must have been in the last century. She also thought of the battle fought at Lansdown, just north of the city gates. Blake had said five of his ancestors died there. He'd seemed so proud of his heritage. Why not? To most Englishmen the name Chesterfield was synonymous with greatness; to Marjorie the name meant misery.

"Is he often in your thoughts?" Beau asked.

His intuitiveness didn't surprise Marjorie; Beau knew her better than anyone except Grandmama. "Only tonight. Good luck in London."

"And to you, Marjorie. Your battle has just begun."

The cryptic statement jolted her. "My battle. What do you mean?"

"I mean," he began on a sigh, "that Blake Chesterfield won't give up, and I won't be here to protect you."

"Now that I know what Blake's capable of, I can protect myself."

He slapped the water. "You know I wouldn't go if it weren't absolutely necessary."

"I know, and I promise to be your welcoming committee."

"You always are. Bath is lucky to have you—and I'm certain that Scottish duke who's coming to visit will find himself especially fortunate."

Marjorie laughed. "Lord Blake is enough nobility for me, thank you."

"He might not like you welcoming a duke. He might cause trouble."

Blake Chesterfield *was* trouble. "Don't forget I have Grandmama."

"She hasn't the power to stop Chesterfield's heir. I'm not sure I do either, but I'd try."

Marjorie slumped against the side of the pool. "Grandmama hates him. She never likes any of my suitors."

"Marjorie, I've never considered it my place to say this . . . but I think Rowena loves besting your father."

"I'm certain she does, but only out of love for me."

Sadly he said, "'Tis more than love for you, my dear. She's had a very hard life, and none of it was of her own doing. She resents men. Modern women like you aren't so dependent on their husbands and fathers."

"Don't forget that I've had neither. Unless you count Papa's cruel games."

He rolled his head toward her "Don't let Rowena

interfere. You need a loving husband and children to care for."

Blake had wooed her with the promise of a home and family. But he would have promised her the Isle of Wight to get her to marry him. "I will pick my own husband."

"Be sure the criteria is your own and not your grandmother's. Times have changed. You have choices. She had none."

Although just above a whisper, his voice was serious, Marjorie knew Beau spoke from the heart. "I can hardly be the child bride she was, Beau, I'm almost a spinster now."

He laughed. "That's because you haven't found the man you want. Have you told Rowena you want to marry?"

She had found a man she wanted, a man she couldn't trust, a man she couldn't have. "I used to talk to Grandmama about marriage."

"And what did she say?"

"That all men are scoundrels and opportunists." At his wince she added, "Except you, of course."

"I'm flattered. Do you share her view?"

"The men my father sends are desperate. Grandmama was treated horribly in her life . . . by men, but not desperate ones."

"She loves you very much," said Beau. "She'll do anything to make certain that your father doesn't choose your husband, even if he is the most sought-after bachelor in England."

"The most sought-after bachelor in England is not courting me because he wants to."

"Good marriages have been built on poorer foundations than blackmail."

"So Grandmama tells me."

"You're all she has, Marjorie. She'll find fault in any man you choose."

Odd, that was the same thing Blake had said. "I

know." As she had so often, Marjorie wished she'd come from a big family with doting aunts, jovial uncles, and boisterous cousins. She wished her father loved her. Immediately she felt disloyal to Grandmama.

Beau touched her arm. "Take one problem at a time, Marjorie. Make your own decisions—especially about Blake Chesterfield."

Despair sat like a stone in her stomach. "He impressed you by catching those cheaters at Wiltshire's."

He scooped up a handful of water and washed his face. "I can't condone what he's done tonight. But I think you love him."

Weary, she said, "Let's talk about something else."

"Very well," said Beau. "But while I'm gone, if you need to talk about tonight, talk to Juliana, not Rowena."

"Lady Masterson's visiting from London. Grandmama's busy with her."

"That's just as well. You'll confide in Juliana?"

The prospect of a new ally pleased Marjorie. "Yes, and speaking of marriage—you should marry her."

He sputtered and coughed. "Let's talk about something else."

The next morning Blake rode alone in the carriage, his fingers tapping on the seat, his mind anchored to the meeting ahead. He hadn't felt so nervous since his first day at Cambridge. What would Marjorie say? Worse, what if she didn't say anything to him at all?

His fingers curled into a fist and pounded the seat. The irony of his situation mocked him.

She loved him. But she wouldn't marry him until he pried open his black soul and hauled out his hideous secret. Then she'd recoil. Love would wither to pity. If he were lucky, she might conceal her revulsion, but it'd be there, in every smile, in every glance. As time went on they'd drift apart, and jokes about ox cheek soup and stitched-up faces would become memories too painful to recall.

His throat constricted. What had he done to deserve such a bleak fate? He'd finally met the woman he loved, and he couldn't express his feelings. Even if he did pour out his love, she'd think his declaration was just another ploy to escape George's trap. How had such a monster sired so comely a daughter?

Seeking a diversion, Blake raised the window shade. Pedestrians lined the streets and chatted amiably on their way to the Pump Room to partake of the customary three glasses of spring water.

But like a cat tormenting a mouse, his mind nagged his heart. He thought of the evening before. She'd enjoyed their loving. He'd reveled in the feel of her long legs around him, his rampant body fitting so perfectly with hers. He wanted to sleep every night with her, wake up to her smiling face, see her nurture his children. What could he do to make it happen?

What had she told Nash?

Blake reluctantly admired the king of Bath for coming to her rescue. Marjorie needed a champion who would keep her best interests in mind. She needed a husband to fulfill her wish for children. All she had now was a huge responsibility, a passel of endearing lads, and a bitter-minded dowager duchess with a grudge against men. And a future with a man she would abhor.

The coach swayed. His stomach lurched. Like an untamed and reticent beast his wicked secret crawled back into the lair of his soul. With sad regret Blake Chesterfield called up the arrogant and confident demeanor he needed to face the world.

Through the window he saw the elegant facade of Hartsung Square. The worn path to the post office came into view. Below the familiar post horn stood Marjorie, dressed in what he now recognized as her working attire: a serviceable blue gown with an unrevealing neckline and modest panniers. He smiled. His postmistress needed no ornamentation to draw attention to her beauty. Her alluring height, her shiny hair, and her enticing confidence made his blood heat and his heart yearn.

Tug, Wick, and Honeycombe stood beside her. Blake wished the day had been colder, for he wanted to see the boys in their new caped greatcoats.

From an upstairs window Cumber Stokes poked out his head and yelled, "Spark in the yard." Inquisitive faces appeared in every window.

Blake chuckled and stepped out. "Heave to, Peddicord," he yelled. "Make her fast."

"Aye, aye, Commodore."

Removing his gloves, Blake approached a welcoming party that looked at him as if he were Attila come to pillage. Odd, since his was the heart that had been pillaged.

"Hello, my love," he said.

Her eyes met his, then narrowed. "Good day, my lord. Thank you for sparing us your time."

Tug moved in front of her; the other boys flanked her. Jutting chins and pursed lips screamed protectiveness. Word traveled fast in Bath. The boys knew how much time Marjorie spent with Blake, and they felt threatened.

With the promise of food and shelter she'd snatched these lads from the gutters of Lilliput Alley. She'd given them a fighting chance to escape the cruelties of life. They could do no less than shield her. He could do no less than allow them their pride.

Ceremony dictated that the lads bow to him, but

Blake had never been one to stand on social protocol. Besides, he had to win over these boys to get to Marjorie.

Hoping for the best, Blake extended his hand to Tug. "Good morning, Mr. Simpson. No sign of Claude Drummond on the heath?"

Stiffly he said, "Nay, my lord."

To Albert Blake said, "How's my boon companion today?"

The lad's animosity melted like butter in the sun. He puffed out his chest and said, "Caught any bandits lately, Commodore?"

Tug cocked his elbow and jabbed the younger lad in the ribs.

"Ouch," cried Albert. "Why'd you do that?"

Tug glared a reply.

Blake smiled indulgently. "I'm afraid not, Mr. Honeycombe. You must have scared them off."

Marjorie rolled her eyes and blew out her breath.

Peddicord joined them. The boys gaped.

Marjorie smiled at the coachman. "That's a fine foxtail in your hat, sir."

Peddicord swept off the hat. "My missus calls it the sin of vanity, my lady."

"And what do you call it, Mr. Peddicord?"

He winked and said, "A foolish man's attempt at character, I suppose."

She laughed, and like a mother hen with her chicks she drew the boys close. After presenting each of them she said, "They're bright, hardworking lads, Mr. Peddicord. I think you'll find them worthy of your time."

Blake's heart did a rolling flip. Every child should have a champion like Marjorie Entwhistle. His children would. But first he had to find a way to earn her forgiveness. She was embarrassed and confused. She was also in love with him.

Still not looking at Blake, Marjorie stepped back. "Then I'll leave them to you, Mr. Peddicord. Good day, Lord Blake." She turned and walked inside the mansion.

Oh, God. Past rhetoric, she wasn't speaking.

Addressing the senior lad, Blake said, "Tug, may I have a word with you?"

The boy sauntered after him. When they were out of earshot of the others, Blake said, "What's wrong, mate?"

He stared up at Blake. "Nothing at all, my lord. Everything's shipshape and in Bristol fashion."

Blake had expected reticence. He would not tolerate sarcasm. "I never took you for a coward, lad."

"I'm no coward."

"Then why are you afraid of answering me truthfully?"

Intelligent eyes studied Blake. Defensively Tug said, "Lady Marjorie doesn't need a husband. She's got us."

Patience, Blake told himself. You command a fleet of ships and hundreds of sailors. Three boys should be easy. "Your words or hers, Tug?"

"You're just like the other sparks. You want to marry Lady Marjorie because her father sent you."

Feeling like a suitor facing a prospective father-in-law, Blake said, "I certainly do want to marry Marjorie. And in case you've forgotten, arranged marriages are a way of life for the gentry."

The lad frowned in confusion. "But she can pick her own spark."

Blake said, "Tell me this, Tug. Don't you want Lady Marjorie to be happy?"

"She's happy aright."

"Don't you think she wants children of her own?"

Tug chewed his lip. "I suppose."

Shark's teeth, but life was odd to Blake Chesterfield.

Who would have thought he'd have to stand in a stable yard and explain himself to a lad of fourteen? Cajoling seemed his best bet. "She'd be a wonderful mother."

"Don't need to be a Mr. Goldsmith to figure that," Tug said, a note of derision in his voice. "Lady Marjorie's the best there is."

"Some say she's on the shelf."

Tug's hands flew to his hips. "Any who says that tommyrot will answer to me."

"I often wonder," Blake mused, "what her children would look like. A daughter, for instance."

"She'd be a beauty and a lady to the core."

Blake rubbed his chin. "You're right, of course. But I guess we'll never know for sure. Since Lady Marjorie doesn't seem inclined to marriage."

That got the lad to thinking. His inquisitive gaze darted here and there.

Deciding to quit while he was ahead, Blake clasped the boy on the shoulder. "I'll just be off then. Peddicord's getting impatient."

With a gentle shove Blake pushed Tug in the direction of the coachman, then strolled into the mansion and up the stairs to Marjorie's office.

When the knock came, she jumped. Her quill left a blot of ink on the ledgers before her. She took a deep breath and said, "Come in."

Blake stepped inside and closed the door. He cut a fine figure in chamois breeches, thigh-high black boots, and a jacket the color of nutmeg.

"May I?" He indicated the bench.

They were alone. In retrospect she wished she'd had the sense to stay with the boys. She felt guilty for dragging them into her problems, but what choice did she have?

Pretending nonchalance, she said, "Suit yourself, but I'm quite busy."

Tall and broad-shouldered, he seemed to fill the

room. The fresh smell of lemons wafted to her nose and made her mouth water and her loins ache.

He sat and crossed his long legs. "If I were truly to *suit* myself, Marjorie, I'd give you a kiss."

Conflicting emotions swirled in her head. Her gaze fixed on his mouth. "You'd have to steal it."

"You mean the way I did last night?"

"You're a troll to bring that up."

"And you're a coward to deny the splendor you found in my arms."

She felt intimidated, and if she didn't watch out, she'd lose control of the conversation. "I'm not afraid of you."

"You're afraid you'll succumb to me again. But I give you my word. I didn't come up here to ravish you."

Remembering the excitement of his body over hers, the fullness of his manhood within her, she steeled herself against him. He was nothing more than a charming rake. "Then why have you come?"

"To see you. To say hello. To ask what you're doing."

Why did he have to be so bloody friendly? Miffed, she said, "I'm balancing the ledgers."

He shot to his feet and walked around behind her. Over her shoulder he peered at the open book. "I'm very good at ciphering—among other things. I could help you."

His seductive tone warmed her, but she was wise to his tricks. "I don't need your help. I can manage just fine."

A knowing grin revealed his elusive dimple. "That's not what Tug said. Perhaps it was the brandy talking, but he did say you'd rather walk the mail to London than add up those numbers."

A boyish cheer boomed through the yard. She

silently hoped the lads remembered their manners. "When were you plying Tug with drink?"

"Ages ago—when I first came to Bath."

"Tug exaggerated. Now, if you'll excuse me . . ."

"Oh, come now, Marjorie," he chided. "Don't be so stubborn."

She stared at his boots and noticed the reflection of the window in the highly polished leather. Poor Everson probably had blisters and a bad back.

"You can't pretend last night didn't happen, Marjorie."

Remembered bliss brought a tightness to her throat. "That would be exceedingly naïve, now, wouldn't it?"

"I hardly slept from thinking about you—wanting you beside me still, longing for the chance to hold you, to talk to you."

His words felt like warm sunshine after a rain. "Well, I really haven't time to talk. Besides, we have nothing to say to each other."

"We certainly do. Before you went to Bristol you agreed that we would spend a month getting to know each other, becoming friends. Will you renege?"

She hadn't expected such persistence. "We got to know each other well enough last night. And you took advantage of our bargain, which makes it null and void."

He sighed, and his mouth widened in a grin that deepened his dimple and sent tendrils of desire up her spine. "There's much more we could learn about each other, you know."

His eyes looked glassy green this morning, and faint dark circles proved he'd had a sleepless night, too. He'd probably tossed and turned in his bed and kicked off the covers. She pictured him naked and chilled, his long legs and tight buttocks against the shiny silk of the sheets. The image shocked her and made her feel wicked. She must stop thinking about him.

"Yes," she said. "There's a great deal more we can learn about each other, such as why my father is blackmailing you."

He flinched. "You're afraid of what you feel for me."

He said it so casually, she wanted to scream. Instead, she smiled and said, "Aren't you afraid you'll slip up and tell me what awful truth my father knows about you?"

His gaze didn't waver. "No."

"You must have some tiny doubt."

"None whatsoever."

"I don't believe you."

Still unmoving, he said, "I swear on the souls of my ancestors."

The softly spoken words held a world of meaning, and as sure as she'd go on loving him, Marjorie knew he'd never tell her. The knowledge ripped at her heart. "It must be something dreadful, Blake."

He looked away.

Any hope for a future with him dwindled. "I'm sorry for you."

He slapped his thigh. "Keep your sympathy, Postmistress, and jump up. In about half an hour Peddicord will allow the boys a turn at driving the carriage —with you and me inside. I'll have your numbers tallied by then."

She sat frozen. "No."

"I was right. You are afraid of me."

The dare set her in motion. She pushed out of the chair and stood against the wall. "Be my guest."

He didn't sit but faced her, bracing his hands on the wall and imprisoning her. Leaning close, he said, "How do you feel today?"

If a broken heart could be an illness, she was on her

deathbed. Lowering her gaze to hide her pain, she stared at his mouth. "I'm perfectly well."

His lips touched her cheek. "You were perfectly perfect last night."

She bit her lip to stifle a groan. "I don't want you to kiss me."

Against her skin he said, "I know. You want me to bare my soul to you, Marjorie. Why should I do that?"

His honesty shocked her. In its purest form the question was a plea. Was Blake Chesterfield asking for reassurance? Oh, why hadn't she considered his feelings? She'd been so concerned with playing her own role, she hadn't stopped to think about his. Instinctively she wrapped her arms around his waist and spoke from the heart. "Because you can trust me."

His lips moved over hers. "Easy words, love," he murmured. "Show me I can trust you."

She hadn't the foggiest notion of how to begin earning his trust, and yet she knew that she must find a way. His predecessors had been quick to reveal their mistakes. But comparing Blake Chesterfield to other men was as foolish as comparing meat to candy.

Taking the easiest and most pleasurable route, she pressed her lips to his. And for the first time felt him hesitate. The enormity of his reaction revealed more than words. Had passion held him captive last night? If so, he was probably sorry for seducing her.

Four heartbeats later he stepped back, his eyes shimmering with regret. "If I didn't respect you so much, Marjorie Entwhistle, I'd forget your ledgers and spend the next half hour worshipping your body."

His false gaiety didn't fool her; beneath the confidence and arrogance lay a vulnerable man. She wanted that man, and nothing would stop her from getting him. "Very well," she declared. "I'll earn your trust, Blake Chesterfield."

He grinned crookedly. "I await your effort, Postmistress. I trusted two women in my life. Both times I was sorry."

"Who were those women?"

As if he'd become shy, Blake let his gaze drift to the floor. "My mother for one. The other should be considered a man's private concern."

"A former mistress?"

He cleared his throat. "A selfish woman in Boston who tried to lure me into a duel with a rival. Suffice it to say neither woman is trustworthy."

"Men aren't trustworthy either," she countered. "My father for one. You could add him to your list."

"He deserves a list all his own."

"I'm not like him."

Enticing green eyes looked her up and down. "No. You certainly aren't. You're curved in all the right places."

Contentment garnered memories of their loving. Her skin grew hot. She had to stop thinking about him. "The ledgers," she said.

With the skill and speed of a human abacus Blake began tallying the ledgers. Marjorie stared in awe. When the task was done he closed the book.

In jest Marjorie said, "Send me a bill for your services."

In answer he pulled her onto his lap. "I demand payment now."

Sweet anticipation filled her. "Name it."

At the least she expected he'd ask for a kiss. At the most she thought he'd demand her hand in marriage. In exchange for the truth she would have given him both.

He caressed her back, his lips turned up in a captivating smile. He seemed hesitant, an odd condition for Blake Chesterfield. "Take me with you to see the mail coach," he said.

Disappointment nagged at her. "Very well, but I thought you'd demand a kiss."

"I want much more than a kiss from your lips," he murmured suggestively, "and I'll expect payment in full when I help you purchase carriage horses. I'm told there's a fine breeder in Monkton Farly."

Marjorie bristled. "I can buy my own."

"I meant select them, not purchase them. I wouldn't dream of treading on your independence."

She laughed "Then withdraw the marriage offer."

"Marriage to me doesn't come with a ball and chain." His grin lit up the room. "It comes with country houses, with big bedrooms, roaring fires to warm you, and silk sheets to comfort you. Me to pour the wine, to give you children and cherish you always."

At his seductive words she wanted to throw her arms around him. That's probably why he said them, she thought. "I don't believe you."

"I'll prove it."

"Then I'll await *your* effort, my lord."

They went to the stable yard. Peddicord held forth from the driver's box, the reins in his hands. Tug sat beside him; the other boys sat cross-legged on the roof of the carriage.

Marjorie wanted to take Blake's hand, but that would be too obvious. Given time to think, she'd plan a course of action. Now that she'd made up her mind to take the offensive, Blake Chesterfield and his dark secret didn't stand a chance against her.

They spent the afternoon in the grand carriage. Tug, Wick, and Albert took turns at the reins. They visited the breeder in Monkton Farly, where Blake instructed her on how to choose the best carriage horses.

Across the Downs and over the hills of Wiltshire, Blake and Marjorie were jostled like melons in a wagon. She despaired of the boys ever learning to master a team of horses. In the valley at Chilcombe Bottom, Wick dropped the reins. Before Peddicord could intervene the carriage slid into a ditch.

"Blast this rutty road," cursed Wick.

Blake clamped a hand on the boy's shoulder. "No need for cursing. Boys, hop down and give Lady Marjorie a hand. Then stand back."

Blake took off his coat and shirt, Peddicord his hat. A bare-chested nobleman and a bare-headed coachman grunted and strained, pushed and pulled to put the carriage back on the road. All the while Marjorie stared in appreciation at Blake's thickly muscled arms and powerful shoulders. The golden compass dangled from a chain around his neck and winked in the warm sunshine. She couldn't stop her gaze from straying to the flat plane of his belly and the line of black hair that disappeared beneath the band of his breeches. She thought of his narrow hips and remembered the feel of his legs sliding between hers. Perfectly perfect, he'd described her. She didn't feel that way now. Perfection would come when he opened his heart to her.

Upon their return to Hartsung Square she was surprised when Peddicord declared that his first mates had weathered the worst. He arranged to train them collectively the following Saturday, then individually, depending on which lad was in Bath on which day of the week.

Marjorie waited for Blake to kiss her good-bye. But he didn't.

On Sunday Blake escorted her to services at Abbey Church. They sat in the Chesterfield pew, a magnificent expanse of Nottingham oak. "Dedicated in fifteen-fifty by my great-great-great-great-grandfather Quinton, the eighth duke of Enderley," he whispered.

Marjorie whispered back, "The Bishop of Wells

trusts me to read his blessings to the unschooled parishioners in Bath."

Blake eyed her curiously. "I know what you're up to, but it'll take more than a recommendation from the clergy for me to bare my soul."

On Monday Blake asked her to take a holiday. In spite of the work that would go undone, she agreed. They ferried across the Avon River to Spring Gardens for the public breakfast. He took her shopping and insisted on buying her a Highland tartan plaid. "In honor of my grandmother, Alexis Stewart," he said, draping the shawl over Marjorie's shoulders.

Gazing into his leaf-green eyes, she said, "Bonnie Prince Charles trusts me to ship him the waters from Bath. He says they help wash down the taste of Italian food."

"I say he's an outlaw and doesn't count."

She shrugged. "Shelbourne trusted me, too."

With mock ferocity he said, "Shelbourne definitely doesn't count."

In the afternoon they visited the carriage maker, who promised to deliver the finished coach within a fortnight. Blake asked what device would adorn the door to the green and gold carriage. When Marjorie said none, he found a stick and in the dirt sketched a design with the rampant lions of England framing a crest that featured a post horn.

"Here," he said, drawing a wavy line across the base of the shield, "I'll put a ribbon bearing the words *Aquae Sulis*. That's the name the Romans gave to Bath, isn't it?"

"You've been reading the local history."

Oddly his face went grim, and he looked away. With a swipe of his booted foot he scratched out the drawing.

Later, when Blake rendered his drawing in pen and

ink, Marjorie glowed with pride over the heraldic crest. She prayed that soon he would bestow his trust as well as his talent at sketching. From past experiences she knew that very soon her father would grow impatient, for none of the betrothals had gone on so long before.

Time was running out for Blake Chesterfield.

On Tuesday she resumed her duties as postmistress of Bath.

Each morning she made rounds, recorded the fees, then took luncheon with Grandmama. Each afternoon she taught reading, writing, and geography to the postboys and labored over her bid for the postal concession. Each evening Blake called for her at seven o'clock. Tuesday they attended a reception at Prior Park. Wednesday they attended a play at the Orchard Street Theatre. Thursday they sat in Horrid Tom's drinking sherry and listening to a visiting poet. Blake always tried to seduce her. She always evaded him. Late each night she took her yearning and her troubles to the solitude of Cross Bath.

Throughout the week Blake spoke frankly about his childhood at Chesterwood. Her heart ached when he said, "My parents believed children weren't fit for society until adolescence. They lived in London, I lived in the country. On important occasions they would summon me, show me off, then banish me to Chesterwood."

Sadly she realized even a family as exalted as the Chesterfields could behave with the cruelty of George Entwhistle.

She asked, "Did they send you away to school?"

With some hesitation Blake admitted to being bored at Eton. Cambridge, he said, had been a nightmare for an impatient young marquess who longed for adventure on the high seas. She invited him to lecture the postboys on the Colonies. He jokingly refused, saying he'd warp their young minds. He did agree to instruct the lads on how to care for carriage horses.

Each time she tried to broach the topic of why her father was blackmailing him, Blake thwarted her attempt. Each time he tried to entice her into his bed, she eluded his seduction.

As the days passed she seemed no closer to gaining his confidence but very near to succumbing to him again. Which would occur first, his confession or her surrender?

She longed to share her concerns with Beau, but he remained in London. Discussing her feelings with Rowena was out of the question; at the mention of Blake's name Grandmama flew into a diatribe about desperate noblemen and the fate of pitiful women who believed their roguish lies. Poor, lonely Rowena. Blake had made Marjorie see her grandmother in a new light.

During morning rounds Marjorie paid a call on the friend who might be her last hope: Juliana Papjoy.

CHAPTER 12

Brawling is out of order in the public rooms of Bath.

—Beau Nash, *Rules of Bath*

STANDING IN THE DOOR OF THE DRAWING ROOM, JULIANA wore a frothy gown of white organza with giant poppies embroidered on the skirt and a wide red sash at the waist. Her blue-black hair fell over one shoulder in a waterfall of spiraling curls. She looked more like a girl of sixteen years than the longtime consort of the king of Bath.

She clasped her hands. "Beau told me you might visit. I'm so glad you did. Do come in."

Marjorie felt the tension begin to subside. "You're certain I'm not disturbing you?"

"Disturbing me? I'm bored silly without Beau. Here. Let me take your satchel."

Marjorie handed over the mail pouch.

Juliana almost dropped it. "How do you manage to tote this heavy thing?"

"I'm used to it, I suppose."

"It must weigh a full stone. Are people mailing bricks?"

"No. Just the weighty correspondence of the peers in Bath."

"At least it's not Dame Surleigh's gossip. Imagine that rubbish in print."

"I dare not."

Juliana hung the pouch on the hall tree, took Marjorie's hands, and pulled her into the parlor. "I'll have Mrs. Bell bring us something monstrously delicious that's certain to ruin our figures. Beau will probably toss me out of his bed."

Any qualms Marjorie had about discussing the delicate matter of her association with Blake vanished. Over plum cakes and hot cocoa she explained her dilemma.

From a drop-leaf table next to her chair Juliana selected one of a dozen ornate snuffboxes. Rolling the tiny gold box in her palm, she said, "Have you had your menses?"

"No. But it's not time yet."

"All right. But remember, if he seduces you again and you conceive his child, you'll have no choice in the matter."

"I'm perfectly capable of raising a child. I've cared for Cumber since he was five."

"I know you have, and God bless you for your generosity. But the king won't abide your bearing a child out of wedlock, Marjorie, especially a Chesterfield. Blake's family is too important."

Although she knew Juliana spoke the truth out of kindness, Marjorie said, "I'm sick to death of the name Chesterfield and all the pomp and circumstance that goes with it."

As if the snuffbox were a coin, Juliana flipped it in the air. "I don't think you're sick of him in the least, my dear." She caught the spinning box. "I believe you love him. And I think he loves you, too. The problem is neither of you likes being forced."

The hopelessness of her situation dragged at Marjorie's good spirits. "He's a smooth-talking scoundrel."

Juliana's crimson lips turned up in a knowing smile. "Would a scoundrel give poor Shelbourne five hundred pounds and an introduction to a businessman in Boston?"

"I'm sure he had his reasons. Men always do."

Juliana laughed. "You sound like your grandmother."

Taken aback, Marjorie said, "I do?"

"Yes, and more often than you think."

Marjorie didn't want to behave as Rowena did. She wanted to trust and be trusted in return. She wanted a husband and a passel of sweet-faced, prank-playing children. Feeling self-conscious, she said, "Thank you for telling me."

"I meant no slight. She's had a bad time of it, Marjorie. But your life—your wedded life—needn't be the exercise in duty hers was." She stared at the box nestled in her palm. "And you might enjoy marriage to Blake Chesterfield. He's most exciting."

Like a banner, her conviction waved in her mind. "Not if he doesn't tell me the truth."

"Oh, pah," Juliana scoffed. "How awful could his secret be? He's surely not a traitor or a murderer."

Marjorie had asked herself the same question. Her answer was always no; Blake wasn't capable of either crime. "Perhaps he got a bastard on another woman."

Juliana held the snuffbox up to the light. "If he did, he'd support the child. But why didn't he marry the mother? Unless she was already married."

A pain pierced Marjorie's breastbone. "I don't

think he'd commit adultery, but I do think he'd seduce a woman he desired." She laughed. "Who knows that better than I?"

"Let's just be glad he didn't marry the mother of his bastard—if that's his secret," said Juliana.

The old confusion plagued Marjorie. "I just don't know what he's hiding."

"Listen to me," said Juliana, all seriousness. "Men keep secrets. It's the way of things. Women do, too."

"Are you saying I'm standing on a shaky principle or invading his privacy?"

"Not if principles and honesty are required traits in the man you choose to wed."

Longing engulfed Marjorie. "I don't want my father's pawn. I want a loving husband."

Juliana said, "You don't think he loves you."

Marjorie wanted to believe he cared for her, but she couldn't. "I don't know."

"You can find out."

"How?"

Juliana exchanged the gold box for an ivory one. "One of his peers arrived yesterday. A Scottish duke named Jamie MacKenzie."

"You've met him?"

"Yes, last night at Simpson's Rooms. He'll be at Wiltshire's tonight. Dance with him—especially a rigadoon." She rolled her eyes. "He's marvelous at those."

"I don't know the steps of the rigadoon."

"Learn. You can kill two birds with one stone. If His Grace of Seaforth knows Blake's secret, maybe you can get him to reveal it. You can also make Blake jealous."

"Blake jealous?" Marjorie chuckled at the humor of it. "I've danced with other men before. Blake never cared."

"Aha!" Juliana held up a finger. "But you haven't danced with a dashing peer of the realm who's eager to find his duchess."

Confused, Marjorie said, "It won't work. Men never tell each other's secrets. And Blake might not like me dancing with a duke, but that's because he's possessive, not in love. There must be a difference."

"There's a world of difference. A possessive man gets angry when another man covets his woman. A jealous man fears he'll get his heart broken." Leaning forward, she said, "Scare him, Marjorie."

She'd spent so many years avoiding men, Marjorie wasn't sure she could pull off the ruse. "You mean flirt with this Scotsman."

"With your looks," Juliana said ruefully, "you won't have to flirt with that Highland rake. Just make his acquaintance. Ask about Blake. Perhaps MacKenzie knows something."

"You don't think Blake will get angry?"

"No, I don't. I think he'll be hurt . . . and very loving."

The paradox of the situation baffled Marjorie. "But I'm trying to avoid his 'loving.'"

Sighing, Juliana said, "When he turns on that Chesterfield charm—and I can almost assure you he will—and you feel you can't resist him, you can guard against conceiving his child."

Marjorie's breath caught. "There's a way to prevent . . ." Embarrassment stole the words.

"Of course there is."

Mentally she slapped her forehead. She should have seen what was staring her in the face. Juliana hadn't conceived Beau's child. Scads of mistresses didn't bear their protectors' children. Relieved, she said, "I would be ever so grateful."

"Very well, but you must promise not to tell anyone I told you. Even Beau."

Marjorie felt pushed and pulled at once. The duties of her position, dealing with the threat of a forced marriage, Grandmama's objections, Papa's indifference, all sapped her strength. The assurance of not conceiving a child would buy her a little time and allow her to concentrate on her other troubles. A sinful thought occurred to her: She could enjoy Blake's loving without risk. "I promise."

"Good. Now I'll teach you the rigadoon. It'll be heavenly fun."

It was hellish disaster.

Later that night Marjorie eased deeper into the warm waters of Cross Bath, but a flood of water couldn't wash away her self-recriminations. When Beau returned and found out about the fiasco, he'd be livid.

Dancing so often with the Scottish duke of Seaforth had been her first mistake of the night. Allowing him to escort her to supper had been the second. Even the humorous moments of the last few hours failed to cheer her.

Juliana had been correct in her assessment of men and their emotions toward women. What she hadn't considered was the third element: indifference. He hadn't even cared that she spent the evening with the Highlander. She wished she didn't care that he'd spent the evening romancing other women.

The sound of footsteps echoed on the stone walls. Someone was entering the bath, but the steam prevented Marjorie from seeing the doorway. It was probably Peg coming to say it was time to drain and clean the bath for tomorrow's raft of customers.

Dejected, Marjorie pushed away from the wall and waded toward the steps.

"Still angry at me about tonight?"

Blake's voice blasted into her melancholy. She

stopped so quickly she almost lost her balance. When he saw her now she could kiss good-bye what little pride she'd salvaged.

She sank to her neck and squinted into the fog. The single torch on the wall behind her shed only a faint light. She couldn't see him. She could only see a huge, ominous shadow. "You're mistaken. I wasn't in the least angry."

Hearty laughter boomed through the chamber. "You were as mad as an undowered bride left standing on her father's doorstep."

The artless analogy triggered her ire. "You're as arrogant as an ignorant nobleman who thinks he can read a lady's mind."

With startling clarity she heard him shed his clothes. He couldn't possibly want her, not after the way he'd acted all evening. "What do you think you're doing?"

"At our first meeting I made the mistake of insinuating that you were obtuse," he said, as if he were discussing which estate to visit. "Ignorant nobleman, am I? In some things I'm a quick study." Quietly he added, "You know precisely what I'm doing."

Apprehension turned her knees to jelly. She couldn't succumb to him—not here, not now, not with her soul already stripped bare. "Someone will see you."

"Not a chance."

"Peg is here."

"No, she's not. I paid her a guinea and sent her home early."

His confidence irked her. "I wish to be alone."

"Come now, Postmistress. Admit that you were jealous, and I'll forgive you for ignoring me all evening."

"I'm not in the least interested in your forgiveness.

Actually, I thought the evening went rather well." She almost choked on the lie.

"If you call a brawl a success, I may have to go back to calling you obtuse."

"You started the trouble."

She heard him splash into the water but refused to retreat. He'd preen like a peacock before a peahen when he saw her, but she was too miffed at him to care.

"Keep talking," he said, "I can't tell where you are."

She clamped her lips shut tighter than the seal on a royal writ. He'd find her, but she wouldn't make it easy for him. She pulled a hairpin from her coiffure and tossed it at the far wall.

When she heard him wade toward the opposite end of the pool, she had to stifle a giggle. She continued to lead him astray. Then she almost ran out of hairpins.

A moment later the fog parted, and he appeared before her. Torchlight sparkled on his golden necklace. His eyes twinkled with interest and appreciation. He stared at her shoulders. "I was hoping you'd wear the robe. Red is the perfect color for you. No, on second thought"— he glanced at the statue of Apollo—"I prefer you naked."

Not for five mail coaches and all the carriage horses in England would she acknowledge the glib compliment or address his preference. "What do you want?"

"I want," he said softly, "to understand why you're angry when all I did was abide by your wishes."

That he cut to the heart of the matter suited her just fine. "I'm not angry. I'm embarrassed for you."

His complexion took on a green cast, as if he were seasick. "Why?"

"Because of the spectacle you made of yourself tonight."

"I see." He floated on his back. "Then please be so kind as to tell me which of my transgressions embarrassed you. Was it that I watched patiently while you danced all of the minuets with Jamie MacKenzie?"

"Now you're being obtuse."

"Oh? You wouldn't perchance be embarrassed because I danced with other women? Or that I played whist and lost to Ralph Allen, or that I escorted Juliana Papjoy to supper?"

Marjorie had been bothered that he danced with other women. All of his partners had been redheads. He was probably lamenting the loss of his last mistress. "Since you seem to know your vices so well, why ask my opinion?"

"Tell me how I embarrassed you."

"You shouldn't have danced the setting with that red-haired tavern wench."

He ducked underwater, then surfaced, shaking his head. "Jealous?"

"Of course not. So long as people *think* we're betrothed, your actions reflect on me."

"Precisely," he said. "Just as *your* actions reflect upon *me.* You should not have danced all evening with the duke of Seaforth."

"Bother the duke. We were speaking of the tavern wench."

He turned up his palms. "How was I supposed to know she waited tables at the White Hart? Or better yet, how do you know?"

"She reads. She gets mail, and wipe that angry glare off your face."

He scooped up two handfuls of water and tossed them at Marjorie. She gasped. "Stop it."

"You haven't answered my question. According to Nash's rules, gentry must mingle with the common folk."

Through her teeth Marjorie said, "Mingle? You

were the only couple on the floor. I suppose you were so distracted by her charms that you didn't notice what was going on around you. No one else danced the setting."

"She didn't distract me in the least. And I didn't know the dance broke one of Nash's rules. He has too many to remember."

She balled her fists. "Then you should read all of them—not just the ones that suit you."

He turned away, his jaw as rigid as stone. The torch flame glittered in his eyes. "Few others were abiding by his rules. You for one."

"I have special privileges. But I don't dance face to face and close enough to rub noses. No one does."

He lifted his eyebrows. "You didn't put up a fuss when the duke of Seaforth spent the evening speaking into your cleavage."

"He can't help being shorter than me. I was nice to him, nothing more."

"Then why is it I have this feeling that you lavished your attention on him on purpose?"

He'd seen right through her. He'd never know it, though. "Jamie MacKenzie is a most entertaining companion. You imagined the rest."

"I didn't imagine you dancing a rigadoon with him, which, I might add, you have continually declined to dance with me because you said you didn't know the steps."

Where she'd learned the dance was her affair. She gazed at the sightless eyes of Minerva. "He offered to teach me. I learned. So?"

"I suppose I should thank him."

"That would be unusually magnanimous of you, but you needn't bother. I thanked him myself."

"By allowing him to escort you to supper."

"You were occupied with Juliana."

"Nash wasn't here. I thought it proper to see she

had an escort. Had you not gone off in a huff, I would have escorted you both."

"I did not go off in a huff. And I resent you saying that I would stoop to common melodrama."

"Melodrama? The meal was a bleeding farce."

"You started the bleeding farce by daring MacKenzie to spear an apple with his knife."

"How was I to know he'd forgo the real fruit and aim for the decorations in Dame Surleigh's wig?"

"You knew," she fumed, "because he's your boon companion."

"Well, I suppose I should have told you we know each other."

Guilt stabbed her, but she ignored it. "Know each other? That's putting it mildly. He admitted to sharing women with you."

"Jamie has no honor."

"Neither," she snapped, "do you. Had you one scruple in that despotic heart, you would have told him we were betrothed. Then I wouldn't have wasted my time trying to make you jealous."

He flinched. "I'm flattered, but I'm still damned either way, I think."

"You certainly are. I heard enough tales of your lecherous escapades to keep you humble for the next decade, Blake Chesterfield. I particularly enjoyed the story about you swearing not to marry until you were forty years old. And when you did shackle yourself to a bride you'd choose a child of ten and five years, so you could train her to be your love slave." Bitterness made her add, "I'm sure you were inconsolable when my father told you I was four and twenty."

"I see." He rubbed his chin.

Why had she thought she could learn his secret or maneuver him into revealing that he cared for her? She'd never been good at pretense. All she'd succeeded in doing was driving a wedge between them. "What do you see?"

"A very interesting aspect of you."

She wanted to slink beneath the water and slither home. If he continued to see right through her, she'd say or do something else she'd regret. "I have no idea what you're talking about."

"So you were trying to make me jealous."

Pride wouldn't let her back down. "So," she mimicked. "You didn't even care."

"Yes, I did."

"You marched off to play whist."

"Disastrous evenings have that effect on me." He reached for her.

She evaded him and splashed water in his face. "How dreadful. You have my sympathy."

"I'm not after your sympathy."

He hauled her against his chest and hugged her fiercely. "I hated seeing you in Jamie's arms. Every time he spoke to you I wanted to break his jaw. I wanted to drag you away and keep you for my own."

The declaration filled her with hope. "Why?" She held her breath.

He kissed her neck, her cheeks, and her closed eyes. "I believed you when you said you wanted my trust. But when I saw you tonight"—his lips lingered a breath away from hers—"all I could think was . . . she belongs to me."

Disappointment shattered her expectations. He didn't love or believe in her. He desired her, that was all. She wanted more. "Trust me, Blake. Tell me what my father knows. I can't belong to you until you do."

"Ask anything of me," he entreated. "But not that. Not ever again. It doesn't matter."

She shuddered to think that this important man possessed a vice so abhorrent that he would beg her not to question him. She shuddered to think how much she loved him.

He pressed his mouth to hers in a kiss that screamed of desperation. With equal ardor she met his need. He ravished her with his lips and enticed her with erotic words.

Then with practiced ease and familiarity he fanned the flame of passion and filled her imagination with promises of the sweet joys they had shared, could share again. She had begun this courtship seeking only to help him escape the bonds of a forced marriage, but along the way she'd fallen prisoner herself.

"I need you," he whispered fervently. "Oh, God, how I need you. Say you need me, love. Say you need me, too."

The plea set her senses swimming, and her body yearned for the feel of his naked skin next to hers. "I do need you, Blake. I do."

When his fingers opened her robe and his hands cupped and lifted her breasts, judgment slipped away like the mist off the bath.

His caresses swept her into a whirlpool of desire. She floated, the warm water lapping around her, Blake holding her tightly and inviting her to join him in a lusty game of ecstasy. Need sang a song in her soul.

In perfect harmony he chanted, "Touch me, touch me. I need you to touch me."

The instant her hand closed around him he groaned and plunged his tongue into her mouth. This was the rhythm she knew, the lifeline that would pull her from a raging sea of want and transport her to the warm shores of fulfillment.

His hands slid up her neck and framed her face. "How is it, Marjorie Entwhistle," he whispered, "that with one touch of your hand you make me feel both a king and an ordinary man."

Engulfed with giddiness, she stared up into his

half-lidded gaze. "I think, Blake Chesterfield, that king or ordinary man, you're a poet at heart."

"If I could, I'd write you a hundred poems." He heaved a ragged sigh and pulled her hand away. "I'm a hungry man who couldn't think of another rhyme even if his miserable life depended on it. Lift your legs and wrap them around my waist."

A thousand reasons why she shouldn't played through her mind. But her body didn't hear.

One of his hands splayed across her back, the other cradled her neck, and as her feet left the hard floor another hardness brushed intimately against her. Eager for him to fill her emptiness, she clutched him with arms and legs and questing hands. Her fingers threaded through his damp hair and freed the ribbon tie.

The mist enveloped them in an intimate bower. They might be the only two people alive in the world. There was no ruined evening behind them, no fateful future before them. There was only the shining present.

She expected him to plunge inside her then, but instead he murmured, "Let your hair down, too. I want to see it floating around us."

Secure in his embrace, she reached for the one remaining pin.

"Lean back," he said. "Let me suckle your breasts while you do that."

Would he never complete the union? "But don't you want to . . ." She gasped when his lips closed over her breast and drew the nipple into his mouth.

The torch hissed and sputtered; the ancient spring lapped at the stone steps. Water dripped in a plinking melody while her heart thrummed the chorus.

"If you insist, Postmistress." He shifted, spreading her legs with his powerful thighs, then thrust up with his hips and moved her down with his arms.

Completeness flooded her. She went lax in his arms, and a soft moan escaped her. "How," she asked, "can anything that feels so right be so wrong?"

Against her breast he said, "'Tisn't wrong, sweetheart. God, you're the rightest thing that's ever happened to me. Let's make a beautiful babe—a girl as pretty as you."

Rapture turned to shock. The sponge that would prevent conception was hidden in her wardrobe at home! Juliana had told her another method, but Marjorie didn't think she could ask it of him. "Wait." She needed a moment to think.

"Why? What's wrong?" he asked.

She could take the easy way out; she could accept him as he was and make the best future she could. She could kiss her pride good-bye for now, but what about next year, or the next? She would resent his secrecy, and their marriage would become a living hell. No. No. No. She wanted his trust, and God help her, she had earned it. She deserved an honest man.

"Am I hurting you?"

Not if she could help it. "No, but we mustn't do this."

"Don't turn shy on me now, sweetheart."

He smothered her mouth with his, and the hand around her neck slithered between them. Before she could protest he found the center of her desire. With deft circular motions he manipulated her tender flesh, and with deep, powerful thrusts he drove her to the brink of rapture. They shared a kiss of searing intensity, of shattered senses and mingled breaths, of echoed sighs and bartered bliss.

He coaxed her with lusty phrases, reminding her of what to expect. A heartbeat before her passion peaked she gasped and clung to him. "Hold your breath," he said. Then he pulled her beneath the surface of the pool and held her there. Suspended in the warm sanctuary of the ancient spring, and snug in the arms of her lover, Marjorie felt the sweet euphoria drench her.

Just when she thought her lungs would explode he surged upward, starting a wave that sloshed over the rim of the pool. He tore his mouth from hers, and all around her the sounds of splashing water and labored breathing permeated the stone chamber. She lay limp within the steely strength of his arms, her cheek against the solid wall of his chest, her loins throbbing with the feel of his manhood, still robust inside her. The cool air restored her reason and focused on one thought: a child.

"Blake," she entreated. "Wait."

He tensed, the tendons in his neck straining like a well-strung bow. "I can't. Oh, God, Marjorie. I can no more resist you than I can pluck the moon from the sky."

His poetic words distracted her. He sucked in a breath, then groaned and jerked against her. "You're wonderful."

Clutching handfuls of his hair, she said, "Please, Blake. You mustn't give me a child."

His eyes fluttered open. She expected a smile of contentment.

She received a glare of contempt. "That's unfortunate," he rasped, "for I can't possibly undo what I just did."

For the next week she returned the notes Everson delivered. When Blake insisted on seeing her, she always made sure several of the postboys were on hand. She sent Cumber on the morning rounds. She even went shopping with Dame Surleigh to insulate herself from Blake. She studied the audit figures and completed her bid. Fearful that her lover would commence his midnight visits, she locked her windows and doors. Equally fearful that he would never come again, she tossed and turned and cried into her pillow.

Dispirited, she waded through days filled with postal duties and wept through nights lonelier than the years of her youth. She'd come full circle, and with little to show for herself. Oh, she'd succeeded in business affairs but failed in affairs of the heart. All she possessed was the inner peace of knowing she'd bettered the lives of a handful of orphaned boys.

And she wanted more.

Seeking strength from the source that always revived her, Marjorie plunged into her work.

Tobias delivered the schedules for the posting stations. She drafted two more broadsides, one for London, one for Bath, listing times and fares for the new mail coach. After braiding her hair she wound it into a figure eight and secured it with wooden hairpins. She donned her lucky dress, the bodice and split overskirt of turquoise velvet, the petticoat of pale yellow satin embroidered with vines and morning glories. As she tied a plain yellow ribbon around her neck she felt a pang of regret for the jewels she'd once owned.

"Better prudence than pageantry," she lectured her reflection in the looking glass.

Secure in the trappings of the postmistress of Bath, she went straight to the print shop of Tobias Ponds.

She entered the lobby of the establishment. The tinkling of a brass bell announced her arrival. The facing sofas and wingback chairs were empty. A sigh of relief escaped her. Her gaze flitted to the backgammon board mounted on a pedestal. As usual, Tobias's trophy stirred a sick feeling in her stomach.

A moment later a pretty parlormaid carrying a silver bowl of peppermints greeted her. Marjorie declined and asked to see Tobias. Alone again, she frowned and thought of Tobias and his obsession with protocol and the part she'd played in helping him achieve success. No other merchant in Bath went to so much bother for the sake of appearances. But then, no other merchant in Bath had acquired his nest egg at a backgammon board.

The side door opened. A smiling Tobias ushered a petite brunette into the room. The woman placed a gloved hand to her throat to draw attention to the jewels there.

"Hello, Marjorie," he said. "I presume you know Mrs. Woodruff."

That he had the audacity to present his mistress to her merely amused Marjorie. That his paramour wore the choker of rubies appalled her.

The satin ribbon felt like a noose around Marjorie's neck.

So, she thought, Ponds wanted to gloat, did he? This was only one of the pieces he'd won from her. She took satisfaction in the knowledge that he'd never have the one thing he coveted: her position and the respectability that went along with it.

She smiled and nodded. "May I say, Mrs. Woodruff, that's a stunning necklace."

"Tobias said it once belonged to you." She blinked and looked up at her protector.

"I always thought it was fetching," said Marjorie.

Tobias's handsome features fell into a sulk. "Run along, my dear." He nudged the woman out the door.

Marjorie retrieved the schedules from her pouch and extended them to him. "I'll need these as soon as possible."

He tugged at the front of his waistcoat, then took the papers. Not bothering to look at them, he said, "No time to stay for a chat and a dish of tea, eh?"

She looked at his well-manicured hands and wondered again how a printer kept his fingernails so clean.

"Thank you, no." She glanced pointedly at the schedules. "I haven't the time."

His polite facade vanished. He sneered, revealing the tooth she'd chipped years before. "Don't expect a discount. When I delivered the first batch of schedules I again warned you that the times were incorrect."

It was her turn to gloat. "You think I've rewritten those schedules."

On a half laugh he said, "We've known each other too long and too well to play childish games. A mistake is understandable, given—shall we say— your father's latest foray into your life. You're not sidestepping this one as neatly as you did the others."

Marshaling her features into blandness, she said, "When will you learn that you can't intimidate me, Tobias? I presume you refer to Lord Blake's sojourn in Bath."

"Sojourn? What an interesting way to describe his forced presence here."

"I do live to interest you, Tobias."

He touched the ribbon around her neck. "Of course, you are accustomed to a more common type of suitor, aren't you?"

She stepped back. "Extremely common, now that you mention it."

"Pity about your rubies." He began perusing the schedule. "But they do flatter Mrs. Woodruff, don't you—" He halted, his hands gripping the paper, his gaze riveted to the words.

"Is something wrong, Tobias?"

He raised angry eyes to hers. "A mail coach? When did this come about?"

"It's been years in the planning. Read on, and you'll see when the service begins."

"That's why the times were so slow on the schedules for the posting inns."

Coolly she said, "An outstanding deduction."

His eyes bulged. "What tricks did you pull to get the money?"

"Perhaps I sold my family treasures."

"Ha!" He pointed to the backgammon set. "You haven't possessed a jewel since you were foolish enough to sit at that board with me years ago."

The jibe still stung. Inwardly, Marjorie, the reckless girl who'd danced into Bath and gambled with the zeal of a hedonist, hung her head in shame. Outwardly, the postmistress of Bath maintained her dignity. "You were a splendid winner at games, Tobias, but a poor loser in matters of the heart. Then again, your heart wasn't involved."

His mouth quivered with rage he couldn't suppress. "I never wanted to marry an old maid like you."

"I know. You wanted to escape punishment for counterfeiting letters of marque."

"Given the choice of prison or you, I took the lesser punishment."

"But I'm the one who saved you from both. Even after you cheated me out of my jewels and tried to ravish me in the private dining room of the Bear Inn."

His hand flew to his mouth and hid the broken tooth. "You went too far in defending your virtue."

"You may have taken my jewels, but I kept my pride, my virtue, and my post. You're a loser, Tobias, in more ways than one."

With jerky motions he began folding the paper. "This mail coach idea is pure folly. It'll bog down in the heath."

"Thank you for telling me. Now I won't have to bother with reserving you a seat, will I?"

He reached back and opened the door. Noise from the street rushed in. "I'll take the seat behind your desk."

"Don't hold your breath, you pompous, braying ass."

"I can't, sweetheart, for you take it away."

Her pulse leapt and her heart sank.

Blake Chesterfield crossed the threshold and stood between them. He seemed to fill the room; he absolutely filled her senses. Now she understood the true meaning of folly: loving Blake Chesterfield.

He looked at her, then whipped his gaze to Tobias. "What's going on here?" he demanded, his tone pure, arrogant Chesterfield.

Tobias retreated to the safety of his backgammon shrine. "'Twas just an amiable business discussion between old friends, my lord. She's a hard woman, as I'm sure you've found out."

Blake scoured her with his gaze. "I've found her quite to my liking."

"We're in the same boat, old chum. So you needn't lie to me. After all, I lost my bid for Marjorie years ago."

Being discussed as if she weren't there pushed Marjorie to say, "That's right, Tobias, and you'll lose again in your bid to become postmaster of Bath. And you, Lord Blake"—she rounded on him—"are out of the *other* bidding. Good day, gentlemen."

As she breezed out the door she caught a glimpse of Blake's stunned and hurt face.

That afternoon she visited the breeder in Monkton Farly and purchased eight of his finest carriage horses. As a bonus the man gave her a sleek sorrel mare. Marjorie called the horse Alma, for she desperately needed a soul mate.

Aching to escape the memories in Bath, she accompanied Wick in the mail cart to Bristol. They returned to Bath Saturday at noon to find the Chesterfield carriage parked in the yard. Peddicord, Tug, and Albert stood nearby deep in conversation.

When she looked inside the coach and found it empty Marjorie felt a flicker of pain. Holding her head high, she marched into the posting room. And ran smack into an outraged Dame Surleigh.

Beet-faced, the woman rattled a sheet of paper and shouted, "I demand your resignation. Here! Sending such filth through the mail is a violation of trust."

Marjorie took the offered parchment. She unfurled it and looked in disbelief at a drawing of herself and the postboys cavorting naked in the King's Bath. The unique style of the artist was unmistakable.

CHAPTER 13

*The maidens of Bath shall enjoy protection
under the laws, lest they visit ill humors on
their protectors.*

—Beau Nash, *Rules of Bath*

TEN MINUTES LATER, THE ROLLED PARCHMENT CLUTCHED
in her shaking hand, Marjorie glided past Sanford,
sailed into Cleveland's house, and ran up the stairs to
Blake's apartment.

He stood before the fireplace, his hands clasped
behind his back, his head bowed. Everson sat at the
desk, a quill in his hand.

"Begin the letter with—" Blake paused and jerked
his head toward the door. His eyes lighted with glee.
"Hello, sweetheart."

A consummate actor, she thought. Incensed, she
marched to him, drew back her arm, and whacked
him across the face with the drawing. "You miserable,
underhanded wretch."

He blinked and stood paralyzed for an instant.
Then he caught her wrist. "Excuse us, Everson."

A shocked Everson waved a hand over the papers.
"But my lord, the reply—"

"Leave it."

Everson stared at Marjorie. She glared back.

"Now!"

The valet shuffled the pile of papers, then knocked over a chair in his haste to obey.

The instant the door clicked shut she focused on Blake. "Let go of me," she said through clenched teeth.

His brows arched in curiosity. "Not until you tell me what's happened to make you so angry that you'd barge in here and slap me."

Suppressed rage quivered through her. "Don't play the innocent with me. You know precisely what's happened." She rattled the paper. "This!"

"I don't have time to read anything now."

"Then make time!"

With his free hand he plucked the tube of parchment, but his eyes never left hers. He flicked his wrist. The crumpled paper wouldn't unfurl. "Stay right there." He let her go.

She watched in livid anticipation, her foot tapping. He unrolled the parchment. The fine lace on his cuffs fluttered. His rigid countenance faltered. He snapped his intense green gaze to her. "Where did you get this?"

The smell of lemons filled her nose. She had tasted the tart fragrance on his skin. Now it brought tears to her eyes and pain to her heart. "This one came from Dame Surleigh. We found twenty-two copies in the London pouch."

"Has Tug left?"

"No," she ground out.

"Good." He grabbed her hand and started for the door. "Come on."

She dug in her heels. "Get your hand off me."

He stopped and studied her as if she were a riddle to be solved. "I want to help you."

"Release me, you scribbler."

He opened his mouth, then closed it. Shocked comprehension dawned over his handsome features. "You think I drew this."

"I love it when you're obtuse."

"Marjorie, I don't know what to say—except I know nothing about this." He studied her closely. "But you think I do."

Holding up her imprisoned wrist, she slapped her free hand against it. "Bravo. What will you do for an encore? Draw you and me in bed together. Is that how you'll force my hand?"

"You cut me to the quick."

She had connived to see sensitivity in him. But that was before he'd betrayed her and disillusioned the postboys. "Oh, please. Spare me your mawkish confessions. I can understand why you'd like to render me helpless and make me dependent on you. What I can't understand is why you'd want to hurt twenty-five young men who think you hung the bloody moon." Her voice choked. "God knows they have few enough heroes as it is."

"For God's sake, I didn't draw this filth."

"Any fool can see that it's your work." Her hand trembling, she pointed to the sultry likeness of herself. "In case you've forgotten, I've seen this drawing of me before."

He squinted at the sketch. "Precisely. This is a copy of my work. At least your face has been copied. The rest of it—" He walked to the window and held the drawing to the light. "It looks like Hogarth's style. Yes, it's Hogarth's work all right." Glancing up, he said, "But you should know that. Come on. I'll show you."

She stayed put, but her mind reached out to embrace his words. She wanted to believe him. But the

288

evidence of his guilt was too conclusive. "Hogarth wouldn't have drawn it, Blake. He knows me."

Sadness ringed his eyes, and his great shoulders slumped. "You won't even give me the chance to defend myself, will you?" When she didn't reply, he said, "What could I hope to gain by this vicious piece of slander?"

She'd been too angry to consider motives. Still, the evidence led to Blake. "You once said you'd go to any lengths to force me into the marriage bed."

The corners of his mouth tightened. "In case you've forgotten"—he flung his arm toward a side door— "our well-initiated marriage bed awaits in that room."

"I haven't forgotten. My stomach won't let me. It churns every time I think about you touching me."

The starch seemed to go out of him. "You truly think I'd stoop to a disgusting trick like this?"

Yes! her battered emotions wanted to shout. Yet her tender heart wanted to trust him. "I don't know, Blake. I just remember what you said about doing anything to force me into marriage."

"I made that rash statement long before you and I decided to trust each other. Back when I thought you were in league with your father. And if you think about it, why would I want to discredit the future duchess of Enderley?"

Her anger subsided. In its wake she felt drained, exposed. "I won't be your duchess. And I think you did it to hurt me."

He sat on the window seat, his legs stretched out, his arms folded over his chest, an imploring look in his eyes. Sunlight limned him in a silvery glow. "The same as your father? Your grandmother? Tobias, and the others George betrothed you to?" He shook his head. "I'm not like them."

She'd heard too many lies from too many desperate men. "Why should I believe you?" she said quietly. "You have to win my trust, too."

"I want to—if only you'd let me." He smiled and patted the space beside him. "Come here. Let's talk. You're too smart to be tricked by such a poor piece of work."

Telling herself she was a fool to give him the benefit of the doubt, she took the first step.

"Come on," he said.

As she walked across the sitting room she became aware of her surroundings, the dark mahogany furniture with brocade cushions, the landscape paintings framed in rich walnut, and the shiny brass lamps. An Indiaman case clock, finished in lacquered tortoise shell, banged the half hour. She stopped at the cluttered desk and righted the chair Everson had toppled. She felt Blake watching her, but rather than meet his compelling gaze she looked at the papers on his desk. "This isn't your handwriting. It's Everson's."

Blake went still. "Of course. He's my personal secretary. Now let's put our heads together and figure out who drew this."

Weariness set in again. Once gossip over the drawing reached the Postal Surveyor, she could say goodbye to any chance of winning the concession again. The postboys would be back begging in the streets, because Tobias Ponds would become the new postmaster.

His name blasted through her brain. "Tobias. I threw the drawing away. He knocked over the trash bin. He must have found the sketch."

Paper slapped wood. "Of course," Blake said. He strolled to the desk. "Ponds. He wants to discredit you so he can win your job. He must have laughed when we were in his shop."

"That miserable cur!" Fifty despicable tortures

came to mind. "I'd like to see him dangling by his thumbs over a pit of snapping alligators."

Blake whistled and grasped her arm. "Poor Tobias. Remind me never to cross you."

She looked up into emerald eyes that glittered with anger. A yoke of remorse weighted her spirits. "I'm sorry I accused you."

He rubbed his cheek. "I know. And that's quite an arm you've got there, Postmistress. I'm glad you didn't use your fist or sentence me to death in a caldron of boiling oil."

A faint red mark streaked his jaw. "I don't know what's happening to me, Blake. I rarely raise a hand to anyone—at least not in anger." She'd had no choice that night in the Bear Inn. How ironic that Tobias had twice been the one to move her to violence.

Blake eased between her and the desk and pulled her into his arms. "I'll have him keelhauled."

A familiar tangy smell surrounded her. His strength seemed to reach out to her and offer shelter. He nestled his cheek against her hair.

"Keelhauling isn't painful enough for him," she said against his neck.

"Well," Blake drawled, rubbing her stiff back, "I could send him in bondage to a sugar plantation in Barbados."

He'd taken her side against Tobias. She hugged him back. "I can't lose my job. The boys need a home."

"I promise you that no matter what happens, the boys will always have a home. So will Rowena."

His assurance was a balm to her battered confidence. "Will you forgive me?"

"Oh, I probably will—given about fifty years worth of friendly inducements."

A thrill coursed through her. In the aftermath she felt stunned and invigorated at once. "Seriously."

"Seriously," he repeated, his lips close to her ear.

"You were angry with me before you stormed in here."

"That's true."

"Was it because we argued in Cross Bath?"

"No."

"Because I made love to you in Cross Bath?"

Separating the person she'd wronged from the lover she couldn't trust seemed an impossible task. And what of the man who was simply Blake Chesterfield, the man behind the family tradition, the man who wasn't indebted to her father? Didn't he deserve respect for the person he was, and bother the misfortune that had brought him here?

When had she stopped seeing him in an objective light?

The moment she'd fallen in love with him.

"Well," he said, "is that why you're still angry?"

Were circumstances different, she would have shared her thoughts. How sad, she lamented, that Blake Chesterfield couldn't be the husband of her dreams. "I'm not angry."

"Talk to me, Marjorie. Tell me what you're thinking."

"Nothing of importance."

She waited for him to pressure her, but he didn't. She waited for him to seduce her, but he didn't. For an instant his arms tightened around her. Then he just held her, the gentle flow of their breathing and the ticking of the clock the only sounds in the room. Seeking shelter in his arms was wrong, she knew, for any moment he'd try to seduce her. The pattern was predictable. All their embraces, no matter how platonic at the start, always ended in soul-stirring passion.

Minutes passed, and he made no move to kiss or fondle her. Marjorie wondered again if she hadn't misjudged him. Had he become so attuned to her moods that he knew what she wanted? Or was his offer of solace merely a new bribe in an old game of blackmail?

Over the broad plane of his shoulder she spied the papers on his desk. With a start she recognized a signature on a letter peeking from beneath the stack. *George Entwhistle.*

The hand of neglect squeezed her heart. She cast it off and pretended to press against Blake. Then she began reading what she could see of the letter.

> . . . *few things give me more real concern than to find that my notions of timely conduction of affairs differ so greatly from yours. You owe to me an explanation of your laggardly conduct. As a man not forgetful of your unfitness in a given arena, you are herewith reminded to conclude, posthaste, the business for which you were sent to Bath.*

Unfitness? Blake was unfit? For what? His conduct in the navy was exemplary. His reputation for command was legend. He couldn't be a bastard; the circumstances of his birth were common knowledge. Compelled, Marjorie read on.

> *I shall avoid the redundancy of enumerating the consequences to the house of Chesterfield should you fail. Thanks to your timely intervention on my behalf with His Royal Majesty, I expect to arrive in England within a fortnight. My dear son, I am ever, with unchanging sentiments of good fortune, most encouragingly yours . . .*

Her stomach roiled. She couldn't decide which news affected her more—Blake's ominous "unfitness" or her father's impending visit to Bath. Yet the latter added a new and dangerous dimension to Papa's game. With Shelbourne, Tobias, and the others, Milo Magrath had been the bearer of ill tidings. This time Papa intended to deal the death blow himself.

Tears clogged her throat at the prospect of her father shouting the details of Blake's incompetence through the streets of Bath. Incompetence. Unfitness. Like a ball spinning on a red and black E. O. wheel, the words rolled in her mind.

She hadn't seen Papa in fourteen years. He would arrive within a fortnight—but of when? The date but must be at the top of the page, hidden beneath the other correspondence.

Wild with the need to know when her father would descend on Bath, she sniffed and nestled closer to Blake. "Oh, Blake. I *was* angry about the Cross Bath. You always try to seduce me."

"Oh, sweetheart," he crooned, spreading his legs and pulling her between them, "I can't help myself. You're so beautiful. But I'll just hold you for now."

She reached around him. Her fingertips danced an inch from the paper. "I'm glad you're so sensitive to my moods. Tobias had me very upset."

He hugged her fiercely. "Don't worry over Tobias. I'll slay that dragon, too."

"Thank you, Blake. I'm beginning to trust you more and more."

What flaw lay hidden in the soul of this chivalrous man? Driven by the desperate need to know, she pressed against him. He leaned back. The pad of her finger touched the letter. She began easing it out of the stack.

Blake groaned, startling her, but she was too close to victory to stop now. Just as the letter slid free Blake cupped her hips and pulled her into the cradle of his loins. Breathing hard, he rocked her against him in a rhythm she remembered well. A yearning emptiness opened inside her, and secret places tingled with need.

With so many layers of clothing between them she couldn't feel his rising passion, but she knew his offering would fill the void within her.

His thoughts had blossomed into desire; hers had wilted into deceit. But he deserved no better. He had been the first to practice deceit.

He buried his head in the curve of her neck and began a trail of kisses she knew would lead to the sensitive whorls of her ear. Knowing she'd be lost at the end of his erotic journey, she raised the letter and strained to read the spidery print.

He pulled back and moved his lips to hers. She tensed with the fear of discovery. He lifted feathery jet lashes to reveal dreamy green eyes. "Marjorie, darling, I feel so much more for you than mere passion. I feel—"

Blake clutched her shoulders and, in one smooth motion, reversed their positions. Paper rattled. He glanced over his shoulder and spied the letter in her hand. As if she were a fire, he jumped back. "What the hell—" Disillusionment clouded his handsome features. "Give it to me," he said.

Swallowing a knot of self-disgust, she said, "It bears my father's signature, so it involves me."

Blake couldn't hear the forlorn expression in her eyes. Damn George Entwhistle for hurting her so. Damn Blake Chesterfield for falling victim to him "You could have asked. I would have let you read it. I thought your aim was to win my trust."

"I didn't know he'd written you until I saw the letter. Remember, he doesn't use the post. Milo delivers his messages."

She offered the letter. Blake took it. "And you don't usually read other people's mail," he said.

"I have a right to know what that letter says."

Frustrated, he couldn't argue the point. He returned the letter to the center of the stack. "It says he's coming to Bath."

She steadied herself by grasping the back of the chair. Her eyes drifted out of focus. "When?"

Blake tamped back the sudden urge to pull her into his arms and apologize, to reveal the ugly truth about himself and end the game. But when the words formed on his lips, his mouth turned bitter. He told her as much of the truth as he could. "Friday next."

"What will you do?" she quietly asked.

Take to the sea? Escape to Wales, slither into a dark corner of his castle and wait out the disgrace? His choices were few and bleak.

The old arrogance reared its head. Out of habit he slipped into the comfortable demeanor that always shielded him from scorn. He shrugged. "Redouble my efforts to win your hand in marriage, I suppose."

She moved so near their noses almost touched. "A moment ago you were tender, open, and loving to me. Now you're acting like a self-righteous prig. Why do you do that?"

She was perilously close to discovering the real Blake Chesterfield. He battened down the hatches. "I have an aversion," he said, "to people who pry."

"Does that include wives? You say I must marry you."

She had him. "I would be honest with you in everything else."

"If I become your wife," she said, "I will pry into every nook and cranny of your life."

She threw up her hands, and her eyes blazed with blue fire. "You have a secret, Blake. It can't be so terrible that you won't share it with me. Not if you expect me to spend my life with you. If I agree to marry you, will you tell me?"

She made honesty sound so easy, but he knew better. "Trust me, Postmistress. You don't want to know."

"I've been trying to trust you, but every time I get close to you, you clam up."

Her astuteness frightened him more than her father's knowledge. Falling in love with Marjorie Entwhistle had been a mistake, for Blake knew she'd hound him until he confessed. Then she'd turn away in revulsion. "Five minutes ago we were extremely close. My reaction to you could never be called clamming up. I was rather blatant in my response, wouldn't you agree?"

Her arms fell to her sides. "There you go again, Lord Arrogance. I don't know why I even bother." She turned toward the door. "Farewell. Good luck dealing with my father."

Unable to let her go, he followed. "What about Tobias and the drawing?"

She opened the door. "The damage is done. But if you feel the need, mount your white horse and ride into the breach."

Blake gripped her shoulder. "Marjorie, please try to understand."

She glanced back. Tears glistened in her eyes. "I don't care anymore," she said. "I've tried all I can."

He watched her go, and for the first time since his mother discovered his repulsive flaw, Blake Chesterfield wanted to cry.

Everson dashed into the room. "You told her, didn't you?"

Without Marjorie, Blake felt squeezed in a vise of loneliness. He tried to take a deep breath, but his chest muscles rebelled. "No," he croaked. "I didn't tell her."

The valet raked sweat off his forehead. "Good. I was afraid you had."

"I'm not that ignorant."

"No." Everson smiled and slapped Blake on the back. "You're smitten with her, though. God, she is a prize, but she's too smart for her own good."

A sick laugh passed Blake's lips. "I don't deserve such a fine woman. Why couldn't my betrothed have been . . ." He couldn't finish the thought, for Marjorie was the only woman who came to mind and heart.

"Bother it." Everson herded Blake to the desk. "You deserve the fairest princess in the realm, my lord. You feel guilty because you haven't outgrown your penchant for lush, red-haired women."

Oh, but Blake had. When his mind conjured a picture of his love he saw a golden-haired, blue-eyed angel, nearly as tall as he, and with a will and a sense of honor to match any warrior.

"What did she want?" asked Everson. "Why did she strike you?"

Blake showed him the drawing. "Tobias's work. He spread these all over town."

"What will you do?"

Blake smiled. "Hang him up by his thumbs and dangle him over a pit of snapping alligators."

Everson screwed up his face.

Blake reached for his coat. "I'll be back."

"What about the other letters?" Everson rifled through the correspondence. "Here's one from Her Grace."

"Go ahead. Tell me her ill tidings."

Everson ripped open the seal. "Sweet Saint David," he murmured, scanning the letter. "She's on her way to Bath. She'll be here in a day or two."

Blake groaned. "And to think I asked her to come."

"There's some good news."

"No such thing exists in my life."

Everson said, "Your father won't be accompanying her. Seems he's fishing in Scotland."

On his way out the door Blake murmured, "Thank God for small favors—like salmon."

By the time he arrived at Ponds's establishment Blake had weathered the shock of his mother's untimely arrival. The anticipation of George Entwhistle's, however, made his soul tremble in fear.

He took out his anxieties on a surprised Tobias Ponds.

The first blow sent the printer crashing into a backgammon board. Playing pieces showered the carpet and furniture. "What the devil?" stammered Ponds, rubbing his jaw.

Blake yanked up his quarry by the lapels and held him off the ground. "Kiss your teeth good-bye, Ponds."

"No!" Arms flailing, feet kicking, he tried to break the hold, but Blake was taller, stronger, and meaner. "Help!"

"No one can help you, Ponds."

The door to the print room opened. The clickety-clacking of a printing press spilled into the foyer and played harmony with Ponds's frantic protests. Wide-eyed, a uniformed maid squealed and clutched the door frame. The noise stopped. Three laborers in inkstained aprons appeared behind the girl.

Emboldened by the audience, Ponds said, "Kiss your heirs good-bye." He kicked Blake in the groin.

A crippling pain shot down to his knees and ripped up his abdomen. His stomach pitched. He let go of Ponds, then cupped his aching balls and doubled over.

The printer landed on his backside. Chest heaving, he struggled to his feet. Blake took slow, deep breaths and tried to ignore the pain clawing at his tender parts. Ponds had gotten in a low blow. No mercy, Blake decided. In return, Blake would take his own sweet time in exacting revenge.

Feigning grave injury, he waited until his opponent moved within striking distance. When Ponds cocked his arm, Blake landed a jab to the printer's stomach. His belly caved in like an old feather pillow. Blake came on with a volley of punches. Ribs cracked beneath his knuckles.

Ponds stumbled backward and fell into a chair.

Blake crooked a finger. "Come on, Ponds. Surely you're not done in yet."

"I'll kill you." Ponds's nostrils flared. His face turned apple red. Ducking his head, he pushed out of the chair and charged. At the last instant Blake stepped out of the way. He snatched Ponds's wrist. With a jerk of his arm he brought the printer to his knees.

"Maybe you'd prefer a few broken fingers," Blake ground out. "That should keep you from forging filthy pictures for a while."

His face now pasty white, his breath coming in gasps, Ponds said, "I don't know what you're talking about."

Blake towered over him and exerted slow pressure on his wrist. "How many of those broadsides did you print?"

The printer gloated. "Enough. King George himself is probably feasting his eyes on that slut."

Blake snarled, "One more word like that and I'll snap your wrist. How many did you print?"

"Let go of me and I'll tell you."

Blake released him.

Ponds yelped, then scooted away, his injured limb cradled against his chest. "You're mad!"

"Damned right!" On weary legs Blake stalked him. "Shall I count to ten?"

"Count all you like, you blue-blooded bastard. Lot of good it'll do you or Marjorie."

"Have you ever seen the hold of a warship, Ponds? Do you have any idea what kind of creature you'd be after six weeks of confinement on a diet of moldy sea biscuit and brackish water?"

"You don't frighten me."

As his need for revenge peaked Blake's imagination took control. "While you sleep, rats will nibble your toes and ears. Your gums will bleed with scurvy. What few teeth you have left will fall out. Your beautiful fingernails will break from picking oakum."

Ponds's throat worked. "The navy doesn't condone such inhumanity."

"You seem to forget who I am. The Atlantic fleet is at my disposal."

"And you're at the disposal of George Entwhistle, aren't you?" The printer shook his head in mock pity. "The high and mighty Chesterfield heir is about to tumble from his throne."

Fighting off a wave of fear, Blake pointed to the maid. "Do you know who I am?"

"Yes, my lord." She bobbed a nervous curtsy.

"Go to the duke of Cleveland's house and ask for Mr. Peddicord. Tell him to bring the carriage here straightaway. Your employer is taking a trip to Bristol." The maid scurried out.

"You wouldn't dare," squeaked Ponds.

Blake sat in a chair and spread his legs to ease the agony in his loins. "Wait and see."

"I'm a private citizen. You can't put me on a ship."

Chuckling, Blake said, "Not only will I put you on

a ship, you worthless bastard, but I'll give orders to have you delivered to the Georgia penal colony. Twelve years of hacking fields of jungle should trim that flabby middle of yours. If you live that long."

Sweat popped out on Tobias's brow. A broken man, he slumped against the wall. "All right," he grumbled. "The list is in my desk—the bottom drawer on the left."

Blake pointed to one of the workmen. "Get it."

"And fetch me a doctor," Ponds called after the man.

"Belay that," Blake said.

The man nodded and scurried away. Blake turned back to Ponds. "How many did you print?"

"One hundred. Now get me a doctor!"

Seventy-seven remained unaccounted for. "To whom were they addressed?"

"To locals."

Blake breathed a sigh of relief. The postboys would be busy the rest of the day, but perhaps the damage could be undone.

"You'll print a formal apology tomorrow, and if I don't see it plastered all over town, you'll be shipped to sea before you can say aye, aye, sir."

Ponds turned green.

"You'll also buy new boots for the postboys, won't you?"

"I'll hire them a damned dancing master," he bellowed. "Just get me a doctor!"

With the list in hand, Blake and six of the postboys spent the evening collecting and burning the drawings. The next day saw the posting of Ponds's formal apology. That night Blake went to see Marjorie. And learned that she and her three young drivers had left for London in the mail coach. Worried sick over their safety, Blake ordered Peddicord to follow and protect them.

The next morning the bells of Abbey Church clanged twenty-four times. Her Grace, the duchess of Enderley, had arrived early.

CHAPTER 14

*The noble visitors of Bath shall conduct
themselves with prudence and discretion.*

—Beau Nash, *Rules of Bath*

THE TEXTURED WALLS OF THE HAMBURG ROOM SEEMED
to close in on Blake. His mother's cloying perfume
and Rowena's cloying personality pecked away at his
good humor. No sane man, he thought morosely,
would intentionally convene such a meeting. But if
his hunch was right, it'd be worth his trouble, for by
the end of this visit Rowena would clamor for marriage between him and Marjorie.

Still, he felt as if he were riding out a storm.

Where the devil were Marjorie and the mail coach?
She'd been gone three days, and it was past noon
already. According to the schedule, they should've
been in Bath by now.

Instinctively his gaze fell on Hogarth's arresting
portrayal of the postmistress of Bath. He smiled.

"Blake!" snapped his mother in her most queenly
tone. She rapped him with her cane. "I fail to see what

304

you find amusing about the Prince of Wales's latest bout of troublemaking. His Majesty's considering exiling Frederick to his apartments again."

"No one else will miss him, Mama."

She began fanning herself. "The older you get the more cynical you become. And don't slouch. The unsuspecting might mistake you for a clerk."

Blake sat up straight.

Rowena tittered. "Imagine that. You still have control over the boy."

Mama preened.

Out of habit Blake laughed, but beneath the false humor his pride stung. In retribution he said, "That would make you a very distressed clerk's mother, wouldn't it, Mama?"

Her jaw tightened, revealing wrinkles at the corners of her mouth. "What you need is a good woman to bring you to heel."

"I'm betrothed to the best there is, Mama."

"If," said Rowena, "she can find the time to marry you."

"Your father and I discussed your upcoming nuptials just last week when we visited the Bolingbrokes. Still, you should have consulted me about the match. I could have advised you." She glanced quickly to Rowena. "I meant no offense, Rowena. I'm certain you've managed the betrothal nicely."

Rowena fiddled with the ivory dragon on her cane. "We've had mountains of experience. Marjorie's been betrothed six—no, seven times now," she said.

"How impressive," Mama cooed. "I'm certain, then, that Lady Marjorie is thoroughly in the main."

Rowena replied, "For a working woman, yes, she is definitely in the main."

Like a hen spying a fat caterpillar, his mother drew up her neck. "Work? You mean charity, I'm sure.

Orphans, the needy, oh, and those poor Irish Catholics, starving in the name of God."

"She champions the meanest orphan," Blake put in, taking pleasure at Rowena's scowl. "She can't bear to see anyone go hungry."

"We give honest work," declared Rowena, "and shelter to twenty-five orphans here."

"How very charitable." His mother's voice sounded as smooth as silk. "I'm sure Lady Marjorie and I shall get on famously."

Rowena said, "You were a Cholmondeley before you wed Blake's father, were you not?"

Had she spouted blue blood, Jane could not have looked more aristocratic. She had a way of drawing attention to herself that had nothing to do with her flawless skin, which Peddicord termed pretty as a baby's bottom, or her sharp hazel eyes, which Everson proclaimed could cut a prince to the quick at thirty paces. Incredible to Blake was how long she could hold attention without uttering a word.

To entrap today's audience she plucked at a bracelet of shilling-size pigeon's-blood rubies. A fabulous array of matching stones adorned her neck.

Satisfied that she had everyone's attention, she finished with the bangle at her wrist and smoothed out a wrinkle in her white velvet overskirt. "How intelligent of you to recall my family, Rowena. Cholmondeley women are highly prized. We have handsome, healthy children and fine breeding."

Blake tried to picture her grunting and groaning to push him out of her womb, her perfectly styled auburn hair dripping sweat, her never-seen legs cocked wide.

He chuckled.

Her fan rapped his knee. "Don't be spiteful. You know very well that the Chesterfields were ecstatic to make such a match for your father."

If she slapped him one more time with that fan, he'd snatch it up and knock the stuffed doves out of her wig. Knowing he wouldn't, he did the next best thing. With absolute irreverence he said, "My father swears 'twas a lucky day for the Chesterfields. To celebrate, he took up fishing in Scotland."

"Our marriage was the talk of the court for years—until you came squalling into the world, nearly killing me in the process. Have you a son, Rowena?"

When she turned away, taking her daggers with her, Blake looked back at the Hogarth. Marjorie's patient smile rained down on him. The moment she arrived he'd take her into a corner and—

"I was blessed with only one daughter," said Rowena. "My poor angel met a bad end at the hands of her husband. Lord Blake knows Marjorie's father well, don't you?"

Fear yanked Blake's attention to Rowena. How much would the old hag reveal about his dealings with George Entwhistle? Wary, he said, "Just so."

"There was some scandal," said Mama. "'Twas long ago." Her hazel eyes grew large. "Oh, my, yes. I recall hearing the story from my aunt. Entwhistle seduced the new king's mistress. Very poor judgment."

Rowena drilled Blake with an evil stare. "His judgment is still poor."

Blake sallied with, "He should have sought your counsel, I'm sure."

Rowena bristled. "He's as despotic as all men."

"Hear, hear," Mama applauded. "Men can be so tiring. Thank heavens for their clubs and hunting lodges."

Hear, hear, thought Blake. Bravo for clubs. The exchange between these old biddies was too amusing to interrupt.

"Thanks to George's narrow nature, my grand-daughter shoulders the responsibility for our welfare. Ends meet slow, you know, Your Grace."

Mama didn't know; the Chesterfield wealth had seen to that. "You mean her allowance surpasses yours," she said. "Pity that Loxburg has come to such dire straits. But there is talk of trouble in Europe."

"Marjorie doesn't get an allowance, and she knows all about the trouble in Europe," said Rowena.

Mama blinked. "She studies politics," she said, as if politics were a puddle of puked beer in her path.

Blake scratched his nose and coughed.

Eyes glittering with challenge, Rowena said, "My Marjorie is a personal friend of Marshal Wade. She also corresponds regularly with Walpole. They are confidants after a fashion."

Mama moved something below the waist, an abso-lute sign that she was displeased. "Sir Robert Wal-pole?" she said. "He's terribly out of the main, you know. You will want to advise her against such an alliance. I assume she still looks to you for such guidance."

Rowena sighed. "She's never looked to anyone for guidance. A bit wild, you might say. She's flagrantly devoted to her common friends, too. On occasion she's stubborn."

Rowena's ploy was as transparent as window glass. By putting Marjorie in a bad light the duchess of Enderley would disapprove of her. Then Marjorie would never consent to marry Blake. It was sad, he thought, that Rowena knew so little about her grand-daughter. It was also sad that the dowager duchess thought she could stop the marriage at all.

To foil her plan he said, "Beau Nash is one of Marjorie's friends, Mama."

"Ah," she purred. "What a delightfully clever gen-tleman. At court we all say so."

"Marjorie delivers his mail," blurted Rowena.

Blake said, "She's administrator of the postal service, Mama. Much the same as you when you supervise the inventory of the family jewels, although Marjorie's position is largely ceremonial."

Mama patted her cheek. "I must confess, 'tis a grueling two-day task counting all those baubles, not to mention the primitive pieces. I'm generally forced to go to the country afterward to recuperate."

"Marjorie's gone to London in the new mail coach," offered Rowena.

"A public conveyance? Oh, my. Has your coachman died?"

"They have three new coachmen, Mama," Blake managed with a straight face. "Peddicord has taken them under his wing."

"You've counseled her well, Blake."

Feeling verbally patted on the head, Blake glanced at Rowena, offering her the lead in the conversation.

She wasn't quick enough, for Mama went on, "How you took such control on your own, Blake, I can't imagine. Unless . . . of course, it's a trait from the Cholmondeleys. My family has very special gifts."

They certainly did, thought Blake: arrogance, indifference, and boredom. The Black Prince would've forfeited Aquitaine before marrying a Cholmondeley.

"After the wedding," Mama said to Rowena, "you should come to London. The court is so lively these days."

That got Rowena's attention. At last, thought Blake.

"Truly?" said Rowena. "I haven't been to court since I was a child. We are quite without resources, Marjorie and I."

"I insist then." Mama glanced at Blake. "I'm certain my son will see that you have your own residence and an allowance befitting your station. One hopes that when he leaves the navy he'll have more time to devote to his family."

Certain she'd keep harping until he replied, Blake said, "I'm ever eager, Mama, to return your devotion. I received so much of it in my youth."

She gave him a slow blink of dismissal. "We'll have such fun, Rowena."

The dowager duchess of Loxburg wouldn't know what fun was even if her maid laced it in her stays. Mama deserved a sour companion.

Carriage wheels rattled over the drive. He turned an ear toward the foyer. A rumbling came from the upper floor of the mansion, then a sound akin to a herd of frightened cattle running down the wooden stairs.

The mail coach had arrived.

Excitement jolted through him. He shot to his feet. "If you'll excuse me, Your Grace and Mama."

Without waiting for a reply he hurried down the mirrored hallway, then raced past the huge kitchen and dining hall to the back of the mansion. In the posting room a sea of coatless postboys milled near the back door, all trying to squeeze through at once.

Barking a crisp "Attention!" he took control. In orderly fashion he marched the boys outside, then followed. The instant he spied the carriage he skidded to a halt.

Wick and Albert sat in the box, one securing the reins, the other setting the brake.

He thought he spied Tug but realized it was Marjorie dressed in one of Tug's uniforms. She stood facing the open carriage door, her arms extended toward an unseen passenger. Blake's eyes were drawn to her shapely bottom and trim ankles, for both were shockingly revealed by the too-tight and too-short breeches.

He took off running. Before he reached the carriage Peddicord appeared in the door of the conveyance, his face a grimace of pain, a lace-trimmed bandage around one foot. Tug crouched on the floor of the carriage and steadied the wounded coachman. Peddicord gave Marjorie his weight. She helped him to the ground, then turned and ducked under his arm to support him.

Splatters of dried mud freckled her cheeks, forehead, and hair. She looked as if she'd been to hell and back, rather than London.

"Wait!" he yelled, running faster.

"Spark in the yard," yelled one of the boys.

Marjorie looked up. Seeing Blake, she spat Peddicord's favorite expletive.

"What the devil happened?" Blake asked, moving under Peddicord's other shoulder.

"You might say we had a spot of trouble," she grumbled.

"Trouble? You look like the losers in a war."

"Not quite," she snapped, blowing a strand of hair out of her eyes. "We made it to London, but we were plagued with one accident after another."

Marjorie stumbled. Peddicord hissed in pain.

"Let go," Blake said. "I'll take him." Then he squatted lower and pulled Peddicord to his side.

"Imagine you seeing to me, Commodore," Peddicord said weakly. "Time was you rode on my shoulders."

"And good times they were, my friend," Blake replied. "What happened?"

"'Twould take hours to tell all of the tale."

"The carriage rolled over his foot," said Marjorie.

"Is it broken?" Blake asked.

She put her hands to the small of her back and stretched. "Several of his toes are black and blue. Cumber!" When the lad appeared she said, "Fetch the doctor straightaway." When he dashed off she turned to the tallest boy in the crowd. "Choose a dozen others. Unharness the horses, feed, and groom them.

311

Then clean up the carriage." To the younger boys she said, "Get the mail bags and start sorting."

Five lads clamored to open the door. Blake carried Peddicord inside and ran smack into his mother and Rowena. The duchess of Enderley frowned in confusion; the dowager duchess of Loxburg smiled in satisfaction.

From behind him Blake heard Marjorie say, "Tell Lizzie to hustle an ocean of hot water to my room."

He groaned inwardly.

Rowena said, "Marjorie dear, may I present Lord Blake's mother, the duchess of Enderley." Turning to her white-faced companion, she said, "Your Grace, my granddaughter, Lady Marjorie Entwhistle, the postmistress of Bath."

Marjorie stopped beside Blake, her shoulders slumped in fatigue. Exhaustion wreathed her face. Under her breath she said, "How lovely to have guests." Out loud she said, "Welcome to Bath, Your Grace."

Blake's mother drilled him with a stare reserved for impertinent princes. "A ceremonial position?" she said, her voice a rumble of scorn that would've carried through Westminster Abbey.

Marjorie whirled on him. "What is she talking about?"

He winced. "Counting the family jewels, I believe."

Peddicord howled with laughter.

At sundown Marjorie propped her elbows on the dressing table and rested her head in her hands. She had soaked in a near-scalding tub until her skin wrinkled; then she'd washed, dried, and styled her hair; then she'd dressed. She still felt exhausted from the trip to London.

Since she'd conceived the idea for a mail coach over a year ago, she had worked and saved to fulfill her dream. From the start, the simple idea had been fraught with complex obstacles: She hadn't the funds for the coach; the Great Bath Road to London was too rutted for fast travel; the inn at Maidenhead burned to the ground; she had no coachman.

She'd conquered each barrier. At last the mail coach was a reality. How could she have been so remiss as to forget the most important factor: fresh horses? How could she have been so gullible as not to recognize her greatest foe: Grandmama?

At the second posting inn from Bath the mail coach had fallen victim to Rowena's betrayal. It still stabbed so deeply that Marjorie felt as if her heart were bleeding. For the thousandth time since the coach left Bath she asked why. Why would Grandmama interfere? And now all Marjorie had to do was walk downstairs and demand the answer.

Like a child facing a caning, she dawdled and allowed her weary mind to settle on the one bright spot in her gloomy life: Blake Chesterfield. For days she'd found solace in thoughts of her lover, the lusty declarations he'd used to seduce her, and his noble efforts to win her trust. She'd accused him unjustly, and he'd forgiven her. Then he'd saved her reputation by organizing a search party and retrieving all of Tobias's drawings. He'd even sent Peddicord to help.

Six men had crumbled in the face of her father's blackmail. What would Blake do when Papa arrived? Would his Chesterfield dignity desert him, or would he meet his adversary head on?

Ironically, she realized she faced a similar dilemma with Rowena. Marjorie wondered if she could win her battle.

Pity hammered at the door of her confidence. Conviction turned the intruder away.

Take one problem at a time, Beau always said.

Marjorie gathered her gumption and went downstairs. In the mirrored corridor she paused. She stared at a dozen images of herself, and each pair of eyes looked ancient, the souls tarnished by disillusion.

You can do it, she told herself. You can face up to that old witch.

Remembering Blake's words stirred her courage. She squared her shoulders and walked into the Hamburg room. Grandmama sat in one of the wingback chairs, her attention focused on a book. The terrier lay curled at her feet.

Marjorie went to the fireplace and stared at the painting that had given her joy over the years. But today she no longer recognized herself in the work. Regretfully she said a heart-wrenching good-bye to Hogarth's innocent girl.

Rowena looked up and frowned. "Your complexion is too sallow today for that yellow dress, child. Everyone will know you failed just by looking at you. My blue velvet would suit you better. I could have Lizzie press it for you."

Blake had observed that Grandmama would fire off a sally, then follow it with praise. Until now Marjorie hadn't noticed. A sheen of tears blurred her eyes. "The mail coach didn't fail, Grandmama."

"Then that'll teach you to depend on a man for your happiness, child," Rowena spat. "Had you listened to me, you wouldn't be standing here playing the watering pot. I told you I'd deal with Blake Chesterfield the same as—"

"You dealt with the others." The words slipped easily from Marjorie's tongue. The realization, however, struck her like a bolt of lightning. Grandmama's treachery extended far beyond the slow pace of the mail coach.

Marjorie gripped the cold marble of the mantelpiece until her fingernails bowed.

Names and events paraded in her mind.

Betrothal to Tobias—Tug found unconscious in a

London alley. Betrothal to Edwin Simington—the disappearance of the clerk in Bristol. Betrothal to Shelbourne—Albert had been mistaken for a cutpurse and arrested in London. The list of dire emergencies went on. One similarity shone through: Marjorie had been absent from Bath every time Milo Magrath returned to France to inform her father that no wedding would take place.

She took a long look at Grandmama. And for the first time she saw the dowager duchess of Loxburg for what she was: a bitter and selfish old woman. "All along it was you, Grandmama."

Rowena plucked at the gold fringe on the lamp shade. "What are you raving about, child?"

Out of habit Marjorie flinched.

Rowena's stern features melted into an expression of sympathy. "Where's that fire and independence you're so proud of? You're working too hard, and it's taking a toll."

Familiar surroundings suddenly seemed alien. "I'm not working too hard, Grandmama, nor am I raving. Perhaps for the first time I'm thinking clearly."

"You should have a nap." Rowena reached for the bell cord. "I'll have Lizzie bring you a tisane. It'll help you rest."

"I don't want anything except answers."

Rowena's hand froze.

Marjorie said, "You made certain the mail coach would arrive late in London because we couldn't get fresh horses."

"Poor dear. But you can't blame me. I had no idea Lady Masterson would be traveling ahead of you."

"And I didn't mention that Lady Masterson was the one who hired all the horses."

Rowena slammed the book shut and tossed it across the room. The terrier trotted after it. "I don't know what you're talking about."

"You made her leave ahead of us. You had no right to manipulate me."

"Tug told me about the lack of horses."

"No, he didn't. He's in his room tending his blistered hands."

"Well!"

Her heart aching, Marjorie said, "You knew how hard I worked to make a success of the coach service. Yet you tried to destroy my most treasured accomplishment. Why?"

A sharp look of resentment sparkled in Rowena's eyes. Too casually she said, "You're overwrought. It's these cursed betrothals. Blake Chesterfield has robbed you of all logic and rationality."

Instinctively Marjorie knew that once all of the deceptions were out in the open, her relationship with Grandmama would change. Feeling as if she were teetering on a rickety fence, self-respect on her left, estrangement from Rowena on her right, Marjorie hesitated.

"You look ill, child. Are you having your menses?"

The start of her woman's time had taken Marjorie completely off guard. That was why she'd worn Tug's uniform. The remembered embarrassment fueled her courage. "Don't change the subject. You betrayed me. You know it, I know it. And worse, I think you enjoyed each of the betrothals."

The dog padded back to Rowena and sat up, the book in his mouth. "You slipped your father's traps," she said sweetly, stroking the animal's ears. "And very admirably, too. I remember telling you so."

Spoken to the dog, the compliment burned like salt on a wound. "And I remember having to go to London to take care of Tug after Drummond attacked him the first time. While I was gone you sent the betrothal announcement and Milo Magrath back to France." Marjorie remembered the blank envelope

Blake had retrieved from Hunslow Heath. "You also paid Drummond to rob the post. Don't deny it, because I saw the envelope with your seal."

"How dare you?"

"But Blake foiled your plan."

Rowena's chin puckered. "Don't throw your lovers in my face. When you came to Bath I gave you my Louisa's jewels. You lost them to Tobias Ponds."

Marjorie's heart ached for the mother she'd never known. "That's typical of your speech. I'm speaking of your treachery with Drummond, and you throw the loss of my jewels in my face."

"That's how Tobias was able to buy his way out of marriage to you."

The truth glared at Marjorie. It didn't matter how the betrothals had ended. They were history. What mattered was the damage Rowena had done. "How could you be so callous as to risk the lives of innocent boys just so you could play a game of revenge with my father?"

"That's absurd. Those boys are far from innocent. They come from Lilliput Alley. Your father is a murderer. I want nothing to do with him."

Suddenly Marjorie understood the reason behind Rowena's hatred. "You blame him for Mama's death, don't you?"

Red splotches bloomed on Rowena's face. "Yes, I hate him. He used my sweet Louisa to get himself an heir."

"So now you use me to get back at him," Marjorie said, her voice thick with tears.

Rowena knotted her fists. "He killed my only child."

Confused, Marjorie said, "She died bringing me into the world. Papa didn't kill her."

"You're a fine one to defend him. Before the holy water dried on my Louisa's grave that worthless swine shipped you off to a convent and took himself off to see the world."

Feeling vulnerable, Marjorie voiced the thought that had plagued her for years. "But you could have fetched me from there and cared for me yourself."

Rowena stared at her hands—hands that had comforted Marjorie, hands that had paid Claude Drummond. "I wanted to, but I'd just wed the duke, and he wouldn't hear of taking in a poor relation."

A hollow excuse, thought Marjorie, for Rowena had never even written. Hurting, Marjorie said, "How terrible for you."

"Don't get missish," Rowena snapped. "Men rule the world, child. They steal, corrupt, and murder whenever the urge strikes. And there's nothing you or any other woman can do to change it."

A broken heart had been at the root of Rowena's cruel machinations. All of the undeserved insults and cruel jibes Marjorie had endured over the years had been payment for the simple crime of being born.

"Look at me, Grandmama."

Rowena lifted her head.

Tortured eyes fixed on Marjorie. She felt very much the lonely young girl who'd bounded into this room hundreds of times and laid bare her soul to the grandmother she thought loved her. Shattered by her own naïveté, she said, "You let me think that you hated Papa because he didn't want me."

Rowena's chin quivered. "He doesn't want you or love you. I'm the only one who does."

A part of Marjorie snatched up the declaration and held it close. Another part of her wanted the truth. She'd come too far to back down now. "You fired the clerk in Bristol, didn't you? Don't lie, Grandmama, because I can find out."

Grandmama hesitated, then thrust up her chin.

"He was lazy, and he kept a woman. You were too young to see what a scoundrel he was."

Rowena's warped reasoning baffled Marjorie. "It was none of your business that he kept a woman—especially if he did his job satisfactorily, which happened to be the case."

Tears dripped down Grandmama's cheeks. "I was only trying to help. I can't do anything worthwhile anymore. I'm just an old cripple."

Unmoved, Marjorie said, "I've heard that ploy too many times before. You can't move me with pity. You made sure I was in Bristol when Simington bought his way out of the betrothal. You never even let me have the satisfaction of besting my father."

"What's gotten into you, child?"

"The truth, Grandmama. You used me."

Rowena jerked so quickly that dust from her wig showered the arms of the chair. "That's ridiculous. I could never do such a thing."

Marjorie now recognized the display of innocence. Still, the insulting trait hurt. She sniffed back tears. "Yes, you could."

"My poor, poor dear," Rowena crooned, her arms held wide in invitation. "You've gone and fallen in love with Blake Chesterfield, haven't you? That's what this is all about."

Tears pooled in Marjorie's eyes. Loving Blake might have caused her broken heart, but Grandmama's betrayal had ground it to dust. "My feelings for Blake have nothing to do with the problems you've caused."

Rowena folded her hands in her lap. "I suspected as much. Although you're not his social equal, you should marry him."

Taken aback, Marjorie struggled for breath. She'd been puzzled by the presence of the duchess of Enderley in the posting room earlier today. Now she understood why the woman had bothered to come to such a lowly room. "You brought her to the posting room on purpose, didn't you? You wanted to make sure I was at a disadvantage when she saw me. How can you profess to love me one moment, then be so cruel the next?"

"You're just feeling self-conscious because you know people will speculate on the reasons for the match. Were it not for your father, Lord Blake would take a high-born woman to wife. Rumor has it he wants a child bride—one he can mold to his liking. How typical of him." Lifting her chin, she added, "At least he won't get his way in that."

Just when Marjorie thought she'd taken the worst blow, Rowena fired off another direct hit. Her pride staggering, Marjorie struggled for balance and logic. Blake Chesterfield was many things, but typical was none of them. He was so very special, she cringed when she considered he might wed someone else.

"Have you nothing to say for yourself?" demanded Rowena. "And don't bother defending him, for I don't wish to hear you chirping his praises."

That did it. For too many years Marjorie had made excuses for such hurtful remarks. She wasn't a bad person. She had scrimped and scraped to offer shelter and promise to the postboys and a comfortable living to Rowena. At least the boys appreciated the effort. "I have plenty to say."

Rowena's brows went up. "That jaunt to London has made you bold."

Marjorie shook her head. The journey to London had made her tired and sore. Grandmama's treachery had made her see reason. "When did you change your mind about the betrothal to Lord Blake? Before or after you undermined my jaunt to London?"

Grandmama seemed enthralled by her pearl necklace. At length she said, "Considering your advanced age, his is the best offer you're likely to receive. What difference does it make when I decided to give you my blessing?"

Marjorie saw red. "Save your cruel blessings and worthless words of wisdom. I've had enough of both of them. Just answer the question."

"Me? Cruel?" Rowena stammered. "I'm the one who loves you, the one who rescued you from that awful convent and opened my home to you."

Love, Marjorie thought, wears strange faces. "Thank you for fetching me from Tournai, Rowena, and offering me shelter in my father's home. You lied about owning Hartsung Square, too."

"You know so much, don't you?" Her voice vibrated with rage. "A rundown mansion is small payment for the life of my daughter."

Feeling like a puppet hung up for the night, Marjorie turned on wooden legs and headed for the door.

"I made you the postmistress of Bath," Rowena shouted.

"You were the figurehead, Grandmama. I did the work."

"That's not so. I covered up all of your childish mistakes."

In the mirrored corridor Marjorie stopped. Dozens of faces stared back at her, and in each pair of blue eyes she saw a forlorn soul in desperate need of a friend. Where, she wondered, will I ever find one?

"I sacrificed for you. I gave you everything, child."

The harsh words ignited a fire in Marjorie. "But not without a heavy price, Grandmama. I refuse to pay it any longer."

"You think you would have fared better with your father?"

Still staring at her own likeness, Marjorie detected a change—a glimmer of hope. And like the elusive answer to a nagging question, she found her friend in the most rewarding of places: within herself. "Hold your head high," the images seemed to say.

Pride swelled within her.

Rowena rapped her cane. The dog yelped. "Your father's a scoundrel, I tell you."

Marjorie turned and faced her Grandmama and the whimpering terrier. "Tell him yourself. He arrives on Friday."

"What? Why didn't you tell me?" Her face a mask of fury, Rowena yanked on the bell cord. "You ungrateful chit."

Bruised and battered, Marjorie turned and took the first healing step to recovery. Smiling, she passed through a gauntlet of cheering self-images.

By the time she reached her room hope surged through her. Someday she would forgive Rowena, but for now Marjorie wanted to put distance between herself and her grandmother. That seemed the most prudent solution.

With the help of the postboys she moved her belongings to an upstairs guest room. That done, she faced her problems.

The postal surveyor had received her bid, and though he could not commit to the outcome of the bidding, he had been duly impressed by the well-sprung coach bearing the fancy crest with the words *Aquae Sulis.* She thought of Blake. Longing squeezed her heart—longing and concern, because time had almost run out for the Chesterfield heir.

Her father would arrive on Friday. What was Blake feeling? She wanted to rush into his arms and tell him not to worry. She couldn't; not until he told her the truth. She wanted to ask how he felt about his mother's arrival in Bath.

Confusion set in.

Then she remembered Beau's good advice. She

sorted through her problems and addressed the ones she could solve.

First she must apologize to the duchess of Enderley. On the stationery of the postmistress of Bath she penned a note to Blake's mother and asked Cumber to deliver it. He returned with an invitation for Lady Marjorie Entwhistle to dine that evening with the duchess of Enderley.

At nine o'clock sharp the Bath mail coach, now cleaned and polished, rolled to a stop at the finest address in Brimley Circle, the home the duchess of Enderley had acquired for her stay in Bath.

Marjorie smoothed the folds of her black velvet overskirt and wished she'd had the extra money for a new dress or a more fashionable wig. Immediately she felt guilty. Squandering precious coin on adornments was a vanity she could neither afford nor justify. She was simply nervous about meeting Blake's mother.

Out of habit she brushed a gloved hand over the padded seat of the coach. She'd selected undyed leather for durability and varnished oak for charm. The coach was luxurious in its simplicity, and she didn't have to worry about cushions fading or lacquer chipping. The one amenity she'd chosen had been extra lamps with opaque white glass. Barring accident and vandalism, and even with constant use, the coach would last a decade.

Cumber opened the door and pulled down the steps. He stood on tiptoe, one hand behind his back, the other extended to Marjorie. Swelling with pride, she ducked and let him help her from the coach.

"Shall we wait for you, my lady?"

Looking down into his eager face, she considered how empty her life would have been without him and the other boys. "Thank you, no, Mr. Stokes. You have lessons, and Tug needs rest. Come back for me at eleven."

He bowed, marched up the steps, and rapped with the knocker. Marjorie followed. A bulbous-nosed butler in Chesterfield livery opened the door.

Much too loudly Cumber said, "Lady Marjorie Entwhistle, the postmistress of Bath, to see Her Grace, the duchess of—" His eyes grew wide and he whipped his head to Marjorie.

She mouthed, "En-der-ley."

He faced the butler again and pronounced the name correctly.

His mouth quirking with suppressed laughter, the butler said, "A very admirable presentation, my good man." To Marjorie he said, "Please come in, my lady. Her Grace is expecting you."

As she glided past Cumber, Marjorie gave him a wink. He rolled his eyes and dashed away.

The butler took her cloak and gloves, then led the way down a wide marble corridor lined with palms in brass pots as big as pickling barrels. She followed him into a lush drawing room. The fancy couches and ornate furnishings faded when she spied the duchess of Enderley rising gracefully from her chair.

As the butler announced her Marjorie studied the woman who'd given birth to Blake Chesterfield. Even with the fashionable wig the top of Jane's head barely reached Marjorie's shoulder. Her skin had the soft glow and hue of a cameo held up to the sun. She didn't paint her face; on that Marjorie would wager a team of carriage horses.

The duchess of Enderley nodded and waved a hand, adorned with a smaller version of Blake's emerald signet ring, toward a chair. "How do you do, Lady Marjorie? Won't you have a seat?"

"Thank you, Your Grace." Marjorie curtsied, then sat.

"You may pour the sherry, Farnsworth."

Silently the butler poured, served the drinks, then left.

Marjorie swallowed back a knot of awe and envy; she'd heard of the Chesterfield jewels. What surprised her was that rumor hadn't exaggerated the magnificence of the walnut-size emeralds circling Jane's neck. The artful way the duchess touched a fingernail to the heavy gold mounting was poetry itself.

Her mouth dry, Marjorie held up her glass and said, "Long live the king."

Surprise rounded the duchess's mouth into a perfect circle. She echoed the toast.

Marjorie wanted to down the sherry in one drink but didn't. She sipped, then cleared her throat. "I'm dreadfully sorry, Your Grace, for the way I was dressed this afternoon. I assure you 'tis not my habit to wear boys' clothing."

Jane stared into her drink, her hazel eyes revealing nothing. "Blake told me you were blunt—a quality he unfortunately admires."

Another apology sprang to Marjorie's tongue, but she repressed it. The episode had been the result of an accident, and she wouldn't humble herself over events beyond her control. "Thank you for telling me about Lord Blake's preferences. I merely thought to clear the air between you and me."

"Rather you did," she murmured. "Now tell me about yourself, and how a gently bred woman comes to such an . . . unfeminine occupation."

How dare she condemn Marjorie for being frank, and then deliver so blatant an insult? Out of loyalty to Blake, Marjorie let the remark pass. "I'm surprised someone of your stature would think my occupation strange. Why, surely you've heard of the late Lady Wells, the postmistress of Aberdeen?"

Clearly she had not, for the duchess blinked in surprise. "The duke of Enderley fishes in Scotland."

Marjorie followed the conversational detour with "How interesting. What does he catch?"

"I'm sure I don't know. Some dreary sort of fish, I suppose."

Marjorie was saved a reply when the butler announced dinner. All through the meal she listened to Blake's mother expound the importance of her family and the endless duties her position required. When they adjourned to the drawing room again and sipped glasses of sherry, Marjorie sneezed to cover a yawn.

During a lull in the duchess's accomplishments Marjorie said, "My grandmother sends you her best."

Jane went back to studying her bracelet. "Such a delightful companion. I do so look forward to her move to London. She'll be quite in the main."

"She's coming to visit you?"

Blake's mother waved a hand. Emeralds glittered in the lamp light. "Goodness no. Blake's agreed to buy her a house there and give her an allowance."

So that's why Grandmama approved of the marriage. Had Blake volunteered his generosity, or had Rowena begun practicing blackmail herself? Either way the move to London would prevent interference from Rowena. Relieved, Marjorie said, "Do you know how Blake and I came to be betrothed?"

She laughed, a tinkling sound that hurt the ears. "What a silly question. The normal way, of course. He approached your father and made an offer for you."

Marjorie rolled the stem of her glass between her thumb and forefinger. Prisms of light showered her black skirt. "My father is not my guardian. The king is."

"Oh, well, that explains it." Jane again performed the graceful gesture of touching her necklace. "Blake went to the king. They're very close, you know. Of course, my family, the Cholmondeleys, are in great favor with His Majesty, too. We've always been in the main."

"Blake did not go to the king, and even if he had, it wouldn't have mattered. I can choose my own husband."

Eyeing Marjorie as if she were a reptile, the duchess said, "How thoroughly common of you."

Marjorie remembered what Jane had said to Blake. The devil left you on the doorstep of Chesterwood What a cold-hearted witch she is, thought Marjorie. "Be that as it may, you haven't answered my question."

"I thought—oh, I'm dreadfully confused. However, then, did the match come about?" Her finely shaped brows rose in suspicion. "Have you tricked my son?"

Marjorie took a deep breath. "No, Your Grace. My father is blackmailing Blake. I had hoped you would tell me why."

"Blackmail? That's ridiculous. Blake has more money than he could ever spend. He pays his debts."

Marjorie said, "I don't think money is at the root of my father's extortion. He knows a secret about Blake."

Jane's face went pale. The glass slipped from her hand and fell to the carpet. "Sweet Saint George," she breathed. "He must have discovered—"

"Discovered what, Your Grace?" Marjorie entreated. "What does my father know about Blake?"

The duchess's hand flew to her forehead. "'Tis too awful. If anyone finds out . . ."

Fear pushed Marjorie from her chair. Her heart hammering, she knelt beside the duchess. "Finds out what, Your Grace? You must tell me."

Haunted hazel eyes met Marjorie's. "I always feared this would happen. How could Blake have been so careless? He knows better than to risk anyone discovering . . . Oh," she wailed, "the damage it could cause."

"What is *it?*" Marjorie said, grinding her teeth.

In a trancelike stupor the duchess stared at her hands. "You can't imagine the shame the Chesterfields will suffer. I'll have to move to the country—forever. We'll be ruined!"

As Marjorie's frustration mounted her patience fled. Finally she said, "My father will spread Blake's secret like the plague if I don't marry him. I will not unless you tell me what he's done."

Jane folded perfect teeth over her bottom lip. Her chest quivered with suppressed tears. "I knew he'd make a slip someday. His father thought the sea was the best place for someone of his kind." With icy hands she clutched Marjorie's arm. All pretense of arrogance vanished from her face. "You must marry him. Oh, please say you will. I'll pay you anything. Name a sum."

"Mother!" Blake bellowed from behind Marjorie. "Control yourself."

Jane wilted in the chair, but her eyes rained cold contempt on her son.

Marjorie's heart felt like a lead weight in her breast. Poor, poor Blake. Unable to face him, she stared at the spilled glass of sherry, her mind a merry-go-round of shocking possibilities.

His hand touched her arm. The shiny tips of his boots filled her vision. Without looking up she said, "I'll marry you, Blake."

He spat a curse that made his mother gasp, then turned and fled the room, slamming the door behind him.

Marjorie called on him the next morning, but Everson informed her that Commodore Lord Blake Chesterfield was dead drunk and unavailable.

Marjorie despaired. Through a haze of gloom she

heard the bells of the Abbey Church ring out. Fear that her father had arrived early blossomed to joy at the sight of Beau Nash. But the king of Bath returned in defeat. Parliament had outlawed gambling. Faro, whist, and other card games using numbers were now illegal.

As bankruptcy loomed on the horizon, the ancient city of Bath fell into stunned silence.

When Blake remained unavailable Marjorie grew frantic, for in forty-eight hours her father would arrive in Bath.

CHAPTER 15

*Men of no character, battered old rakes and
prideful young ones, are an indelible blemish on
the fair face of Bath.*

—Beau Nash, *Rules of Bath*

BY FRIDAY MORNING MARJORIE JUMPED AT EVERY NOISE
and constantly looked over her shoulder. Her neck
ached; her stomach pitched. The silence of the church
bells mocked her anxiety.

Where was Papa?

One moment she doubled her fists and demanded
that he come and put an end to her torture. The next
moment she prayed he'd never set foot in Bath.

Unable to sit still, she marched downstairs and
began sorting the mail. She tossed London letters in
the Edinburgh slot; she sent local packages to Bristol.

Cumber straightened out the mess, then offered to
make her morning rounds. She declined, hoping
against hope that Blake would see her.

He refused. She asked Everson to bring her the
betrothal. He did, and she signed it.

"I'm sorry he won't see you."

Tears pricked her eyes. She'd helped Shelbourne

and the others by giving them money. Scratching her name on a worthless piece of paper seemed a small task in order to aid Blake Chesterfield. "He can't hold me to this betrothal, but if my father sees it, it will buy Blake some time. Perhaps when he comes to his senses he'll talk to me."

"I'm certain he will."

Dejected, she walked back to Hartsung Square. Just as she climbed the steps to the back door the bells of the Abbey Church rang out. Each toll hit her like a blow. Had Papa arrived? Reeling, she raced through the mews to Bristol Road. Just as she rounded the corner the pealing stopped. A moment later Milo Magrath rode past on a pure white horse. Her throat felt as dry as autumn leaves. She stepped back.

A gold and white carriage came into view. Pulled by six lathered bays and outfitted with fluttering banners, the conveyance rolled into Bath. Inside the coach sat a single passenger.

Papa.

Her heart plunged into her stomach. She wanted to close her eyes; pride and curiosity wouldn't let her. Pressing herself against the brick wall of Clarke's Mercantile, she strained for a glimpse of his face. She wondered if she'd recognize him after fourteen years. The brim of his hat shielded his features.

She wanted to race after the carriage. Instead she ran back to Hartsung Square, saddled her horse, and escaped to Bath quarry.

Beau was standing in the stable yard when she returned, his white hat in his hand, his long face pulled into a frown.

Cumber stabled the horse. Marjorie approached Beau.

"Where is he?" she asked.

"He's taken a house in Chamberlain Close."

Beau offered his hand. Marjorie grasped it and felt

his strength flow through her. "You're so good to me, Beau. I can't imagine what I've done to deserve your friendship."

Glancing up at her, he said, "Bother it. You deserve much more than an old gamester with no games to play."

For days her thoughts had vacillated from the impending arrival of her father to the imminent downfall of her lover. What would Blake do?

Heartache and indecision plagued her.

"Cheer up," Beau said. "Things could get worse."

She laughed without humor. "I don't see how," she said, "unless the baths run dry."

He groaned. "Don't even say it. Without revenue from the card tables at Wiltshire's and Simpson's I can stash the treasury in a snuffbox. Our straits are dire in *Aquae Sulis.*"

She'd been so wrapped up in her own troubles, she'd forgotten the plight of her champion. "What will you do?"

Looking like a man with the answer to a riddle, he grinned and twirled his hat on his index finger. "Offer me a glass of brandy, and I'll tell you about my enormously clever plan to circumvent the Gaming Act—legally, of course."

They walked into the mansion and to the Hamburg room, which was empty owing to Rowena's constant attendance on her new confidante, the duchess of Enderley. They deserve each other, thought Marjorie as she served the drinks.

Beau studied the Hogarth. "I look like a pompous headmaster or a foolish old man, don't I?"

"You couldn't look foolish if you wore red satin and peacock feathers."

"And you question why I value our friendship?" He laughed. From his pocket he pulled out a sheet of parchment. Unfurling it, he revealed a broadside. A horn decorated the top of the page.

"This is how I intend to open the gaming tables . . . and stay out of jail."

Blake glanced at the summons, then handed it back to Everson.

"How shall I reply?" the valet asked.

Squeezing his eyes shut, Blake fought the panic that iced his bowels and crushed his pride. "Tell him I'll be there, but I don't imagine I could swallow a bit of food without choking."

"I know," said Everson. "But at least it's lunch, rather than a long-drawn-out dinner."

Blake picked up the quill and twirled it until the feather became a white blur. "That means I just have tonight and tomorrow morning to think about facing him. Where is he staying?"

"In Chamberlain Close. We could walk from here."

Blake inked the quill, then sketched a hangman's noose. "I'll go alone."

Everson sat on the edge of the desk and grasped Blake's wrist. "I beg you, my lord." His voice wavered. "Please change your mind about talking to Lady Marjorie."

An ache of loneliness throbbed within Blake. "One Entwhistle at a time in my life is plenty."

"Lady Marjorie's the one you want."

Jerking his hand away, Blake scratched a broken heart on the blotter. "But she's the one I can't have."

"What will you say to her father?"

"What can I say? I'll show him the betrothal and send him to Marjorie. He's been cruel to her all her life. I just hope he doesn't hurt her too much this time."

Sweat beaded Everson's brow. "I wish I could help you, my lord."

"No one can help me, Everson." He stabbed the quill so hard, the nib snapped. Ink splattered his fingers. "You of all people should know that."

At noon the next day Blake arrived at number six Chamberlain Close. A spring breeze rife with the smells of budding trees and freshly turned earth filled the air. Patches of billowy clouds paraded across a sky the color of Marjorie's eyes.

Blake's heart beat faster than a drumroll before an execution. The morbid irony stung. Why couldn't he have been an ignorant blacksmith? Then he could tell George Entwhistle to take what he knew and run it up a bloody flagpole. Blake would take Marjorie, retire to his forge, and hammer out horseshoes. He and Marjorie would make beautiful baby girls who all looked like her.

His palms were slick with sweat. He shoved his hand into his pocket and felt the betrothal. Although he knew the document offered only a temporary reprieve, he felt better just touching it. He grew warm inside at the sentiment. Marjorie had been willing to brave her father's wrath to save her lover's hide. Even if he could hold her to the agreement, he wouldn't. He'd find another way.

That decided, he found his handkerchief. Spying the familiar chevron embroidered on the silk cloth, he sighed.

Family honor, he thought, is too heavy a burden to bear. Especially if the bearer isn't up to the task. He thought of his favorite ancestor, then dropped his head in shame; he didn't deserve so mighty a forebear as the Black Prince.

Ready to meet his master, Blake grasped the knocker and rapped on the door.

Milo Magrath answered. "Good day, my lord." He stepped back and waved Blake inside. "I'll take you to him."

On stiff legs Blake followed the herald up a flight of carpeted stairs and into a sitting room furnished in shades of blue, white, and gold. Heavenly colors, he observed, for the lair of a devil.

George Entwhistle stood before a bank of windows, his slight form dwarfed by a furlong of drapery. He turned and flashed a confident smile, his thin lips disappearing in a face too wide for a man so small. "Come in, come in, Blake. Sit down," he said, indicating a pair of straight-back chairs covered in blue velvet.

Fighting back a shiver of revulsion, Blake sat. He sought the one topic they had in common. "Have you seen Marjorie?"

"Milo," said Entwhistle, "pour Lord Blake a glass of the burgundy. Quite the finest red wine in all of France, but then you and I shared a bottle during our first meeting, didn't we?"

Blake took the glass and drank. Even if he despised the man across from him, the wine was the best he'd ever tasted. "It has excellent body."

George slid open the drawer of the lamp table and pulled out a piece of paper. "Nash's *Rules of Bath.*"

Uneasiness made Blake shift in the chair. "I'm familiar with them."

George paused in his perusal of the list. "He sounds like a potentate issuing royal commands. And look here." He withdrew another page. "You might be interested in this."

Blake took the paper, illuminated with a horn. He put it in his pocket.

"Not interested?" said George.

Don't get angry, Blake told himself. "I'm more

interested in why you didn't reply when I asked if you'd seen Marjorie."

"I'm sure you are." George held the glass up to the light, his watery blue eyes narrowing as he scrutinized the wine. "The question is, how much of her have *you* seen? A grandchild was part of our bargain."

At the crude words Blake almost choked. "Really, George. She's your daughter."

George's eyes took on a faraway look. "Milo says she favors her mother's side of the family."

The wine in Blake's mouth grew bitter at the thought of Rowena. She'd passed on her elegant appearance and stately height to Marjorie, but nothing else except trouble and heartache.

Looking for some resemblance to Marjorie, Blake studied George's weak blue eyes and small frame. Surly George was as different from vibrant Marjorie as truth from a lie.

Disgusted, Blake said, "Go see her and find out for yourself. I'll even arrange it."

"What's this?" George scoffed. "Are you offering to keep my social calendar?"

Blake's hand shook. The wine sloshed in the glass. He wanted to offer Marjorie his support when she faced her father.

"Fancy that," George went on, "the high and mighty Chesterfield heir stooping to a clerk's task." He tossed down the remainder of his wine, then licked his lips. "But then, I'm certain you'll do many things for me, Lord Blake. Unfortunately, becoming my secretary isn't one of them."

Blake felt like a fly caught in a web that vibrated with the approach of a hungry spider.

"I've heard some disturbing rumors about my daughter since I arrived in Bath," said George. "There's talk of past misfortunes and reckless youth."

Blake's hackles rose. How dare this despicable wretch be so blasé about his own daughter? "Considering the misery you've put her through over the years, why are you surprised?"

George leaned forward. He squinted thick-lidded eyes. "I expect you've put an end to her misery, then. Am I correct?"

Damning himself for a coward, Blake said, "She's signed the betrothal."

George jerked. "Splendid!" He pounded his fist on the arm of the chair. "Wait. I don't trust you. Where is it?"

Blake pulled the document from his pocket. "Here."

George uncrossed his legs and spread the parchment over his thighs. He eyed the signature closely. "Splendid work, my man." He laughed. "Or should I say my son? We'll set the date for a fortnight from now."

"*We* won't set any date," said Blake. "That's for you and Marjorie to discuss."

Later that night Blake stood in Marjorie's room and stared at her empty bed. She'd probably gone to Bristol or to London, or anywhere else she damn well pleased. Better hell than here, he thought.

Guilt tied his gut into knots. She shouldn't be hemmed in by the same boundaries as he; she was stouthearted and affectionate. She didn't need to put on a brave face to get by in the world. She was forthright and confident. She was George's daughter.

Sympathy filled him. She deserved a loving man for a father. She deserved an honorable man for a husband.

She'd offered to sign the betrothal out of pity. For that reason alone he intended to tell her the truth.

She should know the kind of man she'd agreed to wed.

Resignation seeped into his soul. He grasped the bedpost and laid his forehead against the cool wood. Recriminations flashed like summer lightning in his mind. He should never have ordered the *Reliant* to Calais. He should never have visited the vineyard of George Entwhistle.

Oh, God, he thought, pressing his head against the bedpost, why didn't I look over my shoulder before speaking so freely to Everson? How could I have been so stupid as to blurt out the truth?

Blake could still picture the gleeful expression on Entwhistle's face. From that moment on Blake's life had changed. He no longer controlled his own destiny. Like a slave, he'd hurried back to the *Reliant*, then raced to Bath to do George's bidding.

What Blake hadn't counted on was finding the love of his life.

A faint light spread over the floor. Blake whirled.

Wearing a wrinkled nightshirt, his feet bare, a lighted candle in his hand, Tug stepped into the room.

"Is that you, Commodore?"

"Aye, 'tis me, Tug."

"What are you doing here?"

On a half laugh, Blake said, "Talking to myself. Looking for Lady Marjorie."

Tug held the light higher. The flame illuminated his sleep-mussed hair. "She's been coming 'round to see you, but that valet of yours said you were incapacitated."

Blake couldn't help but ask, "Did she teach you that word?"

"Yes, my lord," he said, his chin in the air. "I couldn't read or write when I came here. She says an illiterate is no better than a slave. She gave me a rich man's education."

Envy nipped at Blake's good intentions; this lad and the others had enjoyed years of Marjorie's attention and affection. Blake's time with her had been so short. What would she do when he told her?

Tug stepped back. "Nothing else bad'll befall her," he said. "Not if I can help it."

Such loyalty, thought Blake, couldn't be bought, not for all the Chesterfield gems. "She's very special, isn't she?"

"Yes, my lord, and the sheriff of Wells can throw me in the quod if she doesn't deserve a man as good as you."

Quietly Blake said, "Where is she?"

Tug's young-old face puckered. "She's been awful put-upon lately. You know about the first run of the mail coach?"

The story of Rowena's treachery had brought Blake out of his stupor. "Peddicord told me," he said.

Tug scowled. "The old witch ought to rot in hell. Mr. Peddicord could've lost his foot."

"I'd love to send her there. And don't worry about Peddicord. He's on the mend."

Staring at his feet, Tug said, "Her father's come to Bath, and he hasn't bothered to call on her. Rascally Frenchman."

Blake's head grew light. "I know. England's better off without him."

Cocking his head to the side, Tug said, "I remember what you said about Lady Marjorie having a daughter of her own."

Blake's eyes smarted with tears. "She'd be a beauty, don't you think?"

A proud smile wreathed Tug's face. "A peach. And I think a child would make Lady Marjorie happy."

Dashed hopes flickered to life. "Where is she?"

The lad looked away, but his intelligent brown eyes

showed indecision. A long moment later he said, "In the guest room next to her office."

When Blake headed for the door Tug said, "She ain't seen her sodded father since she was my age."

At the mention of George Entwhistle Blake's stomach roiled.

"You sick, my lord?"

The old Chesterfield arrogance infused Blake. He blew out his breath and said, "No, Tug. I'm fitter, I think, than I've been in a long time." He hoped it was true. He hoped he was doing the right thing. "Go back to bed, lad."

Blake lost his way twice in the dark corridors. When he did reach the right chamber he eased open the door and tiptoed inside. She sat against a nest of pillows in bed, lamplight haloing her.

"Hello, Blake," she said, a bittersweet smile on her face, a book in her hands. "How nice to see you making social calls again."

His courage plummeted. He felt like a country bumpkin standing at the gates to Fenchurch Fair. Admission was tuppence; he had only a penny to his name.

"I came to apologize for being a selfish troll."

As if she hadn't heard the jest, she said, "As Tug would say, that's aright. 'Tis not necessary." She turned her attention to the book. "Good night."

He'd expected anger, but her indifference cut him to the core. Her appearance had the opposite effect on him. The sight of her in a prim white nightgown turned his blood to fire. Her thick, golden braid draped the pillows and mattress and dangled an inch off the floor.

She set aside the book, folded her arms across her breasts, and leaned back against the pillow. Heaving a sigh, she said, "Are you going to tell me what you want, or will you stand there looking like a highway-man who's lost his horse?"

After days of cursing himself to hell and an afternoon with the devil himself, Blake was unaffected by her sarcasm. "When I found your old room empty I thought you'd run away."

A charming, crooked smile lent a girlish quality to her overtly feminine form. "I couldn't, even if I wanted to."

He walked to the bed and sat. She tried to scoot away, but her gown was trapped beneath his weight. "Blake," she entreated.

Stalling, he glanced at the stuccoed ceiling bearing a motif of leafy vines and bunches of grapes. A wardrobe as tall as he and a standing mirror filled one wall; curtained windows filled another. The Hogarth painting rested on its side on the floor in the corner. Why had she taken it from the Hamburg room?

He had noticed during his midnight forays that she kept no family portraits or mementos. He saw none here, either.

Thinking of the centuries' worth of Chesterfield artifacts his family possessed, he said, "In some ways, we're very different, you know."

She traced the binding of the book. "Are you ruminating or working up to something?"

Her frankness made him smile. "You once said my family was vital to the fabric of England." He couldn't resist running his hand over her braid. "I think you're indispensable to Bath."

She lifted one shoulder. "Hardly. Tobias will probably outbid me. Let go of my hair."

Blake's own troubles had seemed so insurmountable, he'd forgotten hers. With absolute certainty he said, "I don't think he'll ever be the postmaster of Bath, and I can promise he won't bother you again."

Her eyes sparkled with determination. "Thank you for getting all of the drawings back. But don't worry over Tobias. I dealt with him before you came. I'll deal with him after you're gone. Now if that's all you have to say, I'm really quite exhausted."

Blake felt mired in a swamp of regret. He'd been strolling along the perimeter of her life, always observing, never truly seeking entrance. Now he wanted in. "I gave your father the betrothal today."

Vulnerability surrounded her. She eased lower in the bed. "What did he say?"

Blake couldn't bring himself to repeat the vulgar speech of George Entwhistle. "He's delighted."

Eyes as blue as the Mediterranean Sea fixed on his. "He also knows something about you that I don't," she said.

He kissed good-bye any chance of happiness with her and said, "Not for long, for I'm about to tell you."

Marjorie braced herself. Seven hundred years of Chesterfield pride was about to be ripped away.

He looked forlorn, his great shoulders slumped, his distinctive brow lowered. Her fingertips prickled with the need to reach out and touch him. Whatever he was about to tell her frightened him as death terrifies the condemned. He'd even worn black for the occasion. But to her, the glossy sheen of his silk shirt and the smooth texture of his leather breeches and vest magnified his masculinity and testified to his strength.

"Blake," she said, "you're not the only one with a secret. Don't you ever wonder why I never go into the gaming room?"

"Why don't you?"

The past rose up to meet her. "Because when I came to Bath I was shallow and lonely. I drank too much wine, and I gambled stupidly. I lost all of my mother's jewels to Tobias."

"That's why he enshrined that backgammon board."

"Yes."

"And why you only wear ribbons around your neck."

"That, too. Now you know the truth about me."

She waited.

He opened his mouth and closed it. Then he lifted a shaking hand, looked at his emerald signet ring, and sighed.

Profound love infused her. Desperate to end his torture, she offered him her hand by placing it palm up on the book. Haunted green eyes, as intriguing as a secluded forest, followed her movement. With his thumb and forefinger he slid the book free and cradled it like a Psalter in his hands.

Their eyes met—hers entreating, his glassy with tears. Her heart constricted. She mouthed the words "Tell me."

"I can't read."

She sat frozen—spellbound by shock and by his abject misery. "Oh, Blake." She reached for him.

He dropped the book, put up his hands and sprang to his feet. "Don't. I neither want nor need your sympathy. Your cooperation in freeing me from your father will suffice."

He'd never sat under a tree on a warm summer day and lost himself in a book. He'd missed the thrill of reading the words of the ancients. "Oh, Blake, you can't mean it."

He looked away. "I can't expect you to understand. Only Everson does."

Through a fog of confusion she said, "But you cipher better than I, and you draw beautifully."

"True, numbers are easy for me, or lines that make a picture, but letters are a jumble of hen scratching. An illiterate is no better than a slave, remember?"

Her mind whirled. "You're the most important man in the king's navy. How did you manage an illustrious career without—"

"Being literate? One doesn't have to read to command men and sink enemy ships."

"How did you survive Eton and Cambridge?"

He rocked back on his heels and stared at the ceiling. "With Everson's help."

No wonder he and Everson were more like father and son than nobleman and servant. "Surely the teachers—"

"No one would dare fail a Chesterfield."

"You took the easy way out, but I won't let you again. I'll teach you, Blake."

He came back to the bed and took her hands. "It's more than just letters, Marjorie. Something's wrong with me." He reached into his shirt and pulled out the compass. "I can't tell north from south—not without this. I can't even read the face of a clock."

She wrung her hands and considered her options. She spent her life solving problems. Was she equal to this one? Yes! "You need spectacles. That's all."

He shook his head. "Please," he said, looking like the Chesterfield he was and not the illiterate he claimed to be, "give me some credit for sense. I can kill a stag with a bow and arrow at one hundred yards. And I can thread your needle as quick as that." He snapped his fingers. "There's nothing wrong with my vision."

"Have you seen a doctor?"

"Indirectly, yes."

"Everson saw a doctor."

"Yes again."

"Give me a minute to think."

"Marjorie," he lamented, "you can't help me."

That sparked her determination. She stuck out her chin and said, "For over six years people have said I couldn't manage the post." She leaned so close to him, her mouth watered at the scent of citrus. "First they said the mail carriers would steal me blind. They were correct. But I found a solution."

He smiled. "Tug and the lads."

She swallowed hard. "Correct. And when I bid for the Bristol package route they said it was too much work. They said I'd botch it to Wales or turn mannish."

"Mannish," he said, "you most certainly did *not* turn."

Giddy pleasure thrummed through her. "Then they said a mail coach would never succeed." He started to speak, but she cut him off. "I know, I know, we had some difficulties, but they are not insurmountable. Nothing is. So, Blake Chesterfield, don't you dare tell me what I can and cannot do."

A look of resignation smoothed out his handsome features. "Very well," he said. "But all the theories from all the great minds in the world— present company included—won't change the fact that I can't read and comprehend more than a word or two. I can't tell the time, or know exactly where I am in the world if I can't see the sun or stars, or consult my trusty compass."

When Marjorie looked back on the times they'd spent together she realized he'd given his secret away on at least a dozen occasions.

Which way is north?

If I could, I'd write you a hundred poems.

I'm not eloquent with the pen.

She hadn't known what to look for. She'd been thinking he'd stolen secrets or sired a bastard child.

"Look, Marjorie, I know what you're thinking, but it's useless."

"I was thinking," she said, "about how far off the mark my speculations were."

"Of what dastardly deed did you accuse me? The French pox? Debauchery?"

Guilt assailed her, but she couldn't lie to him. "Treason."

He winced and bowed his head until his chin touched his chest.

His agony reached out to her. Hoping to break the spell, she said, "I also thought of seduction."

"I'd rather be the willing victim than the guilty rake," he said.

Dear Blake Chesterfield. She thought of his reputation, his charm. He'd probably seduced enough wealthy and beautiful women to fill Bath. What allure could a past-her-prime postmistress and her spiteful relatives hold for him?

None. Except she could teach him to read. "You'll be the student. I'll be the teacher."

"Nobody can teach me. It's useless."

"We'd be outsmarting my father."

Blake would be free to find his princess. Marjorie would be the postmistress of Bath.

The tidy solutions brought her no joy, but she'd learned long ago that happiness was not a requirement of society or a new dress. Happiness was waking each day with pride in her heart and purpose in her life.

"Don't worry," he said. "It's truly not that important. I'll do something—go to the king."

He sounded so defeated. "Are you daring me?" she said.

"Not intentionally."

"Stay right where you are." She jumped from the bed and fetched pencil and paper. When she returned she sat cross-legged, her gown bunching above her knees.

He stared at her legs, his eyes alight with interest. She cleared her throat. He looked up. Grinning sheepishly, he said, "Well, what do you expect from a man accused of seduction?"

"You're the willing victim, remember?" she said. "I'd like your attention, please."

He leveled her a smoldering gaze. "You've got it, sweetheart."

Warmth flowed through her. "That's not the sort of attention I had in mind." She printed all of the vowels in the alphabet, then the consonants. "What do you see?" she asked.

Sliding the paper back to her, he said, "I've tried this before with Everson. It won't work."

"Humor me." She pointed to the "A."

"I see the nose of a canoe."

Confused, she said, "What's a canoe?"

"A small boat." He took the pencil and, by adding a few lines, sketched a boat that was pointed at each end.

She indicated the "E." "Now this one."

He glanced at the letter. "That's easy. 'Tis a pitchfork on its side."

"Print the word 'ship,' " she said.

He curled his fingers around the pencil. She thought of how effortlessly and perfectly he drew pictures and people.

He handed her the paper. "Is it right?"

She tapped her teeth together. The "S" was upside down. "Not exactly."

"See? I told you I couldn't do it. It never comes out right."

Discounting poor vision, she set about learning how his mind worked and discovered that while he could draw a ship to perfection, and say the word "ship" in six languages, he couldn't associate the letters with the sound or the image.

When some of the letters he drew appeared backward she held the paper to a mirror, thinking he might better comprehend the words and thus copy them correctly onto the paper.

He squinted and strained to complete the exercise. The contradiction of him baffled her; hunched over the paper, he seemed so endearingly young, like the postboys during lessons. But the similarity stopped there, for when she thought of the man her heart beat faster, and the woman inside her came scandalously to life. Blake Chesterfield possessed manliness to spare.

The years of frustration had robbed him of patience.

"That's it." He threw his hands in the air. The pencil went flying into the wardrobe; the mirror crashed to the floor. "I quit. I'll never learn." He marched out the door.

Twenty minutes later Marjorie barged into his suite at Cleveland's, a dictionary in her hand, a slate board under her arm. "I've been thinking," she said. "Maybe we're using the wrong tools."

His eyes gleamed with apology and hope. "And I've been thinking about how sorry I am for losing my patience."

Gliding toward him, she said, "Bother it. We've work to do."

He grinned and stared at the bed. "I could spend an hour or two begging your forgiveness. That involves work—of a kind."

She put on her sternest schoolteacher expression and handed him the slate. "No. Here. Write a word."

"What word?"

"Any word."

Rolling his eyes, he said, "I have so many to choose from."

She tapped the slate. "Just do it."

He wrote the word "lips." He left out the "I" and the "S" was backward.

She wiped the slate clean and spelled the word correctly. "Say the word, Blake."

He did, and with such blatant sensuality that her own lips went dry. Fighting back the tide of desire that dragged at her belly, she took his hand and said, "Spell the word this time, but trace each letter as you pronounce it."

"Why?"

Breathlessly, she said, "So you can connect the sound of the letter with its appearance."

He blinked, and the mind behind the glorious green eyes grasped the principle. He slapped his leather-clad thigh. "That's what I've never been able to do. You're brilliant, Marjorie."

Unable to offer him false hope, she said, "It's only a theory. We can't be certain it'll work."

"I know." He gave her a quick kiss on the lips. "And even if I can't learn this way, thank you for caring enough to try and help me."

"You're welcome. Now do it."

Ten minutes later he declared, "Now that I've mastered the lips, let's make up an entire alphabet."

They did, but rather than using childish words such as dog and cat and ship they created a lovers' alphabet. He asked her to write the word "breast."

He spelled the word while tracing the letters. Then his hand caressed her breast. "This visual exercise is working marvelously. Don't you think, sweetheart?"

The lesson was succeeding on two counts: Blake was learning to read; Marjorie was burning with desire.

"Let's go back to the start," he murmured. "I'm anxious to see if I remember the lips."

She knew his willingness had nothing to do with the lesson. He wanted her. She wanted him. But she couldn't risk conceiving his child. "That's enough for tonight. Wick arrives in the morning with the Bristol mail."

Leaving him the book and slate, she returned to Hartsung Square and her lonely room.

Twenty minutes later he strolled into her chamber, a broad grin on his face, a bottle of wine under his arm. "We *were* using the wrong tools."

She leapt from the bed and into his arms. A gesture of gratitude became a hungry embrace, then dissolved into a kiss of passion.

Blake carried her to the bed and laid her on the mattress. Through a fog of desire she watched him undress. And remembered the ladies' sponge. She thought of the consequences and considered her options.

By not protecting herself she could trick him into marriage. She'd given him the means to escape her father's blackmail. But her efforts would go for naught if she conceived his child and forced the marriage.

When he stood gloriously naked before her she excused herself to the dressing room and used the sponge.

Unfortunately, he discovered it a few moments later.

Eyes blazing, he said, "I see I'm not the only one who's learned a new trick."

"Why are you angry?" she asked.

The familiar arrogance returned. "I'm not," he said smoothly, and he put the sponge back where he'd found it. "You don't want this marriage any more than I do. I'm actually quite grateful, because I have a few things to teach you, and they're much more enjoyable if we don't have to worry about . . . complications. Now we can play."

She became the student, and for the next hour he shocked and thrilled her with his stamina and imagination. She lost track of the number of times he brought her to the point of rapture, and when he at last transported them both to release and cuddled her close, she lay in the circle of his arms and wept inside because she'd been right. He didn't want a child by her.

Yet he did want to sleep beside her at least for the night. And she took the solace he offered. Pressed warmly to him, she drifted into the sweetest sleep she'd ever known. But in the morning she woke to an empty bed and the news that her father awaited her downstairs.

CHAPTER 16

*I'm here to hinder people of rank and fortune
from doing what they've no mind to do.*

—Beau Nash, *Rules of Bath*

IN A STATE OF UNBEARABLE ANTICIPATION MARJORIE
dressed in an everyday gown and brushed and styled
her hair. Her heart felt empty, hollowed out by the sad
realization that Blake Chesterfield didn't even care
enough to say good-bye. Perversely she embraced the
pain and clutched it like a shield, for in a moment she
would face the father who'd never loved or wanted her
at all.

From somewhere she heard the faint, pitiful echo of
a lonely little girl weeping for her Papa. Out of habit
she began to soothe the child in her mind by conjuring
a towering giant of a father, his face wreathed in love,
his arms held wide in welcome.

At the fictional picture she sagged with grief. What
terrible crime had she committed to deserve so much
betrayal and heartache? First Grandmama, then
Blake, and always, always Papa.

She lay her cheek against the cold mirror. Her breath clouded the glass. She looked inward but saw no wicked soul deserving of treachery and abandonment.

Life has dealt you a bad hand of cards, Beau had told her years ago. *Will you play them as best you can, or will you bow out of the game?*

Cowards retreated. Marjorie Entwhistle was no coward.

She pinched her cheeks and started down the stairs. At every turn she encountered one of the postboys. Cumber delayed her for ten minutes seeking instructions for tasks he could perform with his eyes closed. Tug insisted on reiterating the qualities and personalities of each of the new carriage horses. Wick stopped her to talk about whether or not they should paint the Bristol mail cart a bright blue.

When Albert Honeycombe rushed toward her and said the stable cat had had kittens, she almost lost her temper.

He grasped her hand. "Oh, please come, my lady, and take a look. 'Tis the pluckiest litter yet. Besides, you always think of the best names."

Suddenly she understood what the boys were about. They were afraid for her, and in their own sweet ways they were trying to spare her the confrontation ahead.

Smiling at the orphan boy with hair as bright as carrots, she said, "Yes, I think we should name them straightaway. But first I must inform my guest that I'll be late."

"Allow me, my lady," Tug said from behind her.

She turned and spied the proud young man. As a child he had dressed in rags and lived in the mews of Lilliput Alley. Now, armed by the lessons she had taught him, he risked his life every time he headed down the Great Bath Road to London.

"Thank you, Tug."

The short excursion to the stables renewed her confidence and reminded her of her blessings. She had a good life, filled with rewarding work and people who cared for her. She was too old to need a father. She could do without a meddlesome grandmother. Would she learn to do without Blake Chesterfield?

A short time later she stood on the threshold of the Hamburg room and watched her father pace. Rowena liked to call George Entwhistle a sawed-off spirits merchant with a title as impressive as a wine cork.

Looking at the stacked heels and gold buckles on his stylish shoes, the padded gray wig, and the expensively tailored suit of pale blue velvet, Marjorie judged him a vain little man who wanted to appear big. She was surprised, though, at how young he was.

"Hello, Father," she said, looking down at the man who'd sired her.

"Good God," he said, his face frozen in shock, his eyes riveted to her face.

Taken off guard, she leaned against the cool marble of the fireplace. The hard edge of the mantel pressed into her back. She missed the security and congeniality Hogarth's painting offered. "Is something wrong?"

Surprise melted into chilly formality. "Of course not." Offhandedly, he added, "I just didn't expect you to look so much like—like Rowena's family."

"Surely Milo told you what I look like." In her own offhanded manner she added, "Thanks to your meddling, he's seen me often enough."

His puffy eyes narrowed. "It's a father's job to choose his daughter's husband."

Years of neglect lashed at her heart. "When have you ever been a father to me? I don't even know you. We haven't shared a birthday or Christmas. I've never sat down to dinner with you. The last time I saw you

you were more interested in bargaining with a cooper over wine barrels than visiting your daughter."

He suddenly became interested in the lace on his cuffs. "I'm a busy man, not some court dandy."

Thank goodness for household gossip, she thought. "According to the duchess of Enderley, you once seduced the king's mistress. That's why he threw you out of England. You forced Blake to ask the king to let you come back."

His eyes met hers, then dashed away. "A man is entitled to a reckless youth," he blustered. "And I won't be raked over by my own child."

"I am not," she said coldly, "a child—yours or anyone's. And I'll choose my own husband."

His forehead puckered. She noticed that the skin there was paler than the rest of his face, as if he often wore a hat and spent much time in the sun. Preposterous, she thought, for her father hadn't worked a day in his life. Or had he? Sadly she realized she knew next to nothing about him.

His gaze flitted over her again. "You don't like Blake Chesterfield?"

Her heart ached, but her pride spoke. "He's another of your pawns."

"Pawn or not, you'll wed him, and that's that, Marjorie."

On his lips her name sounded like a curse he was trying out for the first time. "You can't make me, even if I sign fifty betrothals. You are not my guardian. You gave away that right when you offended the king and left me at the convent."

He peeked at her. "I thought you'd be better off there."

The bruised child inside her wept. "But I was a babe. I needed my father."

He began pacing again. "I was hardly more than a

child myself at the time. My Lou—" His voice broke, and he cleared his throat. "My wife had just died. I couldn't possibly have cared for you."

Hurting, she said, "The years haven't changed your feelings, I see."

He stared at the grosgrain ribbon at her neck. She wished she had a necklace with diamonds so bright they blinded him.

"You'll marry Blake Chesterfield."

Steely resolve hardened her heart. "I will not."

"What's wrong with you? He's the best catch in England."

She considered telling him the truth, but instead she told him a lie. "I won't marry a man I don't love."

"Marrying for love is foolish. I can attest to that. I won't let you make that kind of mistake. You signed the betrothal. Are you backing out?"

Blake would overcome his difficulties. Her broken heart would mend someday. "Yes."

"You should have a wealthy husband," he declared, now engrossed in his hands, which looked callused. "Then you wouldn't have to stoop to delivering people's mail."

Marjorie had learned intimidation at the hand of a master. "I enjoy being the postmistress of Bath. And you'll be happy to know that I only deliver mail to dukes or better."

"I say you'll be the duchess of Enderley."

She sighed. "No, Father, I will not. Blake won't yield to your blackmail."

His gaze whipped to hers. "Blackmail? What are you talking about?"

"You honestly think I'm stupid enough to believe that Blake and the others came riding into Bath eager to marry me?"

His complexion mottled. "There's nothing wrong

with you. Who told you there was? Unless . . . was it Rowena? I'll throttle the bitch."

"You're changing the subject. Leave Blake Chesterfield alone."

"If he means nothing to you, why do you protect him?"

Mustering bravado, she said, "I'd protect anyone from you and your vicious games. You're just like Grandmama."

He smiled vindictively. "I'd call a man out for that insult. She's an old witch with nothing to do but make trouble."

Pain squeezed Marjorie's heart. "And raise me, thanks to you."

"Marjorie, I—" He took a step forward, his hands moving as if to embrace her. Then he stopped. "She had no one, nothing, except sad memories. She convinced me I owed—she promised she'd take good care of you."

Had Papa been manipulated by Rowena, too? Maybe so, but that didn't give him the right to use his daughter for revenge. "In her own way, she did take care of me. Now I can take care of myself."

Through clenched teeth he said, "I'll do what's best for you. You need a husband to look after you and give you children. You'll have Blake Chesterfield for a husband, or the entire world will have Blake Chesterfield on a platter."

Suddenly alert, she said, "I might have expected something like that from you."

"You sound just like Rowena."

"How nice of you to notice."

He withdrew one of Beau's latest broadsides. "Just be at Wiltshire's, and you'll see if I'm not serious about finding you the best husband in England. You have no business living under the same roof with your grandmother."

Marjorie wouldn't argue the point; Grandmama had hurt her deeply. But her troubles with Rowena and the post were at an end. "It's a little late for second thoughts about where I live, Papa. But don't worry." She snatched up a benign truth. "Rowena and I often ramble about Hartsung Square without seeing each other for days at a time."

"I'm relieved to hear so." His eyes lifted to hers, and he seemed to scour her face. Then his expression grew pained. "You're tall—like your mother." He looked away. "Good day. And remember: The destiny of the Chesterfield line is in your dainty little hands."

She watched him leave and had the oddest feeling that it bothered him deeply to look at her. Probably, she thought, because she was a bothersome and unfinished detail cluttering his busy life.

Tucking away her bruised feelings, she looked at the formal version of Beau's plan to circumvent the gaming law. No wonder they called him the king of Bath, she thought as she reread the details of a gala he'd planned at Wiltshire's.

In an effort to save England from vice, Parliament had outlawed card games that used numbers. In an effort to keep Bath out of bankruptcy, Beau Nash had created a new game called Scholar, which used cards with letters and challenged the players to make words.

Her mind locked, but her body trembled with fear. Blake couldn't understand letters well enough yet to create words. Her father knew it.

On Friday evening Blake stood near the backgammon tables in Wiltshire's gaming room. He'd come to face his fear. Terror buzzed in his ears and drowned out the conversation of Beau Nash and George Entwhistle, who stood nearby. Like a jagged reef lying in wait for a ship, the card game loomed ahead.

Bile churned in his stomach, and he sipped tasteless

brandy from a glass he couldn't feel himself holding. He would stop running away and face up to his failing. But oh, God, he wished Marjorie was at his side.

Music from the ensemble seeped through his misery and offered a reprieve, for the game wouldn't begin until the minuets ended.

Even though he knew the effort would prove fruitless, he searched the milling crowd for a glimpse of Marjorie. She'd never enter this or any other gaming room again. He envied her practicality and her strength. She had been a victim here many years ago.

Blake would be the victim tonight. She wouldn't be here to witness his downfall. Perhaps that was best. Marjorie had given him the key. It was up to him to unlock the mystery of the printed word.

Scouring his brain for a scrap of confidence, he relived the past days when he'd worked until his fingers cramped and his eyes ached from trying to make sense of squiggly lines that normal people saw as words. To some degree he had succeeded.

The sudden quiet pulled him from his painful reverie. The music had stopped.

He felt a hand on his shoulder. Looking down, he spied the face of his executioner.

"I'm surprised at you, Blake," George Entwhistle said under his breath. "I never thought you'd fail to win my daughter. Rumor says you can change a nun's mind."

Sad laughter rose in Blake. On the subject of losing Marjorie, who could be sorrier than he? Entwhistle sounded so blasé about meddling in his daughter's life. Blake wondered why. "Are you the one who taught Marjorie to gamble?"

Entwhistle set his chin, a gesture reminiscent of Marjorie. "I've never been allowed to teach her anything," he growled. "'Twas Rowena—and maybe my own neglect—that turned Marjorie against me.

Thanks to that withered hag, my own daughter hates me."

"Why do you persist in these betrothals instead of giving her the love she craves?"

"I couldn't look at her without thinking of my Louisa. So I did the next best thing. I sent her a duke."

"A future duke," Blake corrected, "whom she doesn't want."

"You're slipping, my lord. You should have married her and given me a grandson. Now everyone in the British Isles and France will know your black secret."

Sensing the futility in trying to reason with George Entwhistle, Blake dropped the subject. "How many lives have you destroyed because you can't face your daughter?"

"Don't think you can slither away from responsibility."

The duke of Enderley had made similar comments to Blake. Morosely he realized Marjorie's father was as selfish as his own. Her life had been as lonely as his, too. But the similarity ended there, for Marjorie had put the past behind her. Could he?

"I'll see your family skeletons laid bare on the felt," George threatened.

Half an hour later it seemed the promise would come true. Sitting at the card table with Mama, Tobias Ponds, Beau Nash, Rowena, and George Entwhistle, Blake studied the seven cards in his hand. He recognized the pitchfork lying on its side. The vowel "E." Some of the other cards were familiar: the porthole he now called an "O"; and the yardarm that was a "T"; the nose of a canoe that was an "A." The "L" and the "B" made him smile, for those were the best lessons he'd ever learned. The letters on the other cards were strangers.

Like a blind man feeling his way through a strange

room, Blake fished through his mind in search of words. As best he could, he grouped the cards.

"Chesterfield," said George Entwhistle, who sat on Blake's immediate right, "'tis your turn, and I'm sure you have a word that will dazzle us."

The clock began to strike the hour of nine. Blake began to sweat.

Marjorie stood on the perimeter of the dance floor at Wiltshire's. Shouts and applause from the gaming room crawled over her skin like insects. She shivered in revulsion. Long-buried memories surfaced. She saw a silly young girl, richer in jewels than common sense, laughing as she gambled away her inheritance to a desperate gamester and her first betrothed, Tobias Ponds. She'd believed his friendly declarations, taken his syrupy compliments for gospel.

The immature girl had been desperate to hide from her lonely past and seek the father she'd never known. Hide-and-seek had been a painful game back then, especially when scoundrels such as Tobias were allowed to play.

Resolutely Marjorie walked to the door and peeked inside. Her gaze was drawn to Blake Chesterfield. Wearing a suit of deep blue velvet, he sat with his back to the door, his broad shoulders and pitch-dark hair outstanding in a sea of people garbed in towering powdered wigs and flashy colors.

She studied the other occupants of the garland-draped table. The king of Bath wore his finest white brocade suit and regal mien. Next to him sat Grandmama, decked out in a gown of rainbow-striped taffeta and a wig decorated with bows to match. Diamonds and sapphires draped her neck and wrists. On her left sat the duchess of Enderley, her elegant features pulled into a mask of serenity. Beside her

Tobias stared mulishly at his cards, his face still bearing the scars of his battle with Blake.

The circle closed with Papa, who wore yellow satin and a silly wig designed to add to his height. He leaned toward Blake. Her heart ached, for although she couldn't hear what her father said, she knew he taunted Blake.

When the clock struck nine she couldn't bear the injustice any longer. She lifted her foot, and for the first time since losing her fortune and her self-respect to Tobias, she stepped over the threshold and into her past.

Stalling, Blake downed the brandy and called for another. Like cold steel, fear sliced through his gut. The hour of reckoning had come. He felt a hand on his shoulder. Snatching at any diversion, he looked up.

And spied Marjorie, a tentative smile tugging at the corners of her mouth. "I insist, Lord Blake," she said, "that you allow me to play your hand."

She had to be the most wonderful woman on God's earth. Legs trembling, he rose.

Beau sprang to his feet and bowed. Tobias followed suit. A suspicious frown wrinkled George's forehead. "What's the meaning of this?" he stammered.

"I believe," said Marjorie, "'tis called gentlemanly manners, Papa."

"Oh, do get up, Entwhistle," ordered Beau. "And put on a smile. You *are* in Bath."

"What have you done, George," taunted Rowena, "gone and corked up your etiquette in a wine bottle?"

Caught up in a whirlpool of gratitude, Blake thought he might keel over. A slender hand, devoid of the jewels he'd once hoped to bestow, touched his arm and put him back on course. The sweet fragrance of lavender surrounded him. Fierce love consumed him.

Marjorie pulled him aside and whispered, "Two of the people at this table are cruel and heartless. But they're my burden. Not yours. You've suffered enough at the hands of my family."

So have you, he wanted to say. But longing and pride for her dammed up his throat.

"May I have the cards?" she said.

His hand twitched to do her bidding, but his conscience stopped him.

"I'm afraid not, Lady Marjorie," he said. "Your father and I have made a private wager."

Tobias stepped back. "You can have my place, my lady."

Beau rounded on the printer. "Move from that spot, and you'll never again set foot in this or any other public room in Bath."

Marjorie kept her eyes on Blake. "I must insist."

With three words she'd saved him and his family from the obscurity of shame. She must not be shackled to a man like him. From the very start she had only wanted her freedom. She'd given him his.

Fighting the urge to sweep her into his arms and head north, he did as she asked, and when the cards slipped from his hand and into hers he felt lighter, free. He could do no less than pay her in kind: He would set her free of a husband who might never be able to read his own marriage agreement.

"What is it?" she asked. "Why do you look so pensive?"

Because I love you, he thought, and I'll miss you every day for the rest of my life. "I was thinking of a word I tried to make with those cards."

"I'm particularly fond of the 'L' words," she said.

With the expertise of a sharper she fanned the cards and examined his handiwork. A smile lit up her face and bathed him in warmth. "You've done all the difficult work, Lord Blake," she said, "and left the easy part to me."

She turned to her father. "Lord Blake is very skilled with the written word, you know."

George frowned, his wary gaze darting from Marjorie to Blake.

"He certainly is," Blake heard his mother declare. "He gets his scholarly traits from the Cholmondeleys. My Blake could pen poems as a child."

She lied with the skill of a politician. Affection for her squeezed his heart, even when she sagged with relief.

Blake wanted to kiss Marjorie's feet. He wanted to carry her off to his castle in Wales, raise the drawbridge, barricade the doors, and not emerge till his hair had gone gray and his grandchildren were grown.

His heart brimming with love, he kissed her hand and stepped into the crowd. But with him he took a hundred fond memories of the unforgettable woman known as the postmistress of Bath.

"I need a drink," he said.

Marjorie watched him walk away, his proud carriage setting him apart from a throng of curious bystanders. Praise God, she thought, I'll play Blake's hand. He'll escape humiliation before all of these people. Even if Papa shouted the truth, no one would believe him now.

"Well, child," said Rowena, "will you play or force these men to stand all night?"

"Do shut up, woman," said George.

"Marjorie?" Beau held her chair.

She sat, but she had the oddest feeling that a part of her had been snatched away. She turned and spied Blake standing on the edge of the crowd. There would be time aplenty later to work out her problems with Blake.

He winked and saluted her with his glass.

Deciding her anxiety stemmed from the game ahead, she blew him a kiss and turned her attention to the occupants of the table.

For the next hour she watched her father and her grandmother trade barbed insults and cruel jibes. Seeing them so intent on hurting each other, she made several startling discoveries.

Rowena and George hated each other over a woman who'd been dead twenty-four years. They spent so much time casting blame that they had never mourned the woman named Louisa.

Poor Mama, she thought.

To her further surprise, Marjorie realized her father's powerlessness at the time of her birth. He had been eighteen years old when he buried his wife—the same age as Marjorie when she won her first postal commission and took in twenty-five orphans. He'd never remarried. No woman would replace his Louisa. He couldn't help being the man he was.

Poor Papa, she thought.

Claiming bankruptcy, the Loxburgs had turned out their dowager duchess without a cent. From then on she'd depended on George for her livelihood. She couldn't help being the bitter old woman she was.

Poor Grandmama, she thought.

The last discovery made Marjorie smile: The king of Bath couldn't spell.

Poor Beau, she thought.

Then she took a long look at her own life. Rewards and a happy future stared back at her. She would win the love of Blake Chesterfield.

Lucky me, she thought.

At the close of the game Beau Nash scooped up the pile of winnings and declared that he'd won enough to complete the Mineral Water Hospital.

Marjorie rose and searched the crowd.

But Blake wasn't there.

"He's gone," the valet said.

Caught up in her own happiness, she said, "What do you mean gone? I have to show him this." She waved the official document. "I've won the postal commission."

"My congratulations. I hope it brings you much joy, my lady."

Puzzled by his sarcasm, she said, "What's wrong?"

He stood, resting his hands on the blotter, which was covered with sketches she recognized as Blake's work.

"Why are you surprised?" Everson withdrew the betrothal agreement. "You hypocrite. You signed this, but you won't marry him. You never really cared about him."

She crumpled the envelope. "That's not true. I love him. I want to marry him."

"You can't be the postmistress of Bath and his wife, too."

Everson obviously didn't know Marjorie Entwhistle very well. "Of course I can. In another year or two Tug will be ready to take over. Blake knows that. He likes Bath. Now where is he?"

Through squinted eyes Everson studied her. "What about your father and your grandmother?"

Over a bottle of Papa's finest they'd come to terms. They would never be loving friends like Marjorie and Blake, but they wouldn't hurt each other anymore. "Papa's going back to France. Grandmama to London with the duchess of Enderley. Please, Everson. Tell me where Blake is."

The valet smiled and snatched up the betrothal. "I'll do better than that. I'll take you to him."

At noon she stood on the quay in Bristol and gazed at the warship *Reliance*. In the rigging fluttered a pennon bearing the chevrons of Chesterfield. Doubts and hopes played a tug-of-war inside her.

With a shaking hand she penned a message and handed it to Everson. She waited, hoping to see Blake appear at the rail. But the valet returned alone.

Her heart sank. She'd been foolish to expect Blake to want her now. Fighting back tears, she resigned herself to the lonely life that had once seemed so fulfilling.

Everson handed her a scrap of paper. Her heart hammered as she unfolded the note. Painstakingly printed in Blake's familiar and flawed hand, she read the message, *To the future duchess of Enderley: Permission to come aboard.*

Moments later the postmistress of Bath stepped onto the ship. An honor guard of smartly uniformed sailors lined the deck. At the front of the rows stood Blake, resplendent in his uniform.

She took a step and felt as if she were walking on air. With her gaze fixed on Blake, she seemed to float toward him.

When she was a step away she caught the brisk and welcome scent of lemons. Smiling, she breathed the words "I love you."

He swept her into his arms, threw back his head, and roared, "By all the saints and the Chesterfields that came before me, I love you, too."

The crew cheered. Happiness blossomed inside her. She drew off his hat and pitched it over her shoulder. "Show me."

He chuckled, and pure pleasure glittered in his eyes. "My pleasure, Postmistress."

Then he set his mouth to hers in a kiss of promise and soul-deep love. The crew whistled and applauded.

Passion spiraled and soared until all sound faded save the matched beating of two hearts.

At length he pulled back, his great chest heaving, his eyes smoldering. Dizzy with excitement and love, she gazed up at him.

"Hold that thought, sweetheart. Till we get home to Bath."

AUTHOR'S NOTE

The city of Bath contains a wealth of history and memories of extraordinary people. While Marjorie and Blake and their families are products of my imagination, several of the people you have just come to know actually existed.

Beau Nash lives on today in the writings of Boswell and Pitt, Henry Fielding and Edith Sitwell. Nash died in Bath in 1761, at the age of 86. His mistress, Juliana Papjoy, was so devastated at the loss of her lover that she did indeed live out her life in the hollow of a tree.

Prince Frederick died before he could ascend the throne. His son George III reigned.

In 1745 Parliament repealed the Gambling Act. The English were busy routing the Scots on Culloden Moor.

I love to hear from readers and promise to answer every letter with a personal reply. Please write to me care of Pocket Books, 1230 Avenue of the Americas, New York, NY 10020.

Bestselling Author of *CHIEFTAIN*

Arnette Lamb

❧❧❧❧❧❧❧❧❧

Maiden of Inverness

Available from

POCKET
BOOKS

1066

Judith McNaught

Jude Deveraux

Jill Barnett
Arnette Lamb

A Holiday Of Love

A collection of romances
available from

POCKET
BOOKS

1007-02

POCKET STAR BOOKS
PROUDLY ANNOUNCES

BETRAYED

ARNETTE LAMB

Available from
Pocket Star Books

The following is a preview of
Betrayed. . . .

Rosshaven Castle
Scottish Highlands
February 1785

Sarah traced the wooden bindings on a set of children's stories and waited for her father to share his troubling thoughts. To her surprise, Lachlan MacKenzie, the duke of Ross and the once-notorious Highland rogue, fumbled as he filled his pipe. His hands were shaking so badly his signet ring winked in the lamplight. His beloved face, more ruggedly handsome with the passage of time, now mirrored the strife contained within his goodly heart.

Sadness had begun this winter day, and Sarah wanted desperately to help ease the burden of his loss.

She touched his arm. "Agnes and I used to fight for the privilege of doing that. Let me fill it for you."

His broad shoulders fell, and he blew out his breath. "I'm not your—" Halting, he gazed deeply at her. Affection, constant and warm, filled his eyes. "I'm not your father."

Although she knew she'd misunderstood, Sarah went still inside. He'd acted oddly five years ago when her half sister, Lottie, had married David Smithson. When another sister, Agnes, had left home on an unconventional quest, he'd tormented himself for months. The day Mary demanded her dowry so she could move to London to perfect her artistic skill with Sir Joshua Reynolds, Papa had ranted and raved until their stepmother, Juliet, had come to the rescue.

His vulnerability was born of his love for all of his children, especially the elders, his four, illegitimate daughters, Sarah, Lottie, Agnes, and Mary.

Now he was bothered by Sarah's upcoming marriage to Henry Elliot, the earl of Glenforth, a man whose husbandly abilities he questioned.

But Sarah had made her decision and countered Papa's every objection. "Just because I'm to wed Henry in the spring and move to Edinburgh doesn't mean I'll stop being your daughter."

His blue eyes brimmed with regret. "Name me the grandest coward o' the Highlands, but I'd sooner turn English than admit the truth of it. Oh, Sarah lass."

Sarah lass. It was his special name for her. His voice and those words were the first sounds she remembered— even from the cradle.

"Tell me what, Papa? That I cannot at once be daughter and wife, sister and mother? I'm not like Agnes. I will not forsake you. Yet, I want my own family."

Always a commanding man, both in stature and influence, Papa now seemed hesitant. He touched her cheek. "You were never truly my daughter—not in blood."

She stepped back. "That's a lie."

Unreality hung like a pall in the air between them. Of course he was her father. After her mother's death in childbirth, he'd taken Sarah from the church in Edinburgh and raised her with her half sisters. It was a tale as romantic as any bard could conjure. Those of noble blood were expected to leave the care of even their legitimate offspring to servants. Not Lachlan MacKenzie. He'd taken his four, bastard daughters under his wing and raised them himself.

A stronger denial perched on her lips.

He took her hand. His palm was damp. His endearing smile wavered. "'Tis God's own truth."

Words of protest fled. Sarah believed him.

Moved by a pain so fierce it robbed her of breath, she jerked free and fled to the shelter of the bookstand near the windows.

On the edge of her vision, she saw him touch a taper to the hearthfire and light his pipe. She felt frozen in place, a part of the room, as natural in this space as the books, the toys on the floor, the tapestry frame near the hearth. This was her place, her home. Her handprints had smudged these walls. Her shoes had worn the carpet.

Reprimands had been conducted here, followed by joyous forgiveness.

"You cannot think I do not love you as my own."

His own. And yet not. Bracing her fists on the open pages of the family Bible, she struggled to draw air into her lungs. The familiar aroma of his tobacco gave her courage. "How can you not be my father?"

"I said it poorly." He slammed the pipe onto the mantel and came toward her, his hands extended. "I am your father, in all that counts. You are my own, but"— his gaze slid to the Bible—"I did not sire you."

"Who did?" She heard herself speak the words, but felt apart from the conversation.

New sadness dulled his eyes. "Neville Smithson."

Neville Smithson. The sheriff of Tain, a man Sarah had known most of her life. He lived at the end of the street. She had taught his children to read. Absently, she touched the string of golden beads around her neck. Neville had given her the necklace for her twenty-first birthday. Lottie was married to Neville's son, David. Less than an hour ago, both families had stood in the cemetery and laid Neville Smithson to rest.

His heart, the doctors said. He'd been conducting assizes. He had died in Papa's arms. His unexpected death, which had come as a blow to every household in Ross and Cromarty, now took on a greater meaning to Sarah.

She was neither the love child of Lachlan MacKenzie nor one of his four bastard daughters. Their illegitimacy was common knowledge, always had been. But in his special way, Lachlan had presented his lassies, as he called them, to the world as cherished daughters, and pity anyone who questioned it.

Sarah thought of her half sisters. They all shared a birthday, yet different mothers. As a result, he boasted, of his first and only visit to court. "Did you sire Mary, Lottie, and Agnes?"

"Aye, but it changes nothing. In your heart you are their sister and my daughter."

At ten, Sarah had shot up in height. Although of an age with Lottie, Agnes, and Mary, Sarah stood taller than them. Other differences came to mind. Sarah had always been bookish and quiet. Lottie often swore that Sarah needn't come with them to court, for she'd sooner find merriment in the nearest library. Sarah had been a shy child. Later she held back, not for lack of gumption, but because her sisters were better leaders than she. They were gone now, each pursuing her own life. Soon she would do the same.

"Why did you wait until now to tell me?"

He folded his arms over his chest. "'Twas Neville's last wish. You were still in swaddling when I took you for my own. He didn't even know about you until you were six and we came here to live. When I told him, we agreed 'twas best you did not know."

"Why?"

"We feared your life might seem like a lie."

They could have been standing in the dungeon rather than this toasty warm sanctuary, so cold did Sarah feel. "'Tis one lie for another, Papa." The endearment died on her lips. He always praised her maturity, her sensible nature. But in his heart he did not believe his own opinion of her, for he hadn't trusted her with the truth. Not until now.

Sensible Sarah.

She didn't feel sensible in the least.

Betrayal fueled her anger. "Henceforth, how shall I address you? Your Grace?"

Misery wreathed his face, yet his will was as strong as always. "You canna be angry. Your best interests were at the heart of it."

"If a lie has a heart, it beats the devil's rhythm."

"Sarah lass . . ."

As if she could shove his words away, she held up her hand. "I'm not *your* Sarah. My father is—is dead." Anguish stole her breath. Neville Smithson had entrusted his children to her, yet he'd denied her the greatest bond of all: her own blood kin. And now it was too late to look him in the eye and ask why he had not claimed her.

Other ramifications were endless and baffling. "I stand as godmother to two of my own sisters."

"And a fine influence you are on Neville's younger children."

Neville's children. Her siblings. But Lachlan MacKenzie still thought of her as his daughter. She clung to the comfort. "But they don't know that I'm their sister."

"We'll tell them."

How? she wondered, her pride reeling. But there was no hurt in it for them. Was there? Neville's son, David, would surely rejoice and expect Sarah to take his side in his marital disputes with Lottie. What would the younger ones, her godchildren, say? Would they see her differently?

"Did Neville want you to tell them?" she asked.

"There wasn't time. God took him quickly. He spoke of his wife, then of you."

The information neither cheered nor saddened Sarah. She felt numb.

"You were always so different from my other lassies."

That was true, but Lachlan had given each of his children an equal share of his love. To Agnes and Mary, he exhibited great patience. To Lottie, he gave understanding. To Sarah, he lied. Worse, he was quick to swear that she was the image of his own mother, a MacKenzie. An impossibility.

Sarah marshaled her courage. "It was all lies. Did you also lie about my mother?"

"Nay. Your mother was Lilian White, sister to my beloved Juliet."

Sarah's stepmother was also her aunt, a situation that had always been the cause of great jealousy among her siblings. But all along, she had reason to envy them their blood ties to Lachlan MacKenzie.

"Neville loved you, too. He left you ten thousand pounds."

As a final blow, Lachlan MacKenzie, the only father she had ever known, thought her shallow enough to be bought. Something inside Sarah began to shrivel. She wanted to flee, to cower in the dark and cry until the pain ebbed.

But cowardice was not her way. She was three and twenty and would soon embark on a new life as the countess of Glenforth. Therein lay her salvation from the hurtful world this room, this moment, and this life had become.

You bear the mark of the MacKenzies, Sarah lass.

A lie. No MacKenzie blood flowed in her veins.

In reality, she'd been sired by a man who had toasted her every birthday and visited her when she was ill. A sheriff named Smithson, not a duke named MacKenzie. A man they had buried this morning. A man who sought to buy her forgiveness from the grave.

The cruelty cut her to the bone. "Neville Smithson left me guilt money."

"Nay. You are the same Sarah MacKenzie as you have always been. I would not have given you up."

Even if Neville had asked, she finished the thought. Neville Smithson hadn't wanted her. As a tutor for his children, she'd been acceptable, but not as a treasured daughter.

His fair face rose in her mind, an image as constant as any in her memory. Her father. Neville Smithson, a commoner.

"What are you thinking?"

The sound of Lachlan's voice drew her from the stupor her mind had become. "I'm thinking that I must go to Edinburgh and tell Henry." Yes, Henry and a new life.

"I'll go with you."

Denial came swiftly. "Nay. I'll take Rose." Her maid was company enough.

He sighed in resignation. "If Glenforth is unkind to you or judgmental, I'll make him wish he'd been born Cornish."

The remark was so typical, Sarah smiled. But her happiness was fleeting. Until this moment, it hadn't occurred to her that Henry would do anything other than accept the news with good grace. His mother, the Lady Emily, would not be so generous, but Henry always prevailed in their disputes.

Sarah would take only her MacKenzie dowry to Edinburgh. Lachlan had pledged the twenty thousand pounds months ago and put his seal to the formal betrothal. With Henry's help, she would heal the wounds Lachlan MacKenzie and Neville Smithson had dealt her.

Six Months Later
Edinburgh, Scotland

"Lady Sarah!"

Two of Sarah's pupils, William Picardy and the lad called Notch, dashed into the schoolroom.

Notch yanked off his cap, and the crisp air made his hair crackle and stand on end. "The king is dead!"

Sarah's own troubles fled. "Who says?"

Shoving the smaller William out of the way, Notch hurried to her side. "The Complement's just come off a warship. Everybody knows the Complement wouldn't come to Scotland for any less of a reason." His adolescent voice broke, and he cleared his throat. "I say the old Hanoverian's carved his last button and sent the Complement to give us the jolly news."

The King's Complement was an elite troop of horse soldiers, noblemen all. With great ceremony, the Complement had served English monarchs since the time of Henry VIII. The Hanoverian kings had relegated them to ceremony and foreign service, preferring a Hessian guard. The arrival of the Complement in Edinburgh certainly boded change, but did not harken the death of a king.

Notch's fanciful imagination, coupled with the need to rule the younger orphans, was likely at the heart of the rumor.

Sarah intended to get to the truth of the matter. "Did you hear them say the king is dead?" she asked. "You heard one of the soldiers speak the words?"

He slid her a measuring glance. One eye squinted with the effort. When she did not back down, he withdrew a little. "Didn't have to have it said to me like I was a short-witted babe."

She saw through his bravado. It was how he'd managed

alone since the age of six on the streets of Edinburgh. At eleven, he was as world-wise as a man double his years. But in many ways, he was still a boy. In all events, he deserved her respect and her guidance.

"No one expects you to predict the fate of kings, Notch. Even bishops cannot do that."

He stared stubbornly at the scuffed toes of his too large shoes.

The other children, five to date, preyed on Notch's every word. She hoped to make him understand the responsibility he undertook as their leader.

She leaned against one of the school desks. "But if you are speculating, and it proves wrong, you shouldn't feel a lesser man because you were merely voicing *your* opinion. You could even learn and discuss the views of others in the matter. Such as Master Picardy here."

Eight-year-old William Picardy clutched his frayed lapels and rocked back on his heels. His blunt cut brown hair framed a face of near-angelic beauty.

Wondering how anyone could have abandoned this precious child to the streets, Sarah said, "Why do you think the Complement has come?"

Eyes darting from the school desks to the standing globe to the hearth fire, William considered the question.

"What's it to be, Pic?" Notch teased and challenged at once.

"I believe—" William paused, obviously battling the force of Notch's will. Then he sighed and said, "The king's upped his pointy slippers."

"There it is." Notch basked in his conquest.

Sarah gave up the effort to teach them democracy and shared responsibility. Theirs was a precarious existence; safety lay in numbers for orphaned children.

"Have you ever seen the Complement?" William asked.

"Nay," she said. "They've been abroad for most of my life."

"She's from the Highlands," Notch reminded him, but in a mannerly tone. Then he held out his arm. "Come along, then, my lady. If we hurry we can find a place in the crowd."

Bowing from the waist, William swept a hand toward the door. "Even the gentlemen and ladies have turned out for the Complement. Do come with us, Lady Sarah."

Curious, she reached for her cloak. The weekly lesson had ended hours ago, and if she stayed here alone, she'd spend the afternoon pondering events beyond her control.

But as she followed Notch down the stairs and out of the church, she couldn't fend off thoughts about Henry and the odd turn her life had taken.

Upon arrival at Glenstone Manor in Edinburgh, Sarah had learned that Henry and his mother were on an extended holiday in London. Rather than stay in the family mansion, she'd leased a house in nearby Lawnmarket and awaited their return.

To ease the loneliness and fill her idle time, she'd begun teaching school in a converted storeroom at Saint Margaret's Church. Those who could not afford private tutors sent their children to Sarah.

But then Henry's mother had returned with news that Henry had been accused by the duke of Richmond of cheating at cards. The Lord Chancellor had thrown Henry in prison and demanded twenty thousand pounds for his release. The exact amount of Sarah's dowry —money Lachlan MacKenzie had worked hard to earn.

Now only the orphans attended Sarah's Sunday morning school.

"Look!" shouted William. "There they are!"

Over the noisy crowd lining both sides of High Street, Sarah heard the clip-clop of horses' hooves. An instant later, the first of the riders came into view. The gusting wind, as much a part of Edinburgh as the biting winter cold, ruffled the white plumes in his helmet.

He sat atop a magnificent crimson bay horse. Wearing the traditional uniform of blue tabard, white trunk hose, and a chain of office bearing the Tudor rose, he drew every eye.

George II had added knee boots to the uniform; George III had commissioned fur-lined, velvet capes.

The entire troop, thirteen strong, riding three abreast behind the commander, now filled the street.

Cheers rose from the crowd, but the leader did not take notice. With his chin up, his handsome features appeared carved in fine marble. Yet there was something warm and oddly familiar about him to Sarah.

Impossible, she silently scoffed. She was merely attracted to his rugged handsomeness and commanding air.

"Has the king tucked it in?" yelled Notch.

"Shush!" Sarah grasped the boy's arm.

The commander turned just enough to spy the lad, then look at Sarah. To her horror, she felt herself blush beneath his probing gaze. A slow, sly smile gave him a regal air.

A conceited rogue, she decided, and quelled her admiration. As leader of the most respected collection of horsemen in the British Isles, he was probably accustomed to having women fawn over him. Sarah MacKenzie had better things to do, such as convincing the mayor of Edinburgh to convert the abandoned Customs House into an orphanage.

But hours later when she answered the knock at her door, Sarah rethought her opinion of the commander of the King's Complement. She also knew why he'd looked familiar.

Poised on her threshold, he now wore a brown velvet coat over an Elliot tartan plaid, pleated and belted in kilt-fashion. Henry favored his mother. But this man bore the true face of the Elliots, the same features she'd seen in paintings in the family's portrait gallery.

He had to be Michael Elliot, Henry's younger brother.

Henry. Her pride rebelled at the thought of the scoundrel she'd almost married, and if this second son had returned home to attend her wedding to his brother, he'd wasted a journey.

"You're Michael Elliot."

He shrugged, drawing attention to the breath of his shoulders and his thickly muscled neck. "So my nanny told me."

An odd answer and much too personal to address. Besides, Sarah had had enough of the deceitful and greedy Elliots.

"Why have you come here?"

"For two reasons, actually." He lounged easily against the door frame. "I simply had to meet the woman who preferred to wed a toothless and blind draft horse rather than marry my brother."

Sarah had said that and other disparaging remarks to Henry's mother, but she did not regret her rudeness. The wicked Lady Emily had bullied and insulted Sarah until her patience fled. The woman had gotten precisely what she deserved.

"My sainted mother also said you were a trouble-maker, but she hesitated to mention how beautiful you are."

Was the sarcasm in his tone meant for his mother or for Sarah? Probably the latter, considering the poor manners of the rest of his family.

Bother the Elliots. Sarah was done with them. "You are too kind," she said, meaning nothing of the sort. "You said you came here for two reasons. Beyond repeating my wish to never set eyes on an Elliot again, what is your purpose?"

As bold as a rogue at court, he winked and marched into her home. "To change your mind, of course."

Look for
Betrayed
Wherever Paperback Books Are Sold